THE
FUND

UGO NWASIKE

ISBN: 979-8-9938943-0-0 (paperback)

ISBN: 979-8-9938943-1-7 (ebook)

Published by Dominant Media Group LLC

First edition, 2025

For anyone who ever knew what was expected of them
and said, "nah."

PART ONE

MY FATHER ONCE TOLD ME,

"Son, if you're not in control
of yourself, someone
else surely will be."

1

ADRIAN CHANNING

LIFE AT THE top is exactly how I imagined it.

From the rooftop terrace of this multi-level penthouse, the Manhattan skyline stretches out in every direction. The deal is closed, and for the first time in months, I can breathe.

The party is packed with high-powered investors, entrepreneurs, celebrities, and socialites. Champagne flows freely as they laugh, network, and snap selfies with the city glowing behind them. A DJ plays a blend of house and radio-friendly hip-hop that threads through the undercurrent of conversation and the clink of glasses.

Nights like these are rare. So, I soak it all in, taking a moment to admire the scene before stepping into the fray.

A big screen flashes the logo of Volition Aeronautics and cuts between shots of me and the management team ringing the bell at the New York Stock Exchange. On a dais under the screen, Harry Paxton and Derek Graff prepare to address the guests. Harry and Derek are the Paxton and Graff of Paxton Graff Capital Partners, the largest private equity firm in the world, the trillion dollar investment conglomerate I've helped lead for the last decade.

Derek steps forward with his silver hair perfectly in place, which is fitting for someone born with a silver spoon. He offers a few polished but inconsequential welcoming remarks before introducing Harry.

Harry steps to the podium in a flowing, white Vera Wang gown, and takes the mic in her diamond-encrusted fingers like she owns the place. Because she does. Derek's last name is on the door, but Paxton Graff Capital is her queendom.

"What a rush!" she announces, her British accent diminished from four decades in New York but still noticeable. "Volition Aeronautics! Biggest IPO in history to date!"

She scans the crowd as they erupt in cheers. "This firm has become a leader in the private equity asset class. And together we've made PGC a name synonymous with dynamic and responsible investing—"

"And outsized returns!" Derek interjects, his need to be heard louder than his sense of timing.

Harry glances at Derek just a moment too long and lets out a quiet breath before beginning again. "Tonight, we don't only celebrate the record-breaking IPO of one of our portfolio companies. We celebrate what can happen when you trust your intuition, trust your teammates, take calculated risks, and see them through to the ultimate reward."

The applause lingers long enough for me to take a deep breath.

"I'd like to bring up the man who spearheaded this investment," Harry continues. "One of our senior managing partners who's leading the next generation of this industry. He's a PGC all-star! Adrian Channing!"

I notice a flash of irritation from Derek as I approach the stage, but I put on a smile and take the mic. I feel a touch of anxiety but a single deep breath settles me.

"Thanks, Harry," I begin, gripping the mic firmly. I scan the party, making eye contact with as many as I can. "As investors, we're constantly seeking value. How to unlock it, how to grow it, how to protect it. Volition Aeronautics presents a unique and exciting proposition because while we've opened big and are still climbing—"

"Subject to a ninety-day lockup." Derek can't help but undercut me.

"That's right, Derek." I try my best to brush him off. "We can't cash out our shares just yet... but uh..."

This dickhead knocked me off my flow but I push through it.

"We've only begun to unlock the value this investment will yield over time. When it's all said and done, this will be a true 'never-sell' asset."

I let the applause swell as I reflect on what this moment really means. Five years ago, I recommended to the investment committee that we spend $10 billion to buy the company. Last week, we took it public and we're projecting a $50 billion return. I invested $11 million of my personal savings alongside the firm's capital; it's now worth almost $45 million. However, for the next eighty-six days, it lives in my head, not my bank account, thanks to the aforementioned lockup.

"When we acquired Volition, it was just another aviation company with an ambitious goal of bringing fully electric aircraft to market. That was until Harry Paxton, my dear mentor, and as of this morning, the world's wealthiest woman according to Forbes..."

The crowd cheers for our fearless chairwoman in her fourth decade of market dominance.

"She supported my plan to acquire Blue Rock Industries, a mainstay in my hometown of Maddox, Pennsylvania, a blue-collar city that's been crushed by offshoring. In merging the two companies, we combined Volition's design and tech prowess with Blue Rock's manufacturing engine and became a one-stop shop for all things electric aviation. We're not only reducing the world's carbon footprint, but we're leading the charge in bringing quality manufacturing jobs back to the US."

I leave out the part about how Maddox is a predominantly Black city in dire need of this kind of investment. Five hundred thousand people and counting, boxed in for decades by poverty and bad politics, living with the bones of the factories that once kept the lights on. At one point, my little-known Eastern Pennsylvania city led the nation in quality manufacturing jobs. Then the work went overseas, the money followed, and what was left was crime, boarded windows, and broken promises. My goal in private equity is simple: use investments like this to pull Maddox out of decline and into dominance.

I scan the terrace, the applause rolling in as I see Volition's founder walking in. "I'm proud to say I led this transaction alongside visionary engineer and dynamic CEO, Tim Rouchard, whose mission to utilize the resources of the private sector to save our environment is truly inspiring."

Derek clears his throat, then calls out, "But we're making a hell of a lot of money while we're at it!"

The audience responds with some light chuckles, a few offering polite claps.

I raise my glass. "To continued dominance, maximized profits, and true social impact." A round of applause ensues. I flash a smile, then step off the dais.

Dear God, the code-switching is exhausting. But judging by the excitement from the audience, they're eating that shit up, Harry included.

After a few handshakes with PGC partners and portfolio company executives, I spot Harry at the rooftop bar with Garrett Declan. He's one of our biggest LPs.

Limited partners. They're the kinds of investors who write hundred-million-dollar checks like they're paying the damn light bill. In every fund, there are LPs like him who supply the capital, and GPs—general partners—like us who get paid to multiply it.

I need to talk to Harry about an acquisition I've been looking at, but I smell a networking opportunity.

"Adrian!" Harry air-kisses my cheek. "Great speech, darling."

"Glad you enjoyed it."

"Have you met Garrett?" she asks, glancing up at him.

Garrett Declan, all six foot eight of him, might be one of the most powerful gatekeepers in the investment world. Pensions, sovereign wealth funds, charitable foundations, and ultra-high net worth families all look to him. He controls billions in investable cash. If he backs you, capital pours in. His support will be a game-changer when I'm ready to launch my own fund.

"I know the legend, of course, but haven't had the pleasure." I flash the winning smile and extend my hand. "Adrian Channing."

"Nice to meet you, Adrian." Garrett's southern accent is thick.

His grip is strong, matching my own. He tries to pull me in, but I hold steady.

Harry is smiling, almost like a proud mother. "Garrett, Adrian's one of our most senior executives. He's responsible for nearly every successful buyout we've done over the last decade or so. He also heads our portfolio operations unit."

"So," he says, drawing out the word. "I have you to thank for the superb returns."

It's not the first time I've heard that tonight, but his tone makes it sound less like a compliment and more like he's waiting for Harry to say, 'No, not him. The white guy standing behind him.'

Shit, maybe I'm just in my head.

Before I can respond, Harry jumps back in. "Adrian, Garrett was PGC's first LP ever. He's brought billions into our funds over the years."

"Well, it's my clients' money," Garrett says. "I just tell 'em where to put it."

"So, really, I should be thanking you." I meet the man's assessing gaze, hoping some flattery might win the day. "Without your bankroll, I wouldn't win any bids. Well, I would, but it would be tougher to execute on big winners like Volition."

Always bring it back to the deal. Give him a reminder of what we're doing for him. The truth is, LPs write a lot of checks our way, but we throw more money back to them when we exit investments.

"I like the confidence," Garrett says. "Keep those big returns comin' in, my boy."

I resist the urge to bitch-slap him for referring to me as his "boy." Business first. Feelings when I win.

I give him a practiced smile, which fades as I smell the stink of dog shit wafting in from my left. I turn and see Derek Graff approaching.

"There he is!" Derek bellows, extending a hand.

Garrett clasps it with a subtle grin.

"Good to see you, Derek."

"Hope you're enjoying the party, Garry."

"Another classic PGC shindig," Garrett says. "You, sir, do know how to throw a party."

"We win big, we celebrate big," Derek brags. "But don't worry, we're not charging this one to the fund."

They share a chuckle between themselves.

The moment settles into a quiet pause, just enough space for me to take my shot. "Garrett, deals like Volition are great, but what really excites me is what we're building in the impact space. Our companies are tackling food deserts in the inner city, expanding mental health access, greeni-fying US manufacturing, funding farmers, scientists, veterans, Black and women-owned—"

"Channing, grab me a scotch, will ya?" Derek calls out, his eyes flicking up at me.

This little jackass... I'm a Senior Managing Partner and PGC's biggest rainmaker, not a waiter at the Montgomery Club.

But I can't make a scene, so I grab the bartender's attention, and he approaches.

I glance at Derek, keeping my tone light. "That's who you're looking for."

Derek tightens his jaw, and his eyes narrow, likely in disbelief that I refuse to act as his servant.

Harry looks toward the skyline and then back to the group, taking a deep breath. "How lovely is this? My master fundraiser and my superstar deal maker are talking shop with my biggest LP." She throws her arms around Derek and me.

Derek shifts on his feet and then subtly squirms from under her arm.

"Garry, why don't you join me in the cigar room upstairs?" Derek offers. "I've got those Habanos you love."

Garrett grins. "I do love a good Cuban. Harry, always a pleasure."

He gives her a peck on the cheek before turning to me. "Adrian, nice meetin' ya."

"Pleasure's mine, Garrett." But he's already walking away with Derek before I finish the sentence.

I turn back to Harry. "Thanks for the intro."

"It'll come in handy when you're running things here. Chief Investment Officer Adrian Channing doesn't sound bad to me."

She waves at guests waiting to get a picture. Usually, when she's with me, no one approaches. Everyone knows how seriously she takes business. For her, this isn't just a job, it's a way of life. It's an ethos we both embrace.

"So, is it official?" I ask. "Leora Mencham is retired. The CIO spot is vacant, but still no announcement."

"The board is voting on your promotion at the quarterly meeting. Just a formality, but I'll act as CIO in the interim. It'll be nice to get my hands dirty again in deal flow."

That just means more work she'll put on my desk for her to take credit for.

I grab two glasses of champagne from a floating cocktail waitress and hand her one. "Hey, are you willing to go to 6.5 on Napier Brands? I have Goldman arranging financing. I'll need 1.3 max out of the fashion fund."

"That's a decent-sized ticket for that strategy, no?" Harry takes a sip of champagne as her eyes roam the crowd.

"That's why I need you to push this through the investment committee." I pause briefly to gauge her reaction. "But my projections say it'll be a fourteen or fifteen-billion-dollar company in a few years after I do my thing."

I casually chug my champagne, feeling the bubbles scrape down my throat like the sweetest sandpaper.

Harry glances down the bar at her granddaughter and newest protégé, Reanne Paxton-Mensah. She technically works on my deal team as a senior analyst, but as the heiress apparent, she's never far from Harry's hip.

"Reanne," she calls out.

"Napier's a strong target," Reanne says, exposing her eavesdropping. She pushes her glasses up the bridge of her nose as she taps on a tablet. "Portfolio of fashion brands with consistently high net revenues and significant room for scale."

"Revenue growing at thirty-four percent," I add. "Strong market positioning across verticals… It's a good deal."

"Good." Harry's shrewd eyes meet mine. "Adrian, you know you'll always have my support on a good deal."

She scans the party with a wide smile on her face. "You should be proud. This entire thing is because of your work. Your future here is extraordinarily bright, if you want it."

I smile, and then I register that last part. "If I want it?"

"Come on, Adrian. I know you've always wanted to raise your own fund, build your empire as they say."

She's right, but I play coy. "The thought hasn't crossed my mind."

"Just make sure you give your old mentor a chance to invest when the time comes."

"Listen, if you make me Chief Investment Officer, I'll be more than incentivized to stick around for a while."

"It'll happen," Harry asserts flatly. "And then you can be CEO when I retire. You and Reanne at the helm, a minority and woman-led firm leading the market. That, children… that is my legacy."

Harry may be a posh, British white woman married to a Ghanaian man, but it's her track record, rather than her associations, that's made her a true advocate for women and minorities in high finance.

"I appreciate the support." I chuckle lightly. "And I like the vision."

"As do I, Grandma." Reanne lets out a short laugh as her phone buzzes. I catch her voice as she walks away, instructing an analyst to update the cap table for a company we're about to exit.

It's just Harry and me again.

"How's she coming along?" she asks.

"Good. Reanne's sharp, tough, like her grandma. She'll do well here."

Harry's brow lifts, and a small smile plays across her thin lips as if she's pleased.

It's crazy that after knowing Harry for more than twenty years and making her billions over the last ten, I still feel the need to kiss her ass. But I guess it's warranted. I owe her a lot. Then again, she owes me just as much. I went to business school with her son, Kofi, and that connection opened the door for me. He was the golden child poised to take over for his mom, but for reasons no one discusses, I'm the one taking the reins at PGC.

"Speaking of the future…" I take a sip. "… I have been thinking about what my next ten years look like."

"I know you have," she says.

"You do?"

A slow smirk creeps onto her face. "I know you had a drink with some little shit at Rockpoint Capital."

I pause mid-sip, then lower my glass. "Are you having me followed, Harry?"

Harry chuckles. "When you take meetings with my competitors in a PGC-owned restaurant, word gets to me. But come on, Adrian. You knew that. You wanted me to find out."

Maybe I did. She needs to know I'm loyal but not blind. I have options.

"Are they ready to back you?" she asks but doesn't let me answer. "Who am I kidding? Of course they are. You have the track record to raise your own fund. You'd be their hottest ticket since… well… since they backed me."

"Perhaps. But they're offering—"

"I don't care what they're offering," she says, stepping closer and dropping her tone. "Listen, you can leave now, or you can run things for me for another ten years as CEO."

"Ten years is a long time, Harry."

"Just steer the ship," she says. "Keep your focus on our big picture trajectory. Let Reanne run the day to day on the deal side, with your supervision on the large cap stuff. Keep her as your number two so she'll be ready to take your place when you leave to launch your impact fund."

I shake my head softly. "Not sure I see the upside in staying that much longer."

"The upside is you'll leave as a billionaire," Harry says, scoffing lightly as she takes a sip of champagne. "Beyond that, think of the messaging when you go to raise your own fund: 'the former CEO of PGC in the market with a new social impact fund.' LPs will shoot themselves for the chance to place capital with you. If you go out on your own now, you might raise some money, but you'll get your throat slit on terms."

She's not wrong.

"Well, truth be told, I can't even think about going anywhere until you guys sign off on my carried interest." I'm mentally salivating over my piece of the billions in profits my companies have generated for PGC.

Harry takes a sip of her champagne, almost as if to buy herself time. "Oh yes, of course. Well, I'm not involved in that housekeeping anymore. It's below my pay grade. Derek is holding the keys on all comp-related matters."

"That right there is the reason why your grand vision of me in charge won't work. And why I'm asking for your help with this."

Harry gives a subtly dismissive shake of the head. "I'm sure he'll pay out your carried interest with the quarterly distributions in a few months. Adrian, you've done your ten years, paid your dues, and proven your loyalty. You'll get your payout per firm tradition."

"If I can be frank, Harry…"

"Always."

"I don't trust Derek to do the right thing. He hates me."

And I hate him right back.

Harry laughs off my very real concern. "Don't be paranoid, darling. Derek understands the value you bring to the table. You'll be taken care of."

"It's thirty-two mil, Harry. That's what PGC owes me in carried interest. I know it means little to the ninety-three billion dollar woman but—"

"Don't forget I came to this country with twenty-four quid in my pocket."

"You've mentioned it."

"Don't be a little shit, Adrian."

I let out a soft chuckle. "All jokes aside, Harry. This'll be the first big payout of my career. Given everything, I think you can understand my paranoia. This kind of money it's… it's big for me."

She pauses for a moment, and then she tips her glass at me. "Thirty-two's not shabby at all."

"It's a scratch in the bucket to what you and the other GPs have made on my deals."

"Oh, Adrian darling, I don't doubt that." She smirks as she lifts her hand to take another sip of champagne, showing off a Rolex Lady Datejust and a hand adorned with diamond rings, bracelets, and trinkets.

If I make Chief Investment Officer, I'd receive a seat on PGC's board and a small ownership stake in the firm. That $32 million I'm entitled to after ten years of finding, scaling, and selling profitable businesses would look more like $32 million a year. This is what made Harry one of the wealthiest people in the world. And at forty years old, I'd be the youngest Black man to lead a private equity firm of this size.

The path to the status of billionaire is clear for me. But I don't have it yet. So, I'll take the same approach that got me out of the slums of East Maddox. Go to work.

2

ADRIAN CHANNING

I GRIP THE phone tighter and head down from the penthouse terrace, looking for somewhere quiet to finish this call with my executive assistant. I slip into a darkened hallway.

"Tessa, look, tell the team I say we're not settling for anything less than the twelve billion the company is valued at. Nero Couture isn't just a fashion brand, it's a cultural icon growing at thirty-eight percent year over year. Twelve is actually a steal."

"Vance asked what he should say if they come in under that," Tessa says.

I push open a slightly cracked door and find a room full of middle-aged dudes with frosted tips in designer athleisure, stretching and doing vocal warmups. I make awkward, brief eye contact with one of them before closing the door and backing out.

"Then we tell 'em to fuck off, and we sell the shit to LVMH. Obviously, don't say LVMH, just remind them we have other bidders for this thing."

"I will let him know," she says. "IPO party sounds like a rager."

"Yeah, you could say that." My voice is almost swallowed by laughter, music, and clinking glasses drifting in from outside.

"I heard Derek's team hired the Backstreet Boys to perform," she says.

"I think I just saw them warming up."

"I would have *looooved* an invite," she teases.

I duck into a small alcove, hoping for some quiet. "If it were up to me, the whole team would be here, but you know Derek's rules, 'senior people only.'"

"He's such a pompous ass," she says, almost under her breath.

"I won't argue." I chuckle softly.

"That reminds me. Call my guy at Madison Square. I wanna get the deal team floor seats for Knicks opening night once we close this sale."

"The *boys* will love that." I can't see her but I can tell she's rolling her eyes right now.

"Don't worry. Once I'm running the shop for real, everyone gets an invite to Backstreet Boys."

"It's only right," she says. "Anything else you need from me?"

"Did the analysts calculate our return on this one yet, or are we still guessing?" I ask.

"They did," Tessa says. "They say assuming we sell at twelve billion, we're looking at an 8X return on our initial investment. Just about $2 billion in carried interest for PGC."

"Nice. I'll trust you to get the team over the finish line on this one, but I'm around if you need the big dog to come through and bitch-slap someone."

"I appreciate the confidence," she says, "and you taught me well enough how to do that."

We share a chuckle over the phone as I place my hand on the doorknob of what I hope is an empty bedroom. "Hey, switching gears for a sec, I need the latest financial reporting on Martex Properties."

Tessa is silent for a moment, then continues. "Martex Properties… Sorry, boss, I'm not seeing it in the CRM."

"That's because we own it through Sentry Asset Management, another PE shop I acquired for Harry a few years back. I used Martex to acquire some companies headquartered in Maddox. Just wanna keep tabs on my hometown assets."

I slip into the darkened bedroom.

"I'll have an analyst at Sentry pull the latest financials and send them your way."

"Much appreciated."

I hang up, and immediately freeze at the flirtatious voice of what sounds like an Eastern European woman coming from deeper in the space. "You want?"

I guess this room isn't empty.

"You know I do," says a voice I recognize as Derek Graff's.

The room is dark, save for the faint light streaming through the terrace doors, but I can tell it's the master suite by the expansive space and the foyer-like hallway I'm standing in.

He makes a snorting sound. I can't see, but who am I kidding? He's snorting a line of blow.

As I tiptoe out of the bedroom's mini hallway, hoping to mind my own business, I hear my name.

"That Adrian boy is impressive," says another voice. This one carries a Texas drawl. It's Garrett Declan.

Boy... Again? Seriously?

"Another product of the PGC investment engine," Derek says.

"Is he really the reason returns have been so impressive over the last few vintages?" Garrett asks.

"No, no, Garry. The power of our track record is in our culture, our philosophy, everything we've learned over the last forty years. That's what generates stellar returns. Not any one member of the team."

"Sure, but a senior partner, a rising star that's African American? Y'know? I'll be honest. It checks some boxes for some of my more progressive clients."

"Which boxes are those?" Derek asks.

"Look, I know you don't like to hear it," Garrett says, "but at the end of the day, this isn't just private capital. It's state pension money. Teachers, bus drivers, firefighters, cops... city employees who need their pensions to perform. It's their little reward for when they retire."

I hear a brief snorting sound.

"And yes," Garrett continues through sniffs, "a meaningful percentage of that base is Black, Latino, whatever... So there's demand from some to see more capital flow to fund managers who reflect that diversity. IRR isn't the only priority anymore. They can get attractive returns with any of the thousands of funds in the market. It's about optics."

"Well, we aim to please," Derek says, sniffing profusely. "Channing is a shining example of our DEI efforts—"

"Don't say DEI," Garrett says, chuckling briefly. "But we're on the same page."

"Listen," Derek says, before another long sniff. "I'd love to hear what you're thinking in terms of your capital commitment to our next corporate buyout fund. We're targeting $50 billion on this one."

"It depends on what we see in the data room, but early indications tell me at least ten billion from my various clients."

"That's what I like to hear, Garry."

Derek Graff will do anything to get an investor to write a check. That means flattery, favors, even veiled threats if necessary. In this case, that means playing up the shiny token Black boy at PGC. In reality, I'm everything but a "DEI hire." I'm not a product of the PGC investment engine. I'm the motor. There's no getting around that, even if he downplays my role like I'm some affirmative action case study.

After a few moments, there's an elongated silence. I listen closer, hoping to hear more about how LPs are allocating their dollars in this market, more ammo for when I launch my own shop. But all I hear is the sound of... suction.

I silently back out of the hallway. In doing so, I catch a reflection in a mirror on the wall, and what I see triggers my gag reflex: Derek getting fellated by a young woman I can only assume is an escort while another simultaneously fellates Garrett.

I'm almost too stunned to move. Here's my boss, a man in his late fifties with a wife and a daughter who also works at PGC and is currently upstairs enjoying the party, having a coke-fueled circle suck with our biggest investor, a man in his sixties, also with a wife and kids.

I get the fuck out of there faster than a bullet leaves a barrel, hoping they don't see me.

I return to the rooftop, the image of what I just witnessed still haunting me. I order a shot of tequila from the bar and knock it back, hoping to drown the images in my head.

Before I can even bite back the burn, Tim Rouchard taps me on the shoulder. "We need to talk."

We walk to the glass railing at the rooftop's edge, where the view of the NYC skyline is immaculate and passersby are sparse.

"I think somebody is stealing inventory at Blue Rock," Tim says, his voice hushed.

"What do you mean?"

"I noticed a discrepancy in the Blue Rock quarterlies," he says, handing me an iPhone with a spreadsheet displayed. "The weapons division."

Blue Rock Industries manufactures everything from airplanes and car parts to cereal boxes and ceiling fans. That includes firearms, ammunition, and explosives for the U.S. military, a small detail the public is not necessarily privy to.

I look through the financials, unsure of what he's trying to point out to me.

"What is this?" I ask.

"Blue Rock's Q2 raw metals purchase orders," Tim says. "Scroll down, you'll see the government reporting."

Now, I see it.

"Are you sure this isn't just a clerical error?" I ask.

"Yes, Adrian, I'm sure," he hisses, his northeastern WASP elite accent ringing in my ears. "The Maddox facilities are assembling more firearms than they're reporting to the ATF. Look at how much we're buying in raw metals. This should yield more guns than what we're reporting. Those guys are up to something."

"Those guys? They're your guys, Tim. You're the CEO. You run them."

"They are not my guys," he snaps. "You forced this acquisition on me. When you bought Blue Rock from John Bing and made him COO after the merger, he kept on all of his general managers in Maddox. The guy is a thug, and he runs those factories like one. I started this company to develop the next generation of airplane technology—"

"And you're doing that, aren't you?"

"Not really," he says. "Lately, I've been totally preoccupied with the weapons division."

"It's an important business line for Volition."

"Look, air-to-air missiles for the military? I get that. Weapons of war for the Air Force, fine."

"Right, we can't make electric fighter jets—"

"Without the fight," he finishes. "I get it. But pistols, assault rifles, fucking grenades. This stuff is ending up on the streets."

I eyeball the numbers on his phone again. "This isn't proof of anything but perhaps some sloppy accounting, so what are we really talking about here?"

"You know my daughter goes to Winston Elementary, right?"

"Shit, the school shooting?" My demeanor shifts as my voice softens. "Is she okay?"

He lets out a deep breath. "I almost lost her, man. Because some psycho got their hands on an unmarked Blue Rock assault rifle. We have to plug this leak, Adrian."

"I get it." I let out a genuine sigh. "I don't know what I'd do if something like that happened to my little girl. I'm sorry yours had to go through that. If there's anything PGC can do, you let me know."

I watch as relief washes over him before he quickly refocuses. "The only thing to do is shut down the Blue Rock factories and smoke out whoever's responsible."

I shake my head. "Don't do anything yet. Let me dig into this on my end."

"Fine. I'll send you what I found—"

"Don't." My voice is sharp. "Have you told anyone else about this?"

He hesitates as he glances around the party. "Just Derek Graff. He was in the office last month for a 'portfolio company audit.' He pressed me on whether there were any issues he should know about before the IPO, so I shared my suspicions."

"What'd he say?"

Tim glances around again, his voice nearly a whisper. "He told me to bury it."

Jesus... Derek Graff is nothing but a grifter with a high net worth, sticking his nose—and dick—where it doesn't belong while telling himself he's important. This is an issue that needs to be resolved quietly, not buried.

"But I know you can get Harry to see reason," Tim says.

I scan the rooftop as I think about my next steps. "Okay, from here on out, you don't discuss this with anyone but me. I'll tap my contacts in Maddox and see what's what. I have someone in Bing's office I can trust. But right now, I need you to keep your suspicions and those records to yourself."

Tim accepts my approach because, though he's the CEO, I'm the Chairman. But I'm not convinced the discrepancy he flagged is anything more than some Kevin Malone-esque bookkeeper at the Blue Rock factory who punched the wrong numbers into the system.

I head to the coat check stand, trying my best to sneak my six-foot-four frame past a sea of exiting guests, some of whom are trying loudly to get my attention.

I see Derek hovering around the coat check girl. This guy clearly has a thing for women who aren't his wife and are younger than his daughter. Even though I'd love to avoid him given what I witnessed earlier, I tap him on the shoulder.

"You, me, and Harry need to talk on Monday. Very important."

Derek's lips tighten as his brows furrow. "You don't tell me what I need to do, Channing." He returns to flirting.

I can't stand this guy.

3

ADRIAN CHANNING

LEAVING THE IPO party, I get in my emerald-green Bentley Continental GT, the license plate reading, "BuySell." It's brand new, a little birthday gift for my fortieth. It's a bit flashy and unnecessary in New York City, but I work hard, and it's my money.

I speed across the Brooklyn Bridge with my windows down, Jay-Z's "Can't Knock the Hustle" blasting. The wind whips through the car as I rap along, flicking the roach of this joint out the window. The breeze sharpens the rush of the ride, and the high settles just right as the beat rattles the dash.

As I switch lanes, my phone buzzes. I look down and see it's my daughter, Riley. Maybe she's calling to wish me a happy birthday. At least, I hope she is. More likely, she needs cash, the currency of our relationship, distant as it is these days.

I reach to pick up, but the buzzing knocks my phone off the console onto the floor. I lean over to grab it, but feel the car swerve and remember I had a few, or maybe eight, glasses of champagne and some tequila at the party and just smoked a J. So, I sit upright and let it ring.

Just as I think to myself how I probably shouldn't be driving, the police siren wails behind me, causing my heart to race. The flashing lights fill my rearview, and a cold sweat washes over me.

My hands grip the steering wheel tight as the flashing red and blue lights cloud my rearview mirror. I pull over and can feel my palms sweating as the officer approaches my window.

He pulls me out and makes me blow into a breathalyzer. As it beeps, his eyes turn cold. He reaches for his cuffs, and I can't shake the sinking feeling in my stomach that I'm about to go to jail.

"There has to be something we can do here," I plead. "Looks like my blood alcohol is barely over the limit. I'll park it here and Uber home."

The officer looks me dead in my eyes, unmoved. "I'm afraid that's not how it works, sir. And I can smell marijuana on your person."

He takes a step toward me. I step back, still trying to talk my way out of this. He steps forward again, but stumbles on some loose pavement, losing his footing. We're on the side of the Brooklyn Bridge, and he's close to falling into oncoming traffic.

Instinctively, I reach out, grabbing his bicep and pulling him out of harm's way.

"Get your hands off me!" he barks out.

I comply, letting him fall. His left knee drops to the asphalt, followed by his right hand. But he quickly regains his footing and hoists himself back to his feet. In the same motion, he pulls his pistol and aims it at my chest.

My eyes widen as I raise my arms high. "I'm unarmed!"

The barrel of his gun is still leveled, and every nerve in my body goes tight. My heart is pounding so hard I swear it's rattling my ribs. One wrong move, one wrong breath, and my daughter is fatherless.

But by the grace of God, he's not in enough "fear for his life" to pull the trigger. He holsters his weapon and grabs my arm, twisting me around before slamming me onto the hood of my car.

"DO NOT RESIST!" It's a snarl, cold and violent.

He searches me and finds a small baggy of cocaine in my jacket pocket.

Shock slams into me. I can't believe this is happening. In my forty years, I've never used anything harder than alcohol and the occasional cele-bratory joint. I've witnessed firsthand the destruction hard drugs can cause on lives, families, and communities. It's simply not my style to take them.

I stare at the baggie he's holding up, feeling the heat rise in my chest. The words, *that's not mine, you planted that shit* claw at my throat, but I swallow them down, trapped by the fear of setting him off. All it takes is one bad cop having a bad day, and I'm on the ground with a knee crushing my windpipe, struggling for air I might never breathe again.

"You're under arrest for driving under the influence," he says, his voice low with anger, "resisting arrest, assault on a police officer, and possession of cocaine."

The cuffs lock, and as the officer leads me away, I catch my reflection in my tinted window. My $80 haircut, $8,000 suit, $80,000 Rolex, and $280,000 car mean nothing to this cop. I'm gonna need a damn good criminal lawyer.

4

ADRIAN CHANNING

I TRY TO focus, but it's hard. Work feels different today. Everything is hazy and distant, as if I'm watching myself from outside this glass fishbowl of an office. Monday mornings on the 58th floor used to remind me of progress, like I'd climbed high enough that the world couldn't touch me. Now it feels like I'm still stuck on the ground.

My mind keeps flashing back to that cold metal bench, the damp stink of the holding cell, the embarrassment of having my ex-wife bail me out, the blank stare of that racist prick cop. He planted those drugs. I need to figure out how to prove it.

I've spent years shaking off the chains of being a "kid from the inner city," only to have them railroad me as if I'm still running the streets of East Maddox, Pennsylvania, getting bounced from one foster home to the next.

But I'm here. I've made it this far. I can't let this drag me down. Sure, I'll need to fight this criminal case, and though I'm far from being on my A-game, the work has to get done.

I walk into the conference room for the weekly investment committee meeting. This is where we decide how to spend the billions in our various funds. At this table, we pick apart every investment opportunity until there's nothing left to question.

"What's next, my good people?" The excitement in Harry's voice brings her British accent forward. "I want to see wide margins and hefty exit multiples."

I jump in. "You've all seen my memo on the Napier Brands opportunity. Six point five billion will get us ninety percent of their outstanding shares—"

"Is this another Black-owned company?" Derek blurts out.

An awkward silence fills the room.

Then, Harry says what I'm thinking. "I'm not sure why that's relevant, but no. Derek, if you had read Adrian's investment memo, you would have seen that Sean Napier is a white man just like you."

"I'm only asking because Garrett Declan still seems very focused on DEI," Derek says, "despite the position of the current presidential administration."

"Show Declan the deals Adrian and I have led out of our impact funds," Harry says. "PGC is a market leader in supporting diverse talent. But let's get back to the topic at hand, please."

Harry and I have backed several minority- and women-owned businesses and grown them into giants. It's part of my push to back entrepreneurs that the system still undervalues. I'm proud of that. Hearing her stand on that business to her white male co-owner only deepens my respect.

After I present a detailed analysis, the committee votes and unanimously approves the acquisition.

As the meeting adjourns, my phone buzzes with a reminder: *Get a criminal defense attorney.*

I need to find someone with the skill and influence to make this go away.

A few years ago, my asshole father remarried a woman named Nareeda Palmer, Reeda for short. She has three sons, the youngest of whom, Charles, I met at the wedding. I only went because my then-wife, Brianna, a child psychiatrist, thought it would be "healing" for me to support my dad in his moment of happiness. Bullshit.

25

But Charles is a litigator back home in Maddox and went to law school in New York. He's also a scion of a powerful Black business family that has reach in a few different industries and organizations across the East Coast. He seemed bright and spoke with a commanding yet calm tone. He felt like the kind of guy who could talk anyone into anything, the kind of guy who probably pisses off prosecutors with his ability to woo a judge and jury.

A Google search reveals he spent five years defending white-collar crimes at the Washington, D.C. office of Linder Boykin, a prominent corporate law firm. For the past ten years, he's been running his own criminal defense and civil rights practice in Maddox, and apparently has never lost a trial. I give him a call, and after reconnecting briefly, he agrees to take my case.

ONE WEEK LATER

The early morning light filters through the trees in Prospect Park as my legs pump steadily, wheels gliding along the familiar path to my office. The crisp morning air cuts against my skin, and the rhythm of my ride clears my mind.

Just as I round the next bend, my phone buzzes. It's Charles Palmer. I don't slow down to pick up. But as I reach for my Apple Watch, a rabbit with midnight black fur darts into the road.

But it stops. For half a second, we lock eyes. Its fur catches the sunlight like velvet. Its eyes are unnaturally red, and they seem to burn right through me.

I swerve instinctively, narrowly missing it, only to veer into the path of an oncoming biker. My handlebars jolt as I correct again, skimming the curb by inches. With my pulse racing, I ease off the throttle, hit the brakes, and then drop into the grass.

My phone buzzes again. Charles Palmer.

"Hey," I answer, panting heavily.

"You working out?" Charles asks. "Can call back later."

"All good. What's up?"

"So, I have a client that's a fairly large donor to the NYPD Foundation." Charles's voice has an air of composure that I imagine isn't taught in law school. "I got them to pull some strings. Long story short, the cop who jammed you up is willing to retract his story."

"Holy shit," I murmur, still panting.

"The ADA is dropping the assault and resisting arrest charges, and she's willing to let you walk on a plea. Community service, AA, and a five-thousand-dollar fine. I told her you're good for it."

"Of course I am. But I have to plead guilty?"

"Yes, but I got her to drop the DUI to reckless driving. So, just that and the minor possession. You'll be clear of this in a few months." His tone is nonchalant, as if three months of AA and community service won't completely fuck up my schedule.

"Any other options?" I ask. "I'm getting crushed at work right now, and I'm up for a big promotion. This is going to be an interference."

"We can take it to trial, but it would be a roll of the dice that I personally would not take if I were in your shoes. With the assault and resisting arrest charges, you'd be facing serious jail time."

"I didn't assault him. I tried to help him. A bodycam should show that."

"The ADA's saying the cop's bodycam was turned off."

"Of course it was…" I let out a deep sigh. "The drugs weren't mine, Charles. Someone's setting me up."

"Can you prove it?"

"No." I shake my head in anger. "All I know is I don't do drugs. I left a company party after a few glasses of champagne, but I never bought cocaine, never touched cocaine, never saw cocaine…"

My voice trails off. I did see cocaine that night. Did Derek plant his drugs on me? Is that why he was hovering around the coat check stand? Why would he do that? Does he really hate me that much?

"I'd take the deal," Charles says flatly. "If you find out who planted the drugs and can get concrete evidence of that fact, I can work to get this expunged."

I hang up the phone, fuming at the thought of Derek setting me up like this.

I stand, brush the grass off my shorts, and then swiftly kick over my state-of-the-art bullshit mountain bike, breaking the gear shifter.

As I lean over to pick up the broken pieces, I catch eyes with the rabbit again. I feel like it's watching me from the edge of the forest, like it's assessing the damage it created, keeping score.

"What the fuck do you want?" I mutter.

But then it hops off, leaving me talking to myself.

"Money is like perspiration. The harder you work, the more will come. But the second you stop working, it'll dry up and leave you stinking like shit."

5

HARRIET PAXTON

EDWARD PAXTON RAN the biggest numbers racket in South London in the 1960s. I was sixteen when I watched his jealous business partner stab him in the neck at Chibby's Pub in Basingstoke. I shot the bastard in the face with a snub-nosed .38 and caught the next boat to New York City.

I started in finance the only way I could—as a bookie, taking bets from Wall Street suits in backroom bars. One of my regulars was Arnold Graff, a gorgeous idiot making obscene amounts of money picking stocks for America's wealthiest families while I scraped by collecting slips.

So, I went to night school, got my business degree, and when he initially refused to help me get a job, I threatened to expose our affair to his wife. That motivated him to get me in at Goldman. A few years later, I left and launched PGC with him. The year was 1982, and the name of the game was leveraged buyouts. In fact, I was in the room when that term was coined. Over forty years later, I own the room and everyone in it.

● ● ●

The walls of the Somerset Club on Central Park West don't just soften sound, they absorb it in silk and sunlight. Even the faint clink of silver on china seems to hesitate before breaking the hush. White-paneled walls stretch toward high ceilings crowned with pale molding, while tall windows flood the room with views of Central Park. The air carries the scent of fresh lilies arranged in crystal vases, and the furniture is upholstered in creams and blush tones that glow in the afternoon light. It's elegance without weight, a sanctuary of feminine influence.

Stan Titus, my head of security, stands by the entrance, and a trio of my staffers sit at a nearby table picking at their meals between rapid taps on their devices and hushed updates, the work of managing my orbit of board meetings, media obligations, philanthropic engagements, and academic panels.

Across from me sits Leora Mencham, her dark hair cropped shorter than when she last ran capital deployment for me. She's retired from the day-to-day now, but still sits on the board and is one of my most trusted allies at the top.

I was thirty-three and the only woman moving private capital on the street when she joined me. She was the first hire who understood that I wasn't building some boutique fund. I was building a machine.

"The board's getting restless," she says. "They know you still have a few years, but they want a name."

I stir my tea slowly. "I know what they want."

"And what do you want?" Leora asks.

I raise a subtle eyebrow. "Well, that's not the question that matters, is it? It's not about what I want or what makes sense to me. It's about what will protect this firm for the next forty years. I want the right successor. Not the one the board or the LPs expect."

"Derek thinks the Chairman's seat is already his," she says.

I exhale through my nose. "It's not."

"No?"

"No," I affirm. "Something about him has always unsettled me."

Leora shudders just slightly. "You and me both."

"I don't quite trust him or his tactics. Of course, his father was my mentor, co-founder, on-again, off-again fuck buddy, but I'm afraid he let money raise his children."

Leora succumbs to a light fit of laughter. "But the boy wonder knows the business. He can raise capital, he can charm, he can dress up a pitch deck for the state pension funds and smile for the Financial Times, all while operating the machine."

"But he's not a deal maker. Not like we are. He'd never venture to a defunct copper mine on tribal land in Chile or chase down the CEO of a distressed food distributor in Mississippi. We did, and we turned them into gold."

"That's because he's a heat-seeker." Leora smirks. "He finds the warmest spot and stays there."

I nod, letting out a light giggle. "Exactly. PGC needs to continue to grow. Continue to evolve. I'm not sure Derek is comfortable with anything other than the status quo."

That's what they never understood. The headlines call me a corporate raider, a robber baron with lipstick and an appetite for blood. They whisper it in boardrooms, shout it on social media. As if turning around flailing assets and shedding dead weight is cruelty. What I did created jobs in the long term, rebuilt industries, and delivered real returns. The kind that makes economies grow. I never cared about being liked. I cared about building the world's best companies. And yes, I cared about getting rich.

And now, with nearly two trillion dollars in assets under management, PGC is too big to fail. With that kind of scale comes vulnerability. One misstep at the top, and the whole machine trembles. And at seventy-three, I feel them circling. The board members, media, investors... Power isn't respected when it's held by a woman deemed too old to be dangerous, but too stubborn to die.

Leora lowers her voice. "So, it's Adrian as your successor?"

I smile before I catch myself.

She sees it over the rim of her wine glass. "Christ, Harry. You're going to start a war."

"He's more than qualified. He's got a savant-like mind for business. Risk-taker. Hungry negotiator. Unending work ethic. And his investments might yield the best returns I've ever seen."

"You just described yourself."

"He certainly reminds me of me. Tough. Bold. He grew up in a poverty-stricken, crime-ridden area without a mother just like I did, and he thrived."

Adrian was a student in my "Private Equity Playbook" seminar back when my husband was the Dean of Students at Columbia Business School. He sat front row, challenging every word I said with an unwavering confidence and raw intelligence that I couldn't help but admire. I took him under my wing like he was my own son, gave him an internship while he was in grad school, then told him to go into banking like I did, so he could learn how to price a company and arrange financing. I watched as he skyrocketed through the ranks at Goldman Sachs, practically running their fashion M&A group before I hired him to take charge of my deal teams.

"Perhaps he's too much like you?" Leora asks.

"Perhaps…" My gaze drifts to the window where I can see 57th Street bustling below.

"What is it?" Leora brings me out of my daze.

"Adrian's hunger is thrilling, sure, but it's also dangerous. I've watched him tear apart competitors, turn underperforming companies inside out, and squeeze every ounce of value from a deal that others called doomed. But I've also seen him toe lines I told myself I'd never cross."

"Come on, Harry." Leora raises an eyebrow just slightly, a reminder that she knows where many of the bodies are buried.

"Fine, maybe I did cross them," I admit. "Or maybe I just did it better."

"Have you thought about making them co-CEOs? Let Adrian run the deal side while Derek keeps the investors happy."

"Derek wouldn't go for that. He believes he's the heir apparent. Arnold whispered that prophecy into his ear every day from the moment the boy graduated college until the day he died. He wants to be king."

"He was never even the prince." She laughs. "That spot was reserved for Kofi—" She catches herself and then says, "I'm sorry, dear."

I just sip my tea. "Nevertheless, Derek thinks PGC is his birthright."

"Well, it's not his birthright." Leora's voice sharpens. "It's yours. You launched it. You built it. You control it. You can give it to whomever you wish."

I smirk at the thought.

"And what about Adrian?" she asks. "Do you think a guy like that would settle for just being Chief Investment Officer?"

"He'd take it. But not forever. If I don't make a move to secure him, eventually, he'll leave, go to one of our competitors and then build his own platform."

And that would kill me. Not just professionally but personally. I didn't just mentor him. I molded him. I gave him the edge. He belongs to me. If he launches his own fund, I need to be the anchor investor. That's why I've told Derek to hold on his carried interest payment. If he gets that $32 million now, he'll leave, and I need more time to lock him down.

"So, you promote Adrian to CIO," Leora says, "name him as your successor and then prepare for war."

"I'm not sure, frankly." I shrug. "But whoever takes over needs to see what I saw when I started all this. Not just numbers. Not just leverage. Value… in the little ugly broken pieces no one else wants and the vision and chutzpah to make them winning assets. That's the edge. That's what made us number one."

Leora rests her hands on the table. "Then you know it can't be Derek."

And I know what happens next. The lawsuits, the headlines, the turmoil. Derek won't go quietly.

6

ADRIAN CHANNING

I STEP OUT of my private office bathroom, the steam from the shower still lingering. Today, I wear the gray Tom Ford suit with subtle pinstripes. Understated but unmistakable. As I settle into my chair, I look to my right through the windows that stretch from floor to ceiling and see the sunlight reflect off the East River's surface. The Financial District moves in a frenzy fifty-eight stories beneath me, its constant energy a reminder of the markets always in motion.

My desk is cluttered with pitch decks, diligence reports, and stock purchase agreements I need to sign off on. Behind me, a row of signed jerseys, balls, and deal toys sit beside framed photos of me with icons: the Obamas, Oprah, Mark Cuban, LeBron, and Malala. But none are more important than the photo of Riley and me, and the one of me with my mom.

After a few morning calls with my deal teams, CEOs, and bankers, I flip through a deck for a Hollywood talent agency that's up for sale as Tessa updates me with notes from one of my deal teams on a call I missed while at AA.

"… Speaking of teams," she says. "There's a…" She hesitates.

"What is it?" I ask.

"Martina Hayes has an open role on the PR team," Tessa explains. "Assistant Director of Strategic Communications. I've had the posting open on my screen for hours."

"Plotting to leave me, huh?" I ask, joking. "Jeez, have I not been good to you these last six years?"

"Stop it, boss." She laughs. "I'm not even sure I'll apply. I'm just an admin. I don't have any of the friggin' qualifications."

"You have a masters in communication from NYU."

"But none of the work experience," she says. "Not really."

"Tessa, you've been in the trenches with me on about a dozen live deals—deals that are important to this firm."

"I thought every deal was important to the firm."

"Of course, but if it's on my desk, then it's *the* most important."

"Easy on the ego, boss." She laughs.

"Whatever…" I bite back a chuckle. "…Look, you've handled process calls with sellers, relayed instructions to deal teams, communicated growth strategy to my CEOs, shit you've been my mouthpiece on the work I'm too busy to oversee directly. If that's not strategic communication, I don't know what is."

"I've just done what you've told me to."

"Exactly. And last year, when you told me you wanted to run PR at a major fund or bank, what'd I say?"

"You said if I'm going to shape the public image of the business, I need to know the mechanics of the business."

"And now you know them. That's why I made you board secretary at Arcadian Media. So you can credibly say you've operated at the top tier of media."

"I'm a glorified note-taker there."

"Doesn't matter. Apply for the job. I'll put in a good word with Martina."

"Okay, boss." There's a pause. I can almost hear her smiling. And then the ringing of her office phone. "Just one second."

As I continue flipping through the deck, waiting for Tessa to return, my phone buzzes with a news alert. Yet another shooting. A mall in Michigan this time. Nine dead, four of them kids. Jesus Christ…

Almost immediately after reading the headline, Tessa's voice comes through again on the office line. "I have Tim Rouchard for you. I would've told him you're busy, but I know Volition is top of mind right now."

"Yeah, thanks, Tess. Tell him I'll call him back on my cell."

She chuckles briefly. "One of those calls, huh?"

"Unfortunately." I close the intercom.

I dial his number, and after a single ring, he answers.

"Are you seeing this?" he asks abruptly. "Another mass shooting."

"I know. It's awful, but this really isn't a good time—"

"It'll never be a good time, Adrian. I told you this would keep happening if we don't do something—"

"Tim—"

"They're saying he used a Blue Rock AR-15 with no serial numbers, Adrian. Not scratched off serial numbers, but a proprietary Blue Rock design that was manufactured without a serial number."

"A ghost gun," I murmur, letting the thought slip out.

"Yeah, exactly. We need to do something about this. If a Volition subsidiary is responsible for these weapons, we have a responsibility to the public, to our shareholders—"

"Tim, hold on—"

"We can't keep this quiet," he continues over me, rushing through his words. "I started Volition to perfect electric aircraft technology. To change the world for the better. I didn't partner with PGC so you could turn it into an arms dealer and erase the mission of this company—"

"Tim, shut the fuck up and let me talk."

My outburst draws glances through the glass walls of my office, but I don't care. I've had it with him talking over me. I flash a smile, pull it together, and prepare to tear this guy a new one.

"I don't have time for this shit, Tim. You may not have agreed with the Blue Rock merger, but the weapons revenue is funding your new fleet of electric planes, which, I'll add, is significantly off schedule. You could've quit four years ago when we did the deal, but you didn't, so stop whining about your mission to save the world. This is business. Take your emotions out of it."

"Fine." His tone is curt. "Then business dictates we shut down the Blue Rock factories before someone else connects these dots. I'm pretty sure Bing is behind this. John fucking shady Bing."

"How can you be so sure?"

"I went through surveillance footage. I saw him in the loading dock of the South Maddox factory with some tattooed African American guys in unmarked jumpsuits, loading crates from our facility into their unmarked trucks."

"That's not evidence of anything, Tim."

"Adrian, the timestamps show it was very late at night, and based on their tattoos, I'm pretty sure these guys are RF9."

"RF9?"

"The gang," Tim says. "How are you not familiar with it? They started in Maddox."

I grew up in the Ironbridge District of East Maddox, so yeah, I'm familiar with RF9. I've buried friends because of them. It's a network of violent crews moving black market firearms and designer drugs with Fortune 100 efficiency. No one's ever gotten close enough to pin down who's really in charge—just a name: the Black Gods. A collective with the kind of presence that can bend cities to its will without ever showing a face.

But I'm not letting rumors and stereotypes stop my money.

"So, let me get this straight, Tim. You see some Black guys with tattoos and automatically assume they're gang members?"

He's silent, likely embarrassed, but then he speaks again. "I know how it sounds, but what is our COO doing handling product deliveries? Let alone at two in the morning?"

"I assume he's working hard to create a return on investment." My voice is flat.

"Adrian, he's selling Blue Rock's weapons under the table. I know it. At the very least, I can prove he's cooking the books. We need to pause operations over there and launch an investigation—"

"We're not stopping operations. We do that, not only do we lose cash flow which the Street won't like, but we'll piss off this company's number one customer of guns and planes. You don't breach contracts with the federal government, Tim. It would have a materially negative effect on our stock price."

He lets out a long, drawn-out sigh. "But if we don't do something now, the federal government will shut us down when the public finds out and then our stock pri—"

"That won't happen," I declare. "And you're going to make sure of it."

"How am I supposed to keep the lid on this, Adrian?"

"Figure it out, Tim. Clean up the accounting. I don't care."

"You can't be serious—"

"If any of this comes to light... Well, you were the CEO at the time of the merger. You authored the S-1 statement and insisted we stay silent on the arms revenue. You said it would kill your image and kill the company's image if we told the world Volition is in the gun business."

"You agreed to that plan."

"No, I delegated that workstream to you, Tim. You made that call. When it comes down to it, you and John Bing concealed the weapons revenue from your investors, including PGC. We'll play the victim."

Tim lets out an angry scoff. "You're fucking evil like the rest of 'em."

"No, Tim. I'm a realist. And you? Well, I suggest you find out exactly who's responsible for stealing those guns and shut it down quietly. But Blue Rock stays alive in the process."

"I'll do my best." His words come out a little too quickly, like he's trying to convince himself more than anyone else.

"I don't need your best. I just need you to do what I tell you to do." I hang up the phone.

Perhaps I was a bit harsh, and maybe it's the stress from this God-forsaken, trumped-up arrest of mine, but we can't afford any more issues, not with a $50 billion return on the line. I have a daughter to put through college and an ex-wife with a passion for a job who has become accustomed to the elevated lifestyle I provide for her. With the bulk of my savings invested in this company, I can't afford lost profits.

ONE WEEK LATER

I slip into a meeting at Our Holy Mother Church on the Lower East Side. With a lukewarm coffee in hand, I half-listen as some poor sap spills his heart out about the demons haunting him. My mornings are spent in court-mandated community service and AA, thanks to the bastard who planted those drugs on me.

My thumb scrolls through emails as I try to stay ahead of the nonstop barrage of notifications.

But then my eyes catch an unusual stream of news alerts, texts, and phone calls.

NEWS: Federal agents raid Volition-Blue Rock facilities in Maddox, Pennsylvania. John Bing, COO, arrested.

NEWS: PGC-backed electric aviation company under federal investigation. Calderon pushes for Senate hearings.

NEWS: Volition Aeronautics accused of fraudulently hiding arms manufacturing business in IPO filings.

Derek Graff (text): WHAT THE FUCK IS GOING ON AT VOLITION?

Harry Paxton calling.

Harry Paxton (text): Where the hell have you been? Answer your bloody phone.

I study the article by Nora Hendricks at the New Journal that broke the story, headlined: *Volition Aeronautics or Volition Arms? Secret Revenues, Illegal Deals, Widespread Corruption.*

I scroll down the page and start fuming as I see the words: *Securities fraud… Potential ties to organized crime… federal RICO investigation.*

And then another news alert.

NEWS: Volition Aeronautics (VOAN) stock price down 80%. Analysts project total failure by day's end.

"Oh fuck me…" I don't bother to whisper. I can't.

The room falls dead silent. A few folding chairs creak as heads turn. The woman mid-share stops and stares at me with her mouth open. I ignore them as I continue studying the New Journal article.

Tim was right. Someone has been siphoning off unmarked Blue Rock firearms and selling them on the black market to what they're calling an "unnamed criminal enterprise."

I've been so busy trying to keep my head afloat on the three dozen other transactions I'm leading, while also paying my debt to society, that I never got the chance to really look into Tim's suspicions. And now I'm fucked.

The article confirms their source is a company insider. Fucking Tim Rouchard. I can feel it in my bones. I pushed him too hard, and he went to the press. Now I'm going to push him off my fifty-eighth-floor office terrace.

I storm out of the AA meeting, kicking over a few folding chairs. As I descend the church steps, I call Tim three times, each time with no answer.

I call an Uber and head downtown to PGC's headquarters. The car has a mini-TV affixed to the passenger seat headrest, playing softly. This thing is all over the news.

"…*The insider seems to suggest that mega-PE firm, Paxton Graff Capital Partners, Volition's controlling shareholder, was either complicit in or had knowledge of the illegal arms trading prior to the IPO…*"

That sandbagging piece of shit. I call him again. No answer, so I leave a voicemail.

"Hey Timmy, listen to me, my man. I can't do my job and yours at the same time. Maybe you think we've become friends over the years, but trust me when I say, you have NO FUCKING CLUE who you're dealing with! Keep your goddamn mouth shut!"

7

ADRIAN CHANNING

"MOM AND DAD are pissed," Tessa says, nodding at Harry and Derek in the conference room down the hall. "I told them you were meeting with a potential target."

I step out of the elevator into chaos. It's like everyone in the office is running from a grenade that no one can seem to locate.

Tessa takes my bag and headphones from me while I straighten my tie. We walk past the pristine glass walls toward the conference room.

"Thanks." I straighten my already straight posture. "Do me a favor and pull the diligence report we did for the Volition-Blue Rock merger four years ago and all related email threads. Need it right now."

"On it, boss." She diverts to her desk.

I stop her. "Oh, by the way, I got those all-access tickets for fashion week for you and your mom."

A smile forms on her lips.

"And I spoke to Martina. Send her your application directly. She'll fast track it."

"Oh shit," Tessa blurts. "Thanks, boss."

Always gotta take care of your people, even when the shit's hitting the fan. I've bought and sold enough fashion and retail companies to know exactly who's running New York Fashion Week and how to get what I need from them. And as for the new job, it'll suck to lose Tessa but she's ready for the next phase of her career, and who am I to hold her back?

As I walk into the conference room, I scan the faces in front of me. Harry and Derek sit at either head of the long, glass table as usual. Around them are Terrence Weiss, General Counsel, Martina Hayes, Head of Media and Government Relations, along with a half-dozen other partners. All bickering.

I settle into my chair before Vance Jefferies, one of my junior partners and protégés, leans over to me and whispers, "This is a fuckin' shit show, A.C."

"Fleas to a lion, my friend," I whisper back, doing my best to project confidence.

"Terrence, what's our legal exposure?" Derek asks, continuing the main discussion.

Terrence sighs as he takes off his glasses and sets them on the legal pad in front of him. "Well, there are PortCo issues and there are LP issues."

"LP first," Derek barks out.

"Several of our capital partners draw hard lines against investing in companies involved in weapons sales," Terrence says. "Violating those terms gives them cause for breach of contract."

"The Saudis, the Chinese, the charitable foundations, every single government pension plan whose funds we manage... I know." Derek's voice tightens with frustration. "What if we pay back their investment contributions on this deal?"

"That might help us avoid litigation," Terrance says. "But some will argue that that money should have been invested elsewhere."

"Oh, please," Harry says. "None of my investors would dare bring a lawsuit against me. Talk to me about the portfolio company issues."

Terrence swivels in his chair to face Harry. "If any member of senior leadership at any time knew about the illegal gun sales or the reporting discrepancies, PGC could be subject to liability for criminal negligence, particularly given our control of the board. If the weapons manufacturing pre-existed our ownership of Blue Rock Industries, we need to be clear on what we knew when we made our initial investment."

Harry glances at me briefly before speaking. "We didn't know about any arms trading, let alone illegal arms."

Derek's beady eyes dart to Harry and then to me, trying to read us. "Channing, what did you know at the time of the initial investment?"

I meet his gaze without hesitation. "We didn't know they were selling guns."

"If that's the case, we should be able to avoid criminal prosecution," Terrence says. "However, I can't foreclose the possibility of a prosecutor or civil litigator imputing the knowledge of Volition management onto PGC as the company's controlling shareholder."

"What does that mean, exactly?" Harry asks.

"It means even if we didn't actually know the Blue Rock subsidiary was running illegal guns, they can say we should've known, so we should still be liable." Derek once again shoots a glance my way.

"Correct," Terrence jumps in. "Beyond criminal prosecution, civil lawsuits would run rampant. Anyone who lost money in the IPO, the Volition employees who are now out of work, victims of gun violence who can trace it to an illegal Blue Rock firearm… They could all come after us on a negligence claim."

"And it looks like the Senate Armed Forces Committee will convene a hearing on this," Martina Hayes says, tapping her iPad with vigor. Tim Rouchard will likely be called to testify. I have a back-channel open with Senator Calderon's chief of staff. I'll do my best to keep PGC off her subpoena list, but no guarantees."

"Unbelievable," Derek groans, rubbing his forehead. "Marcia Calderon has a vendetta against private equity. She'll crucify us. It'll be a PR nightmare. Do everything you can, Hayes."

"I always do, Derek," Martina says, her nostrils flaring as she unfurls a portable keyboard and begins typing with fury into her iPad.

Terrence shifts in his seat. "Beyond Congress, the SEC is making inquiries on this. And the FBI's joint task force wants to talk to the entire team that handled the Blue Rock acquisition."

"No," Harry announces. "I won't serve my people up to federal investigators. Lawrence Hadington is an old friend. I'll give him a call."

"He's retired," Derek says.

"But he still controls D.C. for fuck's sake," Harry shoots back. "I'll see if he can give us some cover on this."

"That would make my job much easier," Terrence says. "If we must make a statement to Congress, law enforcement, or the media, we characterize this as a theft of company property, rather than any sort of internal criminal conspiracy. It'll help us in civil litigation."

Derek shakes his head in rage. "How are we even in this situation?" He turns to me. "Channing, how did we not know about this? It should've come up in diligence. If you buried it so we could save another one of your precious Maddox-based companies—"

"I didn't bury anything, Derek."

This guy is a lying piece of corporate waste. Tim Rouchard told me he disclosed this issue to Derek months ago, and Derek made him bury it. I'm sure he's feigning ignorance in case the minutes of this meeting are subpoenaed by any LPs that want to sue us over this.

The truth is, we're only having this conversation because my bullshit arrest pulled my attention before I could really investigate what was going on. Maybe that's an excuse, but it's also reality. I've been stretched thin, and wasting time in AA and community service hasn't helped. But I can't say any of that shit here.

A ping hits my laptop. I click it and see an email from Tessa with everything from our Blue Rock due diligence four years ago.

I study it as Derek mouths off in frustration. Then I find what I'm looking for, and mirror my screen to the conference room television. A pinwheel graph shows, with the header reading: *Company Revenue Breakdown*

42% Aviation

30% Consumer Products

28% Miscellaneous

"The seller must've buried the arms business in this 'Miscellaneous' bucket," I explain.

"You mean John Bing?" Martina asks.

"That's right." Vance nods. "Bing owned Blue Rock before we bought it. We kept him on as COO after the merger."

"Why would we do that?" Derek asks, his tone laced with unnecessary venom.

I jump in, doing my best to shield Vance from Derek's vitriol. "Technically, we bought the company from its creditors. Bing loaded an exorbitant amount of debt on those factories. '08 recession hit him harder than he expected, and by the time COVID shutdown half his factories, they were already nearing bankruptcy. I had our credit fund buy the loans, then we foreclosed on the assets: the factories, the machinery, contracts, licenses, everything. Bing was forced to sell at that point."

"So, you bought the business out from under him?" Derek asks.

I nod. "More or less. But he knew those factories like the back of his hand—"

"And you wanted to take care of your hometown pal after you screwed him," Derek says, not as a question but an accusation. "A man we now know was a fraudster and gun runner."

"No." I keep my voice calm. "It was purely business. Given the world of complexities one might come across when integrating two large enterprises, it made sense to keep him on to run the contract manufacturing business while Tim focused on the aviation development."

Derek doesn't acknowledge my response. Instead, he just focuses on the screen. "So, what am I looking at?"

"The due diligence report we did when we were looking at Blue Rock as an add-on to Volition." I click to the next slide.

"No mention of gun manufacturing, right?" Harry asks.

"No, not in the disclosure schedules."

I display an email from Bing: *The revenues marked as "Miscellaneous" reflect a small set of customer contracts unrelated to our core business which we are in the process of winding down.*

"So, they never wound down the gun business," Vance says.

Terrence leans forward, pressing his eyeglasses to the bridge of his nose as he stares at the screen. "Looks like they never even disclosed it. The bastards."

Harry's gaze snaps to Martina with a realization. "So, they lied to us, and we're a victim in this. That's our story. Marti, sweetheart, prepare a statement. I want to see it in the next hour."

"On it, Harry," Martina replies.

"If that's true," Derek says, "then we have a legal action against the sellers. Right, Terrence?"

Terrence slumps slightly, removing his glasses again and dropping them onto his legal pad. "If there's evidence Bing hid the gun business and snuck it into the sale, then we might have a case for fraud, but he was the only seller—"

"And he's looking at federal arms trafficking charges." I cut in smoothly. "The amount we paid to buy the company went to the creditors. Bing didn't make anything on the deal. Unlikely we'll get a dime back."

"I'd have to agree with Adrian." Terrence says, still fiddling with his eyeglasses.

Derek glances around the table. "So, what the hell am I supposed to say to our investors? Do I really need to remind this room that we are in the middle of a $50 billion fundraise?"

"Of course not." Harry's eyes lock on Derek. "But you're being a tad bit dramatic, Derek."

"Dramatic?" Derek's eyes widen. "Garrett Declan wants to run for the hills over this. If our oldest and largest LP cuts ties, what do you think the rest of them will do? A $10 billion write-off and $40 billion in lost upside doesn't work for them—"

"Enough, Derek," Harry cuts him off abruptly. "You're speaking from a place of fear, and that nonsense is not welcome in my firm."

Silence fills the room, and eyes suddenly drop as the resident douchebag gets put in his place.

"Remind the investors we've collected a bloody lot of fees and dividends from Volition," Harry says. "We obviously won't see the return we had envisioned, but we won't have to write off the entire $10 billion investment. You can also remind them that every other company we've bought with this fund has been a crushing success."

The room falls silent for a moment.

"Someone give Derek our latest exits, for the love of Christ," Harry commands.

Reanne taps her iPad awake, and clears her throat. "In the current buyout fund, we've recorded a 12.4X return on Ravelle Lingerie, a 9.2X return on Cobalt Luggage, 8.2X on DMG Technologies, 6.3X on MelStar Solar, and 4.4X on Iroko Media."

Vance leans forward. "A.C. and I just closed the sale on Nero Couture. 8X return."

"Vance and the team closed it," I correct. "I just supervised."

I always give props to my people, but these are all companies I sourced and practically ran.

Reanne scrolls on her iPad. "We've returned significantly more capital to investors than we've lost, even taking Volition into account."

Derek shakes his head as his lips twitch. "It's not about returns! It's about the goddamn headline!"

The room stills at his outburst.

But then he continues, his rage jumping across the table. "You mean to tell me not a single soul at this firm knew Blue Rock was in the arms business until today? Even after we bought the company and integrated it into Volition? I find that hard to believe."

Me too, Derek, seeing as how you knew also, ya fuckin' dickhead.

"Blue Rock's sales contracts were extremely, and now I realize purposely, vague," Vance says.

"Conveniently vague contracts?" Derek spits out. "You've got to be kidding me." He glances at me. "Channing, you're paid far too well to miss things like this."

I lean forward, keeping my voice even. "Derek, you know I oversee dozens of portfolio companies for this firm, manage hundreds of active bids and exits, all with layers upon layers of workstreams. I don't have time to go through every contract. That's why we have analysts and lawyers."

I let that hang in the air, watching him stew on it for a moment before I begin again. "So, when my diligence team shows me a contract for 100,000 units of 'BRM4 87865' at $4,400 per unit, my work is done, moving the price up to a clean $5,000 per unit. That's why I'm paid what I'm paid."

"Are you seriously trying to explain your negligence?" Derek asks.

I'd love to drop-kick his obnoxious ass right now, but I keep it measured. "Furniture, electronics, machinery, food packaging, sporting goods, textiles, eyeglasses, sunglasses, construction materials, car parts, airplane parts, lawn-mower parts, dog toys... Should I go on?"

I pause before driving the point home, my volume rising. "Blue Rock manufactured damn near every product there is to manufacture. There is no way we would inherently know that 'BRM4' is code for a Blue Rock M4 carbine assault rifle. That's why we ask sellers these questions under penalty of law. John Bing lied."

Vance, visibly uncomfortable, speaks up. "For what it's worth, the M&A lawyers at Linder Boykin didn't flag it either. The team couldn't make sense of the sales contracts, but the customers were real. So was the revenue."

Derek's face flushes. "So now we're blaming the lawyers? Pathetic."

"He's not blaming anyone." I keep my tone calm. "Just stating the facts. We didn't know. But a year after the acquisition, I figured it out during a quarterly audit. Blue Rock's South Maddox factory was assembling weapons for the military and obscuring that revenue in the financial reporting they provided us. I checked the records and confirmed the company had a valid Type 07 FFL License in place, making it perfectly legal to manufacture fire-arms in the United States."

I glance at Harry, sitting quietly at the end of the table, watching the back and forth with her usual calm detachment.

When she speaks, her voice is clipped. "And that's when he brought it to me. I told him to keep it under 30% of Volition's revenue. We keep it under that threshold, we don't need to disclose to the LPs. Isn't that correct, Terrence?"

"That's technically right, Harry," Terrence says slowly. "But this is somewhat of a gray—"

"Exactly." She doesn't let him finish. "We were already pregnant with the thing, so we controlled it. We managed it. The profits were sweet, the synergies were there given Volition's electronic fighter jet development, and our LPs wouldn't care after we exited at a 4X multiple."

Derek's eyes dart from me to her. "You knew about this and covered it up? You both…" He trails off, shaking his head. "And now we're here, responsible for dirty guns on the streets, a $50 billion company reduced to its least valuable bones, litigants lining up to take us to court, and you think we *managed* it?"

"We did nothing illegal, Derek." Harry says. "We did what needed to be done. Protect the return. If we had shut down the arms business, Volition would have taken a significant financial hit."

He scoffs loudly. "Well, your protection plan didn't quite work, did it?"

"The question now isn't who to blame," Harry says. "It's how do we control the damage?"

• • •

A few hours after that meltdown of a meeting, Harry steps into my office alone. No Reanne, no bodyguard, no one to corroborate anything. She doesn't say anything at first. She just walks to my bar cart and pours two glasses of Macallan.

She hands me one as she sits on the leather chair opposite me and takes a deep sip. "You handled that well. I knew you would."

I take my own sip. More like a gulp. The burn cuts through the fatigue.

Harry leans back, the amber glow of the scotch catching in the low light of my office. She's always been a master of making PGC's investment decisions look clean to the outside world, no matter how much dirt lay underneath. Hence, that "we're the victim" façade of hers. She taught me the art of building walls, structuring potentially unsavory transactions with discretion and secrecy in mind. I never objected to her strategies because I wanted my seat at the head of the table. But when I got it, I vowed to do things differently.

"Had I known this gun business would cause such a headache," she says, "I would've let you shut it down like you suggested back then."

I take another deep sip, raising my brow just slightly. "Truth is, without the guns, the Air Force wouldn't have bought into Tim's electric fighter jet model. It made business sense to keep the weapons production in-house."

"None of it matters anymore." Her eyes scan the room before they lock onto mine. "Derek might be right, unfortunately. The media frenzy is shedding an unwelcome light on our entire portfolio. Our LPs will soon start asking difficult questions about our historic investment practices."

I meet her gaze. "PGC has survived worse."

"We have." Harry nods, taking another sip. "But we're in a new day. Stellar returns aren't enough anymore. LPs want a clean conscience. You've got social media and these bloody Gen Z-ers using AI to uncover the skeletons in our closet and make fucking TikToks about them. If we can't change the narrative somehow, this scandal will drag us down."

"So, we refocus. My social impact deals are outperforming the rest of our portfolio. We're hitting our numbers and achieving our ESG goals. Look at RealPoint Medical. We doubled its value in a year and brought cost-effective, quality medical care to inner cities across the country. Job creation, greenifying industrial, investing in minority and women entrepreneurs. We play up that narrative."

"How?" she asks.

"I'll have my CEO at Arcadian Media plant some stories across TV and digital that play up our commitment to positive social impact."

Last year, I acquired one of the largest media conglomerates in the world so we could control the narrative when we needed to. It's not pretty. It's not progressive. It's how the world works.

Harry glances toward the window, her gaze fixed on the city sprawling beneath us. "I agree you've proven the concept of your impact investing program. We've made billions from it, sure, but it won't stop our enemies from coming after us. Not when they smell blood."

"You wanted to shore up your image for moments exactly like this. I gave you the strategy and the deals to do that. Let me start divesting from our ugliest assets so when we're called to testify in front of Congress, we can say with a straight face that PGC is reforming its profit-at-all-costs mentality."

"Don't divest anything yet." Harry is still staring out the window, now lost in the flickering haze of the Manhattan skyline.

"Harry." My voice is slightly more forceful, pulling her gaze back to mine. "It's a smart plan. We can change PGC's image, use the power of its portfolio to create real impact, to solve problems, and still generate rich returns for our investors."

"Turn PGC into a social impact firm?" Harry chuckles softly. "Is that your solution?"

"Why not?"

She flashes an empty smile but then shakes her head softly. "You've always had the workarounds, Adrian. You've done well to insulate us, but I'm just not sure that kind of grand design will do the trick here. If the investors demand a remedial measure, we'll have to give them something."

8

HARRIET PAXTON

As this Volition naughtiness continues to unfold in the news and the pundits continue to criticize my track record, I sit in my office on the sixtieth floor, staring out the window at the city skyline beside the East River. It's a view I never get sick of.

Beneath it, my office is all dark wood walls, leather books, and a velvet chair by the fireplace. It's the kind of old-world British luxury I couldn't afford growing up, so I made damn sure to get it once I could.

A sharp, familiar knock on my office door brings me out of my thoughts.

Through the glass, I can see Derek's face, like a mask of controlled urgency, the kind he wears when he is about to deliver me a headache.

He doesn't wait for an invitation. He never does.

Stan stops him at the entrance. But I wave him through.

"We need to talk." Derek closes the door behind him with a deliberate thud.

I turn my chair slowly to face him, forcing a calm I'm not entirely sure I feel.

"Did Adrian know about the gun running?" he asks. "Volition was his baby for Christ's sake, and he grew up in Maddox. He must have known what Bing was doing."

"We're not speculators, Derek."

"Did you know, Harry?" Derek's voice rises in anger but I ignore him.

"Harry!" Derek barks out.

My eyes widen in genuine shock at his audacity. "Have you lost your bloody mind, Derek? Raising your voice in here like you're the same spoiled child who used to run these halls masturbating in the fucking ficus plant?"

He's suddenly quiet as I remind him, "I built this firm with your father while you were crossing swords with your fellow Boy Scouts of America. I won't be disrespected in this office."

He tries not to glare at me as his cheeks redden. "I don't mean any disrespect, but we need to present a unified front on this."

"You can unify behind me, Derek. This is still my bloody firm and as far as I'm concerned Adrian is still its future."

His face twists into a pained grimace. "You've got to be kidding me. You continue to give him a pass when, time after time, he proves he has no interest in our culture. How can you be so blind? His one-on-five-ball hog mentality has resulted in reckless decision-making and poor oversight of our assets."

I start out the door. "Now is not the time to point fingers, Derek. Let's weather the storm as a team."

Derek scurries in front of me, stopping my path to the elevator. "They're saying our biggest company was selling guns to street gangs, Harry. And that someone at PGC was aware of it and did nothing. We'll need to show our LPs that this isn't an institutional problem, that there is nothing corrupt about PGC's culture, despite what the pundits are saying. Someone will need to be fired, and we both know it's not going to be you or me."

MY FATHER ONCE TOLD ME,

"Son, the only fate worse
than dying is dying a loser."

9

DEREK GRAFF

EXPANSIVE WINDOWS OFFER a panoramic view of the Lower Manhattan skyline. The walls are lined with framed photographs of my father and me standing alongside titans of industry and world leaders. Every surface gleams with polished mahogany, as if the space itself breathes with the weight of the wealth and influence my family has amassed over generations.

I pace in a deliberate rhythm, each step echoing off the vaulted walls. I can sense Channing's anxiety, his discomfort as he shifts uneasily on the marble floor of my office.

"Have a seat." I gesture to the black leather couch in the parlor of my office.

"I'd rather stand. I have a closing dinner in fifteen. What's this about?" His voice is hurried as he checks his phone.

This peon really thinks his time is more important than mine. He infuriates me with his perfectly tailored suit clinging to his broad physique. I'm sure he believes his height gives him a sense of superiority, however deluded that may be.

"I know about the arrest." I keep my tone even. "Driving while drunk and high on cocaine, resisting lawful arrest, and hiding it from us. Not good, Channing."

He blinks rapidly, and his lips part just slightly as if struggling to form words. I drop the case file on the coffee table and watch his stunned reaction as he sits down and thumbs through it.

"Garrett Declan sent it to me," I speak plainly, as if I have nothing to hide. "He always runs background checks on our senior people before he commits to a new fund."

"Why?" Channing asks.

"He advises police pensions, so he has a duty to ensure he's not bringing them into funds run by criminal degenerates like yourself."

But of course, I didn't need Declan to send the file. I paid the coat check at the Volition party to slip coke into his jacket, then had my NYPD contacts pull over his gaudy rapper Bentley. Our policies require all employees to disclose any arrest or criminal conviction, but I knew his ego would keep him quiet. And that Declan would find it.

He places the file on the table and looks up at me. "I can talk to Declan and clear this whole thing up—"

"Not a chance," I exclaim. "You're not going anywhere near any of my LPs. Besides, I've already talked him off the ledge."

"So, what's the problem?" he asks with an eyebrow raised. "Let's just put this behind us and get back to making money for him."

"The problem is… someone has to hang for Volition." My voice sharpens like the crack of a whip.

Channing's eyes narrow as his lips tighten into a thin line. "Someone has to hang, Derek? Do you realize how problematic that statement is coming from you to me?"

Goddamnit, why did I say that? He'll probably sue us for discrimination now. I need to deflect. "It's a figure of speech. Regardless of what the paper trail says, I know you knew about the illegal guns—"

"And so did you. I know Tim Rouchard shared his suspicions with you weeks ago."

"That's a lie, Channing."

It isn't, but he can't prove anything. It would be Tim Rouchard's word against mine, and he's under federal investigation for lying on Volition's IPO filings.

"You've now hidden two potential scandals from this firm, Channing. You can't be trusted with billions in institutional capital."

"Look," he says, "I was going to tell Harry about my arrest, but we've all been distracted by this Volition mess—"

"Resign," I cut in. "I'll write you a check for five hundred thousand dollars right now. Then, you can fuck right off and try to salvage what's left of your career."

I can see that look in his eyes. He wants to snap my neck. I'd love him to put his hands on me so I can put him behind bars again. He stands and steps closer to me, his chin almost grazing the top of my head. What a pathetic attempt at intimidation.

"Or what?" he asks, his voice almost a grumble.

I step forward, reclaiming my personal space. I haven't seen any kind of combat since dorm wrestling at Exeter, but I will not be intimidated.

"Or what?" I nearly scoff. "Or we bury you, Channing."

"No, I'm not letting you fuck me over, Derek. Volition notwithstanding, my carried interest has fully vested. I'm entitled to a $32 million carried interest payout."

I burst out in uncontrolled laughter. "You breached our employment policies when you failed to disclose your arrest and let our biggest LP find out about it first. Carried interest is out of the question."

Channing scoffs. "You think I'll let you do this to me—"

"You know…" I begin pacing again. "I was wondering why you've been out of the office more than in it since the Volition crash. Busy picking up trash on the side of the road, I presume."

"This isn't right." His voice is now devoid of its normal bravado.

I move to my desk, pick up the printed memo, and hold it up as I read. "If Mr. Channing failed to disclose a criminal conviction and hid a drug addiction that limited his ability to maintain sufficient oversight over PGC's assets, leading to a complete write-off of its largest investment, this would present solid grounds for a for-cause termination."

He falls silent.

I place the memo back on the desk. "That's from our employment lawyers."

His mouth stays shut for once. But his pupils drift left and then they still, like he's waiting for a memory to surface. "Derek, we both know who has the drug problem in this room. Does Harry—no, better yet, does your wife know why our LPs love you so much? The parties, the party favors, the escorts."

I nearly laugh at the insinuation. "I'm not an employee, Channing. I'm an owner. I'm not subject to the same standards you are. And you don't know a thing about my wife. You can say whatever you want to her. I'll still be in charge here. And you'll still be terminated."

"This is ridiculous."

"The only thing ridiculous is you driving drunk and then fighting a police officer with illegal drugs in your jacket pocket."

"That's not what happened." His voice carries a lethal coldness. But he doesn't hold the power here. I do.

Then his expression changes. He stares at me as if seeing through me. "It *was* you, wasn't it? The case file says drugs were found 'on my person'. It doesn't say anything about my jacket pocket. You must've put it there at the party. The same coke you were doing with Garrett Declan."

How does he know about that?

"Why the hell would I plant drugs on you?"

"Because Harry wants me as her successor. And because you're an insecure bigot who can't stand to see a Black man with more influence in your daddy's firm than you—"

"Planting drugs, racism..." I scoff loudly. "...Serious allegations you can't prove. But I can prove mine. Take the five hundred K, or I will have you terminated for cause. No severance. No mutual parting of ways. Just the skeleton of what could have been a promising career."

"I'm a senior managing partner, Derek. You'll need Harry's sign-off before you do that."

10

ADRIAN CHANNING

THE NEXT DAY

As I pack my things, I can feel eyes on me through the glass walls, the shock in the faces of my peers. Tessa quietly weeps at her desk as Harry walks by, before stepping into my office.

"I wish you would've come to me." Her voice sounds strained. "We can get past an addiction issue. God knows we've had our fair share, but being dishonest about an arrest? Adrian…"

I really thought she was going to have my back. I should've known better. PGC's governance committee took an emergency vote on my termination. The results were unanimous. I'm out, effective immediately. No thirty-two million in carried interest. No severance. Not even the measly five hundred thousand dollar payoff Derek taunted me with.

"I don't have an addiction issue. Derek set me up."

She raises an eyebrow and gives me a pitiful smile. "Oh, Adrian darling—"

"There's no more 'Adrian darling,'" I snap. "Not when I'm being sacrificed."

"Adrian—"

"No, Harry, your hands aren't clean on this. You need me to take the fall, fine. I'll do it because I'm loyal. It's how I'm built. But you need to take care of the people who are loyal to you."

I turn my back to her and start hastily pulling my deal toys off the shelf. "That's the way of life. In New York private equity, in the projects of East Maddox where I came up, or in the pubs of South London where you did."

I stop packing, then I turn and look her straight in the eye. "Cut me my fuckin' check, Harry. Thirty two mil."

She looks away. "It's out of my hands, Adrian. PGC can't share profits with someone who breached its employment policies. It's a precedent we can't set."

"So, you pay me my thirty-two. Not PGC. You. Personally."

"I can't do that." She shakes her head a bit too hard.

"You paid ten times that amount in taxes last year." I gather my framed photos into a box.

"It's not the bloody amount, Adrian." Her voice quiets as she glances around for onlookers. "Lawrence Hadington pulled some strings. The Department of Justice won't be pursuing any of us over this, including you, but I still have a line of litigants demanding to see my books, claiming I sold my personal Volition stock before the crash and left the public in the lurch. If I paid you $32 million, it might appear as if I'm guilty and parked my profits with you, or—or—or paid you to take the fall."

She's stammering. So full of shit.

"This has to be a clean termination. But I will take care of you when the time is right."

"This is very convenient timing for you and that son of a bitch."

"There's nothing convenient about this," she counters. "I told you just a few weeks ago that you were the future of this firm. Do you really think I want you out like this?"

"I think you want money and power more than anything, Harry. These days, maybe fame, social media recognition, praise from Gen Z-ers, I'm not sure. But I will get what's mine. Even if I need to take it through a court order."

I peer to my left and see Derek and two security guards have arrived outside the door. But as soon as Harry turns their way and raises her index finger, they stop in their tracks and stay outside.

"You won't win a lawsuit on this, Adrian." Harry sighs, turning back to me. "And if you go that route, I'm not sure our friendship will survive."

My lips curl in disgust. "I never fooled myself into thinking we were friends. I just thought that given all the money I've made for this firm, you'd have my back for profit's sake."

"I tried, Adrian, but the board blames you for Volition. Not disclosing your arrest provided the legal means to terminate."

"You could've swayed them but you chose not to," I retort. "You chose to save your own ass instead."

"Stop being a bloody child, Adrian! There are politics at play here. A forty-year-old legacy backed by an extremely conservative LP base. And it's my name on the bloody door. If I'm taken down, this entire firm goes down with it. Thousands of employees, trillions in asset value. Trust me, Adrian. When you're in a position to carry your own water, you'll learn the value of every drop."

"Carry my own water?" The rage in my voice is unmistakable. "I've been carrying my own water, your water, Derek's water, the entire firm's water since the day I stepped foot in this place."

This is the curse of the Black professional in corporate America. You bust your ass to be better than everyone else, sharper than your peers. Unimpeachable. And then your corporate overlord lines their pockets with your labor but then downplays your value the second it's convenient. I kill myself for a decade, barely see my kid, so I can do their dirty work, run their plays, and make them billions. But the second one deal goes south, it's out with my Black ass? Fuck this.

I grab my box of personal belongings, then start toward the door. I stop and glance at my now-former corporate overlord before leaving. "Harry, when it's all said and done, PGC will be nothing more than a place Adrian Channing used to work."

11

DEREK GRAFF

THE MONTGOMERY CLUB is one of the last standing bastions of my father's era. It's a sanctuary of old money and power, a place where the past mingles with the present in a haze of cigar smoke and aged scotch.

The wait staff are all older Black men. Silent and efficient. They're a reminder of the order in the old world: those who served and those who were served. These good old boys are here to facilitate, not grab attention. Channing could learn a thing or two.

I sit back in a deep leather armchair, savoring the rich, earthy scent of tobacco mingling with the peat of the scotch in my glass. Across from me, Niles Tannenbaum lounges in his chair in a dark tweed jacket and a checkered bow tie.

Niles navigated the wild waters of media before he sold his news and entertainment conglomerate for billions. He owns twenty percent of PGC, a substantial stake he acquired during the recession in 1991 when we were overexposed in oil and needed liquidity. This makes him one of the more powerful voices at the table next to Harry and me.

As trustee of the Arnold Graff Family Trust, I control twenty-six percent of PGC's ownership, the shares my father held before he passed. I also received a five percent personal stake when I was named COO. With

Niles on my side, I'll have the majority I need to force her out of the chairman's seat.

"It's not about personal victory, Niles." I swirl the Dalmore 62 in my glass. "I needed Channing out of the way so I could expose Harry's weaknesses, her nonchalance. She's been checked out for years, and he propped her up, attributing his investment record to her leadership."

Niles smirks as he sips. "But you hate him. You can't deny the personal victory."

"Sure, it felt good," I admit. "I haven't forgotten how he embarrassed my daughter. Manipulated her into bed at that exit party in Ibiza."

Niles raises an eyebrow. "Manipulated?"

"My Charlotte was only twenty-eight, still innocent," I exclaim.

"Didn't she say it was consensual?" Niles asks. "If I recall correctly, she initiated it."

"I've always told my daughter to date her own kind," I fire back before I can think to filter myself. "I can't believe she would be with someone like Channing."

"Come on, Derek. The women love him. The media, too. What's it they called him in that Forbes thing? The 'god of PE'—"

"More like devil—"

"Handsome devil." Niles chuckles as he brings the cigar to his lips in slow motion, wetting them first in a way that feels more performative than practical. "I can see why Charlotte fell into the trap."

"Reel it in, Niles. This isn't a private LP dinner, and Channing isn't on the menu. At least not in the way you'd like."

"And you know what I like," Niles smirks as he runs his tongue slowly along the edge of the cigar. His eyes bulge as he strokes it with exaggerated care before letting it hang in the corner of his mouth.

I can't help but shudder. "You can fantasize all you want, but Channing tainted my daughter while he was still a married man. It took everything in me not to put a hit out on him."

Niles's chuckling evolves into full-blown laughter.

"It's irrelevant." The sharpness of my voice quiets him. "I wasn't going to let some flash in the pan, rags to riches diversity case usurp my position at the top. Harry really thought she could make that bastard her successor over me, and I wouldn't do anything about it."

"What an unsophisticated trollop she is," Niles says, still fighting off laughter.

"I couldn't agree more." I take another sip. "Bottom line, I run this firm, not Channing. I was literally raised in this business and know every inch of its infrastructure like my own member."

"But Harry owns a plurality," he says. "She controls the board. She's the 'iconic business-builder,' the 'Queen of the Consumer Markets,' as she calls herself."

"Queen Consumer," I correct him. "That woman just devours everything in her way, no matter the wreckage it causes or who has to clean it up."

"But she's the visionary. The brand name—"

"She's made herself famous, sure. But this firm was started with my father's money and connections. Harry didn't have a penny to her name when she met him. The only reason her last name comes first on the door is because my father trusted her to file the entity formation paperwork when they launched. It was supposed to be Graff Paxton Capital."

Niles laughs in disbelief. "I can't believe Arnold would let that slide."

"It was a different day. Back then, private equity firms thrived under the veil of secrecy. No one gave much thought to branding. My father didn't find it worthwhile to fight his new partner over a name, so he never corrected it."

It didn't help that he was in love with her.

They were co-CEOs and both married with families when their affair started again. Harry let my father believe they had a future beyond their professional partnership. So, he left my mother and tore apart our family to be with her. But Harry never left her husband. When the reality settled in that she had manipulated him once again, he unraveled and called her what she was: "a bloodsucking whore." Unfortunately, it was at our annual Christmas gala in front of the entire firm and some of our key LPs.

Of course, she used the incident to paint him as mentally unstable and convinced the board to force him into retirement. It was presented as a move in the best interest of both his well-being and the firm's. But it was a power play. And just like that, she was the sole CEO. A month later, my father stepped onto the tracks at the Columbus Circle subway station. She may not have pushed him, but it was her doing.

I've never said any of this aloud, but I haven't forgotten. And I won't let it stand any longer.

"You believe you have what it takes to lead this behemoth?" Niles's pointed question snaps me out of my fog.

I smirk, maintaining confidence. "In today's age, the chair of a firm like PGC needs to be someone like me. Someone who understands the power dynamics, the delicate balance of influence and control across arenas."

"Harry and her cronies will say the next chair needs to be a deal-maker," Niles says. "A company-builder."

My eyes flutter upwards as I restrain my annoyance. "Anyone can analyze spreadsheets and calculate deal pricing. We have algorithms for that, for Christ's sake. Do you know how difficult it is to manage conflicts of interest across nearly $2 trillion of assets and thousands of global investors?"

"I imagine you're about to tell me."

"They all want different things, Niles. Some want their money in flashy tech or consumer brands, others want European real estate, Indian private credit, or African oil and gas. We have a fund for every flavor, and I need to know how to sell them. Launching those fund strategies simultaneously? That was my call. Now we're pulling in $30 billion a year in management fees alone."

And it's my name on the email when PGC alerts investors of a major exit and a sizable cash distribution on the way. I'm the one they're indebted to. Not Channing. Not Harry.

"I've seen the quarterly reports," Niles says. "I know how much we've grown since you've been COO—"

"I oversee ten million employees across almost a thousand portfolio companies and twelve other investment firms under our umbrella. It's a complex undertaking, but I've mastered it for the last fifteen years. I've earned my spot at the top."

"I get it." Niles swirls the whiskey in his glass. "What's the latest on this Volition mess? It's turning into a real problem."

"Calderon has officially called for Senate hearings. I got the subpoena last week."

I typically don't let PGC get caught up in congressional crosshairs, but Senator Marcia Calderon is relentless in her crusade to dismantle the private equity industry. Despite my backing her rivals and running smear campaigns against her, she's fortified herself on a platform of fighting for the working man, untouchable in her righteous crusade against our beloved system of capitalism.

Niles winces as he takes a drag of his Montecristo. "Calderon is one spicy Latina. I went toe-to-toe with her when she chaired the media and communications committee. I don't own the New Journal anymore, but I have friends still in charge. They could have buried that story had you asked."

"Channing hid the ball on the guns. My hands were tied. But of course, Harry will leave me to clean up the mess, as always. The firm is at a crossroads, and she's checked out. We need leadership that's fully engaged, not distracted by family drama."

"What family drama?"

I swirl my glass again. "Her son is an addict. She's spent a fortune on rehabs and intervention programs trying to get him clean. Won't take. He lives on the streets now from what I understand."

"Kofi Paxton-Mensah lives on the streets? That's where he went? Jeez, I had no idea. That's awful."

"It is, and she's let it get to her, unfortunately. If my Charlotte had an issue like that, I would step down immediately and devote my full attention to her recovery."

But I raised my daughter better than that. Harry, however, let her African mail-order husband do the child-rearing.

"She's too concerned about her legacy to step down," Niles says. "If she bows out now, she'll be admitting defeat in the face of this scandal."

"Her legacy is secure, Niles. No matter how she got it, no one can take that from her. But her time is finished. I'm ready to take the reins, and the LPs will back me if it comes to that."

"When do you plan to call the vote?"

"I would do it right now if I could, but our bylaws stipulate the Chair can only be removed at the annual shareholders meeting."

Niles lets out a sigh as he crosses his right leg over his left knee. "So, we can't move until next year."

"It just gives us more time to prove Harry is past her prime. She'll flounder without Channing, and I'll be waiting in the wings."

"Sound strategy I suppose," Niles says.

"By the way, I've told every PGC investor, peer firm, company CEO, and reporter who's asked about Volition that Channing is the addict who caused its failure. I need you to do the same."

Niles chuckles as he lights another Montecristo. "Gladly."

"So, I trust I have your full and unwavering support?"

Niles leans forward, his eyes narrowing. "I'll vote your way when the time comes, but I'll warn you, Derek. Harry's not handing over the firm without a fight. Distractions aside, she's still a beast. Not someone I'm keen to make an enemy of. Make sure you have your ducks in a row."

I laugh skeptically. "Niles, did you really let her fool you into thinking she has any actual skills? Harry Paxton is just someone who used to be hot. Someone who fucked her way into every lucrative relationship she could shake her tight ass into and then sucked the profit out of every strong man she could wrap her dirty whore lips around. She screwed my father in more ways than one, and I won't rest until she's out of the way."

And then the name will finally be Graff Capital Partners.

12

ADRIAN CHANNING

THE SOUND OF that doorbell is pissing me the fuck off.

I pull myself out of bed and glance at the naked woman still asleep, her long dark hair splayed across crisp white sheets. I can't even remember her name.

With a heavy sigh, I throw on some sweats and walk down the spiral steps toward the front door. As I open it, warm light spills across the plush rugs and designer furniture of my loft.

"Oh, honey, you look like hell," says Tessa, my former executive assistant. Now, she's just my friend and PGC's Assistant Director of Strategic Communications.

She's wearing a white Celine sweatsuit and matching sunglasses. Her blonde hair is straight and pressed like she just came from a hair appointment.

She's holding two iced coffees and hands me one. I thank her with my eyes as the hangover sets in, leaving my vocal cords momentarily inoperable. I chug the drink as she steps into the expansive space.

This loft used to represent everything I'd achieved: high ceilings, huge windows, designer everything. Now it feels like an overpriced cage.

Tessa scans the disarray: empty whiskey bottles, pizza boxes, and a thin layer of grime creeping over the hardwood floors.

"I've got nothin' to dress up for, Tessa."

My guest from last night stirs, letting out a soft murmur in her sleep.

Tessa glances up, then raises an eyebrow and shakes her head. "And you think drowning yourself in booze and meaningless hookups is gonna fix that?"

I let out a hollow laugh. "There's nothing left to fix. Derek blackballed me. The firms that used to send me Rolexes, trying to poach me, won't even take my calls. I was so fucking loyal to PGC, Tess. Loyal to Harry! And she threw me under the bus."

"I know, honey." A pitying look crosses her face.

I fight like hell to stop tears from falling. "I had it all, and now I don't have shit. Barely a penny to my name."

"Why did you put so much into one deal?" she asks. "You always said to spread your money like roulette."

"I know, but it was a fucking winner, and that's the game, right? You flip your bread, stack it, flip it again until you've got a number big enough to walk away with. I've operated that way since I was twelve years old. And I was supposed to have $32 million coming to me to cover any losses."

I slump onto the couch. Tessa moves around the room, picking up trash like she doesn't know what else to do.

But then she stops, tosses aside an empty pizza box, and then sits on the couch next to me. "Actually, I didn't come here to friggin' clean. I came to get you out of this rut."

"Good fuckin' luck." My hand finds a half-empty bottle of a rare cognac on the coffee table, amidst a sea of empties. I unscrew the top and take it back.

"Adrian, you're the smartest person I know. You will rebound." She grabs the bottle, pulling it from my mouth mid-sip. "But liquor, self-pity, and loose grad students won't help anything."

"I don't even know where to start," I mutter, wiping the spilled brown liquor from my chin.

"You start by facing facts. This place…" She gestures around the loft, "…you need to let go of it. You're not moving forward by clinging to it or that Bentley collecting dust outside. And I know you need the cash."

I glance at the Bentley through the window, once a symbol of success, now just a sinking liability.

"You need to downsize and start fresh," she says. "Sell all this expensive shit. Today. And get rid of the bimbo upstairs."

"And then what?"

"You have a daughter who needs you. Go to Maddox and see her. She has a soccer tournament this weekend."

"How do you know that?"

"We follow each other on social media. Anyways, you need to get out of the city. Clear your head and come up with a plan on how to get your ass back on top."

She's right. The life I built in New York City is over. Wallowing in despair is only keeping me from moving forward. And as for being penniless, the poet known as 50 Cent once said, "In '99, I had a vision and made a decision. Being broke is against my religion."

So, I liquidate everything: the loft and its designer accoutrements, the Bentley, Rolexes, Cartier shades, every piece of swag, every gadget, and every other material item I've ever received from one of my companies, except my mountain bike. After settling debts, I pocket a sum of $79,403.40. I used to spend that on family vacations.

I stand in the empty apartment, the echoes of luxury bouncing off the bare walls as I hand the keys to the broker. Starting over feels like a weight crushing my chest. It feels like failure. But then I remind myself: I'm a mothafuckin' hustler. I've climbed out of nothing before. I'll do it again.

PART TWO

13

ADRIAN CHANNING

I GET TO Maddox and drive straight to Palmer Community Athletics, a massive youth sports complex built years ago by the legendary local businessman, Jerome Palmer. I can't wait to see Riley competing again. She's a natural at everything she tries. From the way she effortlessly controls the soccer ball to the determined look on her face, it's clear that she's the star player.

I sit on the top bleacher next to my ex-wife, Brianna. She's as radiant as I remember, with chestnut brown hair that cascades in waves, almond-shaped eyes, high cheekbones, and smooth features.

We were high school sweethearts and made it out of Maddox together. Granted, Brianna's white, her parents were doctors, and she lived in the affluent North Maddox Hills. When we both got into Harvard, it felt like destiny. We got married after graduation and moved to New York when I got into Columbia Business School and she got into NYU Medical School. Riley was born during my first year in investment banking at Goldman Sachs. At that point, my singular purpose became to make as much money as humanly possible to ensure my kid never had to be confined to the rugged environment I was brought up in. So much for that.

But I suppose Maddox is no longer as rugged as it once was. It's a beautiful day. The sun is shining down on the field, and the fresh smell of cut grass is filling the air. The cheers from the crowd as Riley scores her third goal only add to the electric atmosphere.

"That's my girl!" I shout.

"She needs to pass the ball more," Brianna counters.

"For what? She's the best player out there," I argue, a playful edge to my voice.

Brianna narrows her eyes, already having had enough of my shit. She turns to me. "What are you even doing here, Adrian?"

"What? I can't come to town to see our daughter dominate her soccer tournament?"

Riley attacks the ball for a steal and collides with her opponent. The referee issues her a yellow card.

"Come on, ref! What? You can't be aggressive anymore?" My shouting draws attention from other parents in the crowd. "Shake it off, Riles! You're good, buttercup!"

She looks up at me from the field, clearly embarrassed.

Brianna stares at me like she wants to elbow me in the dick. "She hates when you call her that."

"Since when?"

"She's fifteen, Adrian. Not a little girl anymore."

"Still my little girl," I mutter.

"Are you here permanently?" Brianna asks. "Because if you're not, you need to make that clear to your daughter. I won't cover for you again."

"Do you want me to be here permanently?" I ask, hoping for some warmth from the woman who was once my soulmate.

"Doesn't matter what I want." Her tone is serious but not angry. "I don't know what you want me to tell you. If you're staying in town, great. If you're not, fine. Whatever you do, just be upfront with our daughter about it. Don't get her hopes up that you'll stay only to sprint back to the city when you get bored here."

"I hear you, Bri. I'm done with New York. I'm here to fix what I broke, and that starts with my relationship with our daughter, if that's okay with you."

"It's fine with me, Adrian. Of course, it is, but it's not me you need to worry about. Riley has gone full-on teenager psycho-bitch phase."

"I guess she's at that age."

The game ends, and I walk with Brianna from the bleachers to the parking lot. Riley trails behind as she celebrates with her teammates.

"She starts basketball next week," Brianna mentions. "Can you pick her up from practice? I increased my patient load at the youth center, and things are getting a bit hectic. I was going to ask your dad, but since you're back—"

"No, I'll do it. I don't want my dad driving Riley anywhere."

"You should learn to give him some grace," she says, but I don't want to hear it.

"Listen, Bri, I should let you know—"

"You're broke?"

"Wh-what? How'd you know that?"

"Tessa called me when everything went down. She was worried you might do something crazy. I told her Adrian Channing is way too into himself to commit suicide."

"Thanks... I think."

"And I read the news, Adrian. You're not the only one around here out of work. Blue Rock employed half this community."

"I know." I can't help but wince. "My dad worked the assembly line when I was a kid, before they went bankrupt the first time and laid him off. Before he gave up on working altogether. He got drunk and beat my ass so bad that night."

"I remember the story." Her tone is soft, and she's looking at me the same way she used to look at me when we were teenagers. Like she wants to fix me. "Your mom put him out."

"Then he had the nerve to tell her he was 'just angry.'" I scoff, taking myself back to a memory I've long locked away.

But even after all this time, I remember that night like it was yesterday. While my father drowned in his own desperation, I made a promise to myself that I would never again be at the mercy of things beyond my control. I think that's why I bought Blue Rock in the first place. To seize the power from the company that controlled whether or not I had food on my plate as a child. To run it better and make sure no other kid ever had to deal with that again. This is the first time I've been hit with the reality of what my failure meant to this community.

"So, people are pissed at me?"

"Not at you, specifically," she says. "And I know being back in Maddox is triggering for you, but they are upset. You bought out the city's biggest employer and never even showed your face here. And now you show up after your fancy investment firm throws you under the bus the same way they did this city. It's obvious to those in the know."

I hate the idea that people in my own city look at me like a sellout or even worse, like a dude who ran to the big city, blew shit up, and then ran back home with his tail between his legs.

But I can't deal with that right now, so I change the subject. "Bri, I'm going to need to hit a quick pause on alimony. I can still take care of child support, but I just can't swing $30k a month anymore."

"You know it's never been about money for me, Adrian. You're the one who brought lawyers into it. I just want you to show up for Riley."

"I want that too. And I'm going to. That's why I'm here. I need to rebuild, figure out what's next. But no matter what that looks like, Riley is most important."

Brianna studies me for a long moment. As she does, Riley finishes with her friends and walks toward the car, climbing into the backseat without a word to either of us.

"Excuse me, ma'am," Brianna calls out. "You're not even going to greet your parents?"

Riley backs up and gives me a half-hearted hug. I pull her in for a squeeze.

"You killed it, buttercup." I grin at her, unable to contain my pride, though I'm not sure I want to.

But my eagerness is met with rolled eyes. "Ugh, can you please not call me that?"

"Sure thing, buttercup. Oops, I mean Riles. Wait, can I call you Riles? Or is it Lady Channing, Queen of the Pitch?" My bad dad joke is met with a blank stare.

"Hey, how about we celebrate?" I suggest. "Pizza? Tacos?"

"Do we have to?" Riley asks as she puts in her AirPods.

"You don't have to do anything you don't want to, Riley. Don't ever let anyone tell you otherwise." My tone is steady, though inside I'm disappointed.

"Great," she says, before jumping into the backseat of Brianna's SUV.

"We gotta go anyway," Brianna says. "I have a session. Maybe dinner next time. Take as much time as you need with the payments. We're good."

She heads to the driver's side, then suddenly turns back, grabbing my shirt and pulling me close. For some reason, I think she's about to kiss me, as if this is why God struck down Volition's stock price. So I could give up my pursuit of private equity domination and get my family back.

But then reality hits.

"Just don't be a fuckboy to your own daughter," she warns. "If you're gonna be here, be here."

She lets me go, climbs into the SUV, and drives off. I stand there, unsettled by the fact that Brianna and our daughter seem perfectly content without me, or my money. I expected the loss of it to shake her, to remind her of what she still needed from me. Instead, she looks untouched, as if my absence, financial and otherwise, makes no difference at all.

14

ADRIAN CHANNING

IN THE PARKING lot of Palmer Business Square in Downtown Maddox, I see pylon signs for the Law Office of Charles L. Palmer & Associates, Palmer-Auto, Palmer Printing, Palmer Liquor, Palmer Sporting Goods, Palmer Dry Cleaning, PalMart, and, most notably, Palmer Furniture Emporium.

Stepping into Charles's office, the air carries the scent of aged leather and polished wood. Framed jerseys and signed baseballs, as well as diplomas from Penn State and Fordham Law, decorate the walls. Photos of family, friends, and clients stand on a mantle by the window.

Charles sits behind his desk. He's dark-skinned, with a crisp lineup and a goatee, wearing a tailored three-piece charcoal suit, although his jacket is hanging in the corner and his tie loosened after a long day. But still, he has an easy, confident smile that makes you feel like you've known him for years. I guess I have, but I've only spoken to him in person once at our parents' wedding. Outside of the few conversations we had about my case, I don't really know the guy.

He stands and shakes my hand. I'm slightly shocked at how tall he is, probably six foot two. Just a touch shorter than me.

I hand him a bottle of Macallan-24. "Wanted to thank you for your help with that situation in New York."

Charles takes the bottle, inspects it for a moment, and then sets it on a bar cart in the corner of the room. He gestures to the leather armchair in front of his desk, and I take a seat.

"It's my nature to help a good brother in trouble." He flashes a disarming smile. "So, what finally brings you back to Maddox?"

"A nigga got fired." I let out a light chuckle.

He doesn't join me. Seems like he doesn't love the sound of the N-word coming from my half-Caucasian ass.

After an awkward moment of silence, he finally forces a short laugh. He pours two glasses of the Macallan I brought, hands me one, and we clink up.

"I finally found the time to come home, so here I am."

He sips the Macallan and closes his eyes for a second, enjoying it. "I'm flattered to be the first stop on your homecoming tour, but curious as to why now?"

"I haven't been back to the Mad Dog in forever. The city has grown."

I glance behind him through the bay window overlooking the city. My eyes land on the new luxury apartments being constructed by the riverfront, then they shift to the old plastic plant they're demolishing next door.

"I don't know this place at all anymore. Figured your office would be a good place to start networking."

"It's a fair assessment," he says, nodding slowly. "Is that why you had Volition acquire Blue Rock? Using M&A to reconnect with your roots?"

"Something like that." I laugh off the insinuation that I'm not in touch with my roots.

"Surprised you never came home, even though you were buying companies out here and taking them public."

"Yeah, maybe if I did, it wouldn't have turned into such a shit show." I take another sip. "This conversation is covered under attorney-client privilege, right?"

"If you need it to be."

"We tried really hard to play up the aviation angle and stay vague on the other revenue streams. I mean, growing up in East Madd, everyone knew what Blue Rock was. Contract manufacturer by day—"

"Glocks R' Us by night," Charles finishes.

I chuckle, but he doesn't join me.

"If I had known you back then," he says, "I would've told you buying Blue Rock Industries was a bad idea."

"What do you mean?"

Charles shifts in his seat. "My father had some business with Blue Rock back in the day. Private label furniture. They'd manufacture the pieces, slap on the Palmer brand name. We'd sell as many as we could. It didn't work for a few reasons. The folks who ran those factories have always been a bit... shady."

I wish I had known him back then. Might've saved my career.

I brush past it. "That's right. Big Jerome Palmer, the mattress king with the smooooothest collection on the East Coast." I do my best impression of his deep Barry White-style voice inflection. "I loved those commercials as a kid. He made his sales events feel like the best parties in town. How's he doing? How's the business?"

"The Emporium Discotech..." He says it like he's recollecting a fond memory. "My father knew how to throw a party, and he knew how to sell."

He smiles fondly before his tone turns somber. "He's uhhh... He's no longer with us."

"Oh, I'm sorry. I–I didn't know."

"All good, brother." He shrugs slightly as he takes a sip. "But the business is growing. We opened three new locations this year."

"How many do you guys have altogether?"

"Fifteen across Pennsylvania, Jersey, Baltimore, D.C., parts of the Midwest, Atlanta, and Miami."

"Impressive," I concede. "Especially with Amazon and Wayfair dominating the market."

"I'm not in the weeds on the furniture business outside of managing its legal affairs, of course. My older brother, Rome, has been running the family business for some time now."

"I don't think I've ever met him. Actually, I don't think I saw either of your brothers at the wedding, but maybe I missed them."

I look at the framed photo of the three brothers as boys with their father. I catch him glancing at it as well.

"They couldn't make it," he says bluntly.

An awkward silence ensues for a few moments as I wait for the explanation as to why two sons wouldn't attend their mother's wedding. None comes, so I change the subject.

"Well, look... I've bought and sold hundreds of companies across every sector, but consumer goods have always been my specialty. If you guys are interested in a national expansion, I could help turn the Emporium into a big box player."

He smirks. "I try not to speak for my brother, but I can tell you we're not interested in any private equity money, all things considered."

I stay silent, looking down at my drink, and then I take a gulp that clears the cup.

I can feel him noting my disappointment as he takes a sip of his own.

"In all seriousness," Charles says, "my father was always adamant about keeping ownership in the family."

"Just a thought." I back off.

"Not a bad one, just not for us." He stands to pour me another shot. "But there's a ton of value in this community. Plenty of local entrepreneurs looking to take things to the next level."

I nod in agreement as I lift my glass to my mouth for a short sip. "That's why I bought Blue Rock out of bankruptcy. Hoped it would be a tentpole to bring real capital into the city, save some jobs in the process. Turns out that company's just cursed."

"What you did was bold," Charles says. "Not many would put their reputation on the line for a town like Maddox."

"That's why I got into private equity." I glance back out the window. "To help this place. My plan has always been to learn as much as possible on Wall Street, build enough influence to be able divert some capital to my hood, stack my chips in the process, and then launch my own firm. An investment platform for the community. Capital sourced and deployed in companies that aren't just profitable but are creating positive social impact in the communities they operate in. Real returns, real change, with a focus on underserved, distressed cities like Maddox."

"A noble tycoon, huh?" Charles takes a sip of his scotch and smirks, but then his eyes lock on mine. "I'll tell you what, I like the pitch. Let me know when you're ready to make that vision a reality. I'm always looking for opportunities to put my family's cash and reputation to work. I have some clients looking to do the same."

I pause mid-sip. "I'll keep that in mind."

"But I'm still curious as to why now?" Charles asks. "I had a couple of PE clients when I was at Linder Boykin. I know what you guys pull in. I bet you could've left your firm years ago and launched this strategy, no?"

"PGC is old school. They have a ten year vesting schedule on carried interest distributions to make sure rainmakers like me stick around and don't go work for competitors. I was entitled to a $32 million payout before they fucked me out of it."

"Sheesh!" Charles exclaims in a high-pitched tone, an interesting deviation from his usual stoic demeanor. "I'd be murderous."

I take a long sip. "Trust me, I felt that emotion. Before that, I put everything I had into the Volition deal, so I have no choice but to start fresh. I guess I also wanna try my hand at rebuilding what I broke here."

Charles starts laughing a full-bellied laugh, almost uncontrollable. "This city was broke and broken long before you came through with your private equity money. Maddox needs more than well-placed capital."

His laughter dies down but doesn't stop completely. It's clearly the laugh of a man long-disillusioned by the corruption and inept government that plagues this city.

"I can't say I disagree." I clear my cup. "But Job insecurity, bad infra-structure, food deserts, fuckin' crime. It all starts with money. You wanna change a community, all you need is the capital and the desire to do it. Issue is, those who desire to make change usually don't have the capital."

"And those who have the capital?" Charles asks.

"Usually, they only desire more capital."

15

ADRIAN CHANNING

TWO MONTHS LATER

BRIANNA'S WORDS LINGER in my mind. *Don't be a fuckboy to your own daughter.* So I've been trying to be the dad I should've been all along.

I still can't find a job, which means I have plenty of time to drive Riley to and from school, her various soccer, basketball, and track practices. My baby girl is a star athlete. A star completely. I cheer her on and even cut up oranges for her halftime snacks. She and I used to be so close before the divorce, but afterward, things started to fall apart.

"Why don't you just go back to New York?" she asks from the backseat of the Prius.

"Because you're here. I'm here for you, Riles."

"Whatever."

"Just tell me what you need, buttercup. I'll do whatever it takes to fix this."

"You wanna know what you can do, Dad? You really wanna know?"

"Yeah I—"

"DON'T CALL ME BUTTERCUP!" Her voice is a high-pitched shriek that rattles my bones. "That's what you can do, Dad!"

"Okay—"

"You're just here because you lost your job. I know you'd rather be in New York chasing hookers and doing cocaine or whatever the fuck you do there."

"Hey, watch your mouth."

She's developed a real trucker's mouth. A result of my shitty parentage, I'm sure.

"I googled you, Dad. Found your arrest record. It's pretty rich for someone who drives drunk and takes cocaine—oh and don't forget, cheats on my mom—to be telling me how to act!" The pain in her voice sounds visceral.

"First of all, I don't chase hookers. No one chases hookers. That's kind of the point of a hooker, sweetheart." I pause, hoping my crude humor hits like it used to.

"You're not funny," she announces, though I can see her fighting off a chuckle.

"Riley, I don't spend time with hookers, and I don't do cocaine. It was planted—"

"Yeah sure, Dad." She's clearly not believing me.

"Look, I'm not perfect. I know that. But I'm here now. Let's just start fresh—"

"No!" she shouts. "Why do you think you can just show up and act like everything's fine? Like you're just my loving dad. Like I literally didn't see you for over a year. Maddox is an hour and a half drive from the city. You missed every game, every practice, everything. You weren't there when I needed you. So don't pretend like you care now just because you have nothing else to do."

I flinch at the truth in her words. I have no response that could make up for my actions, and for too long I denied the impact they would have on the person in this world I love most. So, I stay silent, letting her anger wash over me.

•••

Palmer Furniture Emporium in Downtown Maddox is a concrete oasis with its guts spilling out into a cavernous space. The city surrounding it is filled with the frantic hometown energy the Mad Dog is known for. Industrial buildings and office towers loom over bustling streets, where the sounds of construction and commuters passing by can make it hard to hear yourself think.

A vast loading bay sits on the side of the massive building where forklifts and workers are constantly moving. Inside, rows of furniture stretch into the distance like a forest of wood and upholstery.

I pick out a mattress set, living room set, and dining room set to furnish the apartment I just signed a lease for. Just the basics, since I project I'll be out of cash within the next few months. I'm glad to get out of that motel and into an apartment, but the thought of laying down roots in Maddox is haunting. It's another reminder of how far I've fallen.

After I make my purchase, I journey up the warehouse steps. I imagine that's where I'll find the CEO, Rome Palmer, Charles's oldest brother.

I peer through the window in the front door of the top-floor office, my gaze immediately drawn to the bay window that offers a sweeping view of the bustling warehouse below. The room gives a unique blend of casual luxury and old-school charm. An old black couch sags in one corner, while a large mahogany desk dominates the space. By the couch is a sack of footballs with a label that reads: PCA.

Rome sits behind the desk, ticking through a log in a notebook, his concentration palpable. He's dark-skinned like his brother, probably in his early fifties, with a short salt-and-pepper afro and matching beard. He's sturdy with a chiseled face, but he looks tired. The black Gucci sweatsuit and yellow gold chain with a diamond-encrusted whistle pendant hanging around his neck hint that business is booming for the Palmers.

I knock once, then push open the door, but he doesn't even look up to acknowledge me.

"The showroom's downstairs." His voice is deep and hoarse, and his eyes are still fixed on his notebook.

"Oh yeah, I know. Sorry, I'm Adrian Channing, Paul Channing's son."
I offer my hand. He doesn't even glance at it.

"I know who you are," he says, still not looking up from his notebook.

I glance to the left, spotting the wall of TV screens displaying security footage of what seems like every corner of the massive warehouse.

"Okay... Yeah, well, uhh... the store is amazing, by the way. You guys have grown in a major way since I was a kid."

He doesn't respond. Doesn't even look at me.

"Charles mentioned you guys are in the middle of an expansion," I press on. "That's exactly where my expertise will prove valuable to you. I've spent the better part of the last two decades helping companies like yours reach new heights. I know how to position a brand so it attracts not just consumers but serious growth capital. I've built relationships with private equity firms, institutional lenders, and investment banks that specialize in funding this kind of transition. If you're interested in making the Emporium a national, maybe even a global, brand, I'd love to put my network and expe-rience to work for you as a consultant. A small cash retainer is all I'd need to get started."

Rome keeps his eyes on the notebook. "The Emporium is fami-ly-owned and operated. Everyone who works for me, employee or consultant, is a member of my family."

I could believe that if not for his very Caucasian foreman opening the door and brushing past me. Maybe they are family because he's also not acknowledging my existence.

"Ayo, boss man." His South Philly accent is unmistakable.

"Yeah, Frankie?"

"Just thought you should know..." Frankie hesitates as he eyes me up and down. "The last of the private label selection is going out tonight."

"Okay, Frankie."

"Any update on the new shipment?" Frankie asks. "We've got a few customers... uhh... disgruntled by the delay."

Rome lets out a quiet grunt. "Workin' on it."

Frankie sighs quietly, as if to hide his frustration before leaving the office. I'm getting the sense that Rome Palmer is a man of few words.

"Adrian, we're good." He's still not budging from his notebook. "I saw what you did with Blue Rock Industries. We don't need your services."

For a moment, I just stand there. I used to walk into rooms like this to fire guys like him after taking over their companies. Now I'm asking for a chance to help him, and he won't even look up from his notebook. He doesn't see me. He just sees the version the media fed him. The scapegoat. Not the truth. I can't lie. It hurts.

16

ADRIAN CHANNING

My phone sits dead silent on the coffee table. Used to be people were blowing up Tessa's line, damn near stalking her trying to reach me. My CEOs, my deal teams, Harry. But now, no one's checking for me. The world outside keeps moving while I'm stuck on this cheap couch in this pit of unproductivity.

I've gone on fifteen interviews in Maddox, mostly for middle management roles at local industrial companies that I'm wholly overqualified for. But as soon as they see the arrest on my record, the conversation shifts, and suddenly, there's no offer. I can't even get a low-level bank teller job at Maddox Savings & Loan because Derek rat-shit weasel Graff set me up.

Tuesday afternoon, and I'm staring at the ceiling, surrounded by empty beer bottles, until I'm roused by a Google alert.

PGC has been summoned by Marcia Calderon, the senator from Pennsylvania, to testify in the Senate Armed Services Committee, which she chairs. Given Volition's relationship with the military, the scandal gave her the opportunity to renew her attack on private equity. On top of that, Calderon is from the Latin Quarter of West Maddox, so I'm sure this is personal for her.

I sink into the couch, remote in hand, as I click on C-Span. The television reveals the Senate chamber mid-hearing.

"I have the floor, sir!" Calderon sternly shuts Derek down.

His shit-eating grin promptly fades. He sits next to Terrence Weiss, PGC's General Counsel. No Harry in sight.

"The federal government takes its business with the private sector seriously. The capital your firm has injected into Volition Aeronautics—capital which, I'll add, largely comes from the pensions of American workers—has worked to enable corruption, arms trafficking, and mass shootings across America. How do you explain this?"

Despite the Senator's vitriol, Derek keeps a calm expression. "Thank you, Senator. Unfortunately, PGC, as an investor, was a victim of the theft and fraud perpetrated by John Bing in Maddox, Pennsyl—"

"How, Mr. Graff?" Calderon demands. "How does a forty-year-old investment powerhouse like yours fall victim to such a lie?"

Derek leans into the mic. "Our investment in Volition was led by a rogue operator who ran afoul of internal controls designed to deter this sort of activity. He neglected to bring forward the true nature of the revenues being generated by the Blue Rock subsidiary, and failed to disclose to the firm the discrepancy in ATF reporting. This person has since been terminated, and we are taking remedial action to recover as much of this loss as we can for our investors and their pensioners."

"Who was this 'rogue operator' within PGC?" Calderon asks.

Terrence Weiss leans into the mic. "Senator, we are subject to confidentiality and privacy laws—"

Calderon cuts him off with vigor. "Twenty thousand workers in my state are now out of work because of this rogue operator, Mr. Weiss. If you can't name the person responsible for this latest abuse of taxpayer dollars, why should we believe a word of this?"

"While we can't name him," Derek replies, "I can confirm he was integrally involved in the management of our investment in Volition. He was informed of the stolen weapons and withheld that fact from firm leadership, disrupting PGC's long-tenured record of regulatory compliance and responsible asset management. We believe he was dealing with a substance abuse issue."

He doesn't say my name, but two seconds of googling would reveal that I was PGC's representative on Volition's board and that I'm no longer listed on their website.

My phone erupts with news alerts, social media posts, and then a flurry of texts from my contacts in financial media, all alleging that I'm the rogue operator Derek is talking about and asking for my comment. I kick the TV, sending it crashing to the floor.

I call Charles.

"The noble tycoon," he intones. "I take it you'd like to sue PGC?"

He must've been watching.

"Yeah, for every fuckin' dollar. They've been smearing my name across the industry. Now they're calling me an addict on national television—"

"Did you talk to my brother Rome about the furniture business after I told you he wouldn't be interested?" Charles asks, abruptly changing the subject and his tone which is now more serious.

"I-I..." I'm caught off guard. I mean, yeah, I talked to him, but the way he's asking you'd think I walked in there and slapped him around.

"I stopped by the Emporium to pick up some furniture and ran into him. Thought I'd float some ideas his way."

"Don't ever talk to my brother about his business," he says. "You need something from him, you come to me. Do you understand?"

"I can't talk to a businessman about his business?" My tone is stronger than I intended, but I'm fuckin' pissed. "That's all I've done for the last two decades, Charles, and I'm damn good at it. I mean do you know how much money I've made for clients and investors over the last twenty years? The number would make your head fuckin' spin. With respect, you guys would be hard-pressed to find a business strategist like me, let alone one willing to work for crumbs off the table."

"It doesn't matter, Adrian." His tone matches mine in fervor. "My family is very private. I'll say it again. You need something from him, you come to me. Do you understand?"

I take a deep breath and decide it's not worth it. "I do. Didn't mean to overstep."

"All good, brother," His tone is suddenly chipper. "I'll file your lawsuit."

• • •

I step into the H&R Block in Downtown Maddox. The fluorescent lights flicker above, dropping a sterile glow over the tired, beige walls. I used to have the best CPAs in New York handling my taxes. Now, I'm slumming it, trying not to cringe at the smell of cheap coffee and old carpet.

As I wait in line, I hear a familiar voice. "A.C.?"

I look to my right and spot Mitchell Lowenstein, one of my best friends from high school.

I stand in shock before a smile forms on my face. "Mitchie?"

I give him a bear hug, lifting his legs off the ground. He's a stocky, five-foot-four firecracker with dark, graying hair that's thinning at the top. His Maddox accent is unmistakable. Vowels cut off quick, like he doesn't have time for them. Consonants hit hard, every T and K snapping in your ear. There's a sharp edge to every word, making even the driest joke sound gritty.

"My man, A.C. *Always Collectin'* a check." His voice is raspy but full of life.

I haven't seen Mitchie in years, but without his family's help, I may not have escaped East Madd. I practically lived with them when my father was locked up.

"How you been?" I ask. "How's your mom and dad?"

"Can't complain," he mutters, shifting uncomfortably. "But Momma and Poppa Lowenstein are in the heavens with Pac and Big."

"Damn. I'm sorry, man. Why didn't you call me?"

He shrugs. "Didn't wanna bother you."

"It wouldn't have been a bother. Your mom and dad were like parents to me. I owe them a lot. Owe you a lot."

Mitchie nods slowly, his lips pressed together before he lets out a smile. "We took some chances back then, didn't we? Now look at us, getting old. Well, maybe it's just me since you don't look a day over thirty, ya fuckin' Adonis! What the hell are you doin' back in the Mad Dog?"

Mitchie and I duck into a pub for lunch and catch up. I give him the entire download on PGC, Volition, Riley, and Brianna, and the reason I moved back.

"So, what have you been up to, little buddy?" I ask.

He punches me in the shoulder. He always hated it when I called him my little buddy.

"I'll still cut your throat, you tall fuck." He laughs.

I laugh with him as I take a swig of a cheap lager. "Seriously though, last I heard you were in law school?"

Mitch looks up at me as he finishes a bite of his burger. "Yeah, I got the law degree and passed the bar, worked for Linder Boykin for a few years in their tax group in Philly, mainly to appease Poppa Lowenstein. I quickly realized I didn't wanna be another Jew boy tax lawyer in this world, so I pivoted."

"To what?"

"Dabbled in tech for a bit." He pauses briefly as he chews. "Taught myself how to hack together code; do a little day trading here and there. I've got a nice algorithm going."

I smile at the sound of investing. "What're your returns looking like?"

"Not bad. Nothing like the numbers you're used to playin' with."

"Enough to live on?" I ask.

"Nah." He subtly shakes his head. "I keep the day job as an administrator at H&R Block, filing taxes, forming entities, keeping the books for local businesses."

"You enjoy that?" I ask, noticing the displeasure in his description of the work.

"Eh…" He shrugs. "It is what it is. Like anyone trying to get ahead in this world, I've got side hustles."

I raise an eyebrow. "You know I love a side hustle. What do you got?"

"I run my own little 'digital cleanup service,' mostly fixing parking tickets in DMV records, erasing minor offenses from court records, forging business licenses, tax returns… all for a fee."

"Not bad." I smirk. "Not worried about the heat?"

"Nah, I keep it low level and I'm damn good at covering up my tracks. Most of my clients are just regular folks trying to get a job and tired of having to explain some harmless weed arrest from back in the day."

"Commendable."

I contemplate hiring him to clean up my record but can't bring myself to divulge that fuck up of mine. I'm supposed to have evolved out of that part of my life.

After lunch, Mitch goes back to work at H&R Block, promising to push my tax return to the top of his pile. For some reason, even though I'm still fuming at the embarrassment that has become my life, I feel encouraged. Reconnecting with Mitch makes me realize that real friends won't take the word of some piece of shit elitist liar over your own.

As I walk toward my car, I catch a glimpse of a familiar figure in a tailored suit, stepping out of a gray sedan across the street. Looks like Josie Simmons. I met her a few years ago in Paris at SuperReturn, a conference for professionals in the investment industry. She's a venture capitalist out of Palo Alto, which begs the question of what the fuck she's doing in Maddox, Pennsylvania right now. The sight of her stirs something within me. She must be chasing a deal. And if she's chasing a deal, I need to chase it too.

She walks across the side walk and steps into a diner with a walk-up ice cream window that has a line stretching down the street and around the block. Geraldine's Homemade, a local staple. I grew up on that ice cream.

I cross the street, and step into the diner. I scan the large space for her but she seems to have vanished in the sea of customers inside. So, I stand in line.

The queue moves fast and much smoother than I'd expect for a place this crowded. Someone has trained this crew well.

A few minutes later, I'm holding a hot cone with a scoop of their famous caramel crunch. I manage to secure an open barstool and enjoy the ice cream while feeling the energy in the space. They must be doing pretty well.

About halfway through my scoop, I look up on the wall and see framed and autographed photos of celebrities who have stopped in over the years. My eyes pan across them, taking in the history of this iconic local brand.

I stop on a framed article: *Silicon Valley Venture Capitalist Takes Family-Owned Dessert Brand National.*

I look down and see Josie walking out of the back kitchen, now flanked by two Patagonia vest-wearing finance bros who I'll call Chad and Todd. They exchange what seems like a few tense but cordial words and then exit the store. Josie sees them out, and they drive away in their Tesla.

As she re-enters the store, she catches me staring at her, and a smile comes on her face.

God, she's stunning.

17

ADRIAN CHANNING

SHE CARRIES THAT effortless grace and quiet confidence that says she's been through things and came out stronger. Mid-thirties, maybe. Chestnut-brown skin that almost glows with long black braids falling down her back.

"Adrian Channing." Her smile almost lights up the room. "I can't believe my eyes."

"Josie Simmons." I smile back. "I can say the same."

She hugs me tight, and I almost lose myself in the embrace.

She grabs two coffees from the kitchen, and we settle into a booth.

Talking to her feels like catching up with an old friend, even though we've only met once before. I'd just finished a consumer M&A panel when she approached me at the hotel bar to pick my brain. What began as business networking turned into a deep conversation about life and dreams, and we ended up talking for hours. There was a spark, but I was still married to Brianna then and was clinging to the hope of making it work for Riley. So, nothing happened.

"Can't believe I forgot you grew up in East Maddox too. I know I'm older than you are, but we must've crossed paths at some point."

"Maybe," Josie says, "but I went to boarding school in California when I was thirteen."

"And you stayed for a while, I take it?"

"Undergrad and MBA at Stanford. Then I was recruited by Andreessen Horowitz and worked as an investor there for six years."

"What made you leave?"

"I got tired of watching mostly white male founders take capital and make all the wrong decisions with it."

"Figured you could do it better?"

She flashes a confident smile. "I knew I could."

"That why you came back?"

"Not exactly," she says, glancing down at her coffee. "My dad got sick, and no one else in my family had much business sense, my dad included, if we're being totally honest. So, I decided to move home and help him out."

"How's he doing?" I ask.

Her eyes lift to the framed photo of a large man in a chef's apron and a wide smile with a placard reading, *Martin Simmons, In Loving Memory: 1955 – 2020.*

"He died during COVID. The diabetes..." Her voice trails off.

"Oh I'm so sorry."

"It's alright." She glances around the diner, her eyes lingering on the faded checkered floor and the jukebox in the corner, as if searching for a piece of him in the familiar surroundings. "My mother and I decided to turn the brand vegan. Hopefully, he's happy with where we've taken his legacy."

I nearly spit out my bite of ice cream. "This is vegan?"

She laughs. "And one-hundred percent organic. Inspired by my dad's recipe but without all the stuff that's killing our community."

"You've clearly done a great job, Josie. I remember when I was a kid, the walk-up stand in East Madd was the only location. Your dad probably dreamed of strangling me, given how many scoops me and my boy Mitchie ran off with over the years."

She lets out a playful gasp and tosses a crumpled napkin at me. We both laugh when I dodge it.

"But he always served us." I slowly nod my head. "He was a good man... No doubt he's proud of you."

She reaches over and touches my hand softly. "Thank you."

She looks into my eyes, and I nearly melt.

"So, how long are you in town?" she asks. "I can't imagine PGC is opening an office in Maddox."

"I left PGC actually. I've moved back to Maddox full-time."

"Oh, interesting." Her hand is still resting on mine, our eyes still locked, the moment stretching.

But I walked in here to investigate an investment opportunity, not get a date.

"So, are you selling the company to Bonder Foods?" I ask.

She's caught off guard. I can see it in the slight shake of her head as she processes my question. "How'd you know I was talking to Bonder Foods?"

She slowly withdraws her hand from mine.

"I can smell an M&A deal from a mile away, Josie. I saw those two perfectly coiffed Patagonia bros that strolled out of here earlier. Chad and Todd?"

She smirks, an air of disbelief flickering across her face. "How do you know them?"

"Bonder Foods is a PGC portfolio company," I admit. "I sat on the board up until a few months ago. I know their entire corporate strategy team. Shit, I hired some of 'em."

I guess Chad and Todd are their real names. I knew I recognized those white boys.

"Oh wow," she says. "So, what's your take?"

"Well, what're they offering?"

"I'm subject to an NDA. You know that, Adrian."

I smirk, impressed. "Fair enough. How's your wholesale footprint?"

"Growing but not where it needs to be. We have orders pending from Wal-Mart, Whole Foods, and Target, but my father's focus was brick and mortar. Between you and me, he over-leveraged us to open these new locations."

"I imagine the bulk of your profits is being used to service that debt, instead of fulfilling orders?"

"That's why I'm considering a buyout from Bonder. My father's dream was to monetize this brand but I can't do that without a serious bankroll."

"He wouldn't mind you selling his baby?"

"He'd see the value in a deal like this. He was a man of the community but he was a capitalist."

"Sounds like a man after my own heart." The comment prompts subtle laughter from both of us. "His moves make sense. Every business needs cash to grow, especially in retail. The market after COVID hit though..." My face twists into a grimace before I can stop it.

"Yeah..." Her own grimace appears. "That's when we moved into the packaged dessert space. Wholesale and direct-to-consumer."

"How many retail locations do you have?"

"Seven altogether across Maddox, Philly, Delaware, and South Jersey. All owned real estate."

"Impressive. What about social?"

"Just crossed five million followers across all platforms."

I whistle in astonishment.

"Yeah, we were on Shark Tank," she says. "Didn't get a deal but got a huge rush of followers and a surge of orders. Just trying to ride the wave, ya know?"

"EBITDA?"

"Is this a pitch meeting, Adrian?" She laughs.

"It might be."

"We did $3 million last year," she says quietly.

I raise an eyebrow. "You make any money on that?"

"We made a few bucks." Josie says, unable to hide a cheeky grin. "But it's all tied up in debt service as mentioned."

"Nonetheless, you are legitimate." I'm unable to hide my excitement at my first potentially investable asset.

"So, what's your take?" she asks again.

She's looking for free advice from the world's foremost business mind, though, with those eyes, I think I'd give her just about anything she asked me for.

"Bonder is very well capitalized," I begin. "They'll make a cash offer to buy you out and make Geraldine's their marquee brand in the vegan dessert space. I would guess they're offering ten to twelve million for the whole thing?"

"Strong guess."

"I bet it is." I smirk. "The unfortunate flip side is they'll cheapen your dad's legacy with subpar ingredients. They'll replace that homemade quality with a mass-produced mush because that's the only way they know how to scale. But you've got to ditch the bad debt on the brick and mortar and focus on packaged desserts. That's where your scale is."

She looks concerned, not as if it's new information. She was a VC. She understands the reality of scaling and exiting a business. It seems more like hearing it aloud confirmed her suspicions.

"Maybe you just want to cash out, and that's fine. Trust me, I'm the last person to criticize anyone for chasing a check. But if it's a legacy play, I would think deeply about an alternative funding option that allows you to maintain control of the product and operations."

"Other than taking on more debt," she says. "I could raise an under-priced VC round and dilute myself down the drain. Or stay the course and hope this marketing push helps us scale quickly."

"I've invested in a lot of companies, Josie, and I can tell you I've never seen 'hope' sway a financial projection. Have you thought about a growth equity deal?"

"I have, but Bonder probably won't go for it."

"No, they won't," I affirm. "They'll want full control."

She moves a braid from her face before taking a sip of coffee. "I don't have time to find and vet growth equity firms. If I don't sell now, I'll default on the mortgages my father took out to secure the new locations. The only way to save the legacy is to sell it. I don't even know why I'm telling you all of this."

She laughs, but there's a desperation to it, as if she's searching for a lifeline. And here I am, her financier in shining armor, ready to make her balance sheet troubles go away.

"What if I give you the cash to pay off your bad debt and fund your wholesale orders? I'd buy in at the same ten million dollar valuation Bonder is offering. Let's say sixty percent of your outstanding stock. You keep forty, continue to manage the day-to-day, make sure the product quality stays intact. I'll take over the corporate finance and high-level strategy. We grow the business together."

I gauge her reaction as I take another sip of coffee, as if her decision doesn't matter to me. I'll be off with my millions, ready to go invest elsewhere. To her, I'm a private equity executive who retired early with a nest egg. She doesn't know I have no nest egg. No millions. I can raise the funds, though.

I watch her nose and eyebrows scrunch as she considers my proposal. I lean forward. "You can sell it to Bonder today for ten million or we can sell it to 'em in a few years for a hundred, maybe two hundred million."

I had to let her know who the fuck A.C. is. Always Closing.

She smiles, clearly intrigued, perhaps impressed, perhaps turned on. I definitely am.

"Get me a term sheet," she says, "and we can talk more."

18

ADRIAN CHANNING

BEFORE I OFFICIALLY commit to Josie's vegan dessert brand, I need to do my diligence. I set up drinks with my old friend from high school, Mayor Deanie Howard, a Black, openly lesbian Democrat with a strong grasp of the value in public-private partnerships. After a decade on the City Council, she won the mayoral seat in a hotly contested race.

Deanie has her thumb on the pulse of the city and should be able to tell me if I'm dumping my last few bucks into a well-crafted scam. We meet over drinks at the Arlowe Hotel in Downtown Maddox, one of the higher-end hotels in the city.

"Big Deans," I call out as she walks into the lobby bar.

"Only you still call me that, you clown," she says as I hug her five-foot-one frame.

My smile widens. "Ain't so big anymore, my friend. You look good. Thank God for Ozempic, am I right?"

She shakes her head, clearly restraining the urge to pop me in the mouth. "A.C., still an asshole, I see."

Deanie and I came up together in the Ironbridge Homes. Though she stayed in the north tower and I stayed in the south, we walked to school together most days and to our friends' funerals on others. College pulled us in different directions, but when two people survive the projects and rise to

prominence in their own realms, a bond gets created that nothing, neither time nor some harmless fat jokes, can break.

"Seriously, Deanie, you look great."

Her cheeks flush just a bit as she sits down. "I guess it's not that bad to see you, Adrian. What brings you back?"

"I wanted to be closer to Riley. PGC washed their hands of me, and I suddenly had all the free time in the world."

"I forgot Brianna and Riley moved out here to escape your trifling ass." Deanie laughs as she sips her drink. "I've been meaning to catch up with Bri."

Maddox only had two public schools back in the day, so even though Brianna and Mitch grew up well-off on the North Side, they went to high school with Deans and me on the East Side. We were like the four amigos. Mitch and Deanie even had a thing for about two seconds in junior high before she realized she liked girls.

"But I know you, Adrian. You're looking to make a move on something, and it's not just fatherhood."

I explain my interest in investing in Geraldine's Homemade and other homegrown companies through my new investment firm, Community Capital Partners (CCP).

Deanie leans back in her chair, a thoughtful expression on her face. "Maddox is growing, slowly but surely. We're no longer the contract manufacturing capital of America like back in the day, but tech is bringing in jobs. Maybe not fast enough, but they're coming in. We've got a lot of small businesses here that are just beginning to thrive. They definitely need smart growth capital."

"I can sense that."

"But with Blue Rock..." She takes a deep breath. "...I'm wary about big private equity firms and greedy venture capitalists coming in to commandeer the city's talent, get themselves paid, and then cut and run when shit hits the fan."

I settle back into the chair and take a measured sip of whiskey from my glass, trying to project a calm confidence. "I'm not just here to make a quick buck, Deanie. I've always been invested in this city. That's why I put those campaign dollars behind you."

She eyes me warily. Her skepticism is evident. "And I appreciate it, but you're aware that when people like you come back to 'help,' it often feels like a pretext for manipulation, right? How do I know you're not just another player looking to exploit our city's potential?"

I lean forward, my tone earnest. "I'm a son of Ironbridge, Deanie. I've got roots here."

She raises an eyebrow, clearly not convinced. "You'll still have to prove you're different. Maybe not to me, but to everyone else you'll deal with. You know what can happen to you in the Mad Dog if you don't come correct."

"I haven't forgotten."

"This city is a special place, A.C. It can give you life or eat you up."

"I'm not here to exploit anyone, Deanie. And by the way, the Blue Rock scandal had nothing to do with me. It was local operators running that scheme. My only fault was not catching it in time—"

"Doesn't matter," she interjects. "When you convinced John Bing to sell you Blue Rock and then merged it with a company the whole world had its eyes on, you put pressure on a delicate balance that existed in this community. A balance between the business world, the political arena, the public, and the streets."

"What're you saying? You knew Bing was running illegal guns through Blue Rock and didn't tell me?"

"I didn't know shit about shit. Not officially." She sips her drink as if she's using it to stop herself from revealing more. "All I'm saying is, most people in this city didn't even know Blue Rock manufactured guns, so to many, it looks like your big New York private equity firm came in, made it a hub for their battery-powered airplane missiles, played it fast and loose as fuck, didn't heed regulations, and let the city's biggest employer get folded by the federal government, all while letting national news media shit on us, calling Maddox a corrupt and crime-ridden city."

My first instinct is to say that Maddox *is* a corrupt and crime-ridden city, but I feel like that would only piss her off, so I deflect.

"For anyone in this city to blame me for that is bullshit, Deanie. I expect it from the corporate white elite, but not from you." I soften my tone, hoping an emotional appeal scores me some favor. "I just want to make smart investments that help this economy rebound. Of course, I want to make a buck in the process, but I've always been committed to making this city great, fixing the potholes from the private sector. The ones you can't fix due to the corrupt bureaucracy holding you back."

Deanie studies me for a moment, then softens. "Look, I know you grew up in the system like I did. I know your heart's in the right place. But I'll just say, this city can't afford another corporate scandal drawing media attention for the wrong reasons."

"I won't let anything like that happen again in any of the companies I invest in. A.C. now stands for Always Checking."

She laughs. "More like Always Corny, maybe Always Cheating."

"Oh, you got jokes? Don't make me bring attention to that aging head top you got going on." I point to the flat-top afro she's worn since high school.

"Boy, I will beat your ass like I did back in elementary school; don't play with me," she threatens.

We laugh, have some more drinks, and continue catching up.

"So, what's your read on Josie Simmons?" I ask.

"From what I've heard, she's sharp, got a good head on her shoulders, and does business the right way. And I can't get enough of those vegan caramel crunch bars of hers."

The mayor's take on the local market is invaluable, as is her endorsement of Josie's work ethic and the appeal of the product. I'm ready to put in every dollar I have and raise the remaining $5.9 million to make the investment. Derek may have dragged my name through the mud, but I've still got connections who'll believe in my track record over his lies.

19

ADRIAN CHANNING

Sunlight cuts through a sliver in the blinds, landing on my dining table buried in pitch decks and legal pads. I'm on the couch in my apartment, making call after call. Just six months ago, I was closing deals over Michelin-star dinners and luxury boxes. Now I'm here alone, sitting on a folding chair, listening to familiar voices hesitate, then pass. Volition's still too fresh, they say. Too risky.

It's a strange shift, having to scrape for my own capital instead of pulling from PGC's bottomless war chest. Some first-time fund managers build track records deal by deal, raising to buy specific, pre-identified assets until they've built the trust to launch a real fund with discretion to make dozens of investments. That's how I'll have to do it. One clean win at a time until my reputation feels less like a memory and more like leverage. If I hadn't been set up and thrown to the wolves, I could've raised a billion on my first attempt. But nothing good in my life has ever come easy. Why should this?

Next up is Mark Brogdon, an old client when I was at Goldman. He owns damn near every mall east of the Mississippi. He should be worth a few billion at this point, and more importantly, he owes me.

"Mark, long time." I try to push enthusiasm into my voice. "How's Tianna and the kids?"

"Family's good, Adrian." His voice comes through on the speaker-phone, loud and gruff, already seeming uninterested.

"Glad to hear it... Well, thanks for taking the call. As I'm sure you saw in the deck, this is a solid opportunity to get in early on a promising food brand with wholesale orders in need of fulfillment. The company is already entertaining buyout offers, so there's a clear path to exit here. But what really gets me excited, besides the money we'll make, is the chance to help a local economy grow and be a part of solving a real problem in the community."

Mark's married to a Black woman, so I make sure to mention the social impact aspect. Might not be the noblest tactic, but where I come from, you do what it takes to close the deal.

"This company is the next Beyond Meat but for the dessert space," I add. "Black woman-owned and operated and committed to ending the diabetes crisis in the inner city. I'd love to have you on board."

"I saw the pitch materials you sent over," he says. "The samples were a nice touch. The stuff's delicious. But to be honest, I've got some reservations."

"How can I put your mind at ease?" I ask.

"Not sure if you know I'm a PGC LP."

"I didn't."

"Derek Graff brought me in a few years ago," Mark explains. "I didn't love how that Volition deal broke down. I also didn't buy his 'rogue operator' explanation. That guy gives me the creeps, to be totally honest. The whole thing is rubbing me the wrong way, and I'm not sure I want to do business with anyone connected to it."

I feel a pang of frustration. "Look, I understand your concerns and agree Derek Graff is a deplorable character. As far as Volition, I take responsibility for not being so deep in the weeds to catch some low-level execs playing GTA at a subsidiary of a subsidiary of a subsidiary. By the time it rose to my level, it was all over the news."

"How could you miss something like that?" he asks.

"Harry Paxton had me running damn near every PGC portfolio company for her, and regrettably, this issue slipped through the cracks. But that will never happen to me again. I've gone out on my own and now have the flexibility to focus completely on the deals that matter most to me."

"Your reasoning makes sense, but I'm not sure."

"Mark, if you're a PGC investor, then you got the newsletter outlining all the other successful investments I cultivated that'll make the Volition loss immaterial in the grand scheme. Not to mention, I made you a fortune on that Chinese online shopping deal when I was at Goldman. And I'll remind you that was a deal I didn't have to bring you in on."

"I remember."

"So, you remember the company IPO'd for a huge multiple just before COVID put half of your shopping malls into bankruptcy?"

"I do."

"I gave you a lifeline you didn't even know you needed, Mark. Now I'm offering you a piece of something both lucrative and impactful."

"You make good points, Adrian. And I suppose you've always had the Midas touch."

"I appreciate that, Mark. Beyond this deal, you can be a foundational partner of a new type of investment platform, the kind that'll make dollars and *change*, if you catch my drift."

God, I feel like a fucking cornball but this is shit LPs like to hear. He's silent for a while. My heart nearly beats out of my chest as I wait for his next word.

"Okay. I'll come in for the six. Send me the legals."

I'm so pumped I almost break every breakable item in my apartment. "You won't regret this, Mark."

I end the call, beat my chest, and let out a war cry to the financial gods.

Not only will I be able to make CCP's first investment and get back into the mode of building successful businesses, but I'll be able to pay myself with management fees. That's two percent of six million dollars— a hundred and twenty grand a year. It's nowhere near what I was making at PGC but it's a step in the right direction.

MY FATHER ONCE TOLD ME,

"You can't save everyone.
Some folks are just broken."

20
DR. BRIANNA WRIGHT

"How's school?"

Jahlil shrugs, barely looking up from the laminate flooring beneath his sneakers. "Haven't been."

"Why not?" I ask.

His eyes move toward the framed print behind me. It's a neutral beachscape I picked when the Youth Mental Health Center at the Palmer Foundation opened. It's meant to be calming. But still, his hands fidget in his lap, his left thumb grazing the edge of his index knuckle in a slow, steady loop. It's like he's trying to rub something away.

And then he murmurs, "The fuck's the point?"

Jahlil Anderson used to be one of my success stories. At ten, he was bagging heroin on an RF9 corner. By fourteen, he was pulling triggers. His juvenile record is longer than the twisted locks gracing his face. But unlike most of the boys who come to me through the Palmer Foundation's gang intervention pipeline or because the courts force them to, Jah stumbled in on his own. And for someone who's spent her career dissecting the criminal mind, that kind of voluntary act always means something.

When he came in, he was wearing a bloody T-shirt and had a gunshot wound in his right arm. It was nothing too serious from a medical perspective, but it was messy. I patched him up in my office after hours. He didn't flinch at the sutures. But his eyes were screaming.

"I want out," he had said. "I need out. Either they gon' kill me, or I'ma do it to myself."

That was all it took. I made it my personal mission to get Jahlil clear of that life. And the first step was money. Always money. Telling kids like Jah to just stay in school is hollow if you're not also handing them rent money, grocery money, money to buy their sick grandmother's medication, and a few hundred dollars for the emergencies that become routine in South Maddox.

But Jah was different. Ridiculously smart. A genie with numbers. He reminded me of Adrian, so I connected them. Adrian got him and his mother office jobs at Blue Rock, working directly for John Bing. That meant full-time pay and benefits. Adrian even put them both in Volition's stock option pool, so they'd get a decent cash bonus when the company went public. It was clean work, and Jah thrived. For a while.

And then the headlines hit. Volition collapsed, John Bing was arrested, and the Blue Rock factories were shut down. Now, I'm looking at that same expression Jahlil wore the night he walked into my office covered in blood.

"I need bread, doc," he mutters. "School ain't gon' cut the checks I need."

"But a degree will, Jah. That's how you get out of Maddox. Remember the scholarship program we talked about? It comes with a stipend."

He shakes his head. "A stipend they'll give me in two years if I go to college? I might not make it two years. I need help now. Can you help me, Doc, or nah?"

"I help my patients who tell me the truth, Jah."

"I do tell you the truth."

"Maybe." I pause, letting the silence press in for a moment. "But since Blue Rock went under, every time you walk in here, you're a little more hollow. More quiet. More defiant. And every time I ask you what's going on, all I get is—" I drop into his quiet, raspy voice. "Ain't nothin', Doc Wright.'"

"It ain't nothin," he says. "Nothin' I can't handle."

"We used to talk, Jah. Now we just sit in silence, or I'm helping you clean blood off your sneakers. I thought we were past that."

"We were…" His voice trails off. "But Blue Rock's gone. And ain't nobody hiring a sixteen-year-old gang member."

"So you're back to doing what you used to do to make money." My voice is almost under my breath. "I get it."

He doesn't respond immediately, but the clenched fists, shifting posture, and flitting eyes say everything.

"I just need bread, Doc," he says again. "My mom… her lupus actin' up. She can't be on her feet like that no more."

"I know."

"I got two baby sisters. The only way they eat is if I bring 'em food."

"I know, Jah." I keep my voice soft, but he's ramping. I see the flash in his eyes before it even reaches his breath.

"Can your husband hook me up at one of his other companies? I'll do anything. Any job. Please, Doc."

"He's my ex-husband. And he doesn't have any companies anymore. He got fired over this."

"Shit… I'm sorr—"

"Don't do that," I cut him off. "Blue Rock's failure is far from your fault."

He stands abruptly and starts pacing. His breathing is shallow, and his shoulders are twitching. I stay seated, letting him get out whatever he needs to get out.

"I know I fucked up, yo. But I ain't know Mr. Bing was movin' straps wit us. Shouldn't've told Lil Nutty I was workin' there…"

"Stop, Jah." He can't say names in here.

"I was out, Doc. I thought I could do what Adrian did. Leave da hood. Go corporate. Wear shirts with collars and shit. Make real money. Clean money."

He lets out a bitter laugh. Then it breaks, and his voice rises to a near scream. "But then Getz and Slim came to the crib… said they heard about my new job. I told 'em I couldn't, but they said they'd shoot my moms and sisters the fuck up if I ain't help—"

"Jah—"

"They said Bing was double-dippin'. Sellin' straps to the Albanians behind our back."

"Jah, you know the rules—"

"Said I had to be their eyes inside. Had to watch the pipeline. Keep the white man in line."

"Jahlil," I hiss, "Sit down and breathe."

He sits with his hands on knees as he starts the breathing drill we practiced. In through the nose for five seconds. Hold. Out. Again.

"I know what they say about Mr. Bing, but he was good to me. Good to my moms."

His strained breaths slowly escalate into full-blown hyperventilation. His shoulders hitch with each breath as he begins to weep.

"They made me beat that old man damn near to death. Said he was disloyal. Said he needed a lesson. Now they sayin' I gotta smoke his ass so he don't snitch—"

"Jah, stop talking!" My voice cracks across the room.

It came sharper than I intended, but there are rules here. Hard lines were drawn a year ago when Charles and I designed this program. And he's crossing every one of them. No names. No specifics. No information about active or upcoming crimes. Nothing that triggers mandatory reporting. I can't help these kids if the law forces my hand. And if this city's dirty cops do get involved, RF9 will surely find out. And then Jah will be dead, with me right behind him.

"I'm sorry, Doc Wright. I just don't know what to do."

He drops his head into his hands as he continues to sob. "I wanna just leave town, but I can't. My moms. My sisters. They need me. I ain't got enough cash to move us all. I ain't got no options."

His shoulders rise and then fall as the silence stretches between us. He doesn't look at me, and I can almost hear the sound of him desperately trying to hold himself together.

"But I can't kill nobody," he finally murmurs. "Not again."

I move across the room to sit beside him. Not too close but close enough to let him know he's not alone.

21

DR. BRIANNA WRIGHT

THIS CONDO TAKES up the whole top floor of a converted steel foundry. Concrete columns, glass walls, D'Angelo playing through the speakers in the ceiling. Maddox didn't always have places like this downtown. Now, these luxury riverfront properties are constantly popping up between shuttered warehouses and old union halls as part of the city's ongoing attempt to reimagine itself without losing what makes it real.

But right now, we're tangled in his Egyptian cotton sheets. I'm half propped against a pillow with my phone in one hand, arranging session blocks on my calendar. He's beside me, his skin warm against mine, his body lean but sculpted. His goatee is neat, as always, but longer at the bottom today. He has a phone in either hand, likely answering emails or reviewing documents or both.

My phone buzzes, and as I see the name on the caller ID, my vacation into bliss ends. Adrian.

I freeze for just a moment. I look at the name, then at the man beside me. They don't linger but I catch his eyes glancing at my screen before I lock it and send the call to voicemail.

"You haven't told him, have you?" Charles asks, his eyes shifting back to his phone.

"Who I sleep with is none of his business," I reply, a little sharper than I intended.

"That's fair. But I'd rather not lie to him about this. It'd be the honorable thing for me to tell him I'm—"

"Bedding his ex-wife," I finish.

He smiles, but only slightly. "Beyond the family connection, Adrian's my client. There are lines I don't like to cross. I'd rather keep business and personal separate unless everyone knows what's going on."

"I doubt he'll stick around long enough to care." I slip out of the sheets and grab my blouse from the floor. "One thing about Adrian, he always finds a way to make money. It's the only consistent thing about him." I let out a dry laugh but it's more like a scoff.

Charles joins me, laughing lightly, but there's a look in his eye, like his interest is piqued at the sound of cash being folded.

"I'm laughing, but it's not funny. That consistency made me a single mother."

He looks up at me from his pillow and his expression abruptly changes. There's something there, something I can't quite name. Maybe a hint of a deeper intention, like he wants to tell me I don't need to be single any longer. But he doesn't say anything.

God, his stillness, his stoicism... It's maddening. Sexy, yes. But maddening. And who am I kidding? This is purely physical and convenient. Two beautiful people in a moment of mutual distraction. Nothing more.

I finish buttoning my blouse and then put on my blazer. "In any event, I'm sure Adrian will soon find another ladder to climb. Then he'll leave Maddox in his rearview once again."

"Maybe. But while he's here, I'd like to be honest with him about this."

"No, Charles." I zip my pants up slowly. "It may be good, but I don't know what this is. And neither do you. I don't need the friction. Please."

He nods slowly. "Okay. You make the rules."

He shifts out of bed and walks toward the bathroom, stretching as he goes. The muscles in his back ripple, subtly shifting the tattoo on his shoulder blade of two curved horns circling a small center mark. He pushes open the glass shower door, turns on the water, and steps inside.

"Headed to work already?" I ask.

"Breakfast meeting with Judge Phillips," he calls out over the drizzle of the running shower.

Of course. He's probably representing some politician's drunken and disorderly son or a real estate developer's crypto-scamming nephew. He's the most powerful criminal defense attorney in this city. And the most well-connected. He also co-chairs the foundation that funds half my work. He's not just a good lay; he's my partner in all of this, whether he wants to be or not.

I poke my head into the bathroom as I hear the water shut off. "I need your help with a patient."

"Which patient?" he asks as he steps out of the shower, steam curling around him. He towels off his face first, leaving the rest of him bare, completely at ease in his skin.

I blink a couple of times, trying to bring myself back into the present. "Jahlil Anderson."

He squints slightly. "Didi Anderson's boy?"

I nod. "Yeah. He's… special."

"What do you mean special?"

"The kid did my taxes last year." I stifle a chuckle. "Helps Riley with her AP Calc homework. He's an immature teenage boy, but his mind, his work ethic…"

"I knew his father," Charles murmurs, finally covering himself and letting me focus. "Worked for my dad at the Emporium back in the day. Dependable. Well-liked. I remember it shook my brothers hard when he was killed."

My breath catches. "His father was killed? Was he in a gang? I remember your dad employed a lot of ex-convicts."

He shakes his head faintly. "Don't really know the details. But back then, Maddox was different. Less organized. More chaotic. More dangerous."

I exhale. "It explains a lot. Jah shuts down whenever I ask about his father. Now I know why."

"So what's going on with him?" Charles steps out of the bathroom and into the closet. "What do you need?"

"I think he's in trouble. And I don't know how to help him."

He buttons his slacks and then puts on a crisp white button-down. "What kind of trouble?"

"I can't breach privilege. But let's just say that if a sixteen-year-old wanted out of something dangerous, a world you and I both understand very well… I think you, with all your connections, could help facilitate that process. Quickly and discreetly."

Charles leans back, the muscles in his chest tightening slightly as he buttons his shirt. "I've represented a few RF9 corner boys over the years. Petty drugs, weapons charges. Low-level street stuff. I'm not plugged in like that with any shot callers, Brianna. I don't have the kind of influence it would take to pull someone out clean, not without raising flags I don't want raised."

He says it too easily, like it's a line he's rehearsed, even the subtle hesitation between words. It's not that I think he's lying, just that he's calculating. He's so fucking deliberate, so strategic, it actually irritates me. Every word that leaves his mouth is filtered through some internal calculus: risk, reward, reputation. He reminds me of Adrian in that way. Power-hungry. Money-hungry. The kind of man who never enters a room without scanning it for leverage. My type, apparently. God help me.

But this moment draws the line between them. Adrian, as flawed as he is, wouldn't hesitate to help if a kid's life was on the line. Especially a kid like Jahlil. Charles Palmer, on the other hand, looks at the same situation and starts counting favors, predicting what it might cost him. Now I'm starting to wonder not what kind of lawyer he is, but what kind of man.

"Come on, Charles. Don't underestimate yourself."

"I never do. But if I bark up the wrong tree here, they won't just call me reckless and unprofessional. They'll call me a snitch. And then I'm dead on the evening news for trying to protect one."

"Jah is not a snitch."

Charles doesn't flinch. "Not yet. But if I start putting calls in to RF9 shot callers trying to smooth his exit, they'll assume he's soft or that he's flipped or is about to. Or that he'll want to when they deny his request to be released from his… obligations. And when that happens, they won't just quiet him. They'll quiet whoever made the call on the assumption that they know what he knows. These guys don't do liability."

He meets my eyes without blinking. "That means him. You. Me."

I study him for a long moment. "For someone who claims to have no real pull, you seem to know exactly how they move."

A faint smirk tugs at the corner of his mouth as he moves to his dresser and pulls out a tie. "I may not have an M.D. or a Ph.D., but I minored in forensic psychology at Penn State. And I've probably counseled more criminals than you have, although mine were clients, not patients."

I can't resist a smirk. "I doubt it."

"Well, then you know that to succeed in my line of work, you have to understand politics of all varieties."

He's smooth. Too smooth. But I suppose he's right. This kind of intervention isn't without real risk. But Jah doesn't have time for us to be a couple of chicken shits.

"I'll say it again, Charles. This kid is not a snitch. Not a traitor. He's not jumping to another crew or renouncing his ties. He's loyal to his gang. Loyal to a fucking fault! He just doesn't want to hurt people anymore."

"I hear you." He lets out a deep sigh. "But it's not that simple."

"Just talk to him. Spend five minutes in a room with him. You'll see. He's worth the risk."

"There are a lot of bright kids in Maddox, Brianna. I can't insert myself into gang politics every time one of them needs a lifeline."

I exhale through my nose and look him dead in the eye as I prepare to fully take it there. "Let's be real, Charles. No one's taking a shot at the son of Jerome 'Big Palm' Palmer."

That lands. I can tell by the way he pauses in the midst of tying his tie.

He doesn't respond, so I press. "I know the history. And no matter how far you and Rome have taken your family's name, with all your foundations, scholarships, real estate developments, and ribbon cuttings… I know what your father was in this city back in the day... You're like the made men of Maddox or whatever."

He lets out a short laugh, but it doesn't reach his eyes. "Made men, huh? Listen, Brianna, maybe you re-watched Goodfellas recently, I don't know, but my father changed his ways long before RF9 came to prominence. My family hasn't had anything to do with that element for nearly two generations."

"But I've seen how you and your brother shield the young athletes in this city. The chosen few who everyone knows are off limits to the gangs. You guys protect them all the way to the draft so they can name-drop Palmer Community Athletics on ESPN. Well, Jah's not going to the NFL or NBA. But he might be a surgeon one day. Or an engineer. Or a teacher. Or just a young man who actually gets to live long enough to decide what he wants to be. He deserves that chance."

Charles nods slowly. "I get it."

"Do you?" I arch an eyebrow. "I know how you operate. You do well by the community, but only when the community does well by you."

That lands harder than I mean it to. Charles chuckles, but there's something strained in it, like he's choosing laughter over defense.

"If you care about me at all, you'll help him."

"You've made your point." His tone is suddenly as serious as it's been all morning. "Have him come to my office after he gets off school. I need to know where his head is at first, then I'll see what I can do."

"What do you mean where his head is at?" I ask, slightly put off. "I told you where his head is at. He's scared. He needs a life line——"

"I know you say he's not a snitch," Charles says, fastening a set of golden cuff links. "But if he is, then that is a different discussion. A different set of calls. A far more dangerous proposition for all parties involved."

"No," I snap. "He's loyal. And that's a professional opinion, not just a personal one."

"Okay." He exhales through his nose. "I'll talk to the kid. But that's all I can promise."

I lean in, brush a soft kiss against his cheek, then linger close enough to feel the heat off his skin.

"Thank you," I murmur.

His hand finds my waist, and he holds me still for a moment. "You ever think about telling Riley about us? I just figure given our family connection—"

I let out a playful scoff. "You mean the fact that we're in-laws?"

"My mother is married to your ex-husband's estranged father," he says. "That hardly makes us in-laws, at least not anymore. Just family friends. And there's no rule that says family friends can't become more than that."

I pause, feeling the weight of the idea. This is way too early and way too messy. I'm not sure I want to be in a relationship at all right now, let alone with someone both I and my overly-controlling ex-husband work with. I know damn well this isn't sustainable. But I need his help.

So, I nod gently. "I have thought about it. I'm just… waiting for the right moment."

He studies me, searching for the truth in me. "I've never been very good at casual, Brianna."

"I can tell, Charles." I offer a soft smile. "I just need time to work out the best path forward. But I like you. I can see a future where we get to know each other even better."

He doesn't respond, but his hand stays on my waist. I lean in and kiss him, tasting the heat on his tongue as his hand slips down and cups my left butt cheek. He exhales through his nose as he grips it tighter, pulling me in closer. I feel the pressure in his slacks that tells me he wants me again. But I hold for only a moment before pulling back. His hand drops, but his stare doesn't.

My mother taught me that to get what you want from a man, leave him in the space between need and restraint. That's where real persuasion lives, in the tension of wanting something you can't quite have and would do anything for.

Still, leveraging intimacy to get what I need sits wrong in my chest. I could justify it by saying it's for Jahlil, that I'm doing whatever it takes to get him out of RF9 safely. But that'd just be a cop out. I'm not so naïve to think morality is a fine line. Sometimes, we just make messy choices. Not every-thing requires a clinical justification.

And some decisions, you just metabolize and move the fuck on.

22
ADRIAN CHANNING

THE GYM'S ECHOING with whistles, sneaker squeaks, and scattered parent chatter, but I'm locked in on Riley's game. She's cooking these girls right now, crossing them over and getting buckets through contact, but no calls.

I'm halfway out of my seat, yelling at the referee when Josie texts: *Were you serious about working together? Just got an offer from Bonder Foods. There's a ticking time clock on it.*

I reply: *Working on the term sheet. Should have it to you soon. Don't do anything until you hear from me.*

I text Mark Brogdon: *Any update on the paperwork? Need to submit this bid. Can't w/o your signature.*

I see the typing bubbles appear, then disappear. I stare at my phone for almost an hour. No response. I tell myself he's just busy in a meeting, maybe on a jet over the Atlantic or something. I pray I'm right, but there's a pit in my stomach I can't quite shake.

After dropping Riley off at her mom's, I'm stopped at a red light by myself and get a call from that rat shit weasel, Derek Graff.

I should let it ring, but maybe he's calling to settle the lawsuit or, better yet, offer my job back. I heard from Tessa that PGC's deal teams aren't happy with Derek's leadership since I was fired. He's completely abandoned my social impact strategy, and portfolio performance has taken a dip. Makes sense since Derek only knows how to ask for money. He knows nothing about earning it. He's never had to.

"What do you want?" I answer sharply.

"Geraldine's Homemade," he says, slowly and smugly. "Must be some very good ice cream to justify a $10 million valuation. Mark Brogdon's wealth manager happens to be an old friend of mine. She gave me a call asking about you, and I told her you were an addict and a liar. Not to be trusted."

"So, you're defaming me again? I'll have my lawyer add that to the lawsuit."

"It's not defamation if it's true, Channing. I sent her your case file. No matter how good you are at finding deals, LPs don't make it a habit to knowingly entrust their money with degenerates."

"You're the only degenerate on this call."

"And yet, you're the only one with a record," he snaps. "If you call any of my LPs again, I'll countersue for breach of your non-solicit."

He hangs up, and I punch the steering wheel so hard the car honks. The light turns green, and I hit the accelerator. I speed through the city streets. The honking of other drivers fills my ears as I swerve in and out of lanes. My fingers grip the steering wheel, and I feel the anger coursing through my veins. At this point, I feel like driving this fucking Prius off the Destin Street Bridge. I just want to leave everything behind—the failure, the stress, the embarrassment.

I floor it, pushing the car faster and faster. I weave through traffic like my life means nothing. The rush of wind through the slightly open window and the blare of horns fuel my rage. I feel powerful, in control, and ready to go out with a bang.

Suddenly, my phone buzzes. It's Brianna. And as quickly as the anger came, it fades. My foot eases off the accelerator as the thought of what I have to live for enters my mind. Riley.

I park at a convenience store.

"FUUUUCCCCCCCCCCCCCCKKKKKKKKKK!" I scream at the top of my lungs as I shake the steering wheel so hard the car is shaking. I feel the taste of salt in my mouth, the blurring of my vision, the moisture down my cheeks.

After a few minutes, I wipe away the tears and look up. The poor clerk inside the store is looking at me terrified, probably thinking I'm hyping myself up to rob him.

I take a few deep breaths and read Brianna's text: *Sorry I missed your call this morning. But we're having dinner tomorrow night at Paul and Reeda's. 7 p.m. Come and spend time with your kid. And see your dad.*

• • •

My father, Paul Channing, was always a drunk, a liar, and a degenerate. One night when I was a kid, he wanted to go to a bar to watch a basketball game. My mother, Adanna Channing, the original A.C., couldn't find a sitter and wanted to stay home with me. But he refused. "I need my dancing partner, or the Sixers won't win," he had said.

My mother was an immigrant from Anambra State, Nigeria, with a soft and melodic accent, from what I remember. After being sold into slavery by a rebel warlord during the Nigerian Civil War, she was eventually smuggled out and brought to the United States under the guise of domestic work. She settled with a wealthy family in Philadelphia, working as their housekeeper. That's where she met and fell in love with my father, who was employed by the same family as a groundskeeper. That was before he got a job at Blue Rock and they moved to Maddox.

My mother was perfect. Her only flaw, as far as I'm concerned, was staying married to the charming Irish asshole who is my father.

I sat in a corner booth at Lorenzo's Bar & Grill and played with my Teenage Mutant Ninja Turtles while my father drank and danced the night away with my mother in his arms.

Afterward, my mother begged to drive us home since she'd only had ginger ale. But my father was stubborn and self-righteous and insisted he wasn't drunk. He refused to hand over the keys and then drove us into a cement traffic barrier.

The car flipped twice before landing hard on its side, passenger door down. Miraculously, I walked away unscathed. My father, the Irish drunkard, survived with a mangled leg and a concussion. My mother died on impact.

I was seven years old. And the Sixers still fucking lost.

My father was convicted of manslaughter, and since it was far from his first DUI, he spent eight years at Riverville Correctional in upstate Pennsylvania while I bounced between foster homes. When he got out, he got custody of me but kept partying and generally just being a dick. I was fifteen at the time.

To honor my mother, he made sure I stayed off the streets and focused on school. He stayed out of trouble until I left for Harvard, but after that, he started pulling small cons for the Irish mob, landing himself in and out of jail until Riley was born. That's when I gave him an ultimatum. No drinking, no jail, or he wouldn't see her or get another penny from me.

He says he's a new man and found God after meeting Reeda at a church event six years ago. He claims he hasn't touched the drink since, but I don't trust him.

When I got married, I vowed never to be like my father, a man who sacrificed his family on the altar of his recklessness.

As I approach the front door of his and Reeda's elevated Craftsman home in North Maddox, its quaint front yard garden adding a touch of charm, I feel a presence behind me. I glance left and see nothing. And then right. Nothing again.

I turn around to see Charles Palmer in the dark of night, almost like a silhouette. I didn't even hear his footsteps. The sudden sight of him startles me, and I nearly drop the bottle of red wine I brought, fumbling it in my hands before securing it.

"The noble tycoon." He greets me with a pat on the back. "Didn't mean to scare you."

"Don't worry, man. You didn't."

"Still got those hands, I see."

"Once an athlete, always an athlete." I chuckle, trying to shake off my unease.

"I know that's right." He brushes past me and climbs the cobbled steps to the house as Reeda opens the door.

She's a thin, tall, elegant Black woman in her late sixties. My father certainly has a type.

"Hey, Momma," Charles gives her a kiss on the cheek and continues into the house.

I make my way up the steps, extending the bottle in my hand as I see her. "Hey, Reeda."

She ignores the bottle and wraps her arms around me, pulling me into a tight hug. "Adrian! So good to see you, honey. Paul is thrilled you're back."

Reeda and my father sit at the heads of their dark oak dining table. Brianna and Riley sit on one side while Charles and I sit on the other. Behind Riley's head are a few hanging photos, some of me during my high school football days, others of my father and Reeda, and one of my mother and me.

"Good to *finally* have you back home, son." My dad stretches the word "finally" as if I'm the world's worst son and have no possible reason for wanting to stay far away from him.

Just the sound of his raspy voice, burned by years of alcohol corrosion, makes me want to slice his pale, wrinkly neck with my steak knife.

I bite down my anger and focus on my plate. "This lamb is delicious, Reeda."

My father keeps talking, oblivious to how hard I'm trying to tune him out. "My granddaughter tells me you've been back a few months now. And only now you come to see me and your stepmother? Is that really how I raised you?"

I scoff as I drop my fork. The clank of the metal on the ceramic causes the table to freeze for a moment.

"You didn't raise me, Dad. It was the state of Pennsylvania and the streets of Ironbridge that did the child-rearing."

"Why you gotta bring up old history, huh?" he grumbles. "That's why you never made it D-1. Never learned how to just let the past go, move on to the next play."

"No, I didn't play Division 1 football, but got a full academic scholarship to Harvard. Made it real easy on you." I let the sarcasm rise in my voice.

"Oh no," he says. "I didn't have to pay for your college but nothin's easy with you, Adrian."

I drop my fork again. "You're a real piece of shit, Dad, you know that?"

"Adrian, come on," Brianna says gently, always the peacekeeper.

"Then what's that make you, son?" His voice is a grunt. "You think it was easy after your mother die—" He stops himself. He knows that if he continues, I'll remind him she didn't just die. He killed her.

An awkward silence consumes the dining room for what feels like hours. Riley picks at her food while Brianna shoots me looks that say, *Get your shit together.* It's a look I know far too well.

After a while, Reeda clears her throat and glances my way. "Adrian, honey, I hear from Charles that you're starting one of those venture capital funds."

"Private equity, Momma," Charles corrects, taking a bite of mashed potatoes.

"Oh, sorry, I know little about these things." Reeda smiles. "Only what I see on Shark Tank. What is the difference, anyway?"

"Think of it like this," I begin. "Shark Tank? That's venture capital. They're betting on someone else's dream, taking a tiny sliver of the pie and hoping it takes off. Private equity firms don't bet on other people. We buy full control and bet on our ability to run the dream better than the last guy. One's about hoping for an outcome. The other's about making it happen."

"Sounds exciting," Reeda says. "So, tell us about your fund."

"Can he please not?" Riley scoffs. "No one gives a shit about his failed career."

"Riley!" Brianna scolds.

"It's okay, Bri." I can hear my tone betraying how defeated I'm feeling.

"No, it's not," Brianna says. "Riley, you need to watch your mouth and speak to your father with respect. Apologize right now."

"Sorry," Riley says, her voice clipped.

"It's okay, buttercup."

"Can I just be excused?"

"Go." Brianna says.

Riley gets up from the table, taking her plate to the kitchen.

"And wash your plate!" Brianna calls out.

"She's actually right," I slowly admit. "My career in private equity is over. No one's hiring me after Volition. I found a promising company I'd like to buy into but none of my old money contacts want anything to do with me anymore, so that's that."

The dinner continues more or less the same. Awkward silences fill the gaps between insubstantial bouts of small talk.

After dinner, Reeda and Brianna clean up while my dad dozes off on his recliner and Riley does her homework.

I step outside, feeling somewhat at peace in the backyard. I admire the manicured lawn and luxury patio furniture, another product of my father marrying up.

Then, I glance to my left. Through the window, I catch Charles leaning against the counter, saying something to Brianna as she rinses a plate. She laughs and says something back that makes them both smile. I watch them for a second longer than I should.

Brianna glances up mid-rinse and catches me staring. Her smile quickly fades, then she looks down and starts washing dishes again. Charles seems to catch the tension because he turns and locks eyes with me briefly before I look away. I pull out my phone to pretend like I'm occupied, but out of the corner of my eye, I see him amble to the bar.

The fuck was that?

After another minute or so, Charles joins me with two glasses of the wine I brought. He hands me one, we clink up, and sip quietly.

"So…" I clear my throat, breaking the silence. "… you sleepin' with my ex-wife?"

He draws his sip out longer than normal. It's nearing a chug at this point. But then he lowers his glass, smiles, and lets out a light chuckle. "Of course not. But would you have a problem with that? Just curious."

I take another deep sip, thinking about how full of shit he is. "She's not my wife, man. What I have a problem with does not matter."

"Good to know."

Truth is, I don't quite care. If Brianna can find happiness here, who am I to object? And Charles seems like a good enough guy.

We take a few more quiet sips, exchanging awkward glances as the minutes go by.

"So, what's the deal with you and your dad?" he asks.

I think about that question for a moment, unsure of how much of that history I want to share right now. I quickly decide I don't at all. "What's the deal with your mom and your brothers?"

He chuckles lightly. "Touché… Well, tell me about that company you found."

I forgot Charles mentioned he's interested in investing.

"It's a promising regional food brand in the process of scaling nationally. I can send you the pitch deck if you're serious about investing."

"I'm always serious, Adrian."

"Well, this could be the perfect first investment to launch that platform I told you about."

"How much are you looking to raise?"

"Six million."

He doesn't even react to the amount. "Let me make some calls. I know some folks who are always looking for opportunities."

"That would be great, but I need it ASAP. The CEO is under pressure from another buyer and doesn't wanna lose the deal."

"I'll see what I can do. But Adrian, I must say. Getting you out of that charge with a slap on the wrist, filing that wrongful termination suit, and now arranging capital for this deal on short notice. That would make three favors in a row from me to you."

"I thought it was your nature to help a good brother in trouble?"

He smirks. "Also my nature to get paid."

"I can respect that. What do I owe you?"

"Keep your cash. I know you're having some liquidity issues right now."

Liquidity issues... fuck this guy for throwing that in my face. "So, what do you want?"

"I'm just looking for an intro," Charles says. "I'm representing a group of mothers here in town who've all lost sons to gun violence. It's a class action against PGC for their negligence in funding John Bing's gun-running scheme at Blue Rock."

I raise an eyebrow, intrigued at the thought of making PGC burn. "You need my testimony."

"We will," he says. "But first, I need to prove those guns actually came from Blue Rock."

"How?"

"The unnamed source mentioned in the New Journal article. Do you know who that is?"

"I do, but I don't know about this, Charles. I'm subject to a non-solicit. Can't really talk to PGC people like that."

"Why stay loyal to those people? They took $32 million that was rightfully yours, tossed you out, defamed you—"

"Trust me, I know, but..." My voice trails off as I think it through.

"Look, I just want to talk to the source," he says. "Maybe he or she can point us toward some concrete evidence on what was going on at Blue Rock, maybe convince them to testify in the civil case. You do this for me, I'll get you the cash you need for your deal. We'll get your fund launched in a real way."

After a brief moment of consideration, I look Charles in the eye and shake his hand.

23

ADRIAN CHANNING

"ADRIAN, YOU KNOW I can't talk to you. I'm in litigation against PGC."

I can hear Tim Rouchard's kids playing in the background over the phone. Must be nice to blow up your own company, screw over thousands of people in the process, and then retire to your Upper East Side brownstone to enjoy your life with kids who don't seem to hate your guts. I would love to pummel the guy, but I need him, so I lead with contrition.

"You and me both." I plug my AirPods in as I stand on the side of the court while Riley finishes basketball practice. "PGC pushed me out and blackballed me over this. I'm a pariah out here, man."

"I'm sorry about that."

"It is what it is." I pause. "Look, I understand why you did what you did. And I don't blame you."

He's quiet, perhaps processing my vulnerability, something I never used to show.

"I don't know what you're talking about, Adrian." I hear the hesitation in his voice.

"You can cut the act, Tim. I know you're the whistleblower. Like I said, I don't blame you. I went too hard at you and should've listened instead. Should've taken your suspicions more seriously. I apologize."

Tim is quiet for a moment. "Adrian, I appreciate that but I'm not the whistleblower. I am glad this all came out though. Those kids, man…"

My patience is beginning to wane but I keep my tone as friendly as I can. "I get it, Tim. You did the right thing going to the New Journal."

"Adrian, I'll say it again. I did not speak to the press." The sincerity in his voice is evident.

If he wasn't Nora Hendricks's inside source, then who the fuck was?

"Doesn't really matter, man. You know I moved back to Maddox full-time, right?"

"No, I didn't."

"Yeah, I'm trying to clean up some of the wreckage of Blue Rock. That's why I called."

"Oh?"

"Yeah, there's an attorney here putting together a class action against PGC for their role in the scheme, on behalf of a group of mothers who lost children to illegal Blue Rock firearms."

"Wh–wh–what does that have to do with me?" Tim stammers.

"He needs your testimony. If you can help him trace those deaths to Bing's operation, the case against PGC becomes far stronger. I'll have to testify as well that I knew about it but PGC forced me to keep quiet in order to preserve our return."

"Adrian, I'm not sure I can get involved in this. I'm working with the FBI, and they've told me to lay low while they finish their investigation."

My head jerks back in shock. I step outside, away from other parents, as I lower my voice. "The FBI is still investigating this?"

"They thought I was in cahoots with Bing. I obviously wasn't, but the only way they'll drop the fraud charges against me for the IPO filing is if I cooperate fully against Bing. I'm not sure I should even be telling you this, let alone some civil lawyer. I think they're even looking at a case against PGC."

I shake my head. "PGC was like five levels above any gun sales. Terrence Weiss assured me there's no case. And Lawrence Hadington is a longtime LP. He's not going to let the DOJ prosecute his friends. Not for securities fraud and definitely not for arms trafficking."

"That's not what I've been told by the agents in charge—"

"It's bullshit, Tim. Do you know how insulated PGC is? How many state governments and federal agencies invest with them? Politicians and foreign dignitaries? They make too much money for the powers that be. Only way to hold that firm accountable is through a loud civil lawsuit."

He exhales slowly. "I don't know, man."

"Just meet with him. He's a good man and a great lawyer. You want to do the right thing? This is the right thing."

"Maybe we should let the criminal process play out first," he suggests.

"No, Tim. Even if PGC is prosecuted criminally, they'll pay a fine to the government. If they lose in a class action, they pay the victims' families."

"That money won't bring back their loved ones."

"No, but it'll do something in the way of compensating the communities that have been decimated by Blue Rock's ghost guns. This is the entire reason you let Volition crash. It was a necessary byproduct of doing the right thing, I get that now. But don't let it be for nothing."

He remains adamant he didn't speak to the press but agrees to drive down to Maddox for the meeting. So, I call Charles to finalize it.

"I set up the meet. The witness you need is a guy by the name of Tim Rouchard. He has all the info on the illegal guns."

"Tim Rouchard? Volition's founder?" he asks. "Why would he blow up his own company like that?"

"I guess he caught a conscience. All these school shootings, mall shootings, church shootings... too many shootings." My voice trails off.

The carnage this past summer got to me as well. I have a kid in this world. It wasn't easy seeing that tragedy, knowing my companies were helping to bring instruments of death to the world. But I had a bottom line to worry about. So much for that now.

"Anyway, just do me a favor and make this as painful as possible for PGC." I feel a surge of righteous anger flood me. I bite it back.

"That won't be a problem," he replies with that classic Charles Palmer confidence.

"Any word on the capital we talked about?"

"We're all set there, Adrian. Let me know when you agree to the terms with the company, and I'll shoot it over to you."

I nearly gasp. "Whoa. How'd you come up with that amount so quickly?"

"It's my family's money. We'll come in through our trust."

Holy shit, I'm about to be back in business. The first step toward the Adrian Channing comeback story is in full effect.

"There's now just a matter of fees," he continues. "I know you private equity guys are used to your standard two and twenty, but my people think something closer to ten percent on the carry makes more sense on this deal. And no management fee."

Charles knows I'm desperate, and he's squeezing me. I'd probably do the same thing in his position.

"Could you do one percent on the management fee and fifteen percent on carry?" I ask.

He's silent for a moment. "We can do twelve percent. No management fee."

I soften my tone, leading with sincerity. "Charles, I have a kid to feed. I'm not making money on the management fee. I'm using it to keep the lights on. I'm going to work my ass off for you to make this investment shoot through the stratosphere. A 10X return. But without a fee, I have to take a job, and that means I'm not spending every ounce of energy I have to make this company a winner."

"Take a job, I don't care," Charles says, his voice chilly, almost curt. "Based on your pitch deck, it's Josie Simmons who's doing the work here. She's the company. I can approach her myself and offer this deal. Plus, I know what Brianna's making. Riley will be fine."

Is this sandbagging son of a bitch threatening to cut me out of my own deal? In my old form, I'd have him lanced in the streets for that type of threat. But wait—

"How do you know what Brianna makes?"

"I guess she didn't mention…" He hesitates. "She's spearheading the youth gang intervention program at the Palmer Foundation."

"The Palmer Foundation?"

"That's right," Charles says. "Rome and I set up a youth center on the south side years ago. We're trying to steer kids away from the gang element in the city. We give them a place to study, play ball, and hang out in peace. Brianna had the idea of offering mental health services, anger management, group therapy, that sort of thing."

"So, she works for you?"

"With me. Well, she more so works with my team at the foundation. Really, she works for those boys."

I never loved the idea of Brianna in closed-door therapy sessions with emotionally volatile gang members, but I'm not surprised. This is her life's work, and she's the best at it.

"Would you meet me at point five percent on the fee?" I propose. "I need some cash to do my job. I'll do the twelve percent on carry, that's fine. There'll be more than enough to go around after we exit."

"No management fee, Adrian. My family isn't comfortable paying a fee for a deal we can do ourselves. We're not in the business of giving away free money. This is a deal breaker, so let me know if you need to think about it."

"Okay." I can't help but roll my eyes. "No management fee."

"Good. I'll get your paperwork signed up. Just give me a ring when you close the deal with Josie, and I'll wire you the money."

"I don't expect closing to be a problem."

"Sounds good," he says. "And Rouchard?"

"He's driving in from Manhattan as we speak. I told him to meet you at the lobby bar at the Arlowe Hotel at seven p.m."

"Much obliged."

24

ADRIAN CHANNING

DINNER WITH JOSIE at Fiana Bistro on North Market. My attire is a study in understated power. A Brioni suit, charcoal gray, tailored to my frame. It's one of the few pieces I didn't sell before I left New York. A black turtleneck softens the sharp lines of the suit. Fall is in effect, and I can feel the wind chill.

As I enter the restaurant, I check my watch. Seven p.m. Charles should be meeting with Tim right now.

I check my phone and see a text from Josie, saying she's running a few minutes late, only heightening my anticipation.

The restaurant is intimate, with low lighting warming the worn brick walls. A jazz pianist plays in the corner, entertaining the handful of local professionals dining here tonight.

The door chimes, and there she is, a vision in black. Her dress is a sleek sheath that hugs her curves with precision, showing off just the right amount of cleavage. Her hair is in braids, long and flowing. Her skin reminds me of Godiva milk chocolate, and it's glowing in the soft lighting. She's objectively gorgeous, but there's an edge to her, a sharpness that hints at a woman capable of controlling not only her own destiny but the destiny of whoever she aligns herself with.

I stand to greet her, giving her a hug and a light peck on the cheek. Her skin is incredibly soft, and her fragrance is sweet. We sit, and after some small talk, a waiter takes our drink orders.

"I'll have the Sancerre." The elegance in her voice reflects that of her wine choice.

"I'll have the same."

After a few moments, the waiter pours two glasses. We clink in cheers, and her eyes meet mine.

"I'm glad we could meet," she says. "I've been looking forward to this."

"Me too." I glance up from the menu. "Especially since we're about to make history together. I imagine you've had a chance to look over my formal offer."

"I did," she says. "The terms generally look good, but I flagged a few things to iron out."

"Naturally." I smile.

"I'm open to a sixty-forty equity split your way, but I want to make sure we're clear on control and approval rights. It's important I retain the freedom to run the day-to-day operations as I see fit."

I raise an eyebrow, swirling my glass. "That's fair, but I'm not just looking to be a silent partner. That's not really my style. I'm happy for you to continue running the day-to-day, but I typically look for approval rights over material business decisions. If I'm putting up the cash, I need to know the ship is being steered in the right direction."

Josie's gaze sharpens, but her tone remains steady. "So, will I need to solicit your approval anytime I need to make a call on something? I know how you PE guys are about control. Would you like consent over my son's nap schedule as well?"

My smile quickly turns to laughter. "Only so I can tell you to let the kid sleep in."

"Not on my watch," she says, laughing. "Momma runs a tight ship."

"I can tell."

"In all seriousness, my team and I built Geraldine's packaged dessert business from the ground up. We have a system that's been working."

"That's why I'm interested. But with respect, Josie, we wouldn't be here if it's been working as well as it could be."

I take a sip as I notice her gaze subtly dropping.

"Look, I'm not asking to run the day-to-day. That's all you. But I need some oversight so I can ensure we're on the path to greatness, and that path ultimately needs to run through me. But I'm gonna go to work for Geraldine's as well. My full rolodex. Two decades of business-building at your disposal."

Josie leans forward, her eyes never leaving mine. "I, of course, know the value of having Adrian Channing, the 'god of PE', on my cap table."

I smile. "Oh, you saw that article?"

"It came up in my diligence." There's a slight flirtation in her tone. "But what's more valuable to me is a partner who respects what I've built and doesn't come in like a wrecking ball trying to mansplain to me or my team how business is done. We know our product, we know our market, and we know how to execute."

"Fair enough." I lean back with the smirk of a man genuinely impressed. "But if you want my full commitment, I need to know we're in this together, with me having the final say on the major moves. Let's say any expenditure or contract worth more than ten percent of the quarterly budget?"

She pauses as she thinks it through. "I can work with that."

"Great."

She scrolls through the notes on her phone. "Let's move to exit rights—"

"I need full control over exits." My tone is sharper than I intended. "When we're ready to sell, I'll broker that deal and pull that trigger. Too many times, I've had to fight with CEOs who wanted to wait just a little bit longer before putting the company up for sale. It's a headache I don't want to deal with at this stage in my career."

"I hear you, Adrian, but I need to be involved in any exit discussions."

"You'll be cc'd on every email, but I need to drive the transaction. And I guarantee the deal I make will benefit you fully. If the numbers don't work, we walk. You want to keep a piece of the upside? Retain a minority stake so you keep winning when Bonder Foods, Conagra, or General Mills takes the $200 million brand we sell them and turns it into a two billion dollar brand? I'll make that happen."

I get caught in her big brown eyes before continuing. "I'll take care of you, Josie. And when it's all said and done, you'll be a multi-millionaire. Mark my words."

Her smile comes slowly but triumphantly. "You make a strong pitch, Mr. Channing, and I'll admit I'd much rather work with you than those Bonder snobs."

"Trust me, I wish more of my CEOs looked like you."

Shit. Was that inappropriate?

"I just mean… not old white dudes," I clarify.

Her cheeks flush slightly, then slowly, her expression straightens. "That actually kind of brings me to my next question… Volition… I saw the Senate hearing, did some Googling. I know you didn't just 'leave' PGC. Above everything else, I value integrity and honesty in business and otherwise."

Inside, I'm seething. Derek Graff's lies are going to be the death of me. But keep it cool, A.C. She's just protecting her company.

I flash a smile, hoping it comes off as confident, but as I open my mouth, she cuts me off politely, placing her hand on mine and flashing a look that tells me *it's okay*.

"But I also asked around," she says. "My friend, Mimi Lewis, runs the NYC Black Businesswomen Network."

"Small world. Mimi's great. She helped me source several minority-owned companies to invest in when I was at PGC. Some of my favorite deals."

"Yeah, she put me in touch with a few entrepreneurs you've worked with." She softens her tone as her eyes lock onto mine. "Adrian, everyone I've talked to about you, without exception, says you're the partner they'd trust with any venture. Sharp, principled, visionary, and beyond supportive. I've seen addicts. My son's father, for one. Uncles, aunties... I don't believe the rumors for a second."

I lean back, surprised. Our gazes meet, and I let myself linger there. There's a quiet glow in her eyes, like she's searching for something.

"That means more to me than you know, Josie. Not many people bother to look past the headlines these days."

She doesn't look away, even when the silence stretches. There's something unguarded in her demeanor, as if she's just made the calculated decision to work with me.

"Business, to me, is life, Josie. And life is about trust. If you're willing to trust me with your dream, there's not a thing in this world I won't do to make it a reality."

"I can see myself trusting you, Adrian."

A quiet warmth settles in my chest. This kind of validation is a rare thing—knowing that the years of honest partnership, of putting everything I had into each deal, each handshake, wasn't for nothing. And here's Josie Simmons, as sharp and methodical as they come, willing to look past the ugly search results when you Google my name.

As the evening continues and the wine flows, we keep negotiating, each word a step closer to sealing a deal. And beneath it all, the underlying current of attraction makes the stakes feel higher.

"I'll have my lawyers draw up the paperwork." Her laugh rings out, warm and effortless. I find myself grinning before I even realize it.

"Shall we toast?" I raise my glass. "To a promising new partnership amongst old friends."

"I can drink to that." She smiles before clinking my glass and looking me deep in my eyes in a way that makes me feel like she knows my every little secret, my every move. She's spellbinding. And after that negotiation, I might be in love.

As dinner arrives, we start getting to know each other more personally. I learn more about her dad, her experiences as a Black woman venture capitalist, and that she's a single mom with an eight-year-old son. I tell her everything.

Riley and Brianna. My dad. I open up about Volition and how my mentor threw me under the bus after the play she called went up in flames. I obviously don't share that I'm broke because of it, but I'm honest about how painful it was to be lauded as the "future of the industry" one day and called a "rogue operator" and "DEI hire" the next.

The night gets deep. It's incredibly easy to talk to her. She won't stop smiling at me, and I'm lost in her eyes. As I signal for the check, a grin tugs at my lips. I walked in here to close a deal, but I'm leaving with something deeper.

Exiting the restaurant, I call an Uber since we're both tipsy. We don't say much as we wait. We just stare at each other, smiling like kids at camp.

I gently pull her closer to me, but it's not even a pull. It's like she's already gravitating toward me. Our lips meet, soft and slow, and it's like nothing exists but us.

But then she pulls back.

"Is this smart?" she asks, her voice innocent yet seductive. "Mixing business and pleasure."

"I think your lawyers still need to send me the paperwork. We're not business partners yet."

I hope she sees that as cute, rather than reckless.

Her gaze flutters upward like she's weighing the risk. "Let's sell the company first."

She steps away and orders her own Uber.

I'm disappointed, but now I have even more respect for her. She knows her boundaries and sticks to them. Besides, a woman like Josie Simmons must be savored, no matter how much I want to devour her.

I watch her enter the car and vanish into the night, and then I go home and sleep the best I have since Volition crashed. Maybe it's the sense that I'm finally rebounding from that ugliness, or perhaps it's just getting back into the mode of dealmaking, but I feel invincible.

Once Tim gives Charles the information he needs for his civil case, Charles will provide his family's capital, and I'll make the first investment out of Community Capital Partners, a private investment firm for the people, backed by the most influential family in Maddox.

MY FATHER ONCE TOLD ME,

"Son, your life changes
after you kill a man."

25

CHARLES PALMER

I TRULY HOPE Tim Rouchard can't name RF9 as John Bing's buyers.

Tonight I'm in my black BMW 760i, with my uncle Mac behind the wheel. A war is unfolding on the streets, and Rome has made it clear that I don't travel without protection. Mac may be older now, but he's still sturdy and lethal with a .45. As one of the original Black Gods, alongside my father, he carries institutional knowledge about this business that can be beneficial to keep close.

Parked around the corner from the Arlowe Hotel sits an early-2000s black GMC Denali. Blacked-out windows, no plates. My other older brother Truck is at the wheel.

His given name is Tracy, but we've called him Truck since we were kids, mostly because he's always been built like one. And he's never had a problem steamrolling anyone in his, or our, way. Officially, he's in the music business. Unofficially, he's the chief enforcer of the Black Gods and the co-founder of RF9 alongside Rome. At forty-four, Truck is the epitome of the term "OG." Surviving this long in his line of work without getting eliminated by a rival crew or incarcerated is nothing short of legendary.

As he winds down the window, the thick smoke from his blunt billows out in a slow, heavy cloud.

"Chuckie, get in."

The nickname is a trigger for me. But I suppress the twitch in my jaw and get out of my car. As I move across the front of the SUV, I can see his right hand, Getz, is in the passenger seat, and two more of their guys are in the back.

Normally, I wouldn't be caught in public with Truck, let alone in a vehicle packed with illegal weapons and four known gang members, all marked with RF9 ink. But these aren't normal times.

The Blue Rock gun factory has been shut down, the family business is under pressure, and the FBI's investigation into RF9 is starting to gain real traction. If we're not careful, we risk them uncovering my family's involvement at the helm of it all.

Getz steps out of the front seat, tipping her head down to me in a nod of respect to a Black God, before climbing into the backseat.

As I settle into the front passenger seat and shut the door, Truck turns to face me, and his diamond earrings catch the glow of a nearby streetlamp. "Where's the mark?"

"He'll be here in a few minutes," I confirm. "Listen, don't do anything until I give you the word."

"You don't give me orders, Chuckie," Truck snaps, blowing a plume of weed smoke in my face. "Rome was clear on this shit. He said to clean it up. So, if the white boy is talkin,' we need to pull the plug on him."

"I'm not giving you orders, Truck. I'm just doing my job. If the CEO of Volition is killed in Maddox, the feds will not go away, and Adrian will know I was involved. I'll find out exactly what Rouchard knows, but if he can't name RF9 as Bing's buyer, then we don't need to take this risk."

"Fine." I hear a note of disappointment in his tone. The man enjoys killing people, a dangerous but necessary tool in the line of business our family is in.

Getz leans forward from the backseat. "We got Slim Choppa workin' valet. If it's goin' down, you give him the nod, and he'll let us know which whip to follow."

"If it needs to be done, do it discreetly," I remind them both. "It should look like he skipped town."

Truck takes another puff of his blunt, the ashes falling onto his black but graying beard. "We'll grab him up and do it at the chop house. Pigs won't find a body."

"Good." I reach for the door handle but the name Getz mentioned triggers something in my memory. "Slim Choppa? That's the rapper you've got making waves online?"

"Yessir," Truck says, his voice filled with pride. "Boy finna be the first big rap nigga out da Mad Dog."

I let out a brief sigh. "Yeah, I saw the 'Gang Shit' music video. Do you know there's a shot with your RF9 tattoo clear as day on the damn screen?"

Truck shrugs. "Must've missed that in editing."

"You missed a full close-up of your RF9 tattoo on your arm while you're turning the wheel in a rented Lambo?"

"Who said it was rented?" He smirks, his blunt shifting between his lips. "Ay, so what? I give no fucks about no cover. I been out here. Niggas know what it is."

"That's the problem, Truck. They're not supposed to know what it is. Not with everything we have in motion right now."

Truck turns toward me, leaning his elbow on the center console. "And I'm supposed to hold back my brand over some bullshit line you and Rome drew in the sand? The rap game and the dope game have always moved hand in hand. We real. The music real. The streets see that shit and fuck with it. That's why we movin' units."

I exhale, slow and quiet. No point in pushing harder. Not here.

"Okay. That's your business."

I'll just fix it on my end. I'm sure they didn't clear that Temptations sample. Probably didn't even try. I'll get the music video pulled for copyright infringement by morning. If we get dragged down over this, I'll make the case that Truck's the only one with dirt under his fingernails. Rome and I covered our RF9 tattoos years ago, and since then, I've worked countless angles insulating us for this exact reason.

I open the door and shift my body to exit.

"And what about your boy, Adrian?" Truck asks, prompting me to shut the door, delaying my exit from this felonious vehicle. "Rome said he popped up on him. Was askin' too many questions."

"I dealt with that. Adrian doesn't know anything about our business, and it'll stay that way."

Truck shakes his head. "This dude comes back to town after years away and first thing he do is try to get into our books? You sure he ain't working for the feds?"

"I highly doubt it. He has no reason to."

"So what the fuck he want with the Emporium?"

"He just wants back into the world of big business, and I'm gonna give him that. And then, he's going to make this family more clean money than we've ever seen. He's a member of the legit Palmer network, so no one touches him without my approval."

Truck laughs, and his crew joins in, eager to echo his amusement. "Ain't no such thing as the legit Palmer network. Yo shit exists to cover our shit from the feds. That's it."

"Regardless, you know the division of labor our father insisted upon. Clean business is within my purview."

"Okay, Chuckie, I do, but if this light-skinned nigga Adrian becomes a problem, then that's *my* purview. And if I need to, I'ma pull the muthafuckin' plug on him. I don't give a fuck if his white daddy is married to our momma, and I don't give a fuck how you feel about it."

"Fine, but it won't come to that." I take a deep breath as the Adrian discussion naturally brings Brianna to mind.

I turn to Getz in the backseat. "Do you have a boy named Jahlil Anderson working for you?"

"You mean Jah-Kill?" she asks. "That boy used to be one of my best shooters 'til he started fuckin' wit ya shrink bitch and got soft."

I blink once, then let it pass. "Did you put him inside Blue Rock with Bing?"

"Nah, he got that job on his own," she says. "But once he was in, we figured why not use him to keep tabs on the fat man?"

"And look how well that worked out," I mutter.

"The fuck you trippin' on, Chuckie?" Truck asks.

"The boy is gonna spill, Truck."

There's a pause in the car. Then I feel the rage bubbling up beneath the calm I work so hard to maintain. "You put a corner boy with severe PTSD inside the engine of our operation. You gave him access to logistics, supply flows, and sourcing. That's high-level Black God trade secret."

Truck rolls his eyes and scoffs. "Man, how many times I gotta tell you this ain't fuckin' Washington D.C? Turn off that fake-ass white boy voice."

The car erupts in laughter. Getz howls like she's watching some sort of comedy special. I just ignore it. But when it quiets, I switch my approach.

"Look, your 'lil shooter ain't wanna be a shooter no more." I relax my vernacular. "Had the barrel in his mouth. Wanted to blow his brains all over his momma's studio apartment. Instead, he walked into the foundation for help."

"And the white bitch made him squeal?" Getz cuts in.

I catch the way her hand tenses on the pistol on her lap, already itching to take her retribution.

"I didn't say that."

Truck squints. "So, how do you know all this?"

I lie, clean and easy. "He didn't tell Dr. Wright any specifics, but she's not stupid. She knew he was involved in something heavy and was scared he was about to end up in jail or worse. So she referred him to me, thinking I could get him out."

That part's true. The rest isn't. Jahlil admitted to me that he told Brianna everything. She knows our gun supply ran through Blue Rock Industries. She knows Getz, Slim Choppa, and Lil Nutty pull the strings for Truck at the street level. I can't guarantee she doesn't know the entire mid-tier structure, given how many RF9 youth she counsels now.

And after our last conversation, I'm almost certain she suspects my family never truly left the game. She didn't say it outright, but I could hear it in the way she pressed me, asking how I knew so much and why I spoke with such clarity about how RF9 moves.

She's not stupid. She's trained to read the subtleties, the gaps, the tone shifts most people miss. That's why she's dangerous. But even in light of all she knows and all she could say, Brianna's not a snitch. She loves those boys too much. She knows if she betrays their trust, even once, she loses her credibility, her program, and her purpose. But more importantly, dead civilians are bad for business. So I lie because that's the only way to maintain control over this situation.

"And?" Truck asks.

"And the boy is broken." I let those words hang. "Took all of five minutes and a fried chicken sandwich before he was naming names in my office. Getz, Slim, Nutty, Bing and his whole circle. This is why I told y'all to stop using kids to do dirt."

Getz kisses her teeth. "But he don't know who the Black Gods are, though. He don't even know Truck. The Palmer name stays protected on the block. We know the drill."

"Yeah I know. And that's the only thing protecting us. But if that boy turns State's evidence, he has enough to seal a RICO conviction. That'd gut RF9. Whether or not the Black Gods are specifically implicated, the heat won't stop there. It'll reach all of our business and political interests."

Truck flicks ashes from his blunt and exhales a plume of smoke. "We'll handle the 'lil nigga. And your shrink bitch too."

"Not necessary." I keep my voice smooth. "You don't touch Dr. Wright."

Truck grins. "You fuckin' the bitch?"

"No," I lie again without blinking.

"So why you care?" Truck asks.

"She's a civilian. That's a Rome-level decision."

Truck scoffs. "But the 'lil loud-mouth is my call. I don't need big bro to sign off on no bitch-made ex-shooter. That's RF9 business. Ain't got nothin' to do wit you or Rome if we're keepin' shit a buck... not anymore."

I take a deep breath and look through the car window as the city lights glimmer in the distance. My instinct is to push back and try to protect Jahlil for Brianna. But that instinct is rife with emotion, and emotion is weakness in this business. Jahlil's a scared kid with too much in his head and no discipline to keep it sealed.

That's why I've been quietly sending boys like him to Dr. Wright. The ones who couldn't stomach the weight. And the ones who are too reckless and too eager to kill without thinking. It's both compassion and containment. Better they cry to a therapist I control than run their mouths to the police. But Jahlil's way too fragile, and he's bleeding secrets that are far too important. That makes him a risk to the family. And the family comes first.

"Do what you want with the kid. But Dr. Wright is on me and Rome."

Truck tenses. "She knows too much, Chuckie."

I shift in my seat and drop my tone. "Leave her be, Tracy."

His eyes snap toward me. "Don't fuckin' call me that."

"I'm serious. Everything she knows is sealed under psychotherapist-patient privilege. Legally, she can't testify against us."

"That don't mean she can't point them pigs in the right direction," Truck snaps. "You know how them muhfuckas move. Dirty as hell in the dark, but when they bring the courtroom lights up, it's only our shit that get exposed."

He's not wrong. But a dead doctor with our name all over her program is what I'd call an unacceptable incurrence of liability. Truck won't understand that language.

"You make a decent point. But think about how much more fed heat we'll get if the head of our gang intervention program is murdered. Doesn't matter how clean you leave it. The optics alone will make the federal government rain fire on our heads. I'm sure they already think the foundation is a cover."

"It is a fuckin' cover, Chuckie." Truck chuckles, prompting his cronies to placate him in laughter.

Yes, we use it to launder money and build our narrative. But I built that place with intention. We've slowed RF9's youth recruitment and cut teen gun deaths in half over the last five years. It may be a tool, but it's mine. And I won't let Truck's paranoia burn it down.

"Look, if you touch Dr. Wright, you and I will have a problem."

Truck narrows his eyes. "Yeah? And what the fuck you gon' do? You wanna settle this shit like Pops and the OG Black Gods used to? Cuz I got five minutes right now."

I shake my head, tired and annoyed. "Fistfights don't solve problems, brother."

"So what? Charles Leroy Palmer, attorney at law, gon' take his own brother to court?" He cackles again.

I let him and his lackeys laugh for a bit before I strike. "Nah, lawsuits don't solve problems either. Not efficiently, anyway. But money does. And don't forget I control yours."

That makes the car go quiet. I don't stop. "Y'all like those nice, clean distribution checks from Palmer Holdings that magically show up in your account every quarter, turning your street money into properly taxed investment income that you can dump into your artists? You like stuntin' on Instagram for whatever BBL beauty you tryna put in rotation for the week? That's me. You hurt Dr. Wright, I'm done. The machine stops. And then it won't be the FBI, ATF, or DEA that takes you down, brother. It'll be the IRS."

He doesn't move. He only exhales as he keeps his eyes forward. I can almost see his mind working. He knows I'm not bluffing. I've spent the last fifteen years building a bulletproof laundering infrastructure, tested by former federal investigators and scrubbed by top white-collar law firms. It works because I built it to. Truck may not have my degrees, but he's not dumb, and he knows his gangster history. He knows how Capone went down. How the biggest fish get fried not because of the bullets, but because of their books.

"Aight nigga, she off limits." He takes a long drag of his blunt, lets the smoke roll out of his mouth as if it's hanging on his last words, before blowing it out in a smooth, steady stream. "Until she ain't."

I nod once, but don't reply. There's no use in me arguing with Truck over what he can or cannot do. Only Rome can successfully do that.

26

CHARLES PALMER

I SIT AT the lobby bar of the Arlowe Hotel, waiting for Tim Rouchard to arrive for our meeting. It's a modern space with low lighting and comfortable armchairs, and on a quiet weekday evening in Downtown Maddox, hotel guests are few. I order a seltzer with lime and wait for him to arrive.

I pull some photos on my phone while I wait. Looks like a white male in his fifties, skinny with dark hair and glasses.

There he is.

"Mr. Rouchard?" I offer a hand. "Charles Palmer."

After a few moments of small talk, I explain how I'm planning a class action against PGC on behalf of mothers of gun violence. A fabrication.

"To build a civil case," I begin, "I would need to first establish that Blue Rock did indeed have an inside operator knowingly selling guns to criminals. Can you tell me what you discovered?"

He takes a sip of his scotch. "Blue Rock was legally required to disclose to the government exactly how many firearms it was producing. The amount of raw metal firearm components the South Maddox factory was purchasing should've yielded more units than what Bing was officially reporting. I did some digging, put two and two together..."

I take notes to enhance my cover, but I'll shred them at my first opportunity. "What'd you find, exactly?"

"John Bing, Willis Graham, and Julian Farth," he says. "This crew of corrupt execs and foremen assembled the unmarked guns themselves overnight and sold them to RF9 for what seemed like decades."

"And you've told the investigators?" I need to know the extent of the exposure.

"Not yet. I have an official meeting with the FBI tomorrow morning. I plan to tell them everything and give them all the files I backed up before Bing deleted them from the servers when I confronted him, the fraudulent government reporting, surveillance footage of known RF9 members at the Blue Rock facility in South Maddox, Bing's confession—"

"Wait. John Bing confessed to you?"

"More than confessed," Tim admits. "He offered to cut me in to keep me quiet, but I sold my company to PGC for billions. Granted, my VC investors took most of that money, but I don't do what I do for financial gain. Not anymore…" His voice trails off as if he's trying to place an emotion, or maybe escape one. "Anyways, that ogre didn't know I had my phone recording in my pocket."

"Would you be willing to share this recording with me?"

He hesitates, clearly uncomfortable.

"Or at least describe what's on it," I soften my tone, almost pleading. "I can't stress how helpful this will be to our civil suit."

"He just admits to cooking the books."

"Does he say who he was selling those firearms to? Did he say RF9 specifically?"

"No, not specifically. He just insinuates he has buyers he can't disclose to PGC. I told him I wanted no part, and I left. Next thing I know, the servers are corrupted and the evidence of forged reporting is practically gone. Luckily, I had already backed everything up on my phone."

"Do you have the phone with you?"

"I do, but Mr. Palmer, before you ask, I don't think it's smart for me to share it with you before I share it with the FBI. I'm happy to tell you the facts informally so you can get a jump start on prepping your civil case, but the criminal case needs to come first."

I put on a trained smile, doing my best to keep him at ease. "Of course. This is just research. I still need to validate if there's even a case here. Can you tell me if anyone else at PGC knew about what you found?"

"I flagged the reporting discrepancy to Derek Graff, PGC's COO," he admits. "I thought someone was just stealing raw materials, but at the time, I didn't know who or why. He told me it was nothing and had me bury it. By the time I figured out the specifics, we had already IPO'd. And then kids started getting killed with those ghost guns. That's when I went to Adrian."

"And you told him your suspicions regarding RF9's involvement?"

"I did. He didn't believe me, thought I was overreacting. Then things blew up so quickly. I never got to show him the security footage or the confession."

Shit… And I hate cursing. I think it's the lowest form of human communication, but if Adrian can connect RF9 to the Blue Rock guns, that makes him a liability that Truck would need to take care of. But I have plans for Adrian. I need him alive.

After I conclude what would be a useful interview if I was actually suing PGC in a class action, I pick up the tab and we head out of the hotel toward the valet. As I step outside, I see Getz's guy. He's not hard to miss if you know what to look for. Black kid, probably no older than twenty with the top of an "RF9" tattoo on his neck, poking out of the collar of his valet uniform.

I turn to Tim who's holding his valet ticket. "Let me get that for you."

I take the ticket from him so I can pay for it. Even though I have a cover story and Uncle Mac already paid off hotel security to scrub their surveillance footage, best to limit any credit card charges indicating that Tim was ever here.

I hand the valet the ticket, giving him a slight head nod. That's all it takes to send the message: *the white man behind me needs to die.*

Moments later, Uncle Mac pulls up in the BMW. I shake Tim Rouchard's hand and thank him before getting in the backseat.

We swing around to the side alley where Truck is parked. He winds down the window.

I roll mine down. "Make sure you destroy his phone."

Truck blows a cloud of blunt smoke in my direction. "Nigga, you think this our first fuckin' rodeo?" He laughs with his crew, imitating what he calls my "white boy voice" as he rolls up the window.

I just shake my head as Uncle Mac peels off. As we drive through downtown, he peeks at me from the rearview mirror.

"You're doin' good, nephew." His West Philly accent is strong and his voice is gruff. "Your daddy would be proud of how you're helpin' your brothers clean up this mess."

"You talk to him lately?"

"Here and there."

"Can you set up a visit?"

Uncle Mac shifts in the seat as he turns onto North Market, headed toward my penthouse on the riverfront. "You know Big Palm don't want you boys seein' him like that. You start visiting someone you love in prison, someone you look up to, slowly, maybe subconsciously, you start to normalize that shit. Start to think it's okay to be held down in captivity like an animal, okay to get caught. Big Palm wants you out here, focused on protectin' the family name, keepin' it clean just like you doin, son."

● ● ●

MY FATHER ONCE TOLD ME,

"Son, you ain't never gon'
be shit but a thug."

27

TRUCK PALMER

Slim shuts the door of the Denali, still wearing the valet jacket we bought online. "Blue Audi, plates ending in 2TUV."

I glance at Getz. "Hit Nutty. Have him scoop the 'lil nigga my brother was talkin' bout. I want him to pull the plug on Bing. Need to know what the boy about. And then have 'em meet us at the chop house."

"Say less," Getz says, already pulling out her burner phone.

I tap the steering wheel lightly, keeping my eyes on the exit of the hotel valet. We're just around the corner, tucked in an alley off a side street that don't see much action. Downtown Mad Dog is movin' tonight, but our mark is headed where the streets narrow and the factories sit dead. A decent place to grab a nigga up.

By the way, I call everybody nigga. Black niggas, Caucasian niggas, Mexican niggas, Asian niggas. If you don't like it, blow me. When I was fourteen, I called my momma nigga, and she put me out the house. I just said, "Whaddup, my nigga," and she kicked my ass out. Not long after, I pulled my first plug. It was on the corner of Franklin Ave. & 9th St. in South Madd where my career began. That was thirty years ago.

Chuckie was raised on the North Side by our momma, but me and our big brother, Rome, was raised on Franklin & 9th by our pops with dealers and killers. Rome's the new mattress king, youth sports icon, man of the community, and whatnot, but I'll never give up this RF9 shit.

I see the Audi pull out of the hotel driveway. I turn the ignition and the engine growls low as we lurk forward.

He turns right onto 11th Street, and we slide in behind him, a good distance back. We follow behind like a ghost, past the empty rows of rusted metal fences and abandoned warehouses. The streets 'round these parts are deserted. Nobody around to see shit.

We follow him through the isolated corridors of the Riverwalk, waiting for our moment. He turns north onto Rawley Street, slowing as the industrial wasteland looms ahead. No lights, no witnesses, nothing but the smell of oil and the sound of distant freight trains.

"We on," I tell my squad calmly as my fingers clench the wheel.

Their fingers clench pistols and uzis as they pull down their ski masks. My blood's pumping, but I ain't nervous. I'm ready.

We tail him until the city lights fade into the darkness of the old industrial district. And then I floor it. The engine roars as I swing this murder wagon across his path. Tires shriek against asphalt, and my niggas move before the car stops. Straps out, barrels leveled.

I stay in the driver's seat while Getz, Slim, and two other soldiers handle the work. My eyes stay on the mirrors, watching for pigs and pedestrians. They rip the door open, nines and submachine guns raised, aimed steady at Tim Rouchard's head.

They pull him out and pistol whip him. But his bitch ass whimper is cut short by the gag they jam in his mouth. He squirms, but it don't matter. He's nothing now, just a problem that need to be solved, a plug that need to be pulled.

I scan the street behind me and see headlights coming up in the distance. "Let's go! Grab that nigga! Move!"

My crew drags him to the back of the Denali, binding him tight at the wrists and ankles before tossing him in the trunk.

Getz jumps in his Audi and speeds off. We're gone just as fast, both whips burning rubber in opposite directions before those distant headlights get close enough to see what's happening.

We pull up to the warehouse by the Port of Trenton. The building's got old bricks dark with age and rusted metal doors. This is an RF9 slaughterhouse. It's quiet, isolated, and close to the port, making for easy disposal.

I kill the engine and step out. The night air stinks of saltwater and decay. I can almost hear the whispers of dead niggas echoing off those cold, stained exterior walls. The mark in the trunk is breathing heavy, muffled by the gag.

Inside, the warehouse is dark. Steel beams stretch up to the ceiling. A few old lights buzz overhead, flickering onto the concrete floor as my soldiers drag him in.

His eyes are wide, and his voice is shaking as they force him onto a large blue tarp on the floor. "Pl-p-please, please I have a family."

"Yeah... So do I." I lift my Desert Eagle to his dome and pull the trigger. The shot rings out loud, bouncing off the walls and fading into that sweet ringing in my ears. His head snaps back, and blood sprays as his body slouches.

"Get him wrapped up." I give the order, already turning toward the exit as I light a blunt.

I step outside and see Getz pulling up. Now, she's in her black 1989 Chevy Caprice. She steps out wit Lil Nutty and he's dragging somebody behind him. Skinny kid wit dreads who can barely stand upright. His face is swollen to shit. He got one eye puffed shut and his lip cracked wide open. Blood on his teeth. Shirt torn down the middle, showing an RF9 chest tat like a badge he earned but forgot how to wear.

"The Audi a soda can," Getz tells me. "I wiped the GPS and his phone's geo-data before I smashed it up. Ain't nobody trackin' him to da Mad Dog."

"Good shit."

"But Rouchard was leaving a voicemail for that Adrian nigga when we got him," she says. "We ain't say shit but he might have heard us jack him."

"Shit! He got my voice on tape. I was barkin' at y'all slow asses to move faster."

"Ayo on da gang, I'll pay his ass a visit tonight." Getz taps the RF9 tat on her arm twice. "Dead the light skinned nigga and wipe the voicemail. Let me know what you wanna do."

I squint and rub my temples. "Nah, hold off. He got business with the Black Gods. Need to connect with my brothers first."

"You handle the other white boys?"

"Yeah, Chuck's people at MPD got us the location on Bing and his two boys," she says. "Tracked 'em to a safehouse on the westside. Had to get creative to distract the 'lil piggies on watch but we slid through and got the job done. They ain't finna do no more talkin'."

"Aight, good work," I blow a drag of weed smoke out the side of my mouth and as I look over, I see the kid again. "That the 'lil nigga?"

"Yeah," Getz says. "Jah-Kill."

"He handle the work like I said he should?"

"Nah, the boy froze up. Couldn't pull the trigger on the fat white man. I had to do 'em myself."

"Whatchu think?"

"Your brother was right," she says, shaking her head like she's ashamed. "He ain't got it no more. Hate to say it, but he weak. Can't hold this RF9 shit."

I take another short pull of my blunt. "Lemme holla at him."

She turns and waves him forward.

Nutty pulls him closer. "Bow to da Black God, bitch!"

Then he throws a quick uppercut into the kid's stomach. He doubles over with a tight grunt, then stumbles forward and almost drops but catches himself on instinct. His face is twisted in pain, but he doesn't cry out. Doesn't fold. Just breathes through it.

That's the thing about some of these young bouls these days. They talk that tough shit, but they usually break easily. But this one? He absorbed the pain. Let it sit in his chest like it belong there, like he want it there.

The boy looks up at me, confused. Then he looks behind me and sees the body we just dropped. He sees my niggas wiping up blood and wrapping up the corpse.

"Shit, they ain't lyin'," he says. "Palmers really do run the streets. The Black Gods are still alive."

I can see the fear in his eyes as he makes the connection. But something else is kickin' in too. Awe.

I look at him with a blank stare. "And we ain't ever gon' die."

The kid just stands there, doesn't say a word.

I lower my head, trying to get eye to eye with him. "You ain't gon' beg, 'lil nigga? Tell me how loyal you is? How you ain't mean to spill company secrets? How you ain't gon' do it again?"

He shakes his head slowly and I see that look in his eye. I know that look well. I've seen it in the mirror more times than I can count. It's a look that says, it'd be better if I'm dead anyway.

Jahlil looks me in the eye without a trace of fear. "I already told my momma I'm sorry."

I pause mid-drag, letting the smoke burn through my nostrils into the air. His voice was almost peaceful when he said that shit, like the kind of peace that come from finally facing the moment you been waitin' on. I'm almost envious. For a second, in my mind, I see my own mother. I see her face the day she found the piece our pops gave me and told me I wasn't welcome. She said I wasn't her son. And she meant that shit. Worst beating I ever took was when Big Palm found out I let her find it.

I used to carry that pain, that rejection. Thought maybe one day I'd do enough to fix it. But those days are gone. I could dedicate my life to spreading the gospel. I could build churches, hospitals and basketball courts for poor children like Rome and Chuck do. Or I could get a hundred more niggas zipped up. It don't matter to Reeda *Channing*. She buried the version of me she loved a long time ago.

So fuck it. I give Getz the nod, and with a cold quickness, she raises her piece and puts three bullets in Jahlil's chest. He drops hard to the concrete and spasms once as blood pours out.

I step forward and see he's still breathing, but it's shallow and wet. He's gurgling through his throat, choking on his blood.

His eyes are twitching like he's searching for something that ain't coming. Like he's still tryin' to hold on to life. Or maybe he's seein' the 'light' they talk about.

"Once the 'lil nigga bleed out, put him on the boat wit da other rat." I turn back toward the door as the blunt burns slow between my fingers.

Getz nods as she puts her piece back in her waistband. "Gotchu, OG."

My soldiers load the bodies onto the yacht. We motor out to the usual drop site, tie four ninety-pound dumbbells to both of 'em, and toss the carcasses overboard, making sure the snitch bitches hit the river floor and stay there.

28

ADRIAN CHANNING

FOUR A.M. BIKE ride around Upper Maddox Valley and back. I go thirty miles along the countryside before I even look at my phone. I take in the sights and sounds of the early morning, the cool breeze against my skin, birds chirping in the distance, the dewy grass, and even the lowing of cows across the fields.

As I make my way back home, the sun has fully risen, and the city around me buzzes with life. Amidst it all, I feel at peace. My mind is clear.

I head back inside, the air still cool on my skin. The ride leaves me sore legs, sure. But it also gives me the edge I'm chasing. Most people are just getting up, and I've already notched a win. I turn on the TV to catch some news before stepping into the shower. A reporter appears, speaking with a sorrowful tone.

"It was a particularly violent evening in Maddox Pennsylvania last night. A witness safehouse was brutally attacked. John Bing and two other executives at the now-defunct Blue Rock Industries were found murdered in what police are calling 'execution-style killings.' As you may recall, the men were arrested for selling Blue Rock firearms on the black market. According to inside sources, they were expected to testify against the leaders of the national crime syndicate believed to be the buyers of those weapons. According to a source at the FBI, the previously unnamed group is believed to be RF9, the Maddox-bred street gang…"

I turn down the volume to collect my thoughts. Before I can, I look down at my phone and see a missed call from Tim Rouchard from last night. I had my phone on silent during dinner with Josie and then came home and passed out. He left a voicemail, but I never saw it.

I press play. *"Hey, Adrian, I just met with Charles. Seems like a good lawyer. I just wanted to..."*

Tim's voice trails off. And then I hear a loud screeching of tires, followed by muffled, frantic movements. Then come his screams of utter terror, as if he's staring death itself in the face.

Suddenly, I hear a distant voice that isn't Tim's. It's a tough, raspy, burly voice, a voice I can tell belongs to a man much larger and much Blacker than Tim Rouchard, the skinny white man from Wilton, Connecticut.

"Let's go! Grab that nigga! Move!" the voice barks, followed by the sounds of car doors slamming shut and then more tires screeching in the distance.

The voicemail ends. I call him back. It goes straight to voicemail. Doesn't even ring.

Slightly panicking, I dial my lawyer.

"Adrian," Charles answers, out of breath.

"Hey man, sorry, I know it's early."

"Not early. Just getting off the row machine. What's up?"

"I just uh... I got a weird voicemail from Tim. It sounded like he was in trouble."

"What kind of trouble?"

"I–I–I don't know," I stammer. "Like a carjacking or something."

"When?" Charles asks, his voice calm.

"Last night." I check the timestamp on the voicemail. "8:13 p.m. You met with him, right?"

"I did. At the Arlowe, like you set up," Charles confirms. "Finished up at around 7:45."

"Do you think I should call the cops? I saw Bing and his guys were killed last night. Maybe this was related? Seems like his buyers are cleaning up loose ends."

"It's possible," Charles says calmly.

"But how would they know where to find him? He doesn't live in Maddox."

"It wouldn't be hard to follow him from New York."

Then, an eerie realization hits me. "Do you think I'm in danger?"

"No," he says. "I'd assume they'd only target people who were complicit in the conspiracy. Or people with evidence of the buyer's involvement and are cooperating with the federal government. Do you fall into either of those categories?"

"I don't know anything about any of that. I worked for the parent company of the parent company of the parent company of the entity that was making those guns. I didn't get granularly involved with sales. I mean, Tim told me he suspected RF9 was involved, but that was pure conjecture at the time. The whole thing blew up before I could look into it. I never saw any real evidence of a conspiracy. Just some numbers that didn't make sense. I couldn't testify against RF9 if I wanted to. And I absolutely don't want to."

"Why's that?"

"I may have gone corporate, but I'm still from Ironbridge, Charles. We don't deal with police."

"Then I wouldn't be worried about being targeted," Charles says.

"But how would they know Tim was working with the feds?"

"From what I understand, RF9 is extremely well-connected for a street gang. I'm sure they have members of law enforcement on their payroll. It's likely how they got Bing's location."

"Jesus Christ," I mutter.

"Not for nothing, violent crime has been on the rise over the last year or so. This could've been a totally random carjacking for all we know."

"Either way, I think I need to give this voicemail to the police."

"I agree…" His words are slightly hurried. "…But why don't you let me handle it? I deal with MPD all the time. Send me the voicemail, I'll get it to the right detective."

"Okay yeah, I appreciate that. I fuckin' hate the police."

"As do I, but it's a hazard of the job so I'm used to it," Charles says. "In any event, I need you focused on managing my capital. Did you close on the Josie investment?"

"That's not a question you ever need to ask me, Charles. I always close. That's why they call me A.C."

He chuckles. "Okay, A.C., the noble tycoon. I've got something coming to you right now. Oh, and like I've said before, my family is extremely private, which makes us very concerned about confidentiality, as I'm sure you can understand. Our participation in your fund should stay between us. Even with Josie."

"Of course," I tell him. "Last thing I need is a company trying to go over my head and court my investors directly."

"Great. Talk soon."

He hangs up, and less than a minute later, my phone vibrates with a notification from my bank.

Community Capital Partners SPV I, L.P. – Wire Transfer – The Palmer Family Trust ($5,930,400.00).

My excitement is overshadowed by my concern for Tim and the eerie possibility that RF9 is on a murder rampage to silence anyone and everyone who may have known about their Blue Rock gun connection. John Bing and his cronies were criminals. I won't say they got what they deserved, but they knew the risks of working with gangsters. As for Tim, I wanted to slap the guy across his mouth for killing my career, but I don't want him dead.

I'm just glad Charles is willing to help me through this chaos. As the city's top litigator, he knows the system, the cops, and the politics better than anyone. He'll have my back. After all, he's my attorney. And now, he's my investor.

● ● ●

MY FATHER ONCE TOLD ME,

"White, Black, Brown, or other,
a criminal is a criminal."

29

SPECIAL AGENT REGINA COURTLEIGH

SIX MONTHS LATER

JOHN BING AND his accomplices have been murdered, and Tim Rouchard has gone missing without a trace. His ex-wife told us he dropped their kids off a day before he was supposed to and told her he had an 'important meeting.' No details, which wasn't unusual for him. He was divorced, lived alone, and was known to keep his work to himself.

So, we pulled his phone, his car logs, his laptop. Everything was wiped. No tower pings, no GPS history, no plate-reader hits along any route out of the city. Either he's fleeing prosecution or RF9 got to him.

This task force has spent countless hours chasing down leads trying to find a pattern or link that might uncover the identities of the "Black Gods," the group we believe is pulling the strings behind RF9, but without John Bing and Tim Rouchard, we hit a wall. I wasn't about to sit around waiting for a miracle. So, we put two undercovers in with RF9. Now, the intel they're feeding us is keeping our investigation alive.

But here we are, months of wire taps, physical and digital surveillance, and the only theory we're confident in is that someone related to Jerome Palmer Sr. is in charge of RF9 but we're no closer to real evidence.

Senator Marcia Calderon and two of her aides enter the task force command room of our FBI field office. This place is mostly steel and vinyl, stuck between old factories and abandoned warehouses in South Maddox.

Calderon shakes hands with my boss, Special Agent in Charge Davis Rondell, exchanging pleasantries. I stand next to my partners, Agents Jabar Galloway and Winnie Ortiz at the front of the room.

Calderon makes her way down, scanning the three of us. "Special Agent Courtleigh, how's everything coming along?"

"Senator, it's been a long road, but we're closing in."

Her smile tightens. "That's what you said last time."

I can see the impatience bubbling beneath her calm exterior. She wants results, and I can't blame her. The Black Gods aren't ordinary criminals. They're deeply embedded, shielded by money and connections. It doesn't help that most of the city sees them as upstanding citizens.

"We're building profiles on the Palmer brothers." I gesture to the screen behind us with photos, charts, and lines connecting the dots. "What we need now is a smoking gun that ties them to RF9's illegal activities."

Calderon glances at the board, her lips pursing as she reads the names. "Walk me through it again." She folds her arms across her chest.

I step up to the board, my voice flat, clinical, but underneath it, fury still burns. This isn't just another case for me. These people killed my father.

"Jerome Palmer Sr. aka 'Big Palm.' Seventy-two years old." I keep my tone as professional as I can. "Currently serving a life sentence at Riverville Correctional for the murder of Special Agent Kevin Courtleigh..." My breath hitches.

Rondell notices and jumps in. "Big Palm started as an enforcer for the Philadelphia Black Mafia. He's rumored to have taken part in the Hanafi child murders in D.C. back in '73."

One of Calderon's aides gasps softly. "The baby drowning massacre?"

"That's the one," Rondell says. "His reputation was one of violence. Kidnappings and home invasions were his prime revenue stream back then. But after a stint upstate, he came home and launched Palmer Furniture

Emporium, marketing himself as a reformed convict who learned the trade of upholstery in the joint."

"He became a local icon," Ortiz says, "hiring ex-cons in his stores and warehouses, helping locals with checkered pasts make an honest living."

"But as we know, that's all a farce," I say. "When he wasn't filming cheesy 'mattress king of the disco' commercials, he was establishing the Black Gods, a smuggling outfit under the Black Mafia. But Big Palm didn't make it a habit of staying under anyone's thumb."

I make eye contact with Calderon before she flicks her eyes back to the board. There's something about her I don't quite trust, but I can't put my finger on it.

"After the Black Mafia leaders were assassinated in '82," Galloway says, "Big Palm took control of the East Coast market for synthetic narcotics and then later, firearms. Before long, the Black Gods became an empire and ruled the streets from Maddox to Cleveland."

"That is, until he pled guilty to my father's murder." Rage builds in me at those words.

"But it's not clear why none of his family or any other members of his organization went down with him, or why the case records remain classified," Galloway says. "As far as the public is concerned, Jerome Palmer Sr. died a wealthy furniture magnate in 2004. Senator Calderon, you were the U.S. Attorney at the time..."

Calderon steps forward. "We had his two eldest sons dead to rights on trafficking charges. They were just kids at the time, high schoolers, maybe college-age. Their father used them as puppets. His hands were clean, but he was the one ordering the violence. We needed him off the streets."

She crosses the room and glances at me. "Special Agent Courtleigh, your father's murder was unfortunate, but it gave us a break in the case. He was undercover inside the Palmer home in South Maddox, acting as Reeda Palmer's handyman, when a black Escalade with spinning rims pulled up and opened fire on him. We had a surveillance team on a nearby roof but they couldn't ID the shooters. Still, we were sure it was one of his sons who pulled the trigger."

"How were you so sure?" I ask.

"It was sloppy, clearly unplanned or the work of inexperienced operators," Calderon explains. "The car was registered to one of Palmer's legit businesses, and that gave us what we needed for an arrest warrant. We knew we'd have a fight on our hands in court, so we offered a deal. Big Palm agreed, knowing we wouldn't stop until we had him behind bars. He confessed to the murder on the condition we didn't pursue his sons or any of his family and allowed him to serve his time under a pseudonym so that his kids and grandkids wouldn't be haunted by his reputation. I'd get my kingpin off the streets, and the Palmers would be left to lead legitimate lives."

"But why give such a concession if you had the sons on trafficking charges?" Rondell asks.

"The evidence was muddy," Calderon says. "The Attorney General wasn't convinced we could win on RICO. And I didn't care about politics or headlines back then. I just wanted a violent man off the streets. But the Black Gods would end with Big Palm, that was his promise."

I can't believe her naivete. "I'm afraid he lied to you, Senator. The Black Gods are very much active, and based on what we've uncovered, one or more of his sons have taken over leadership. We have surveillance up on Rome and Truck Palmer, as well as members of their immediate circles."

Senator Calderon's face turns into a cold scowl, and her body tenses up. "We are running out of time. The people of this state—hell, the whole country—are watching this investigation. The implosion of Volition Aeronautics exposed Maddox, Pennsylvania, as the country's number one source of illegal guns. I expect results. If you can't make RICO stick, I'll have to bring in a team from New York or Chicago to handle this, a team more experienced with this level of organized crime."

Rondell shifts next to me, likely feeling his career on the line. He clears his throat. "We understand your concern with the pace here, Senator, but—"

"No buts, Davis. I don't care how you do it. Just take down the Black Gods."

30
CHARLES PALMER

TODAY'S MY NEPHEW Jordan's tenth birthday. It's a football-themed party in the backyard of Rome's mansion in the North Maddox neighborhood of Berry Hill. The house is cloaked in aged stone, sharp hedges, and iron gates that command the secluded corner of this upscale suburb. Massive windows reflect the afternoon sun, and the lawn is cut so clean it looks like it was painted on. It isn't just big, it's tasteful, the kind of place where money whispers instead of screams.

As I ease up the driveway, I spot the federal agents in their unmarked sedan. Their lack of subtlety would be laughable if they weren't dangerously close to tying us to RF9.

The backyard is alive with kids playing, footballs flying through the air, Palmer kin mingling, and laughter mixing with the smell of barbecue. Inflatable goalposts frame the lawn, and a giant inflatable helmet stands by the pool.

Uncle Mac and I give hugs to Rome's wife, Shanita and their seven kids. Shanita and Rome have been together since I was a kid. She's like a sister to me.

We pass through the party, trying our best to greet the nearly fifty Palmer cousins, nieces, nephews, uncles, and aunties enjoying the family gathering. I wish my mother would join us at these, but she's gone "no-contact" with Rome and Truck, still maintaining hope they'll leave the life. She doesn't know how involved I am. To her, I'm just a lawyer.

Rome mans the grill. People move around him like planets orbiting the sun, careful not to get too close but drawn to his gravity all the same. He's the embodiment of the phrase, "the Black man is God," a phrase my father raised us on. It's the phrase that laid the foundation of our family moniker, "the Black Gods."

As Uncle Mac and I walk over, Rome glances up. Frank Madigan is standing next to him, drinking a beer.

We give each other handshakes and hugs, then I step to the side of the grill. Out here in the open air, we don't have to worry about listening devices, even though we religiously have our people conduct sweeps of every inch of our homes, cars, stores, warehouses, and various hangouts for bugs. The trees around us stand like sentinels, guarding the secrets we convene on. But of course, armed guards protect each entrance.

"Our situation with the government seems to be subsiding," I start, keeping my tone light and casual as if we're just discussing ribs and sauces or a set of tax filings I need his signature on. "Chief Collins tells me the case on RF9 was predicated on testimony from former Volition-Blue Rock insiders, and they've all been… persuaded into silence. It's been months now with no subpoenas, no grand jury movement, no field activity. I think we're in the clear, at least for the moment."

Rome doesn't look up. He keeps working the grill, flipping a slab of ribs. "Guess somebody forgot to tell the agents posted across the street."

"Probably a reduced detail at this point. Optics more than anything. The surveillance units on me and Uncle Mac were pulled weeks ago. No drones, no tails, no wire taps we can detect. They're watching you out of habit now, maybe spite. But not strategy. My guess? They're just keeping the file warm, hoping something new surfaces."

Rome grunts. "They still got eyes."

"They always do," I admit. "But you haven't touched street business in years. The powers that be at the FBI will eventually realize there's little return on investment watching a man grill burgers and coach football games."

That earns me just the traces of a smile.

"Okay, C." He finally glances up from the grill. "But I don't want you tied to anything Truck does from here on out. Gotta keep you clean from that dirt."

"I know, but... desperate times..."

He looks at me as if he can sense the stress in my voice. Since Volition failed and our gun connect got shut down, protecting the family's interests has become increasingly difficult.

Rome looks me in the eye, and I can feel the weight of his concern. "Yeah, but that should be the last time you handle a mission like that, you hear me? You can't represent us in court if you're a co-defendant."

"I hear you, brother."

Truck finally arrives, loud and carrying a stack of gifts for Jordan, along with a cloud of burnt marijuana aroma. He greets Shanita and the family members and spots us at the grill across the lawn.

As he jogs toward us, he playfully interrupts the game of flag football, intercepting a pass and running for a touchdown. Given his size, one might think he's one of the many NFL players who came through Palmer Community Athletics, making a guest appearance at Jordan's party. But no, it's just a big Black, bearded, tatted murderer. The confirmation of those ugly stereotypes. But I suppose we all are.

Truck gets to the barbecue patio and gives quick daps to Rome, Mac, Frank, and me. With the five of us, we have a quorum.

"We're losin' ground in the streets," he says. "Losin' corners to the fuckin' Albanians. Shit is hotter than ever, and we runnin' out of plays."

"If we lose corners, we lose 'em." Rome says, his eyes fixed on the grill. "We don't make our money on the streets. Not anymore."

"If we stop pushin', then no money's comin' at all," Truck shoots back. "The gun business is down. Our wholesale customers on the dope side buy from us because we force them to if they wanna buy our guns. If we don't control the guns, then they'll go elsewhere for dope, and then we're done. Rome, you know this, my nigga."

Frank steps forward. "Yeah, Rome, this is what I was trying to tell you when that Adrian guy was in the office. The Triads, the Jamaicans, and the Italians aren't happy with the delays. Even the Irish Twins are making threats. They need their guns."

Although he's a white Irishman from South Philly, Frank Madigan is an honorary Black God. My father took him in as a foster son when we were kids and trained him in the family business like he did Rome, Truck, and me. We don't share blood, but he's our brother. My father never told my mother he was a distant nephew of the "Irish Twins of Boston," Tanner and Cooper Madigan, heads of the Boston Irish Mob and longtime allies of the Black Gods.

Officially, Frank is the head of distribution at Palmer Furniture Emporium. Unofficially, he's in charge of smuggling our contraband across the US and Canada, hiding it in the interiors of various pieces of furniture.

Frank coordinates wholesale shipments. Truck supplies RF9 soldiers to protect them while also running our direct to consumer business. Rome oversees it all while I manage legal affairs and legitimize the income. That's the division of labor my father declared when he left the Black Gods to us.

Truck turns to Rome. "Chinese, Irish, Italians, Jamaicans, the fuckin' Russians, the bikers... If we don't make good, they'll buy from our competitors. This Albanian Kodra Krew is back, Rome. Tell 'em, Frankie."

Frank sighs. "Yeah, the Albanians are posturin' for war, boys. They jacked two of our trucks out of Detroit last month. Two thousand ARs and Glocks gone."

Rome finally looks up from the grill. I can see a glint of concern in his eye. "Uncle Mac, what do you know about 'em?"

"Arjun Kodra heads their US business," Uncle Mac starts. "Based out of New York, he moves guns, dope, pussy, stolen cars, everything. His uncle is Valmir Kodra."

"Who the fuck's that?" Frank asks.

"A certified terrorist-for-hire," Uncle Mac says. "He's on practically every most-wanted list there is. Got a few bombings in Europe and some high-profile political assassinations in the Middle East on his name. His network is well-capitalized, extremely violent, and willing to do whatever to win market share."

"Rome," Truck says, "they movin' in on our territory across the fuckin' country, offering better prices on everything. They know we don't have the firepower to control the market anymore. They're gonna try to knock us off the board for good. I can't protect this family without clean artillery, bro."

"I hear you, T." Rome loads another rack of ribs onto the grill.

Uncle Mac turns to Rome, his voice low and raspy. "Hate to add to the pressure, nephew, but Big Palm is losing ground in Riverville. Got a rival prison crew causin' trouble for our business in there."

"Albanians?" Rome asks.

Uncle Mac shakes his head assuredly. "Nah, it's a nigga crew. One of the few not under the blessings of the Black Gods. Thinking they can take advantage of our current instability. It's a ripple effect."

"We gotta get a new gun supply, kill these fuckin' Albanians, get our customers back in line, and let the markets know the Black Gods are still in control," Truck says.

"It ain't that easy, T," Rome says, wiping sweat from his forehead with the bottom of his apron. "I got federal agents damn near livin' outside these gates, watching my every move. I can't set up a new connect with that kind of attention on me. New relationships. New logistics. It all takes time. One mothafucka forgets protocol, says my name on a wiretap, we in a RICO."

For a moment, the only sound is the sizzle of meat on the flames and children calling for the ball in the distance.

And then a realization hits me. "We need someone to do it for us. Adrian might be able to broker a new supply. He acquired Blue Rock not long ago and could still have access to its supplier records. He gets us the parts we need. We buy the Blue Rock factories out of bankruptcy and put him in charge on paper. Then we grab some warehouse guys from the Emporium to assemble the product. It would be like business as usual, except we'd own the process completely."

Uncle Mac takes a swig of beer, flashing a smile as he swallows. "It's smart, nephew. Like the dope labs your father and I set up in '82. Get the raw shit from the white boys, cook it up in-house, cut out the middleman, keep margins down."

Sometimes I forget that before he was a Black God, Uncle Mac was a chemical engineer. He and John Bing worked together at Canderton Chemicals, which produces everything from bleach and liquid drain cleaner to pharmaceutical precursors for MDMA, methamphetamine, fentanyl, LSD, dopamine, and more. Decades ago, Mac cut an under-the-table deal to buy Canderton's off-spec precursor chemicals. My father then bought up abandoned industrial sites and built hidden drug labs across the country, thus vertically integrating a synthetic narcotics empire.

When Bing took over Blue Rock Industries in '95 and moved into weapons manufacturing, my father struck a similar deal with Bing: unserialized firearms off the books, straight from the assembly line. Between the labs and the guns, they quietly seized control of the two most profitable sectors of the American black market. But now that control is slipping away.

Truck paces, likely still fuming at the notion of Adrian getting involved. "Hell nah. I got a bullet for that light-skinned sellout. He knows too much."

I take a deep breath. "We discussed this, Truck. He's not going to talk."

"How do you know that, C?" Rome asks, still focused on the grill.

"I got him off on an ugly assault charge in New York. I'm helping him sue his old firm. I got him to deliver the Volition snitch. And he came to me with that voicemail with Truck's voice on it, clear as day, during the grab."

"That's why we need to pull the plug on him," Truck says.

"We don't. The voicemail by itself isn't enough to convict you on anything. I'd get that thrown out less than a minute into pre-trial hearings. But the point is, he brought it to me, and I buried it. He thinks I'm his friend and loyal advisor, so he'll come to me first with any suspicions and I'll make sure they go nowhere. I told him Maddox PD doesn't think the voicemail is evidence of anything and he accepted it. If he were gonna talk, he would have done so by now."

"I don't know, C." Rome subtly shakes his head. "Still a loose end."

"Adrian Channing knows how to make money, Rome," I argue. "Legitimate money. The kind that can put this family on the Forbes list. But his reputation is shot and he needs support. If we're his benefactors and give him a lifeline back into a career managing capital, he'll be ours."

Rome finally looks up from the grill, a hint of intrigue in his eyes, one I haven't seen in a long time. "This that investment opportunity you told me about?"

"It is. I moved forward on it."

"How much?" Rome asks.

"Just about six million."

Truck's eyes nearly leave his head. "Six million? Are you crazy, Chuckie?"

"It'll come back to us tenfold. He promised as much. A 10X return. And his track record is clear. The man has never bought a company that didn't at least double in value before he sold it. Other than Volition, of course, but for obvious reasons, I think we can say that was an anomaly. He'll return our money and then some. And in the meantime, we control him and can leverage his contacts to get our gun business back up."

"Rome, we're gonna need that bread," Truck says.

"We have more in the trust. Right, Chuck?" Rome asks.

"That six was most of it. But we have a backlog of cash off the street that needs to be cleaned."

"Yeah, but with the feds watchin' our every move, the laundry has to move slowly," Rome says.

"All the more reason to work with Adrian. Private equity isn't exactly a high-transparency space, nor is it heavily regulated. Money moves easily and quietly through funds like his."

"Fuck all that." Truck moves to the patch of lawn behind the grill and stands face to face with Rome. "If these Albanian niggas come for our heads, we gon' need guns and soldiers. That shit cost money! Chuckie gave our rainy day fund to some fuckin' shyster ass nigga without telling us, and Rome, you just flippin' burgers? What the fuck is goin' on here?"

I don't let Rome respond. "What's going on here is evolution, Truck. The future is falling right in our lap with this investment. In any event, we agreed a long time ago how this thing would work. How we invest our clean cash has nothing to do with your role. You'll get your distribution checks as scheduled."

"Boy, I will crack you over yo shit 'fore you try and tell me what I do for this family," Truck says. "You don't put in no fuckin' work for this family. I put in work for this family!"

"And what about that undercover agent?" I keep my voice low. "The one you thought was just a snitch and forced me to kill when I was only fourteen? That's the reason Big Palm's in prison. The work you put in for this family is only going to get this family put behind bars. Need you to let me and Rome do the thinking here. We all know that's not your strong suit."

Truck's expression twists into rage. "You keep disrespecting me, I will beat the shit outta you, boy—"

"Truck, relax, son," Uncle Mac says.

"Nah Unc, this nigga put on a suit and forgot who his big brother is—"

"Enough."

With one word from Rome, Truck quiets.

"The more legitimate streams of revenue for this family, the better." Rome glances at me. "C, what kind of returns did he promise? And how long until we see 'em?"

"Private equity is a longer play," I explain. "Not like the real estate flips. Three to five years, maybe longer, maybe shorter, but when it comes back, it'll be times ten."

"Sounds like Adrian feedin' some bullshit," Truck says as he lights a blunt. "He's gon' skate off with our bread like the last money manager Chuckie brought through. I don't trust it, Rome."

"Ay put it out," Rome says. "I got kids and white neighbors in this bitch."

Truck pinches the end of the blunt with his thumb and index finger, while grumbling to himself about how "the Black God don't give no fucks 'bout no got damn white neighbors."

Rome sighs briefly. I can tell he's trying to keep a cool demeanor, but he's stressed, perhaps annoyed. "C, we can't afford to lose any more clean money on these investments."

I shake my head. "This won't be like the other fund. I guarantee. Adrian's the real deal."

"Okay..." Rome draws out the word. "... I trust your judgment. But if he becomes a problem, Truck gotta handle it. No debates."

Truck's shoulders drop as the tension fades from his face.

I shake my head. "It won't come to that."

"Who wants burgers?" Rome hollers as he prongs a stack of patties onto a serving platter. A chorus of happy screams echoes across the field. "T, take these to Shanita for me."

Truck takes the platter and hikes toward the house. Despite his bravado, he typically does what he's told.

"Uncle Mac, Frankie, let me talk to Chuck right quick," Rome says.

As Uncle Mac and Frank walk toward the basketball courts where some of the original Black Gods have gathered, I turn back to Rome. He's no longer watching the grill. His eyes are fixed on, Jordan, who's sitting cross-legged in the corner of the end zone, quietly tracing lines in the turf while the others play around him.

"We got the results back," he says. "They say Jordan has autism."

"Shanita mentioned... I'm sorry."

He crosses his arms over his chest. "Feels like... I don't know, man. Like some sort of karma."

"Can't think like that, brother. You're a great father. And not just to your own kids. Ever since Big Palm went away we've all looked to you. What you do provides for the next generation."

Rome nods, his eyes never leaving Jordan. "I know. But I want out of this shit, C. I need to focus on my family and leave all this other shit behind. All this shit that'll get me lined up like Pops, or worse. I just wanna raise my family and coach my teams in peace."

This is the first time he's said it directly, but I've known Rome wants out. I can hear the weariness in his voice when we talk. I see it in the way his shoulders slump under the weight of these discussions. He's tired of the life. And I don't blame him, given the rock and hard place we're sitting between.

"My job is to protect this family's interests. That becomes a lot easier if we're no longer in the contraband business."

"That's why you went in with Adrian behind my back?"

"Wasn't behind your back. You gave me authority over the accounts, so I made the call."

"Six mil's no chump change, baby bro."

"No, it's not. But the world is changing. The question is whether we'll change with it. We've taken far bigger risks. But this one would put us on the right side of legitimacy."

"And you're absolutely sure about this? About him?"

"Adrian's our way forward. With his skill and our backing, we'll get in on the ground floor of the next billion-dollar investment firm. He does the work while you coach and raise your family. I can run my firm, and Truck can do whatever Truck does. It'll be totally separate from our other business. Feds won't be able to touch it. These private equity guys are playing with billions like it's nothing. No reason we can't exist in those rooms."

"A gangsta with a long-term investment plan." Rome slowly smiles. "I guess it is a new day."

"You deserve as much, Rome."

"Just keep an eye on this Adrian nigga. I don't trust him either."

"No need for concern, brother. Adrian Channing is desperate. And a desperate man can be controlled."

31

DR. BRIANNA WRIGHT

My NEW PATIENT sits on the sofa with one arm draped across the backrest, her long legs spread wide, right ankle balanced over her knee like she owns the room. She's dressed in black jeans, wheat Timberland boots, and a black windbreaker with the letters "BTE" embroidered on the left chest.

My office at the Palmer Foundation is painted in soft pastels of mint green, baby yellow, and warm charcoal. It's designed to feel safe and inviting. There are hand-drawn posters on the wall with glitter glue affirmations, and a basket of fidget toys by the door.

It's a space meant for children. Teenagers, maybe. Not grown women with murder in their eyes. But she said she works for the Palmer family, Charles referred me, and that she needed help, so here I am.

I press the record button on the device tucked between sheets in the notepad on my lap. "Morning, Theresa."

"Call me Getz."

As she says the name, my heart skips. Jahlil was terrified of a person named Getz. I suddenly notice the RF9 tattoos crawling up her neck and spilling past her sleeves onto her hands. Symbols I've seen sketched in crime reports and gang databases.

I assumed this Getz was a man. But now I know. She's the reason he went missing. Whether she pulled the trigger herself or gave the order, it doesn't matter. Part of me wonders now if she's here because she can't live with what she did or simply to do the same to me. I suppose I'm about to find out.

I glance down at the intake sheet on my notepad. "It says here your name is Theresa Legette."

"Yeah, but everyone calls me Getz. You can too, Doc."

Her smile is casual and a little too comfortable. It's performative, like she's playing a part and wants me to notice.

"Why?" I ask.

Her eyes flick around the room. "Legette... Getz... I *getz* to the bag. I *getz* to that action... I thought you had to be smart and shit to be a doctor."

"No, I get the wordplay." I force a chuckle. "It's clever... But I mean why insist on the street name in therapy? This is a confidential, safe space. There's no need for any mask or shield. You can just be Theresa here."

"That one of your rules?" she asks.

Does she want me to know she's spoken to my RF9 youth patients about this program? She does. She's threatening them.

"It's not a rule. Just a suggestion."

"Alright, Doc. You can call me by my government if it make you feel betta."

"Wonderful." I glance down at my notepad. "So... what brings you in?"

She leans further back on the couch and crosses her arms. "Just thinkin' about some things, I guess."

"Would you like to talk about those things?"

She gives me what I can tell is a practiced smile. "Yeah. I guess that's what I'm here for, right?"

Nothing about her seems like someone who actually wants therapy. No visible anxiety, no vulnerability, no hesitation. Her affect is flat but her gaze is deliberate. She's here on assignment. And I don't know whether it's to gather intel, send a message, or both. But I suppose I have a duty while she sits in my chair.

"So, what exactly have you been thinking about?" I ask.

"I've been thinkin' a lot about control. Over people. Over results. Over myself. I used to be real good wit it. But lately…" She trails off, letting her unfinished thoughts float in the air. "Lately, I been wonderin' what it might feel like to just… let go. Crash out completely. On anything and everything I'm supposed to have peace wit. Stop holdin' it together."

I nod slowly. "Control can mean a lot of different things. Sometimes when people feel out of control, they overcorrect. Do things that make them feel powerful in the moment without realizing they have real consequences."

"Consequences…" She smiles again. "That's cute, Doc."

"You said 'crash out.' I know the lingo. And I know that crashing out almost always carries consequences. But can you tell me what it means to you?"

Getz shrugs and lets out a condescending chuckle. "Tunin' out the noise. The world tryin' to tell you what's right and what ain't. But most don't know what it's like to carry what I carry. They talk like they know. Like they'd do better if they was in my shoes. But they wouldn't. They'd fold."

Her tone is too smooth. There's clearly something she's not saying. But I need her to say it. That she killed Jahlil. Or ordered it. Or knows who did.

"What is it you feel you're carrying?" I ask.

Her eyes fix on mine for a second longer than I'd like. "Loyalty. Duty. Some other shit I ain't got a name for… regret maybe."

Regret. That's an interesting choice of words, but I won't focus on that yet.

"And what is it you feel loyal to?"

"The usual," she says. "Family. Friends. The job. People who looked out when no one else did. People who put you in position to be more than that nappy-headed 'lil girl gettin' finger popped by her foster father."

The words land hard. Trauma always does. But I keep my face neutral. She's watching me too closely, measuring me. Testing me. I can't tell if she's giving me the truth or something rehearsed, like a scar she's weaponized, part of the story she tells to keep people off balance, to win sympathy, to justify the violence. Either way, I won't give her what she's looking for.

I just smile gently. "Loyalty is powerful. But it can get complicated when those loyalties start pulling us in opposite directions. Has that been happening to you?"

She doesn't answer right away. Instead, she leans back again, this time with her head tilted back, studying the ceiling. "You ever wonder, Doc, if maybe it's just easier to not feel shit at all? Like what if you could just shut it off. That little voice that tells you you're crossin' a line."

"Are you trying to shut that voice off right now?"

"Nah." Her lips twitch into a smirk. "Just wonderin' what it feels like. Some people say guilt eats 'em up. I think that's only if they weak."

"I don't think guilt means someone's weak. I think it means they're human."

She exhales sharply through her nose, like she's holding back a laugh. "And maybe that's just it…"

"What?"

"Maybe I ain't human, Doc. Maybe I never got the chance to be. Black girls in South Madd don't have the luxury of bein' soft."

Her voice trails off, and then she lets out a low chuckle. But it's not amusement. I can almost see her reliving the abuse in her head.

"You cry, they call you dramatic," she says. "You run, they say you need a man to protect you. But when those same grown men who supposed to protect you put they hands all on you? Well, that's your fault too."

"Your trauma is not your fault. It may be your burden to carry, but it didn't start with you. That's important to remember."

She scoffs. "I know that shit, Doc. I deal wit my shit like the muhfuckin' soldier I am."

"Like so many Black women," I murmur, more to myself than to her.

"There you go," she says, scoffing again.

"I mean it with respect."

"Fuck your respect. Y'all love callin' a Black woman strong like it's some badge of honor. Like 'strong' mean we was designed by Jehovah to take more bullshit than everybody else. We supposed to cry in silence, bleed in silence, and smile while everyone around us give us they shit to hold."

"You're right. It's not okay."

"No, it ain't. But you wanna know the real shit, Doc?" Her voice shifts with a rising energy. "After the streets, the system, the media—all of 'em—keep tellin' you how strong you is, how much you can handle... you start believin' it."

She shoots up from the couch and starts tapping her chest rapidly with her palm. "Like maybe I am built different. Maybe I can take anything I want. From anyone. I'm so fuckin' strong, right? Try and stop me. Try and kill me. I bet you can't. I bet you drop before I do. Can't nobody touch me. Can't nobody tell me shit 'bout shit 'cause I'm a muhfuckin' superhuman, Doc."

"Superhuman, huh? Invincible."

She doesn't respond, but her body stills. I see the recognition in her face as she sinks back onto the couch.

I wait a breath, then lean in slightly. "I get that. I really do. It's a powerful coping mechanism, turning your wounds into superpowers. Convincing yourself the pain makes you better, sharper, above it all."

"But?"

"But there's a line. Between coping and delusion. Between being resilient and thinking you can do whatever you want without there being repercussions."

"Says the superhero shrink tryna save every little broken Black boy in Maddox, PA. You don't think there are repercussions to that shit?"

She's trying to antagonize me, but I've heard that criticism at every step of my career.

"I don't think I'm a superhero. I know I can't save everyone. But trying isn't delusional. It's what keeps me grounded."

Getz raises an eyebrow as the corner of her mouth twitches. "That's the only thing that keeps you grounded? Not your daughter?" She draws out those words, like she's chewing on them. "Riley, right? Pretty, light-skinned basketball star with a mean crossover. Real poised. I guess she don't need saving, do she?"

There it is. The line between veiled and direct just blurred. But this bitch doesn't realize I'll gouge her eyes out with my bare hands if she even breathes in my child's direction. I don't care who she's killed or how many people in this city bend the knee to her gang.

But my face doesn't move. I can't give her the satisfaction.

She studies me for a moment, then leans in, her voice dropping a register. "But I wanna hear about the 'lil niggas you couldn't rescue out the trenches. The ones who, even though you tried ya hardest, still ended up in the clink, shot the fuck up… or just… disappeared."

I shift back in my seat just a hair, keeping my breath as even and my eyes as steady as possible. But inside, my chest tightens because we both know who she's talking about. She's trying to be cute, bringing up my daughter and then referencing Jahlil like a reminder of the awful things that can happen to kids in this city. She wants me rattled. But I've sat across from worse monsters than her. And I'm still here.

"I do the best I can for every person who sits in that chair."

"I ain't doubtin' that," she says. "But some people don't want to be saved, right? Some of 'em are already too far gone. You ever think maybe it's not on you? And that maybe if you keep trying to disrupt the natural order, you'll end up the one in need of saving?"

She's baiting me. Watching my reactions. Picking at the wound. I think about Jahlil's quiet desperation, the bruises he tried to hide, the fear he expressed last time I saw him. I think about how I haven't heard from him in months. I think about the hollow feeling I get every morning that tells me I know why that is. And then I look at the woman across from me. Calm, composed, and covered in ink that tells a truth she never has to say out loud.

"I think everyone has a line of acceptable risk, Theresa. The trick is knowing when you're getting close to it and whether you're willing to cross it."

Getz leans forward again, placing her elbows on her knees. "You think you'd ever cross yours?"

I hold her gaze. "Only if someone gave me a reason to."

We stare at each other in silence for what feels like an eternity. And then the timer on my phone buzzes.

"Looks like that's our time for today."

She doesn't move. "I got a question, Doc."

"Sure."

"How far does that doctor-patient privilege thing of yours go?"

"Unless there's a risk of serious physical harm to you or someone else, everything said here is confidential. I can't repeat anything you share without risking my license."

"So I could tell you I killed three niggas last night." She pauses before a sly smirk comes onto her face. "Hypothetically... and you'd have to keep it to yourself because they dead already?"

"Technically, yes. If it wasn't a threat to someone's life going forward, you'd be able to report me to the medical board if I said anything to anyone about it."

Getz finally stands, slinging the hood of her windbreaker over her head. At the door, she pauses and looks back.

"That's real good, Doc. But if anything you know about me or my friends gets out, I ain't reportin' you to no medical board."

She lets that threat hang, then walks out. I lock the door behind her and press my back to it, before sliding down to the ground, breathing harder than I have in years.

Calm yourself, Bri. You're tougher than this. Just think.

I could go to the police and report my suspicion. But what would that change? These are the same cops who beat boys like Jahlil unconscious in poorly lit alleyways. The same ones who look the other way when someone from a rival gang goes missing, if they weren't the ones who made them vanish in the first place. RF9 doesn't just own corners. They own badges, judges and systems. And I know exactly what they're capable of. I have a daughter to protect. That's the reality. That's the line I can't afford to cross.

But still, I can't stop the thought: What would it look like if someone actually took them down? And what would it take to survive it?

32

CHARLES PALMER

As I STAND in the courthouse hallway awaiting a verdict I'm certain will be returned in my client's favor, thanks to a judge squarely within the Palmer network of influence, I catch movement in my periphery.

I turn to my left and see Brianna in a beeline toward me.

"Dr. Wright."

She doesn't say anything. She just grabs my arm and pulls me into a shadowed alcove near the emergency exit.

"You could always stop by my office like that one time."

"I'm not here looking for daytime dick, Charles." Her words are rushed. "I'm here about your friend. Getz."

My eyes dart before I can stop them as I try to figure out how she even knows that name. "That person is not my friend."

"Well, she showed up at the youth center saying she works for your family and that you referred me to her."

I bite down a sigh as I shift on my feet. "She works for my brother."

"She's not a goddamn furniture salesman, Charles. Please don't insult me."

"Not Rome. My other brother, Tracy. He owns a rap label and has a few ex-RF9 members signed as artists. They had some legal issues preventing them from going on tour. I got them off as a favor to my brother, to protect his investment. That's the only reason I know any of them."

That cover should hold since it's not entirely a fabrication and there's no official record of me ever running with RF9.

"So, this Getz is a rapper?" she asks.

"No, but sometimes they bring friends around and put them on payroll as security. That's all it is."

Brianna steps closer. "Did she know Jahlil?"

"I don't know who she knows," I lie.

"Did she kill him?" she asks through gritted teeth, glancing toward the hallway.

"I have no idea. We don't even know if he's dead. He might've skipped town. Happens all the time." I look toward the courtroom door, pretending to check if the bailiff is about to call us back in. "But I'm afraid this is going to have to wait—"

She grips my chin and turns my face back to hers. "Charles, his mother and sisters haven't heard from him. He wouldn't just leave like that."

"I don't know what to tell you, Bri—"

"The truth," she snaps. "Did he tell you anything?"

"Like I said before, he never made it to my office. I waited all afternoon before I had to be in court. You can ask my receptionist if you'd like."

Another lie. My receptionist is my cousin. She'll hold the line.

Brianna studies me, searching my face. "If you're telling me Jahlil never came, fine. But don't pretend you're powerless. You told me you didn't have any pull. And yet your brother employs a woman I'm nearly certain is an active RF9 leader. Not former. Because why would a former gang member show up in my office to threaten me?"

I obviously can't answer so I deflect. "I'll make sure she finds a new therapist."

"That's it?" She lets out a bitter laugh. "You're not going to do anything else?"

"There's not much else I can do."

"Bullshit," she spits out. "You're either afraid of them or you're protecting them."

"I can assure you——"

"Just stop it, Charles." She shakes her head in a way that tells me she's disgusted. "You're a liar. I can see that clearly now——"

"Brianna, I——"

"If it isn't about the youth center, stay the fuck away from me."

"You approached me today, Dr. Wright. But if I may offer some parting advice... I would be cautious with the kinds of accusations you make about these people. This city isn't always gentle with truth-tellers."

She stares at me for a long, tense moment. It's as if she's trying to decide what's left of the man she once thought I was. But she never knew the real me. No one does. In any event, this was just a physical release. I know that now. I let myself pretend Brianna could fit into my world. But this life requires full disclosure, and that's a luxury I don't have.

I keep my expression still as she turns and walks away.

• • •

Uncle Mac and I arrive at the rear parking lot of Truck's office. It's an old gym in South Maddox he's converted into a recording studio for his gangster rap label, "Big Truck Entertainment," a newfound obsession he's dumped over three million dollars into. The company promotes music and concerts. And, of course, supplies the pills, coke, weed, whatever, to the crowd, artists, influencers, producers, and entourages. He's got a few artists gaining some steam on social media but to me, it brings unwanted attention to our business.

Truck is out back, smoking a blunt as usual. RF9 soldiers patrol the alley as I step out of the backseat.

"Big Mac." Truck greets our uncle with a handshake and hug.

"What's goin' on, nephew?"

"Different day, same shit, Unc, except now we at war. But you know how that goes."

"All too well," Uncle Mac drawls.

I don't have time for pleasantries. I'm due back in court. "What are you doing sending your people to my youth center without running it through me?"

"Whaddup to you too, Chuckie," Truck says. "God damn, you rude, boy."

"Can you tell me why Getz is wasting Brianna Wright's time?"

Truck shrugs his shoulders, his demeanor flippant as ever. "I don't know, Chuck. Mental health matters, don't it?"

I let out a hard, dry scoff. "That psycho isn't seeking therapy. We both know that. But she walked in there, telling civilians she works for the Palmer family. I've told you, you don't send people through my network without talking to me—"

Truck interrupts me with a plume of blunt smoke to my face. "How many times I gotta tell you, Chuckie? I don't take orders from you."

"Yeah, you take them from Rome and he said to leave my network be."

"That's what he said to you. You not the only one having sidebar conversations with our big brother. Rome told me to keep tabs on Adrian."

"So, why is Getz bothering Brianna?"

"That's his baby momma, right?"

"She is but they're not together."

"Don't matter much and you know that, little brother. The shrink and the daughter will help us keep the light-skinned nigga Adrian in line when it comes to our bread. I need a soldier I can trust close to her so he knows it ain't a thing to get to his people if he tries to steal our money. Past that, she need to know what happens if she work with the feds. You keep puttin' my shooters into her therapy seat—"

"I put *kids* into therapy," I correct, "kids who were shooting each other for no reason, selling our guns to other kids who shot up classrooms and shopping malls with them, bringing the worst kind of attention to our organization."

"Nah nigga. Adrian Channing brought the attention when he convinced his slave owners to buyout Blue Rock and make it the fuckin' Tesla of airplanes."

My brows lift as I stare at him.

"I read the news, nigga," he says. "Especially when they talkin' bout the Mad Dog."

"You might be right, but the feds wouldn't have gotten involved if our product wasn't tied to those school shootings. You dropped the ball on that."

"How you figure, nigga?" Him and his boys chuckle at the accidental rhyme.

"It's called KYC, Truck. Know your customer and make sure they don't bring drama back to us—"

"Don't matter, Chuckie. The feds want a headline. They always do. And 'lil ol' Blue Rock Industries wasn't a blip on nobody's radar until it became a part of Volition Aeronautics. Your boy set all this shit in motion."

I hesitate to respond. He makes a valid point.

"And besides," he continues, pausing to blow another plume of blunt smoke in my face. "I can't control where every piece I move ends up at. Niggas buy straps, use 'em and sell 'em when they need to, just like they do wit the family furniture. I can only control what I can control. My people. And you got my soldiers sharin' company secrets wit a civilian—."

"It's a calculated risk, Truck—"

"Bullshit," he blurts, coughing on his last pull. "You wanna protect this family name so damn bad but keep bringing outsiders close to the family fuckin' secrets. You think I wanted to kill that white boy money manager you brought in? No, Chuckie. But the nigga fucked wit our bread then ran to snitch, so I handled him. You think I wanna kill Adrian's fine ass white baby momma? No, Chuckie, I don't. But if the feds go after her and she tells, I'll have Getz pull the plug and that blood gon' be on your hands. Those are the risks you not calculatin'."

"I assure you I am. I already told you she's subject to psychotherapist-patient confidentiality. She can't testify to anything as long as your crew follows protocol. Let 'em learn how to manage their emotions, channel their anger into making us money. Don't divulge details or talk to her about ongoing or upcoming activities."

"Again, it don't matter, Chuckie. She ain't dumb. She know what we got goin' on. Only you're so delusional to think the whole damn city don't know who we are and what we do. My young bouls in her chair makes her a potential witness. That shit'll get us all locked up."

"Not if you follow my lead, Truck. I have a plan to get us clear of all of it: the disgruntled customers, the turf wars, the feds, everything. Out clean."

Truck shakes his head as he takes another long drag. "I ain't no nine to five nigga, bro. You and Rome wanna go fully legit, be captains of industry, community leaders or whatever, and that's cool. Y'all go do that. I'll hold down the street shit like I've done my whole life. But don't leave me a burnin' ship. No gun connect, bleedin' corners, and loose ends that'll feed me right into a muthafuckin' fed case."

I pause, taking in his very legitimate concern. "Listen, bro, I hear you. No matter what happens, I won't let you see time. You know your little brother runs circles 'round these white niggas in a courtroom, right?"

Truthfully, I believe the N-word was designed to subjugate Black folk, so I typically don't use it, but he laughs and his temper calms. And I need him under control.

"Nah, seriously though," I continue. "The shit you and Rome built up over the past twenty years is more than impressive. It's the shit of legends. The Black Gods need to live on, I get that. And I'll call in every mothafuckin' political favor I've collected to make sure my brothers stay out of prison."

Truck flicks the roach of his blunt, and with a practiced ease, reaches in his jacket pocket for a new one, lights it and pulls. "And you know I'd murder the whole fuckin' world for my brothers, stand on a million life sentences. But if you not gon' let me pull his plug, you need to get your boy, Adrian, to open the gun connect for us."

"I'm working on an angle, but I don't know how to broach the subject without him figuring out what we do."

"You the smartest nigga I know. The sneakiest too."

I join him in laughter even though I resent the insinuation.

"You'll figure something out," he says. "If not, just tell him who I am, and that he'll end up in the river like his boy Rouchard if he don't fall in line."

33

ADRIAN CHANNING

THIRTY-TWO STAFF, SEVEN locations, and a modest headquarters in Downtown Maddox, each piece held together by Josie's vision and impeccable work ethic.

My first order of business after coming aboard was renegotiating the company's co-packer arrangements, utilizing relationships I developed at PGC. Her cost of goods sold has shrunk by thirty-eight percent, Vegan Caramel Crunch is flying off the shelves, and revenue projections are trending in the right direction, but we need to push momentum.

I walk into Josie's office and see her sitting at her desk reviewing some print ad mockups. The vision of a gorgeous woman fully engaged in the process of building a business... Let's just say I have to remind myself to remain professional. She's stunning, and I'm becoming more attracted to her with each meeting.

"What's up, partner?" She sounds like she hasn't slept in days but is trying to power through.

"Not much." I glance at the reminder flashing on my phone. "Oh, I have a call with Tatiana Craig's people in five. You free?"

"What? I love her! Her first album got me through so many stupid breakups." She laughs. "How?"

"When I was at PGC, I was chairman of a company called Arcadian Media, which sits at the top of a long chain of companies that control her record label. I might be able to bring her on for an ad campaign for Geraldine's."

"Adrian, that would be a game-changer… but we have no money in the marketing budget to pay an R&B icon."

"Yeah, I thought about that. How do you feel about giving her a small equity stake? It would be worth it given her eighty million followers on social."

"If it's a true partnership, then I'm okay with a small equity stake." She pauses for a moment. "Social media posts, a TV and print campaign, in-store pop-ups, the whole nine. But no more than five percent."

"I was thinking no more than three percent, but let's see how it goes."

She smiles as she nods. "I'm good with that. Let's also structure her equity as a warrant with a short exercise period. That way if her people forget to exercise the right to purchase those shares, she gets nothing."

I laugh. "Shrewd. I like it."

We sit in the conference room, the glow of the laptop screen illuminating Josie's determined expression beside me as I pull up the video call with Sheff Rucker, CEO of Streamline Records and Tatiana Craig's manager.

The room feels charged as I stare down this legendary music executive through the screen. He's positioned like a fortress with Grammy awards and platinum plaques displayed on the walls behind his desk.

"Adrian," he says. "With all due respect, this is too small for Tatiana. I'm not seeing the value for her or for my precious time."

I keep my tone steady, letting a confident smile play on my lips. "This isn't just another endorsement, Sheff. She'd be the face of our fight against diabetes in the Black community, alongside a dynamic Black woman CEO. That aligns with Tatiana's advocacy, and it's a story the media will love. And when it's said and done, she'll make a pretty penny for just a few days of work."

He raises his eyebrows, clearly unimpressed. "Your pitch would make sense if you were offering some cash up front. But equity only? She's not going to waste her time on a company without the budget to stick around. I can't put the next Beyonce behind a brand that'll go bankrupt."

I can see Josie's anger flare as she leans forward. I place my hand on her wrist, letting her know I've got this. "Sheff, I'm not some two-bit serial entrepreneur, you know that. I sit atop industries. I was chairman of Arcadian Media, which owns Atlas Records. And although Streamline is technically publicly traded, Atlas owns sixty-three percent of your outstanding stock."

"So what? PGC owns damn near everything under the sun. I'm not surprised. But you were shitcanned from that place, weren't you? Something about a 'rogue operator'…"

I smile, holding back the urge to cuss this bald-headed caveman out. "I left PGC, but I still run that machine. Vance Jeffries manages Arcadian now and I taught him everything he knows and still counsel him informally on strategic decisions. Perhaps at our next tee time, I tell him that I think the public markets would react well to a change in CEO at Streamline Records."

"Are you really threatening my job?" he asks, his bravado wavering.

I smile, maintaining an air of professionalism. "Or I can tell them that a round of surprise C-Suite bonuses would boost morale and do good for employee retention. He'll go in whichever direction I advise."

His expression softens.

I press on. "I still have influence, Sheff. I'm offering a minority stake in the company for Tatiana and you, personally. Rest assured, it'll pay off in spades when we hit the scale we're projecting."

He leans back, clearly weighing his options. "Equity in a startup?"

"Not a startup," Josie says, her voice sharp. "Geraldine's has been a regional staple in the dessert space for five decades. We're not just another food brand, we're part of a necessary conversation about health and sustainability. This isn't just a chance for Tatiana to earn millions, it's a chance to drive real change."

"So, it's an ESG play?" he asks. "You're trying to save the world, but I could give two shits unless it translates to profit."

"You're not in private equity, Sheff, but you've been in business long enough to know my track record. Ask your board. I put them all in position.

Or ask any motherfucker in your rolodex with nine figures in their net worth. They'll tell you I don't do small deals. And I don't get involved with companies that aren't winners."

Sheff looks at us with a shit-eating grin. "What about Volition Aeronautics?"

Josie leans in with a confident smile playing on her face. "You mean the company that revolutionized the world of aviation? Its failure had nothing to do with Adrian and it's something that'll never happen here. We make vegan ice cream, frozen yogurt, cupcakes, and cereal bars. Not assault rifles and grenades."

God dammit, I'm in love with this woman.

"More importantly, Josie Simmons is the real deal," I add.

I glance over and see Josie's cheek flush. We lock eyes briefly as I return to the pitch. "She's already rebuffed a buyout offer from one of the largest food conglomerates in the industry. She has the blueprint to exit this company at a significant multiple."

Sheff uncrosses his arms and leans forward just slightly. After a few moments of him stroking his goatee, he speaks. "Send the paperwork. We'll get it done."

I end the call, close the laptop, and glance at Josie, who's beaming with excitement.

"That was awesome," she says. "You're impressive."

I smile as I lock eyes with her, but then my gaze drops to her lips. "As are you, Madame CEO."

We stand opposite each other in an almost feral heat of passion from the excitement of winning the deal. Josie wraps her arms around me in an unrestrained moment of celebration. Her playful bear hug turns into a warm embrace. It's both unexpected and electrifying. As our bodies press together, time drags on, simmering with intensity. Our faces are nearly touching, the heat between us almost electric.

I hesitate, reluctant to move closer. I don't want to cross any lines. But as I stay still, her lips meet mine. It feels like peace in almost a year of chaos.

I pull her tighter as our lips part, and our tongues barely meet before the door swings open.

An older Black woman walks in. I can tell it's Josie's mom. They're practically twins. In front of her is a young boy no older than eight, wearing a dirty baseball uniform. Their entrance cuts through the charged moment like a cold splash of water to the face, and we're forced to separate, the tension hanging awkwardly in the air.

"Hey, Mom," Josie says, trying to brush past it.

Josie crouches down to her son. "Hey baby, I heard y'all couldn't pull out the win."

"You didn't come," he says, his face fixed on the ground.

"I know, baby, I'm sorry," she says, caressing his cheek. "Mommy had to work, but I'll make it up to you."

Josie looks up and sees me standing there like an awkward idiot. "Adrian, I'm sorry. This is my son, Allen. And my mom, Geraldine."

"Pleasure to meet you, ma'am," I shake her hand, and then Icrouch down to Allen's level. "What's up, buddy? How'd you hit?"

"I'm a pitcher," he says curtly in between sniffles.

"Allen, manners," Josie says.

Allen grumbles something inaudible and then runs into his mother's office, shutting the door behind him.

Josie sets her hands on her hips as she sighs. "I'm sorry about that."

I chuckle lightly. "No worries. I hate losing, too."

I turn my attention back to Josie's mom. "So, you are the famous Geraldine of Geraldine's Homemade. It's an absolute honor to finally make your acquaintance. I've been a big fan of your family's product for something like thirty-five years now."

"Mm-hmm, I've heard about you, Mr. Channing."

"Good things I hope."

"Good things from some." Geraldine thumbs through the print ad mockups on the conference room table as she speaks. "My friend Doreen was a floor supervisor at Blue Rock. She thought she was soon to retire. Now she's seventy-three, cleaning houses and waiting on some arbitrator to decide if she'll get even a sliver of her pension back. And making me pay the entire tab on margarita nights." She giggles softly but there doesn't seem to be much happiness in it.

"I'm sorry to hear that." My voice is low.

I resist the urge to tell her that if it weren't for me, her friend's pension would've disappeared five years ago before I stepped in and bought the company out of bankruptcy. That if I was still at PGC I'd push out a cash settlement to make the employees whole. That I used to have that kind of pull and I used it differently. But something tells me she wouldn't understand. Or care.

"I just thought that…" Geraldine hesitates, as if she's contemplating how much to share. "You know, when we heard that some big New York firm was buying Blue Rock, we were nervous. We thought you'd lay everyone off, bring in robots, and send everything else to China. But then my Josephine told me the purchase was being made by a Maddox man. I did my googling and saw a Black boy from Ironbridge. I told all my friends… Then we thought, 'we're in good hands… he's one of us…'"

"Momma—" Josie tries to jump in but her mother raises a hand and Josie quiets.

"You didn't take care of those people at Blue Rock and that's okay," Geraldine says, eyeing me closely. "Maybe you couldn't. I mean why else would you be back here if that machine you brought to town didn't swallow you up along with all of my friends—"

"Momma, Adrian had nothing to do with—"

Geraldine's eye's snap to Josie's. "Don't interrupt me again, baby girl."

Josie's eyes shoot downward as she murmurs, "I'm sorry, Momma."

Geraldine moves closer to me. The look in her eye is strangely both fierce and calming. "Just make sure you do right by my daughter."

"I have only the purest of intentions, ma'am." I give her a practiced smile, hoping she doesn't see right through it. "Profit-seeking intentions."

"Mm-hmm… But while y'all are seeking profits, make sure you're also seeking protection."

Josie covers her face with her hands as she turns away. "Oh my gosh."

"Oh hush, girl, I don't mean it like that. I just mean… Well, this ain't Silicon Valley or Manhattan, baby. Disruptors don't always get rewarded here. Maddox doesn't admire ingenuity. It absorbs it, dulls it, or turns it into something it can exploit. And if it can't, it casts it out altogether."

I shake my head softly. "Well, maybe Maddox needs some changing. Or someone willing to change it."

"Now that ain't the problem," Geraldine says. "That's the thing about places like this—people like this. They know they need saving, but they ain't ready to be saved. They've survived for too long with too little help to think they need any."

"Surviving isn't the same as winning," I say. "Maddox could compete on the world stage in terms of innovation, economic growth—"

"That I can't argue with, Mr. Channing." She takes a deep breath as she sits down at the table. "My husband used to say Maddox, Pennsylvania is like a stew that's been simmering for far too long. A recipe thick with secrets and heavy with history. Packed with flavor." She lets out a soft laugh, almost as if she's remembering the way her late husband used to tell it.

"Every now and then," she continues, "some smart folks come along thinking, 'We don't need to simmer this stew that damn long. Let's just turn up the heat, add our own spice and make it ours.' And sure, maybe the stew taste just the same for half the effort. It might even taste better. But to those who've lived on that slow, familiar, developed flavor—the one built on the secrets its carried through generations—well, they'll spit it out. Then they'll burn down the restaurant. But I suppose, Mr. Channing, you already know all about that."

She pauses for a moment, her eyes locked with mine. It's like she's staring directly into my soul. "Change doesn't come when it's needed. It comes when it's wanted. And I'm just not sure this city is there yet."

A heavy silence fills the room. I glance at Josie. She's watching me, searching my face.

Geraldine smiles, breaking the stillness. "But I suppose that shouldn't stop you two from selling a whole lotta vegan ice cream."

She stands, turns to Josie, and kisses her on the forehead. "I'll take Allen home. Just needed to get his schoolwork. I'll see you soon, yes?"

"Yes, Momma. Thank you."

"Let's go, boy!" Geraldine calls. "And don't forget your bookbag again!"

Moments later, Allen comes running out with a black Sixers backpack on his back.

They leave the office, and it's just me and Josie again.

She lets out a sigh and slowly shakes her head. "I'm sorry about them. My mom is... protective."

"And profound." I force a smile that doesn't quite hold. "Don't worry about it."

Silence takes the space between us. I scan the room, thinking of something, anything to change the subject to.

"Don't tell me your son is named after Allen Iverson?"

She bursts out laughing. "His dad is an A.I. superfan. I couldn't get a word in edgewise when it came to naming my own son."

"I mean, I can't blame him." I laugh with her. "He seems like an awesome kid."

"He really is." She smiles. "The love of my life."

Another semi-awkward moment passes of us staring at each other.

My eyes linger on her lips. I want nothing more than to taste them again. But I have to set that feeling aside. No matter how mutual the attraction, my focus has to stay on growing and selling this company as fast as possible. That kind of win won't just redeem me. It'll prove that Volition was a fluke, not the pattern. That I wasn't the problem. And then I'll have what I need to raise a real fund to back twenty more companies like this one, each built to drive real change.

And yet, Geraldine's words hang in the back of my mind. Maybe Maddox isn't ready for the change I'm trying to bring. Maybe she's just beholden to an outdated school of thought. Either way, I don't have time to simmer.

34

ADRIAN CHANNING

As soon as I return home after a day of chasing investment opportunities from Maddox to South Philly to Newark to Wilmington and back, my phone rings. It's Harry Paxton, my old boss and fake-ass mentor.

"Adrian, darling, I told you a lawsuit was not the way."

"What is the way, Harry? How do you expect me to get any type of job in this industry with your little attack dog fabricating stories to the world about how I'm the cokehead who snorted away Volition's stock price? Only way I can feed my family is to bring a suit."

"I'm sorry, Adrian. I want to make this right. Why don't you come to New York? We can sit down and hash things out. I'll send a helicopter."

The nerve of this old bag to think she can just summon me like I still work for her.

"I can't," I respond. "Riley's playing in her championship basketball game tomorrow."

"Sounds like a bit of fun." Her voice is suddenly more chipper. "I'll come to you."

● ● ●

My watch tells me it's nine in the morning when Harry's helicopter touches down on the soccer field at Palmer Community Athletics across from the basketball gym. The helicopter's rotors kick up dust as it settles in the field.

Harry steps down, looking every bit the polished predator she's always been. Her charcoal Givenchy pantsuit, sharp and unmistakably high-end, feels jarringly out of place at a kids' basketball game in suburban Pennsylvania.

Following her is her granddaughter Reanne Paxton-Mensah, a team of assistants, and her bodyguard, Stan Titus. Their presence both shocks and annoys me. We could've discussed this shit over the phone.

She strides up the steps, her eyes scanning the surroundings with an air of controlled excitement like a child on a field trip, as if the ongoings of normal life are so foreign to her. I can hear Reanne in the distance on a closing call, reminding me of everything that was taken from me.

Harry greets me with a wide smile and a hug that I reluctantly reciprocate. "I see you've embraced the 'girl dad' life, as they say."

"Riley's a superstar athlete," I reply, struggling to mask my irritation.

"Like her father, if I recall correctly," she exclaims. "Come, let's sit before the match begins."

"Game, Harry. Not a match."

"Oh whatever."

We walk the perimeter of the old blacktop courts, now fenced off for renovation, and find a bench tucked between the courts and the soccer fields.

She looks over her shoulder, and calls out, "Giovanna!"

One of her assistants rushes ahead of us, pulling a travel-size spray bottle from her coat pocket. She gives the bench a few aggressive spritzes, wipes it down with a "H.P." branded microfiber cloth, then returns to Harry's army of assistants sitting on the benches behind us.

"God knows what sort of things people do on these," she mutters, before finally sitting.

I raise an eyebrow. "I thought you came here through Ellis Island?"

"You're still a little shit, Adrian, aren't you?"

Harry explains how they shut down Ellis Island in the fifties and she's "not that bloody old."

I then listen to the ravings of an out-of-touch billionaire who is sitting on a park bench likely for the first time in decades. Harry has a way of taking three right turns to get to her point when she can just turn left. I'm going to miss Riley's tip-off listening to Harry's "bloody this" and "bloody that" complaints about how hard it was to get clearance to land her chopper at PCA.

My rage starts to bubble, but I hold it in.

"You know your case is a loser," she says. "But you're obviously not just another litigant. Your letter or your lawyer's letter, that Charles Palmer. He writes like a bloody thug. Is this really the type of attorney you want speaking on your behalf? Making threats to divulge confidential information?"

"Charles is one of the best lawyers in the city, Harry. And you might want to think twice about calling a Black professional a 'thug' when you're being sued for discrimination."

"Oh, you know I didn't mean it like that. My husband is West African for Christ's sake."

I shake my head in disbelief at her I fuck Black dudes excuse. "I don't care. Derek killed my career . I can't raise institutional capital. I can't get another job in finance."

"Come on," she goads. "It can't be that bad."

"I got rejected for a teller job at a fuckin' savings and loan, Harry. Because Derek set me up and continues to shit on my name to everyone he knows."

"Adrian, I get it, and——"

"I know where the bodies are buried. And I will talk to the media if that's what'll get my life back. I've seen the cancel campaign against you. The TikTokers love shitting on you these days."

"I'm their favorite punching bag. Even that bloody Simpsons cartoon did a parody of me."

"I saw." I bite back a laugh.

She exhales, long and slow, then raises her hand in the air and lifts two fingers. One of her other assistants rushes over and slides a cigarette between her fingers. She brings it to her lips, and he lights it before stepping back without a word.

"Landing your chopper here won't help." I nod to the looky-loos snapping photos of her and the luxury chopper stamped with PGC's logo, parked on a field in the very town they believe PGC ruined.

"You can't afford any more bad PR."

"Well, that's why I'm here to offer you a deal. I know you need money, and I'm willing to settle this case if you agree to not pursue further claims and sign an NDA."

"What are you offering?" I ask.

"Two million."

All I can see is the three-quarters of a million dollars in diamond rings wrapped around her wrinkled fingers as she raises her cigarette to her lips. Today, she dons the Audemar Piguet Royal Oak Offshore, white gold. It complements the white of her hair and contrasts with the black of her heart.

I can't help but scoff. "That's probably not even what you spent gassing up the choppers and jets this quarter."

"So, what's your bloody counter?" she snaps. "You've been out in the wild less than a year. You haven't forgotten how to negotiate, have you?"

She laughs as if we're friends who tease each other. We're not.

"Ten million."

"That's excessive, Adrian."

"I was entitled to thirty-two before Derek set me up."

"You allege it, but I don't know anything about a setup, and I'm sure you can't prove it in court—"

"You don't know what I can prove."

She doesn't respond immediately. She just eyes me as she draws from her cigarette. Then she says, "We can do five mil. Best and final."

"Fine. But I also need a signed statement from PGC that clears my name of the Volition failure."

"A statement, Adrian?" Harry falls into a condescending fit of laughter. "Terry Weiss would have a coronary. Our position is simply 'we were a victim of fraud' and we don't know a bloody thing else about it. You just need to give it time. Before long, the LP community will forget all about this and your return to glory will be swift. Take the cash, put it in the market, and flip it the way you know how."

I think for a moment about what that piece of paper would do for me. At every corner I turn, someone asks me about Volition, damn near hinting that I was the one who orchestrated the whole conspiracy. I'm a victim just like anyone else, dammit.

"I need the letter, Harry. I need my name cleared. The money is actually secondary."

"The money is never secondary, Adrian. I thought I taught you better than that. The letter is a non-starter."

"Fine, then five million dollars and you personally agree to stake the next deal I find. You'll pay full fee and carry as my lead LP."

She pauses for a moment, and then smirks. "Now that's the Adrian Channing I know."

The next week, we handle the paperwork, and Harry wires my cash. I set aside enough of the five million dollars to take care of Brianna and Riley and feed myself for a year, and I invest the rest into Geraldine's Homemade. Josie has a new line of vegan ice cream cones and wholesale orders are already coming in. Although I couldn't get a statement clearing my name of Volition, I have a multi-billionaire committed to funding CCP's next acquisition.

35

CHARLES PALMER

I'm LEANING AGAINST my BMW outside PalmerSpaces, a co-working space we bought a couple of years ago. We gave it a modern, minimalist look to attract the city's burgeoning tech scene. But it's a front, of course. A shell of legitimate construction to launder RF9 income. I gave Adrian an office for free as a show of good faith after refusing to pay him management fees on the Geraldine investment.

I watch from the parking lot as he pushes through the door, his laptop bag over his shoulder and a look of purpose on his face. He's headed to pick up Riley from basketball practice at Palmer Community Athletics. Truck's people have his routine locked down.

"Adrian," I call out, flashing a rehearsed grin. "I've got a weekly pickup game down at PCA. Got a few lawyers and judges, a couple of real estate developers on the roster. One of my regulars couldn't make it tonight. Down to get in a run?"

He pushes his lip out and shrugs his shoulders. "Let's get it."

We walk down the street, enter the gym, and step onto the court, the smell of sweat and varnish hitting me. I watch him as he laces up, trying to keep that cool facade. But I know he's desperate for a win to fill the void of his recent losses.

The game kicks off and we're matched up against each other. I drain a three-pointer right off the bat, just to set the tone.

On the next possession, he drives hard to the basket, muscling through me with that overblown aggression. He's all physicality, slamming his body against mine like it's some sort of redemption arc as he forces in a floater.

I sink another shot and watch the frustration mount in his facial features. The back-and-forth escalates as we trade buckets. He has the height and strength, but I have the technical shooting touch and the finesse.

As he drives, I swat the ball away, catching his wrist as he drives the lane for a layup.

He resorts to trash talk. "Play defense, Charles! You just foulin', homie!"

I only chuckle.

As the ball is being inbounded, Adrian bumps me. "You played at Penn State, right?"

"All-time leader in three pointers," I confirm.

"Didn't wanna go pro?"

I run to my spot at the top of the key. "Two torn rotator cuffs my junior year killed that dream, so I focused on law instead." I catch the ball.

"Good choice." He rips the ball from my hands and surges down the court with it.

I sprint behind him, attempting to position myself between him and the basket. He gathers momentum before launching into the air, soaring high over me. He crashes into the rim with a thunderous dunk that resonates through the gym. The small crowd erupts in awed gasps.

"You dealin' with an athlete, son!" Adrian hollers as he high fives his teammates.

After the game ends, we catch our breath on the sidelines. I grab my water bottle, taking a long swig. Adrian sits on the bench next to me, icing his knees.

"Good shit, Charles. You're nice from long range. Wasn't enough to get the win... but impressive."

"You had me with your post-game." I do my best to ease him with flattery. "Looking like Carmelo when he played in Denver."

After some more back and forth, I make my pitch and his skepticism is palpable.

"So," Adrian says, his brow furrowed, "your client wants to resurrect Blue Rock out of bankruptcy, but needs someone inside to verify contracts the bankruptcy filings don't cover?"

I make sure to sit comfortably, casually, my body language loose. Everything about me needs to feel like an opportunity, not a question.

"Exactly. From what I understand, it's standard practice for this Japanese investor. I was just brought on as local counsel to help with their diligence process."

"I thought you were a criminal defense attorney."

"Well, I handle some discreet corporate matters from time to time. When the money is right, of course."

He gives me a half-smile. He's not buying it, not yet. I can see it in the way his eyes flicker, calculating.

I casually shrug. "Look, I get it. It sounds like a lot to ask. And trust me, I don't want to keep making you dip back into the PGC world, but all they're looking for is reassurance. They're nervous after the scandal and don't want to buy the asset if there are any other hidden liabilities that haven't come out in the wash. I'm sure you have some contacts at PGC who can dig up those contracts so we can fact-check against what's been disclosed in bankruptcy court."

"Of course. I practically ran that firm and still have folks loyal to me. But I don't know, Charles. You're asking me to ask people I care about to violate confidentiality, to risk their jobs and potentially prosecution."

I can say it now, tell him who my family really is and what happens to people who say no to the Black Gods. I can lean forward, lower my voice, and let him know in no uncertain terms that refusing me is not an option, then maybe have Uncle Mac pistol-whip him in the parking lot.

But no. Not yet. That has to be a last resort, a blunt instrument.

Instead, I smile again, playing to his ego. "I understand why you'd be hesitant about this. I get it. But listen, I told them about you, and they're impressed. I could get them to offer you equity in the deal, on top of a cash consulting fee. Perhaps a seat on the board of the new company."

I see it in his eyes, just for a moment. That hunger. Adrian's a man who's been in exile for too long, watching from the sidelines as others make the moves he used to make. He misses it. The high stakes, the power, the thrill of pulling off a deal no one else can.

As it seems he's ready to say yes, Riley walks over, her backpack slung over one shoulder and a look of teenage annoyance on her face.

"Hi Charles." She turns to her dad. "I'm done with practice. Can you take me home now?"

Adrian nods and then turns to me. "Let me think about it."

I smile. "Take your time, brother."

36

ADRIAN CHANNING

As I leave the gym, Charles's pitch gnaws at me. That guy is too smooth. The way he leans in with that courtroom confidence, like he can see the desperation creeping through my new beard. And maybe he can, but I wasn't born yesterday. Even though I dunked all over his ass, Charles was all smiles for the first time since I've known him. I can tell there's something else underneath it, something that's not sitting right.

He wants highly confidential PGC files for some foreign buyer looking to acquire Blue Rock's assets out of bankruptcy. It's illegal, but it's tempting. The opportunity to take back a company that ruined my career, to do it right this time, to reopen a chain of factories that employed half of this city, to reengage in the world of high-stakes deal making.

After I drop off Riley at her mom's house, I park at a metered space outside of PalMart and do some shopping. With my groceries in hand, I step outside, replaying the whole conversation in my head. Suddenly, my attention is pulled. My piece-of-shit-Prius is being towed away.

But I paid the fucking meter.

I rush toward the tow truck, but it's too far gone. I glance at the parking meter. It's broken. I look at the one next to it. Also broken. The one next to that? Broken.

I call an Uber. When I get in, I make small talk with the driver.

"Damn city's falling apart." I let out a quiet scoff. "Even the parking meters are screwed. I paid my hard-earned dollar fifty but still got towed."

"Yeah, that's been happening all over the place," the driver says. "Meters are broken everywhere. Real problem in the city. They've been saying they're going to fix 'em for months now, but you know how that goes."

Then it clicks. The city's parking meters are a disaster, and I'm old friends with the mayor. This isn't just a civic issue; it's a money problem waiting to be solved.

I've never done a public-private partnership, but I've studied them. With the right vision, I can turn those meters profitable in months. But the real upside is in advertising. In a city of half a million, every meter, kiosk, and garage wall is prime space I can sell to consumer brands. That's how I scale it and flip the operation for five times my money. It's the kind of deal that puts you on the map in private equity and exactly what I launched Community Capital Partners to invest in.

I change the Uber's destination to City Hall. When I get there, I more than likely piss off Deanie's secretary by dropping my groceries on his desk before I barrel into her office with all the finesse of a bull in a china shop.

She looks up from her desk, startled. "A.C., what the hell?"

I hold up my hands in a small surrender. "Hear me out."

"What do you want, man?"

"This parking meter issue? I have a solution. Let me acquire the city's meter system. You won't have to worry about a thing. My fund will buy new meters, install them, and operate them. The city gets the revenue rolling back in, fewer people disputing parking tickets, and we profit-share. It's a win-win."

She leans back in her chair, eyebrows arched, tapping a pen against her chin. "I like the idea, Adrian. So much so that we've been working on a program to do just that. My committee on public works is putting together a contract proposal for local companies to bid on. But not just meters. The contract will be to renovate and operate all of the city's public parking infra-structure. So, street parking, lots, and garages."

"That's even better. You can save the effort and just give CCP the contract."

Deanie shakes her head. "I can't just hand you a government contract because we're friends and because you think you're so brilliant that you're the first and only person to think of it."

She's too damn principled, but maybe I can get a sense of what the winning bid would look like from her perspective. "Okay, what kind of numbers are you looking for?"

"I need to run a fair process, Adrian. You're on record as one of my campaign donors. It would look too much like cronyism if I gave you an advantage, and I ran on an anti-corruption platform, remember?"

"No one will know, Deanie." I scan the empty office, fixing my eyes on the shut door behind me. "And it's not cronyism if I'm qualified to get the job done and we strike a fair deal. I'm more than capable of running this project."

She arches an eyebrow. "I know what you're capable of, A.C. The city knows all too well."

She's alluding to the Volition-Blue Rock scandal, and I'm getting really sick of this.

"Don't do that, Deans. Don't blame me for the next man's fuck up and overshadow two decades' worth of good business because of one failure. I've moved past the Blue Rock nightmare."

"You have? Great!" Her eyes widen and she flashes a fake smile before returning to her previous stone-cold demeanor. "The city hasn't, A.C. I can't sell a deal with the guy who worked for the private equity firm that many believe caused this upsurge in unemployment. You're welcome to put in your bid, but I can't show you any favor."

"Come on, Deanie. How many times have I taken care of you when you needed campaign funding? How many dinners did I host for you in Manhattan? I brought you out-of-town corporate donors with no strings attached. No favors to be repaid. I helped you get this seat. Just tell me how I win this deal."

It doesn't feel good to throw my help in her face. I didn't do it for leverage. I did it because she deserved the job. But in this life, favors are meant to be traded in.

She sighs and then sits up in her chair. "Look, my opinion is this. If you somehow showed that you've done something to address some of the fallout from Blue Rock's shutdown... that might help your chances."

Do I want to commit to Charles's deal without even ironing out the details with him?

Fuck it. Empires are built on back-room deals just like this. Well, at this moment I'm standing in the middle of the mayor's office. So, very much a front room deal, but that's beside the point.

"What if I told you I was working with a group looking to reopen Blue Rock?" I ask. "Plan is to rehire all of the old employees and get back to business as usual, without the firearms production."

Her raised eyebrows and half-open mouth betray her intrigue. "You serious?"

"We're in the early stages, but yeah. I have a line on a Japanese investor. They like the price given the bankruptcy, and we're starting on due diligence. Would that be enough to convince the city council I'm the right guy for this parking deal?"

"A.C., if you can restore those jobs, I'd think the city council would be delighted to be in business with you." She glances at a map of the city on the wall. "As a matter of fact, if it works out and we tell the press we hatched this plan together to get those jobs back, that would go a long way when reelection time comes around."

"I'll tell the world it was your idea, Deans. You can hold rallies and speeches at the factory amidst hundreds of happy employees who I'll make sure vote your way."

Her face shifts again with intrigue.

"But help me out here," I plead. "What's the number?"

"Twenty million for the upfront payment," she says quietly. "You get Blue Rock back up and make sure your bid is solid, I'll go to bat for you."

I smile, knowing the red tape has been cleared.

"Wipe the cock-sucking grin off your face, A.C." Her phone rings, and she motions for me to get out.

There it is. I deliver Blue Rock to Charles, and Charles delivers me a manufacturing company. I deliver manufacturing jobs to Deanie, and Deanie delivers me a lucrative parking contract.

Everybody wants something. Everybody gets something.

37
HARRIET PAXTON

THE SCENT OF jasmine oil lingers in the air, mixing with the soft sounds of classical music as the steam rises from the marble bath behind me. This spa day has been long overdue. I've just returned from a week in Davos where I attended a conference of global financial leaders. After deplaning my Gulf-stream 800, here I am, seated in my Brooklyn brownstone's private sunroom, its expansive windows overlooking the cobbled street below. It isn't my largest home, but it certainly is the most intimate.

Derek Graff's wife, Michelle, and their daughter, Charlotte, are with me today. Michelle, an elegant but tired woman in her fifties, sits across from me in a plush armchair, her posture stiff, betraying the tension she's carrying.

Michelle and I have been friendly for years. She worked as a senior analyst for PGC years ago before she and Derek got together. Michelle retired to raise Charlotte who later spent some years working for her father in our Investor Relations department. She's off being pampered with manicures, massages, and the works.

Michelle shifts in her chair, her eyes tracing the outline of her wine glass. "I don't know how to thank you, Harry. If I hadn't found out, God knows how long Derek would have continued lying to me, continued putting me at risk. I can't believe I was so blind."

"It happens to the best of us, darling. Trust me."

"But you're right." She sighs like a woman who's been through too much. "Only thing to do now is take him for everything."

I lean forward slightly, my tone empathetic yet measured. "You're doing the right thing, Michelle. Protect yourself and your daughter. You deserve better. You have my support. Whatever you need."

I know Derek Graff and Niles Tannenbaum are plotting a coup against me and have the votes to force me into retirement at the shareholder's meeting next month. So, I anonymously sent Michelle evidence of Derek's usage of escorts and illegal drugs. The photos were unfortunate but she had to see them.

What's important is I knew she would divorce him. I encouraged her to sue him for the five percent of PGC stock he owns personally. They're the only shares that are actually his. The other twenty-six percent he plans to vote against me are owned by the Arnold Graff Family Trust, of which Derek is the sole trustee. Michelle can't touch those, but she can take the rest.

Under PGC's bylaws, if a shareholder gets dragged into a messy divorce or an estate fight, whether it's a scorned spouse or greedy kids going after PGC shares, I can swoop in and force them to sell me those shares at market value, rather than allowing a judge to force a sale on the open market. It's a protective mechanism to keep outsiders from getting a seat at my table or competitors from getting a peek behind the curtain.

Michelle filed the papers last week and Terrence Weiss initiated the buyback the next day. Derek and Niles's fifty-one percent has just become forty-six percent, and the rest of the shares are owned by my allies and me.

The conversation lulls as Adrian arrives, just as Michelle and Charlotte are leaving. He looks polished, the lines of his tailored suit fitting his tall and built frame perfectly, his beard trimmed to a sharp line that somehow makes him even more handsome. As he enters, Charlotte lingers near the door, her lips curling into a teasing smile as she cast him a glance.

Adrian respectfully addresses the mother first. "Michelle, good to see you." Then, he glances over. "Charlotte, long time."

"Adrian," she purrs, "it's been a while. You look good. I still remember that night in Ibiza at the Ravelle party. I'm available if you ever wanna catch up."

She gives him a doe-eyed look as she subtly presses her cleavage together. She's clearly had a touch too much champagne. I watch the exchange, silently amused. Adrian flashes a winning smile, though he seems uninterested.

Charlotte finally leaves with her mother, but not before making sure Adrian catches one last flirtatious look.

As soon as the door closes behind them, Adrian wastes no time diving into the purpose of his visit. He sent me his pitch deck on the Maddox parking deal. I'm intrigued, but I never make an investment without looking the sponsor in his eyes.

"I'm raising $50 million to fund the bid and renovations," he says, "but the upside? Parking fees, advertising, tech partnerships. We'll 2X in less than five years."

I lean back, swirling the wine in my glass. "I like the deal, Adrian. Municipal services are steady. I'll come in for thirty."

"Harry, if you want to maximize the potential here, you need to go bigger. Put in the full amount. This deal's not just about parking and advertising. It's a chance to invest in a rapidly growing city and others like it. A potential fifty million dollar ticket-turning into a multi-billion-dollar prize. Think of the ESG points and the headline value you'll earn."

"That's why I'm investing thirty. But I can't be the sole investor. I need others to validate this opportunity alongside me. Show me you can raise the other twenty."

I catch the look on his face, a rare mix of frustration and relief. "Okay, Harry."

I tap the arm of my chair with my finger. "Since you're here, perhaps I can use that strategic mind of yours."

Adrian smirks. "I was waiting for that. I heard you're in a tussle with Derek."

"How did you hear that?"

He laughs. "I have more friends at PGC than you do."

"Perhaps. Well, he's tried his best to take me out, but I've neutralized him. Now, I want him out for good."

A slow smile tugs at Adrian's lips, followed by a look of curiosity on his face. "How do you propose I help with that?"

I lean in closer. "Derek's daughter. You shagged her and she clearly wants more."

"I tend to have that effect on women, Harry," says the pompous little twit. "But that was a while ago. What are you getting at?"

"The bulk of Derek's voting power comes from his family trust. He controls it, but they're not his assets. They belong to the beneficiaries."

"Charlotte."

"Exactly. Arnold formed the trust for the benefit of his grandchildren. He placed Derek in charge, but he doesn't see a dime from those shares, he just controls how they're voted. If you can convince Charlotte to sue her father for control of her trust fund, it would trigger my buyback right on Arnold's founding shares. I'd be able to push him out completely."

"So, you want me to seduce Charlotte into suing her own father?" He raises an eyebrow. "Harry, this feels wrong to say the least, and like a long shot."

"Charlotte already hates her father. That's why she quit the firm. She didn't want to be around him. You just need to plant the idea in her brain, perhaps after you plant your pecker up her ass, if that's what the little whore likes—"

"Jesus Christ, Harry." He blinks rapidly.

"You get what I bloody mean. Make her bend to your will by any means necessary. The way I taught you."

I fan myself briefly. I'm getting flustered at this kind of talk.

"She doesn't even need to go through with it," I continue. "The filing by itself will trigger the buyback. And then she can drop the suit."

Adrian shifts in his seat, still clearly uncomfortable. He's always had a conscience.

"Look, Adrian, I don't love the idea of manipulating the girl, but I have no other choice. If I don't move Derek out of my firm, he will keep vying for control, and once he has it, he will drive PGC into the ground."

He remains silent. I can sense his discomfort with the approach, so I dangle something that will move him.

"Once he's gone, I'll make a path back for you. The markets will have forgotten about Volition by then. I'll acquire your shop and give you the Chief Investment Officer title at PGC, as promised. I'll retire in a few years and then you'll take over completely as chairman and CEO with a full equity package. You'd be a multi-billionaire before you turn fifty."

I can see the fire of ambition burning in Adrian's eyes as he says, "I'll get you what you need."

38

ADRIAN CHANNING

SITTING ON THE terrace of this rooftop lounge, the Midtown Manhattan skyline unfolds in a sea of lights and glass towers. The last time I had a view like this, Tim Rouchard had just tipped me off about the scandal that ended my career in New York. A year later, and honestly, I didn't think I'd be back this soon. Definitely not for this.

Charlotte Graff is seated next to me and her body language couldn't be clearer. There's a subtle shift in her posture, a far-from-subtle crossing and uncrossing of her legs, and a playful tilt to her head. Her strapless black dress barely covers her breasts and legs. If my feelings for Josie weren't so strong, I probably would entertain her advances.

"It's been a while," she says, her voice low and seductive.

I can feel her eyes on me, appraising me like I'm a piece at an auction. She places her hand on my thigh and starts caressing it gently. I pull out my phone and pretend to check an email, trying to rebuff her as naturally as possible.

Charlotte leans back, taking a sip of her extra dry martini. "Adrian Channing... always hard at work."

"Money never stops." I draft a fake email to myself only briefly lifting my gaze to meet hers. "You know that better than anyone, Charlotte."

"Sure… but even after PGC? Wait. Why did my asshole father fire you anyway?"

"Because he's an asshole." I take a sip of this Japanese whiskey. "And racist."

Charlotte smirks. "He did always tell me not to fuck Black boys. Look where that got me." She slips her hand back onto my knee but only for a split-second before she moves it to my crotch. I shift abruptly. Her hand falls away and her face tells me she gets the message.

"Adrian, why the hell did you ask me out?"

I give her the best bullshit I can think of. "I heard about the divorce and wanted to check up on you. I know what divorce can do to a kid."

She rolls her eyes as she reaches for her purse. "Thanks, but I'm thirty-two and single in a city where dating is hardly worth it anymore. I don't need emotional support. I need dick. But you don't seem interested in helping me with that, so I'm gonna go."

"Wait." I stand with her, gently placing my hand on her arm. "I also wanted to connect with you on an investment opportunity. I know you just launched your own venture fund. You might be interested."

I give Charlotte the pitch on my parking play.

"It's smart," she says.

"And I'd love to bring in an old friend like you."

"What's the minimum investment amount?"

"Twenty."

She shakes her head stiffly. "Twenty million is too rich for my blood. Not for a single investment"

"Too rich for the granddaughter of Arnold Graff?" I ask, chuckling lightly. "I'd imagine you've got a nice inheritance tucked away."

Charlotte takes a slow sip of her martini. "I only invest what my father lets me have from my trust fund, only a few million here and there. The fucking misogynist."

There's my opening. Truth is, I don't want anyone named Graff anywhere near my business. I know she can't invest twenty mil without her dad's blessing. But the pitch worked to get her to open up about her trust fund.

"Ah gotcha," I sip my whiskey as if this specific topic of conversation means nothing to me. "Well, if your trust fund is fully vested can't you take control from your dad?"

"The only way to do that is to take him to court," she says.

"I guess… But if it's really your trust fund, then it's your money, not his."

"I don't want to sue my father, Adrian. He deserves to be miserable for what he did to my mom but he's still my dad."

"I'm not suggesting you push him off the Empire State. Just saying you knock him down a peg."

She stops mid-sip and places her glass down. "I'm not an idiot, Adrian."

Shit.

"I know how close you are with Harry," she continues. "And I know she and my father are at war."

I stay quiet, occupying myself with another slow sip.

"If you want me to sue my father for those shares so Harry can take them from us, then I'll need something in return."

"Charlotte, you'll get upwards of thirty billion dollars for those shares when Harry forces her buy right."

"I mean I'll need something from you," she says slowly.

"You can't be serious." I laugh.

"I can be." She doesn't laugh with me.

"So if I sleep with you, you'll sue your dad?"

The seductive grin returns to her face and her hand returns to my thigh. I don't brush it away this time. Am I really about to do this?

"Not just that," she says.

"What else?"

She suddenly straightens her expression, though her hand lingers in my lap. "I want a baby."

I nearly spit out my last gulp of whiskey. "Absolutely not."

"You don't have to raise it. But I want a child with your kind of genes, Adrian. Tall, dark, handsome, athletic, smart."

"I already have one kid who hates me. I can't make another one. Besides, your father would disown you if you birthed my child."

"He'll disown me if I sue him," she says, scoffing out a chuckle. "What's the difference? I mean, think about how enraged he'd be at a sweet little Black baby Graff inheriting all of his money. That might even be better revenge than taking PGC from him."

I consider the proposition, contemplating how much I really want to make Derek burn. And then it hits me. This bitch with all her 'athletic Black baby' talk actually disgusts me. Messing with her cost me my marriage.

I down the rest of my whiskey in a single gulp and stand as I button my blazer. "The difference is whether or not I sleep at night."

As I leave her in the lounge, I text Harry: *Charlotte's not our in, but I'll deliver Derek another way.*

Harry: *Fine. Just do it quickly.*

Me: *I don't work for you anymore. It'll happen when it happens.*

39

CHARLES PALMER

ADRIAN PITCHED ME on the parking deal, but my brothers won't sign off on any more cash going to him, let alone $20 million. I need him to get me those Blue Rock files so we can identify whoever was supplying John Bing with gun parts and then reestablish our firearm operation. So, I agreed to help him raise the capital, introducing him to certain clients of mine with deep pockets.

I told Adrian they were entrepreneurs who ran into some white-collar trouble which I helped them out of. But because of it, they can't get into the types of ultra-conservative, risk-averse private equity and venture capital funds that generate the best returns.

"Good thing I'm not ultra-conservative," he said to me.

The Bonetti Family discreetly controls the Philadelphia Italian Mafia with a lucrative heist operation as their leading source of revenue. Of course, their organization buys their guns and drugs from RF9. Publicly, they operate jewelry stores and high-end art galleries, and that's all Adrian needs to know.

What sets Tori Bonetti apart from the rest of her family is her knack for finance. She's invested in several real estate deals alongside our family trust. She runs the Bonetti organization's finances under her father, Don Daniel Bonetti, and she's responsible for the majority of their legitimate revenue streams as well.

With Don Bonetti's dementia regressing rapidly, Tori is positioning herself to be the first ever "Donna" of the Philadelphia Mafia.

We meet her at a private Bonetti Jewels showroom in downtown Philadelphia. She's seated behind a desk, sipping an espresso. She has long, dark brown hair and is dressed in a black jeans and blouse set. Today, like most days, she's adorned in diamonds and secured by two black leather jacketed members of her organization. Everything about her reflects a radiant confidence that says she knows how to play powerful men like chess pieces in a game her father taught her to win.

"Charlie," Tori says smoothly, her thick, South Philly Italian accent rolling off her tongue. "Good to see you again, love."

Her eyes flick to Adrian, a playful intrigue glinting in them. "Hello handsome. I hear you need money."

Adrian flashes a smile, looks over at me, and then back at Tori. "Rest assured, I don't need your money, Ms. Bonetti. But I have an investment opportunity that I'm looking to de-risk with third-party capital. Prime real estate, parking spaces, advertising——"

Tori holds up a hand, silencing him. "I've seen the materials. I know what the deal is. But what's not clear is when I'm getting my money back."

"Well, we could be looking at a return timeline of anywhere from three to seven years. I can't make any guarantees, but this is a long-term investment that I believe will offer outsized returns over time."

"Seven years?" Tori cuts in, her voice like ice. "I can't do seven years."

Adrian looks at me again and then back at Tori. "Well, then, maybe this isn't the best fit." He starts gathering his pitch materials. "Ms. Bonetti, I can't make any guarantees around returns. And it would be unethical for me to accept capital from anyone who can't bear the risks of an investment of this nature. You could lose your investment completely. That is the unfortunate reality of this business. Or you can make enough on one deal to retire your grandkids."

"Charlie, what's he talking about?" Tori's voice is sharp, almost angry. "I'm not worried about the risk of investing, I just don't like waiting around for assets to mature while shady fund managers run off to the Seychelles with my money, ya know?"

I can sense Adrian getting offended at the "shady fund manager" reference so I lean forward. "Tori, this deal is different. And I'm personally vouching for Adrian. He's far from shady. He's of the highest quality of business mind there is, and he will return your capital. But it's going to take time, and you know there are no guarantees in business."

Tori purses her lips briefly, clearly considering the statement.

"Adrian has the right strategy," I continue. "Maddox is growing at an extraordinary rate, and we believe this company will become the go-to provider of municipal services in blue-collar America. In the meantime, there's a great deal of real estate at play here, quite a lot of construction to be done. I know your father dabbles in construction. We can see about swinging subcontracts your way."

After a short pause, Tori lets out a quiet laugh and turns to me. "Charlie, given the profitable relationship our organizations have shared all these years, I'll take your word on this. For now."

I should clarify. I lean toward Adrian just slightly, keeping my tone calm. "The Bonetti's source fine art, Moroccan rugs, tapestries and such. We sell them at the Emporium."

Tori smirks. "Exactly." Her eyes flick back to Adrian. "But I don't know him like that, and I don't trust Wall Street types, no matter how easy on the eyes they are." She winks at him. Adrian just smiles as if he gets that kind of comment all the time.

"So, I'll invest four million," Tori says. "But I want a promise on construction contracts, plus an exit option after three years. You'll buy me out at five million or fair market value, whichever's higher. No matter what happens, my family sees a return."

Adrian nods. "I'm okay with the exit right. But I can't promise any contracts just yet. Not without running a process on subcontractors."

I can sense Tori's building frustration. The contracts de-risk the entire proposition for her family.

"Adrian will run a bidding process to appease the city. And then you'll get your contracts, Tori."

I can feel Adrian's eyes burning toward me, but he stays silent. He's desperate enough not to object.

Tori smiles again, this time with warmth. "Good. We're in."

I set up meetings with a collection of my "small business clients," each holding excess cash they're eager to legitimize. It's an opportunity to draw them further into my sphere of influence. When Adrian not only cleanses but multiplies their money through his fund, their dependence on the Black Gods deepens. We already control their guns and drugs. Now we control their excess cash.

There's the Lloyd Posse, a Jamaican drug-running syndicate with operations stretching from Miami to New York. On paper, they own herbal medicine stores across the Southeast. They come in for $4 million.

Then there's the Zi Wan, a network of Chinese Triad groups specializing in counterfeit goods and cybercrime. They deal in everything from fake luxury handbags to hacked credit card information, operating on a global scale. They put in $3 million from their technology repair business.

Finally, Black Metal M.C. is a Black motorcycle club based in Southern California. Their roaring sport bikes are a prelude to a sophisticated drug trafficking operation that spreads RF9 narcotics across state lines. The IRS, however, agrees their income is derived from their vintage motorcycle and car dealerships across the West Coast. They promise $2 million.

The remaining $7 million comes in from a collection of similarly situated investors, some legitimate, others not, but all under the control of the Black Gods.

40

DR. BRIANNA WRIGHT

I TIE MY hair back in a loose bun, glancing at the clock. The morning is slipping away, and I have to get Riley to basketball practice before heading to work. I'd prefer to be there already, getting a head start on the mountain of paperwork waiting on my desk and patients lined up all afternoon, but mornings with Riley have become precious moments I'm not willing to sacrifice, even if she barely speaks to me these days.

She used to be so open, so full of energy and enthusiasm. I used to see so much of myself in her, the way she cared so deeply about people. But now, at fifteen, she's become more like Adrian. Driven, competitive, always striving to be the best. But at what cost? I worry about her, about the way she seems to close herself off from the world, from me, from her dad.

"Riles! Are you ready?" I call out, the sound of my voice echoing through the halls.

This house is too big for just the two of us. It was Adrian's demand when Riley and I moved back after the divorce. If we're living in Maddox, it has to be on the North Side, far away from the dangers of East and South Maddox.

Every inch of this suburban McMansion screams of his need to prove something, to himself, to the world. This place wasn't for us, it was for him, a subtle monument to his ego, a symbol of the wealth he had then, back when the three of us were a family.

I can't lie. I miss the togetherness we had in Manhattan, but even without the infidelity, I think we would have still ended up divorced. He was completely consumed with work, always chasing the next deal, the next board seat, the next billion-dollar exit. I started to feel like a ghost in my own marriage.

Yes, he cheated, but what I'm sure his ego won't allow him to disclose, probably even to himself, is that I cheated first. I'm not proud of it, but I'm human. We were growing apart, and the distance had already settled in by the time either of us crossed that line.

We tried counseling, but he felt the need to get back at me by sleeping with at least six different women, including someone he worked with. Our divorce was inevitable at that point.

Still no response from Riley. I sigh and glance at the clock on my bedside table. It's just after seven a.m., and we have about twenty minutes before she needs to be at practice. I can hear her footsteps pounding down the hall, a clear signal that she's not in the mood for conversation.

"RileyBear, can you come in here for a minute?"

She appears in the doorway, dressed in her basketball gear, her long, curly brown hair pulled back into a tight ponytail. She looks so much like her father, with sharp cheekbones and determined eyes, though her olive skin is a few shades lighter. And tall. She towers over me now.

"Can you PLEASE stop calling me that?"

I pat the bed beside me. "Sit with me for a minute."

She hesitates, but eventually sits down with a dramatic sigh.

"I know you're frustrated," I begin, "and I know things have been hard with your dad."

"Hard?" She scoffs, crossing her arms. "He's been a ghost for over a year, Mom. Now he suddenly wants to play Dad again just because he got fired? It's pathetic. He only cares about himself."

"I know you're angry with him. And you have every right to be. But you know he loves you more than life itself, right? You're probably the only thing he cares about more than his career. Even if he doesn't always know how to show it. Just give him some grace. For me, please."

"Why?" Riley snaps. "He's a forty-year-old man. Why should I be the one to give him grace? You guys have made me go to therapy since I was a kid, but he can't get himself an appointment?"

"You have a point, sweetie. It's not easy for him to admit when he needs help—"

She rolls her eyes and stands. "You know what, whatever, Mom. Can we just go?"

It saddens me that this is where their relationship is. They used to be thick as thieves. Two peas in a pod, sometimes to my chagrin, when they'd gang up on me in their playful teasing, calling me the 'only Channing in the house without any African blood.' They've always had the same strange sense of humor.

As we head downstairs, I hear the doorbell ring. I see Adrian's familiar figure through the app on my phone. He's dressed in a crisp button-down shirt, blazer, and slacks, his usual polished appearance intact. But I can see the strain in his dark blue eyes, the tension that has settled into his features since his world shattered. The beard is a new development, likely a result of no longer working for the ultra-conservative PGC.

Riley pushes past me to open the door, her expression betraying her annoyance. "What are you doing here? It's not your day."

"I have a meeting near PCA," Adrian replies, flashing a hopeful smile. "Figured I'd give you a ride to practice and back."

Riley's eyes jump to me, seeking some sort of escape.

"Stop it, Riles. Go with your dad."

She's clearly not thrilled, but she grabs her bag and heads out the door. "Thanks for squeezing me in between your precious business meetings, Dad." She rolls her eyes as she stomps toward his car.

Adrian watches her go with sadness in his eyes. "She won't cut me any slack, huh?"

"She's hurt, Adrian. It's gonna take time."

He nods absently, his gaze still focused on Riley as she tosses her bags into the car.

"I know." He finally turns to me. "I'm trying, Bri. Trying to be here for Riley and rebuild myself a bit, ya know? But I don't want to lose her."

"Then you need to be more consistent." I cross my arms as I lean against the doorframe. "I appreciate you moved here, but the timing made it feel insincere."

"But it's not insincere—"

"Can you really say with a straight face you're not gonna run back to New York if PGC comes calling again?"

"Yeah, Bri, I can."

"How?"

"I'm laying down real roots here. I launched Community Capital Partners, made my first investment, and have eyes on a second one. Trying to build out the platform."

"Well, that's a start." I soften my tone. "You've been talking about that idea since college. Where did you find the capital? I know you were having trouble."

"Charles helped me raise a few bucks with some of his clients."

I narrow my eyes. "Which clients, Adrian?"

"His family trust and a few other regional investors."

My heart sinks, and I immediately shake my head. "Adrian, no. You can't take money from the Palmers."

"Why not? Aren't you taking money from them? I know they're bank-rolling your youth counseling program."

"And that's why I'm saying you shouldn't be in business with them."

"What do you mean, Brianna?"

I hesitate. "I can't breach privilege."

"Bri, what is it?"

"Do you remember the rumors about their dad, Big Palm?" My tone is getting more frantic.

"Yeah, I remember the stories, but Bri, you'd be hard pressed to find a businessman in South Maddox without some type of record. It's well documented that he turned his life around."

"Okay, Adrian." I sigh, giving up. "Just be careful."

"I'm always careful, Bri."

He isn't always, but I don't have the strength to argue with him. After fifteen years of marriage, I know there's no use trying to get Adrian to see your side of things when he has his mind made up.

"I don't have a choice," he says. "I can't get a job worth a damn. I need to earn a living, and the only way I can do that is if I build my own business."

"Look, I know you think you're desperate." I try to keep my voice calm. "But those people... Adrian, Charles's brothers are dangerous."

"Rome's just mean, but he's fine."

"Not just Rome. Their other brother. I've heard Charles talking to him on the phone and I've counseled people who work for him. I know how this sounds coming from a 'North Side white girl' like you like to call me, but I've also spent my adult life studying the criminal mind, and he is clearly a gang member."

He stops, and I can see the wheels turning in his head.

"Charles did say his brothers and his mom have some issues and don't talk. You think it's because this other brother is in a gang?"

"That would make sense to me, Adrian. Reeda's a no-nonsense woman."

He shakes his head. "I don't know, Bri. I don't like to speculate."

I sigh because I can't with him anymore. "Just... here." I google Truck Palmer on my phone and hand it to him.

Adrian eyes the search results. "Tracy 'Truck' Palmer. Big Truck Entertainment. BTE. He owns a rap label."

"All of his artists rep RF9, Adrian."

He studies the screen, pulling up news articles of various BTE rappers, all with visible RF9 ink and claiming the gang in their lyrics.

"Come on, Bri. These rappers are almost always just playing a role for entertainment. They're not really about that life."

"Scroll." I lean in as the screen floods with articles of violence, arrests, and drug conspiracies. "Now play one of the music videos... that one. Slim Choppa, 'Gang Shit.'"

A mixture of trap drums and East Coast drug rap blares from my phone, bouncing off my front porch steps.

Adrian bobs his head to the beat, completely lost in it for a moment. He pushes his bottom lip out. "Not bad."

I direct his attention to Truck in the background sitting behind the wheel of a Lamborghini, arm casually draped over the steering wheel.

"Pause it." I lean closer to the screen. "Zoom in."

He does, and there it is, an "RF9" tattoo inked on his inner forearm.

"Hmm." He pauses the video, squints at the screen, then shakes his head like it's nothing. "Bri, maybe you forgot that at one point in my young life, I was classified as a gang member."

"How could I forget, Adrian? As if I wasn't your alibi on several occasions when we were in middle school."

"And I'll love you forever for it, Bri. I got lucky and got out, went corporate. Isn't it possible this Truck guy did the same? Plenty of guys with that kind of background turn their lives around and get into the music business."

"And some of them just get into the music business and forget to turn their lives around. Adrian, this is different."

"How, Bri?" he asks, his voice growing in emotion as if I've touched a nerve. "I still rep EMSK and have the tats to prove it. When you're raised in that tradition and survive it, when you bury your best friends behind a flag or see them get locked away forever, it's not just something you can erase from your identity. Trust me, I've tried."

"I know, Adrian." I place a gentle hand on his arm, trying to calm him.

We spent countless hours talking about this when we were together. Adrian may have been my first case study. When his father was convicted for the drunk driving death of his mother, he had no other family, so Adrian was orphaned. After his fifth foster parent in three years wouldn't stop abusing him for "being a smart ass," he ran away. He lived on the streets before joining the East Maddox Stronghold Killaz—"EMSK" or "Stronghold." He found a home and a family in that gang. I knew he sold drugs, but he was always vague on what he had to do to earn his place. But I've studied that world enough to know that the father of my child, a man I'll always love, struggles with a variety of demons.

"Look Bri, even if Truck is an active criminal, as far as I can see, neither Charles nor Reeda has a relationship with him."

"Reeda, no. But Charles, yes. They work together. I'm not sure in what capacity, but they have a relationship. I think he's trying to guide some gang members away from that life and using my program to help, but now I'm not totally sure if that's all it is."

"Then you need to stop working with them." The concern in his voice is almost tangible. "I don't want you dealing with active gang members. "

"I'm helping a lot of kids, and they're all harmless. Did you forget I earned my stripes at Riverville, treating mental illness in death row inmates?"

"Of course not. How could I forget my badass, fearless North Side white girl." He flashes that seductive smile that seems to always cut the tension and remind me of the face I used to want to punch and sit on at the same time.

I turn away, subtly trying to hide my blushing. "The Palmer's 'funding' is just free rent. I work out of their youth center, but I pay for everything else myself. You, on the other hand? You can't take millions from them."

"I couldn't get out of this if I wanted to, Bri. I've made commitments with that money. Besides, Charles is the only investor I've come across that doesn't care about Volition or my arrest."

"That can't be true, Adrian."

"I spent two weeks in New York chasing down old so-called friends." He scoffs almost hysterically. "None of those bitches wanted to take a chance on me. I thought I might be able to borrow the money. I had a loan lined up with my old boss at Goldman until compliance flagged my arrest and killed the deal. I don't have the luxury of being picky about who I do business with anymore."

I can see the conflict in his eyes, the desperation warring with his better judgment.

"This isn't about business. It's about your life. Your freedom." I step closer to him. "Adrian, you might be getting involved in something that you can't walk away from."

"I think you're overreacting, Bri. I don't think Charles would give me gang money to invest if that's what you're concerned about. Whatever Truck is involved in, it must be separate from their family business. I did an anti-money laundering search on the entity they invested with, and it came back clean. I did my legally required due diligence. I don't need to ask any other questions."

"Charles isn't as honorable as he presents, Adrian. Don't you think you're being just a little reckless?"

"No, Bri. Do you know how many sanctioned Russian oligarchs and human-rights-violating Saudi princes PGC takes money from? Why should I be more careful than the biggest PE shop in the world?"

I open my mouth to tell him he's an idiot when his car honks, loud and long.

"Helloooo! I'm late!" Riley shouts from the passenger seat window.

"Gotta go," Adrian says, forcing a grin onto his face.

He kisses me softly on the forehead. "I appreciate you, Bri. But don't worry about me."

41

ADRIAN CHANNING

As I DRIVE Riley to basketball practice, the streets of Downtown Maddox blur by in a mix of crumbling brick and gleaming glass, signs of creeping gentrification. The skyline hints at an industrial hub rising from the ashes of old factories and mills. Nostalgia weighs on me as I sit next to my mini-me, but she's lost in her phone, earbuds in. The distance between us is heavy.

The silence swells as I glance sideways. "I watched some highlights from your last game."

I'm hoping basketball gets her to open up but she just ignores me.

"The mechanics on your jumper are lookin' clean," I continue. "You just gotta keep being aggressive in the paint, and it'll open up your outside game. Soon enough, it'll be Caitlin Clark who? Nah it's Riley Channing! Number one high school player in the nation. My buttercup on the Wheaties box. Wooh wooh wooh wooh!" I pump my fist with my free hand.

"Dad, stop." She rolls her eyes, dismissing me, but the flush of red in her cheeks betrays her delight at my hyping her up. I'll never stop.

The silence returns as we turn onto Destin Street, passing by a corridor of newly renovated luxury row houses. Just as I'm about to retreat into my thoughts, the car's Bluetooth connects to Riley's phone. Riley looks around, surprised as Kendrick Lamar's HiiiiPoWer floods the interior of the Prius.

"Sorry." She pauses the music. "My AirPods died."

"No worries. Leave it."

She hits play and I can't help it, I bob my head and start rapping along. *"Visions of Martin Luther starin' at me. Malcom X put a hex on my future someone catch me..."*

Riley's eyes widen. "You know this?"

I chuckle hard. "You Gen Z-ers think you discovered everything good. My generation created hip-hop, kiddo, and Kendrick's been a staple since you were in the womb."

"I know that," she says, rolling her eyes again. But then her tone shifts to a more curious note. "This song just came on my playlist. I've never heard it."

I shake my head softly, a wide smile on my face. "Nah, you've heard it. This album was your mom's soundtrack when she was pregnant with you. I think this was actually playing in the hospital room when you were born."

She snorts in laughter. "I don't believe Mom would want that."

I join in her laughter. "Then you don't know your mother."

"What do you mean?" she asks, her wall of teenage resentment starting to fall.

"Your mother loves hip-hop, Riles. Gangsta rap in particular. How did you not know this?"

She doesn't say anything. She just keeps giggling and shaking her head.

"Ask her about the time we went to your Uncle Mitchie's Halloween party as Dr. Dre and Eminem. She was obviously Eminem."

Riley practically erupts into an uncontrolled series of giggles and snorts that seem to be competing with each other.

"No, seriously. At her request, your birthing playlist was nothing but Jadakiss, Beanie Siegel, Cam'Ron... but then Kendrick hit the scene and your mom became obsessed."

"She only listens to Beyonce when she drives me. Or NPR." Another burst of laughter ripples through the car. God, I love that sound.

I glance over. "Nah, your mom's a... well, she's a nerd, but she's a hip-hop head, too. I think hearing all that hardcore rap in the womb might be why you don't take shit from anyone. You've got that fire."

Riley looks over at me, blushing. "Really?"

"Absolutely," I reply, my heart pulsing with hope. "I mean it's obvious on the court, but you're strong, Riley. You stand your ground and never back down. Don't ever lose that. You're growing up so fast. And doing it in a tough world.. But Channings are tougher. Always."

We pull into the gym parking lot as the song finishes. I catch her studying me, as if she's contemplating whether or not to forgive me.

"Thanks for the ride." She grabs her bag and opens the door.

"Anytime. Love you, kiddo. Have a good practice."

"Thanks, Daddy. Love you too," she murmurs hastily as she shuts the door, running into the gym.

It was soft, like it slipped out before she could catch it, or like she didn't even realize she said it. Daddy. She hasn't called me that, let alone said "love you" since before the divorce almost two years ago. I told Bri. She's still my little girl.

42

DR. BRIANNA WRIGHT

THE SESSION HAS gone well, just like the others over the past few months. I've spent countless hours with Jordan Palmer, and today, we focused on a game designed to build social skills to understand others' emotions.

Through the window of the youth center, I can see the tension on Rome Palmer's face as he descends from the backseat of a black Range Rover. I watch as he walks past his caravan of black SUVs and his guards posted like statues. They're RF9. These guys probably have their tattoos covered, but I've been studying gang psychology long enough to spot a member.

He usually keeps a low profile, but the temperature in Maddox these days is hotter than normal. My teens won't stop talking about some war with the Albanians. When Charles told me his brother hires RF9 for "security," I started digging on the internet. I found Truck's connection to the gang first. And then I started looking at Rome a little closer. How he moves. He doesn't have any visible RF9 tattoos like Truck has, but he's not just the "mattress king of Maddox" and a youth sports coach. I'm almost certain now. Because the image is slipping.

The goon squads he travels with now don't help. The soft-spoken mentor act doesn't hold as well when you have a caravan of bodyguards shadowing you at every engagement. But he still shows. He's always here for his son. Always on time, saying little but always watching.

Though I'm fully qualified to treat it, autism isn't my specialty, so I referred Jordan to a colleague. But then Charles stepped in, asking me to do it as a favor. That was back when I thought he was just a clean-cut defense attorney trying to help his nephew.

It was Rome's wife, Shanita, who booked the sessions and asked all the right questions. We made Jordan's plan together. Rome just showed up for pickups.

For months, I figured he was just a normal father keeping tabs from a distance, trying to be involved in his own way. But over the last few visits, that changed. He started asking me about my background, how long I'd been back in Maddox, and where I trained. When I told him I had done a post-graduate fellowship at Riverville Correctional, he asked if I had worked for any other government agencies. At first, I thought it was just a father trying to catch up on his son's care, finally stepping into the process his wife had handled alone. But it wasn't that. Not really. He was assessing me, trying to decide whether I was a liability.

Today, he's wearing a maroon Nike sweatsuit and a gold whistle necklace. Even with a lollipop in his mouth and surrounded by the soft pastels and cheerful décor of my youth clinic, his presence is imposing.

Jordan spots his father through the window and instantly lights up.

"Daddy!" he shouts, rushing toward the door.

I follow him out, watching as Rome bends down and scoops him into a hug, his large hands gently ruffling the boy's short locks. There's a softness in the way he holds him, a brief vulnerability, perhaps even happiness, before he straightens, guiding Jordan into the car without a word to me. And just like that, I think the interaction is over.

But then he hesitates and tells one of his guards to escort Jordan into the SUV before turning and stepping inside my office.

"How's he doing?" His voice is flat, but the fractional hesitation between each word tells me he's not comfortable.

"He's progressing at his own pace, making small improvements every day. It's a process, but he's working it well.."

Rome nods, his eyes fixed somewhere behind me. He shifts on his feet, and I can feel him pulling back, retreating into the wall he always puts up. But I know there's more. I've seen it in his eyes during pick-ups, during the rare moments when his facade cracks just enough.

"You don't believe it's helping?" I'm probing but I keep my tone light and nonconfrontational.

"Whatever will help him grow out of this."

I offer a small, understanding smile. "Autism isn't something you 'grow out of.' But that doesn't mean he can't learn and thrive. You've seen his progress."

He lets out a breath, glancing back toward the window where his son is waiting in the car. "My wife's the one who believes in all this. She's the one who keeps pushing me to come here."

I nod slowly. "She seems like a great mom."

"She has to be. Seven kids. I barely have time to be home. What choice does she have?"

There it is. The crack.

I sit down, motioning for him to do the same. For a moment, I think he'll just walk out, but something holds him there. Reluctantly, he sits across from me with his arms crossed as if to shield himself.

"I'm sure it's hard on her." My voice is soft. "Balancing everything. Your business, the kids, the pressure."

His eyes narrow slightly, studying me. "My business?"

"I know the furniture stores have been growing," I say, perhaps too quickly. "PCA is huge now. You and Charles are doing a lot in the community. Lots of Palmer Real Estate signs—"

"I'm not naïve, Dr. Wright. I know your proximity to my mother may have let you in on some family secrets."

"Reeda and I have gotten close."

"And you're friends with my wife." He says it not as a question, but as a statement for me to confirm. "I know my daughter Nia and your Riley are on the same basketball team now."

"Shanita's the only other mom anywhere near my age. The only one I can have any kind of entertaining conversation with, if I'm being honest."

"And what exactly have they told you?"

I glance around the room as I contemplate how much truth I should reveal. Riley's always been close with her Grandpa Paul, Adrian's dad. But we got closer when we moved back to Maddox two years ago. Reeda has opened up to me about her marriage to Jerome Palmer Sr., how he was a violent sociopath who lied to her about being a reformed criminal, and forced their sons to do the same when they were teenagers, all the way until his death. She's shared how she's struggled to forgive them for it. But she's always been sparse with details. Shanita's the same, never giving with the details but specific in her questions.

As I glance back at Rome, I realize my silence is entering the realm of 'awkward,' so I deflect. "I have a professional responsibility to keep patient information confidential. That includes information regarding their home lives. As long as they don't pose harm to Jordan, no family secrets will leave these walls."

He looks down at his hands, starts twisting the silver ring on his pinky. "'Pose harm to Jordan...' Everything I am poses harm to Jordan, to all my kids. It's ironic, really. My mother won't talk to me because of the business my father, her husband, forced me to take over."

Did I just trick this guy into admitting he runs his father's criminal empire? Or is he talking about the Furniture Emporium? But why would Reeda have an issue with him running a furniture business?

"I get it." I nod slowly, pretending like I know everything. "Family traditions can be complicated. Yours clearly shaped you into who you are, but your mother lived through something most people can't imagine. Being blindsided by the truth about someone she trusted with her life. She made the choice to walk away, for herself and maybe for you too."

"I make my own choices," he says flatly. "I don't see how my mother's refusal to meet her grandchildren is for me."

"Sometimes, not speaking is the only power we have. She might think it's the only way to push you toward something different. Something safer. To get you to visualize the kind of future you want for your family."

"You think I haven't done that?" His voice trembles, and then breaks. "I've visualized every angle, every scenario, every outcome."

I don't respond immediately, giving him time to keep sharing. But he purses his lips and crosses his arms.

"I know how much you care about your family. Your wife does too. I know she's been trying to hold everything together at home for you."

There's a spark of something behind his eyes that looks like remorse, but it's gone as quickly as it comes. "What's your point?"

"Only that the people who love you might see the same future in mind. Maybe Reeda and Shanita are more alike than you realize."

Suddenly, he clenches his fists. The tension is almost radiating off him. "Why are you saying it like that?"

I subtly raise an eyebrow, confused. "Saying what like what...?"

"Like you know something I don't," he says. "Has Shanita been talking to my mother?"

I hesitate, not wanting to betray anyone's confidence. "Well..."

He stands to adjust his jacket, deliberately revealing the grip of a gun jutting out of his waistband before sitting back down. "Dr. Wright, if you know who I really am, then you know you shouldn't lie to me."

"I think Shanita is just trying to reconcile you and your mother. But a couple weeks ago during a game, she asked me whether generational trauma could be used as a criminal defense. She said she was listening to a true crime podcast and got curious. But her questions were those of someone who had done research, someone who was invested. But she hasn't told me anything specific."

Rome's face tightens, and his silence stretches like a taut wire about to snap. His voice, when it comes, is low and dangerous. "You should stay out of my family business, Dr. Wright. I'll remind my wife that regardless of your connection to my family, you are not a Palmer. And neither is my mother."

251

I exhale slowly, contemplating my approach so as not to anger him further. "Look, Mr. Palmer. I understand that you're a man caught between two worlds, a father who wants to protect his family, but also someone deeply entrenched in something much more complicated. I can help. I've dedicated my life to helping people work through tragic histories so they can see a different future. You can trust me."

For a moment, he says nothing. Then, slowly, he stands and locks eyes with me. "You can't help me. And the only thing I'll trust is that you now know exactly what'll happen to you and yours if you tell anyone what you know about me and mine. Not even Adrian."

43

ADRIAN CHANNING

I OPEN THE door to find her standing there with takeout bags in hand, a bottle of wine tucked under her arm, and that familiar smirk that always seems to catch me off guard. The smell of Thai food fills the air as she steps inside, kicking off her shoes and heading straight for the kitchen like she's been here before.

Josie and I have weekly status meetings. Her demand. Tonight, we sit at my dining table, working while we eat. She's on her laptop reviewing sales projections while I work on a fundraising deck for whenever the LP markets forget about Volition, but all I can think about is how comfortable she looks in my space as the glow of screens reflects off the dark glass windows of my apartment.

We're mostly quiet, but every now and then we sneak glances at each other while we work.

She breaks the silence suddenly, her eyes still on her screen. "You know, if you're trying to make that more compelling, you might want to rethink that slide."

"What do you mean?"

She looks up, gesturing toward my laptop. "The third slide on track record. The one with all of the *glorious* companies you've bought and sold?" Her tone feels playfully sarcastic. "It's clear, but it's not grabbing. You're leading with numbers before you've even sold them on your vision. You should hook them first, make them care about what you're building. And why you're the best person to build it."

I chuckle softly, running my fingers through my beard. "Alright, let me hear it. How would you fix it?"

She leans forward, resting her elbow on the table as she stares at the slide, her voice calm but confident. "Start with the story and tell them why this strategy matters. It's clear you have the experience, so they already know you can find good companies. What they need is to believe in the vision and in you. Who you are and why CCP is going to change communities and bring in great returns at the same time."

I nod slowly, her words sinking in. She's right. She usually is. And she makes it sound so easy.

There's something else here, something that's been building between us for months now. I mean, we've kissed a couple of times, but we promised to keep it professional for the sake of a harmonious working relationship. Shit can get ugly mixing business and pleasure, she once said. She doesn't cuss often, but when she does, it's always unexpected and always makes me laugh.

Josie tilts her head, and her eyes meet mine. A soft, knowing look passes between us and then a hint of a smile forms on her face.

"I think you just made my entire deck better. And here I thought I had it all figured out."

She lets out a light giggle. "You're still probably the best dealmaker I've ever seen. I'm just giving you another perspective."

"Probably?" I smirk.

"Okay, the best..." She draws the words out while briefly rolling her eyes.

It's as if my face is frozen in a smile. She's something I haven't experienced in a long time. Something real. A balance in my life of constant chasing, a reminder that the journey is better traveled with a companion.

We go back to our screens. Minutes pass, maybe hours, not sure. I glance at her again, catching the way the light hits her face.

"I'm glad you're here." The words slip out before I can stop them.

"Me too," she replies, her voice just above a whisper.

We move to the couch, and I put on Tatiana Craig's latest album. Josie leans back, tucking one leg underneath her as she swirls her glass of wine, her eyes following the motion of the liquid.

And then, she glances around my quaint apartment as curiosity emerges in her eyes. "I have to ask... for a private equity rainmaker, you live pretty modestly."

"Honestly, I just got tired of the excess." I try to keep my tone even and as honest-sounding as possible. "When I moved back, I thought I'd live a little simpler, spend only on necessities, and invest the rest. I have enough space for my daughter when she comes over. That's all that matters right now."

She tilts her head, smiling softly. "The 'god of PE' turned minimalist? That's kind of charming. I guess you're full of surprises."

The conversation gets deeper. I tell her all about my current struggles with fatherhood.

"Girls are tough," she says. "You've just gotta keep showing up."

I guide the conversation toward her romantic history.

"I've never been married. Allen's father was probably the most serious relationship I've ever had. After that situation, a man just didn't seem worth the stress. I only wanted to focus on my baby and my career."

"How'd it end, if you don't mind me asking?"

"We were—I was... young." She corrects herself. "Thought I could save him. Thought the birth of our son would fix all of his... quirks." Her voice is strong, but there's a weight to it, something sad. "I was wrong. He was a liar and an overgrown child. Always in and out of trouble. I thought if I could just keep him steady, if I could just be there for him, it'd be enough."

She shakes her head, and the corners of her mouth lift in something like a smile, one that speaks not of joy but of surrender. "I was wrong."

There's a pause. She's staring at her glass, lost in the memory. It feels like she's pulling back layers she didn't intend to pull back. I don't say anything. I can tell this is more about her finding her way through the words than anything I can add.

"I had to come to terms with the fact that he didn't love me, and I didn't love him. So, we co-parent when he's not too preoccupied with his work, and that's about it. I learned the hard way not to mix emotions with doing what's right. He loves Allen, and what matters to me is that my son has a relationship with his dad."

Her eyes meet mine, but now there's a sharpness there. "But all of that other drama? The inconsistency, the lies, the deception, the cruelty? I won't entertain any of it again."

"I get it." I nod, keeping my tone light. "I respect it more than you know. I'll be honest. I'm in awe of you, Josie. I mean, look at what you've built, and all on your own."

"I didn't build this," she says. "This was the brand my daddy built for my momma long before I was even a thought. It's their product."

"Maybe, but I didn't invest in a brand or a product, I invested in Josie Simmons. And I can already tell it's the best decision I've ever made."

She glances away, a full, unabashed smile overcomes her, before she turns back to me. I can see that she's flustered. "Adrian, I've always been good at sticking to my rules. But with you, it feels like I'm toeing a fine line. Like the risk of letting myself fall for you might not be that risky, but I don't know. The complications are endless."

"Complications don't scare me." I lean forward, looking into her eyes. "I can handle whatever comes my way. I feel like you can say the same thing."

She laughs, and for a moment, I see her soften. Maybe, she's imagining what it'd look like. Me and her together. Then she catches herself.

"I'm extremely careful about who I let in." Her voice is quiet, almost apologetic. "I can't afford to get distracted by a man who doesn't have his shit together and is looking for a woman to do that work for him. I'm not saying that's you. I hope it's not. But I can't do that again."

"I understand. I have work to do. That much I know. We all do. But I don't think we necessarily need to do it alone. So long as both parties have a mutual understanding."

"You're so formal," she says, giggling softly, "like everything's a business deal. But I agree, Mr. Channing."

"In all seriousness, I know we've had our moments in the past. The last thing I want is for you to feel uncomfortable."

"I don't feel uncomfortable, Adrian. If anything, I feel too comfortable with you."

She looks at me as if the tension between us is something she's trying to fight off. But there's no denying the pull. I can feel it in the way she looks at me and the way she lets her hand linger on mine.

"It's getting late," she says. "I have to pick up Allen from my mom's."

I help her pack her things and then walk her down to the garage.

"He has his first football game tomorrow afternoon, if you want to stop by." She clicks open her trunk. "No pressure, of course."

I smile. "Are you kidding me? I would love to see him play."

"He's warming up to you. He wouldn't stop talking about the pointers you gave him last week."

"I'm glad to share the wisdom of a washed-up wide receiver. Can't wait to see him do his thing."

I load the boxes of Vegan Caramel Crunch cereal bar samples into the trunk of her Jeep.

"Thank you, Adrian. For everything."

She stares into my eyes. I lean in, my heart pounding in my chest. I can feel my cheeks burning as our lips meet. A blaze of passion that ignites within me, and I pull her hips closer to mine. The taste of her strawberry lip gloss lingers on my tongue. Time stands still as we lose ourselves in each other.

She pulls back, her voice a whisper as she says, "I think we're breaking the terms of our agreement. You know, mixing business and pleasure."

"You're right. But I don't really care anymore. Do you?"

She smiles, her eyes sparkling with affection as she pulls me in for another kiss, and then asks, "I'll see you tomorrow?"

"You will."

"Okay." She gets in and drives away.

I turn toward the parking garage elevator with the rare feeling of true joy lightening my steps, only to freeze at the sight of a black muscle car idling near the entrance. Two Black kids are inside, probably no older than nineteen or twenty. Their eyes meet mine briefly before they look away, and then I notice the marijuana smoke billowing from the windows.

For a moment, a cold unease creeps up my spine. The car feels familiar, like I've seen it before, but I shake it off. They're probably just two kids who live in the building, smoking weed in their car to avoid pissing off their parents.

• • •

THREE MONTHS LATER

Josie and I have been moving slow, mostly on purpose. No drama, no chaos, just showing up for each other every day. Work has become an extension of that rhythm. The Tatiana Craig endorsement turned Geraldine's into the hot new thing. Her phone doesn't stop lighting up with offers, orders, and social media praise.

We're pacing toward seven million dollars in sales this year and holding close to two million in profit, but every dollar is going back into the company. Another year or two of this kind of growth, and we're looking at a high eight-figure exit at least. But even with that on the horizon, I find myself more focused on us than the upside.

Outside of work, it's been youth sports games, dinners, bike rides, and brunches. Allen's football team calls me "Coach A.C." now, sometimes to the actual coach's dismay. Josie's been to every one of Riley's basketball games since we got serious. She brings homemade muffins and teases me about yelling at the refs. Josie's a skilled chef, but what wins my heart is the way she lets Riley take over her kitchen like she owns the place. They bake while I pretend I don't hear them laughing at me in the other room.

Riley's definitely softening toward me. She still has a sharp tongue and won't let me slide on any of my shit. But that old connection, the bond we had back in Manhattan before the divorce, it's coming back.

After one of Allen's games, he leaves the team dinner with one of his friends for a sleepover. Josie and I stay behind at the pizza parlor, lingering over sodas and garlic knots. The crowd thins and the lights dim. We talk and share that full-body, soul-level kind of laughter that makes hours pass like seconds, until the waiter gently lets us know they're closing.

Outside, the autumn air is cool against my skin. The streets are mostly quiet, just the faint sound of traffic in the distance and the smell of roasted chestnuts from a cart down the block. I walk her to her car and place my hand on the small of her back as she unlocks the door.

She turns toward me, and her smile is soft but electric. She leans forward and our lips meet. Slow at first, then fuller. I run my fingers through her braids, brushing them back to see her face more clearly. The kiss deepens. It's not rushed, not messy. It's perfect.

I whisper, my voice hoarse with desire. "I want you. I want every piece of you."

"Come over," she says softly.

I follow her home and as I step inside her house, we waste no time. Our passion guides us, our kisses become more intense, our touches more urgent. Josie's eyes sparkle as she whispers my name, pulling me closer. She takes off my shirt and unbuckles my belt. I unzip the back of her white sundress and watch it fall away. I run my hands over her curves, admiring her natural beauty and the work she's put in to maintain it.

We make love for the first time, our bodies moving in perfect sync. The warmth of hers against mine, the sound of her breath in my ear, it all feels incredibly right.

In the afterglow, we lay entangled, our hearts calming.

She leans closer to me and whispers, "That was amazing." She places a soft kiss on my chest before she snuggles closer.

I pull her in, holding her hand and kissing it softly. "You're amazing. I've never felt like this before."

"Me neither."

Our lips meet again with increased fervor. We spend the night making love as if that's what our bodies were designed for.

When morning comes, I wake and she's still in my arms. I don't want to leave. Ever.

44

TRUCK PALMER

I LEAN BACK in the driver's seat of my Escalade, windows down, letting sunlight shine through. I keep this one matted out in black with twenty-eight inch chrome rims. Some might call it old school, but I came up in the early 2000s. At least the rims ain't spinnin'.

My eyes scan the streets outside. Corner boys and lookouts signal to each other as customers approach. The corner of Franklin & 9th in South Maddox is hot this afternoon. The sun is out, my windows is cracked, but this is the kind of heat that has nothing to do with weather.

Soldiers keep coming, one after the other, like they're punchin' a clock at some nine-to-five. Only their timecards are bags of cash, and their boss ain't some middle management ass nigga. Nah, this is my kingdom, every inch of it. And a king gotta touch the people every now and then.

Getz sits shotgun in a vintage Sixers jersey, designer jeans, and freshly twisted dreads. Looks like she got a new RF9 tat on her shoulder, matching the ones on her forearms, neck, and face—badges representin' the lifetime of work she put in behind this shit, every war she's survived, every body she's helped me bury or dump in the river.

"Why in the hell you wanna sit in on cash drops?" she asks, chuckling in shock that a Black God is on the street. "This shit way below yo' pay grade."

I keep my head on a swivel, my eyes scanning behind my LV shades. "Call it nostalgia, my nigga."

"Nah," she says. "You need to be laid up in the studio wit some bad bitches, henny, and weed. Shit, that's where I need to be."

"There'll be time for that, G. Had to tap in witchu on some other shit though."

"Ay, hold that thought, OG." Getz looks out the window. "We got Zaida comin' through."

Zaida's a fine ass Dominican with perfectly round big titties that Getz got runnin' pills out one of my nightclubs. She struts over to the whip with short shorts, one of them tank tops showing off everything she workin' with, and a pink fanny pack wrapped around her waist.

I glance in the rearview mirror at her. "What's good, Zaida?"

"Everything's always good, big Truckie," Zaida says, giving me a sexy ass look.

"Who you callin' Truckie, girl?" Getz scoffs as she takes the fanny pack from Zaida and counts the cash inside. "It's 'OG' to you. Don't disrespect the Black God."

Zaida just smirks. "No disrespect, OG Truck."

"It's all good, baby." I catch her eyeing me in the rearview and shoot her a wink.

Getz finishes her count and tosses the fanny pack in the trunk with the rest of the pile. "You gotta go, baby girl."

Zaida's basically eye-fuckin' me through the rearview at this point. But then she climbs out. "Bye, OG. Hit me up later, baby."

"Fasho." I watch her bounce that fine ass out the whip.

"You not fuckin' my new bottle bitch, is you?" Getz asks.

I chuckle. "Workin' on it."

"Well, I hope you enjoy my sloppy seconds," she says with a nasty grin.

"You full of shit, nigga." I laugh.

"Ay maybe I am, but don't let her get too close," Getz warns. "When a new bitch get too thirsty, my trigger finger start to itch, nahmean?"

"You think she funny?" I ask. "Workin' for 12?"

"Nah, I ain't sayin' all that. I wouldn't let her 'round you if I thought that. But just fuck the bitch, don't trust the bitch."

I laugh. "We should get you in the studio. Them some bars right there."

"Nah," she says, laughing. "Rap game can't handle a real nigga like me."

We crack a few more jokes before I shift back to business. "Ay, what's good with the light-skinned nigga?"

"I got soldiers watchin' his ass," she says. "I can put blood on his button-down whenever. Just let me know."

"Good." I light a blunt and take a few pulls until it starts hittin'. "His baby momma and kid too."

"Yup I got soldiers watchin' 'em," she says. "Keepin' tabs like Rome said."

"You still in the bitch shrink chair?" I inhale deep and hold it.

"Just had one session wit her. I ain't gon' lie. She smart. Don't take shit. Ain't afraid of shit. And she fine as hell. I can see why the young bouls like her."

I stop scanning the street and look her in the eye. "Don't get soft, G."

"Nah never that." She takes the blunt from me and hits it once. "Y'all let me know. I'll put that white bitch in the ground today. On da gang, nigga, I don't give a fuck. Shit, her and the barely Black daughter."

"Aight, keep it easy. No more therapy, nigga. I don't need her twistin' ya head up n shit."

"Won't happen, OG."

"And don't ever speak my family last name, you hear me?"

"My bad," she says. "Only way I could get an appointment was to name drop."

I shake my head softly. "It's aight. Just keep watchin' for now. Way too much at stake to have loose ends running around wit our bread. Need to keep Adrian from thinking he can run off like the last money man my little brother brought in."

"What happened?"

"Remember that 'lil ol' Jewish nigga I had Slim and Nutty fuck up a couple years ago?'"

"Ray Fitz," Getz says. "Yeah, I remember him."

"I ain't tell you back then 'cause Chuck was embarrassed, but the dude stole our shit. By the time Slim and Nut pulled his plug, his wife and kids had already blew the country wit fifteen mil of Black God bread. Vanished. No traces."

"Gotdamn!" Getz hollers as she rolls a new blunt, sprinkling some white in it. "Fifteen Ms ain't light, OG."

"Can't let no shit like that happen again, so I need surveillance on him and his family." I glance over, waiting until she looks me in my eye. "Keep it quiet. Don't scare 'em, but when the time comes, I need Adrian to know we got insurance on our six mil."

Getz nods, and then passes me the blunt. "I gotchu."

I take a slow pull, the smoke hitting me for a second, a buzz creeping in before I pass it back to her. "And if the therapist get any ideas about talkin' to the feds, we'll need to pull the plug anyway."

"No stress, OG. I'll stay on her."

The carousel of cash drops continues.

"We got this nigga Kareem comin' through," Getz says. "He a new nigga but he been movin' big weight for us down in Miami. He solid."

"How long he been tapped in?"

"Just a few months, but he came through on referral from one of my hitters outta Charleston. Said they did a bid together down at Marley Hill and he held it down on many occasions."

"All good. Bring him in."

Getz cracks the window and hollers, "Ayo 'Reem, you up."

Kareem hops in the back and drops a duffel bag on the center console. "G Getta, OG Truck, what's good, God? How's the family?" he asks.

"Ain't shit," I say.

"Fasho fasho," Kareem says. "Ayo, give my blessings to the Black Gods."

Getz unzips the duffel and starts pulling out stacks of neatly bundled hundred dollar bills. At least a couple million in the bag from the look of it.

I turn back, looking him up and down. His eyes are hidden under a bright blue Marlins cap pulled down over his face. Seem like he don't wanna look me in the face. Few do.

"You say you from Miami?" I ask.

"Yessir," Kareem says. "Carol City to be exact."

"Well, up here in Maddox, if you raised on Franklin & 9th…" I tap the RF9 tattoo on my inner forearm. "…you don't give blessings to the Black Gods. The Black Gods can give you life and prosperity, or they can give you death—"

Just as those words leave my mouth, an Oldsmobile screeches behind us with its windows down.

I hear one of the corner boys yell, "Oh shit, Albanians!"

"Get down, Truck!" Kareem pulls my shirt, forcing me to hunch over the center console as gunfire rips through the air, riddling my whip. With his other hand, he pulls his piece and fires out his window, taking out the first shooter who was about to take my head off.

Two motorcycles burst from the alleyway with riders uppin' pistols as they speed toward us. They open fire without hesitation, dropping corner boys and customers without discrimination.

These European fucks are coming for my head.

"Shit!" Getz shouts. She returns fire from her 9mm.

More of Getz's corner boys let loose with submachine guns and pistols, each taking cover behind their whips parked just up ahead. My soldiers tear out of my recording studio down the block, firing AR rounds, while our lookouts in the row houses lay down cover fire from above.

Kareem's like a marksman with the 9mm, taking out shooters coming through on foot. But still, the sound of bullets ricocheting off my bulletproof windshield fills my ears.

"G, take the front!" I holler before I climb past Kareem to the trunk where I have Big Betty, an AA-12 automatic assault shotgun. Chuckie got it for me for my birthday.

I grab it out of the case as the whip keeps getting riddled with bullets. Thank God I got this bitch wrapped in Kevlar.

I crack the back window and start blastin' at the Oldsmobile. "I know they ain't coming for the Black God!"

I squeeze off as many rounds as the metal will allow. Another Albanian drops, his body crumpling to the ground.

I hear another car accelerate toward us. I lower my head as I feel my truck rattle from assault rifle rounds shuddering the back hatch.

I up the automatic shotty again and pull, no release. I blow two heads off and take out a tire before the driver crashes out, hitting a light pole.

Corner boys run up and unload into the car, making sure they all dead. Finally, the gunshots stop.

"Y'all good?" I ask in between heavy breaths.

"I'm straight," Getz gasps, enraged. "Bitch ass niggas can't touch a RF9 soldier! K, you straight?!"

"I'm aight," Kareem yells. Then, he turns to me. "Oh shit. Truck."

I see it before I feel it—the dark stain spreading across my white tee. Then, a sharp, burning pain in my chest and shoulder. I falter back into the trunk, landing on a pile of backpacks, duffel bags, and fanny packs stuffed with cash. My blood seeps into them.

"Shit! Truck, you hit!" Getz's voice cuts through the chaos, but I can barely hear her. The world is tilting, my vision is blurring.

Kareem presses a shirt to my wound.

"Fuck," I gasp, the pain growing, forcing me to release my grip on the shotgun.

I can see the fear in Getz's eyes as she looks back.

"You ain't goin' out like this, God," she says as she slides into the driver's seat and guns the engine.

My eyelids get heavy, and the cool wind from the open window hits me, cutting through the heat as the darkness sets in.

45

TRUCK PALMER

I WAKE UP from surgery and the doctors are all worked up, throwing around medical talk like it's supposed to scare me.

"He took bullets to the chest and shoulder," they say to Rome. "He needs time to rest under medical supervision."

What I need is to get out this hospital. I can't let my enemies or the streets see me down. One call from a nurse affiliated with a rival crew, that call turns into a text, a post, a DM, and before you know it, our enemies think it's open season on RF9 territories across the country because Big Truck got popped. Fuck nah.

The bullets missed the vital spots. Some bad bruising, a whole lotta pain, but nothin' I haven't felt before. I'm only forty-four. Still young.

I walk out the hospital on my own two, surrounded by an army of RF9 soldiers. Ain't nobody takin' me out on some ambush shit. Only way to kill a nigga like me is to die wit him. And they ain't bring enough.

Rome and Shanita set me up in their crib. They got an entire private clinic. Doctors on call, nurse staff, the whole nine, all paid to keep me alive and not ask questions.

The room itself is calm, with dark wood paneling, leather chairs, and lofted windows that let in enough sunlight to remind me I'm still above ground. It's secure. High walls, gated entrances, and armed guards who don't blink and don't hesitate. This house is a gangsta's fortress, the type niggas bleed for. In my big brother's case, the type you bleed niggas for.

Rome settles into the chair across from me, his eyes scanning the room.

"T," he says. "You should be resting."

I shift slightly, trying to find a comfortable position. "Rest won't get us what we need, Rome. We got problems that won't wait."

He doesn't respond immediately, just nods, weighing his words as he tends to do. That's his way, never rushing into anything, always thinking three steps ahead. It's what makes him the leader he is, and why we been on top for so long. But the top ain't lonely anymore.

"I know," he finally replies. "But they almost took you out, little brotha. This was too close, T. Gotta get you out the field, let Getz and the other shot callers step up."

"White man can't kill a Black God, bro. We been through worse." I try to push past the pain in my chest and the fog in my head. "But this, this wasn't just a message. You know that, right?"

"I know, T—"

"They think we weak, Rome. They know we got no more gun supply. They've taken all our wholesale customers and keep knockin' off my corners. Not because they want a street-level dope business but because they wanna see what we'll do. They wanna see if we still willin' to go to war over this shit."

"I know, T—"

"They came for me on fuckin' Frank & 9! These niggas gotta die, Rome."

Rome's eyes darken, a flash of the old him trying to come through. "I know, T!" But he keeps it in check, keeps himself controlled. "And it's on me. I've been... hesitant."

"I know you been thinking about retiring."

He takes a deep breath. "I thought maybe it was time. We've made more than enough. Thought we could pull back, start to live a different kind of life."

I shake my head. "Only one life for me, Rome. Only one death."

"I wish I could convince you that wasn't true, bro."

"Ain't shit to convince. I told pops when I was fourteen I wanted to play football. He told me I wasn't ever gon' be shit but a thug. Momma kicked me out the next week and nobody came lookin'."

"That's a lie, T. And you know it." His voice carries force, and he finally looks me in my eyes. "I came lookin'. I came and got you. We built RF9 together. Wasn't just you."

"Yeah, we built RF9, then you gave it to Big Palm. He showed you the furniture game, showed you how to do legit business, made Chuckie go to law school. Only thing he showed me was how to move weight and put holes in niggas."

I can see Rome shifting in his seat as if he's trying to dodge the truth I'm laying down.

"I ain't complainin', big bro, don't get me wrong. I'm just sayin' we all have a role to play in this shit, just like Chuckie love to say. And I'm good with that."

Rome sighs. "I'm tired of my role, T. Tired of looking over my shoulder, constantly checkin' for wires, forcing my wife to raise seven kids without help because I can't trust a nanny she hires ain't workin' for the feds. Tired of needing an armored caravan just to pick up my kids from school. Tired of what this all means for them... the shit they'll have to face for my actions."

"You don't think I get that? You don't think I wanna watch my son play ball at PCA? I can't be seen in public with my own family to keep the cover that you and Chuck care so much about."

"It's Pops's rules, T. Protect the family name."

I'm the only nigga in this family not lying to the world about who he is. I might sign some artists, sell a few records, but I'm a gangsta first and always, a Black God in the truest form. I don't give a fuck who knows it. So, Maddox, PA views me as the "black sheep," the rebel Palmer shunned from his influential family. To keep people thinking we legit, I stay away from public events and only see my family at Rome's house or at discreet locations we own. But we can't afford to worry about a damn cover, not with this war reaching its tipping point.

"They sent shooters at my head, Rome. They came for us on a block we've owned for damn near four decades. What happens if I got my son wit me next time? What happens if they come for you when you wit Shanita and the kids? We're exposed and we gotta clean it up!"

My anger's boiling. I wince from the pain.

Rome notices. "You gotta take it easy, brotha. But you're right. I'm gonna get this fixed. It's not what I wanted, but it's what we need right now. I'll call in some favors, get us some temporary firepower while Chuck sets up the factory with the Adrian nigga. I'll make sure the streets know the Black Gods and RF9 remain untouchable."

I nod. "Time for war, big bro. Can't leave a nigga standing. You taught me that."

He looks at me, and I can see both pride and sadness in his eyes. "I taught you too well, maybe. I never wanted this for you, T. Definitely never wanted it for Chuck. But you're your own men. And you've always held this family down. Always held me down."

"And I'll never stop."

"But I need you to get your rest, aight? I don't know what I'd do without you, dawg."

I stay silent, letting the moment hang between us. There's nothing more to say, really. Rome knows I'd die for this family. I'd eat a million years in solitary if it meant my brothers could keep goin'. So, he's gonna do what needs to be done, even if it's not what he wants.

"Where's Chuck?" I ask.

"Dealing with police. Workin' his contacts, making sure they don't come at us over the illegal straps and cash they found in your car."

"He wasn't gonna visit his big broth—"

"Stop," Rome says. "He stayed in the hospital all night with you."

I give Charles a lot of shit, but he's a real one and a killer in his own way. "Anyone tell Mom?" I ask.

Rome looks down like he's hesitating. "Yeah, Chuck told her."

"What she say, Rome? She ain't come?"

"Nah, she ain't come, baby bro."

"What she say, Rome?"

"Chuck said… uhh… she said to tell her when your funeral is."

"Damn."

My mother and I never saw eye to eye, but to hear that burns. I haven't talked to her in over fifteen years. Even still, I would do anything for her, anything to protect her. For her not to give a damn that I almost just got killed hits hard. But fuck it, this is the life I chose.

Actually, it's the life Jerome Palmer Sr. chose for me, but I guess it don't make no difference.

Rome leaves, and I drift off to sleep.

A few hours later, the door creaks open. My son walks in, his small frame moving slowly as if he senses the tension in the room. His eyes widen as he sees me awake. Then he makes a beeline for me.

"Dad!" he shouts, climbing onto the bed and gently hugging me, afraid of the wires.

I pull him close, shuddering at the pain in my chest, but I don't care. I need to feel him there, solid and real.

"Whaddup, baby boy?" I squeeze him and feel my first real smile in a minute.

His mom stands in the doorway with her arms crossed, not saying a word. She doesn't need to. Her presence alone is enough, a reminder of everything outside this life that I sacrificed.

I look at her, my eyes weary as they lock with hers. I pray I see something warm, the feeling we used to share. But there's nothing, just a cold distance that's grown between us over the years. She wants nothing to do with me. That's been clear for a minute.

"I can't believe you're still doing this at forty-plus years old," she says. "You know what? It's none of my business. We heard what happened, and he wanted to see you. I'll be back in a couple of hours to pick him up. Given the army of guards outside, he'll be safe, right?"

"Of course. Thank you for bringin' him, Josie."

46

ADRIAN CHANNING

With $50 million in capital commitments secured, I put in my bid on the parking contract and now I need to make good on my promise to Charles.

Getting PGC's Blue Rock files was easy. Tessa got them for me within a couple of days of my request.

If I'm coming in as a strategic partner on the new Blue Rock, I need to spearhead it. That means doing my own diligence and making sure the deal makes sense. This should be easy enough since I've bought this company once already, but this time the stakes are different, way higher.

Hours pass like minutes as I dissect the company and its assets from top to bottom. I build a business plan and marketing deck in my head, then on my laptop, along with a pricing model optimized for today's market realities and financial projections that account for every market shift. I break down the operations from manufacturing to distribution, identifying key customers, and pricing strategies.

I get to the contracts and records relating to Blue Rock's firearms assembly business and stop. There's no way in a million slaps of the ass I'm including that business line in these models, but something tells me to keep them. Harry taught me to never delete an email or record of anything that has money attached to it. So, I archive them in a separate file in my encrypted data room and keep going.

When I finish, it's not just a file of contracts and records, it's a roadmap to running a successful company. For a few hours, it felt like the old A.C. was back. No private equity fall from grace, no smear campaign, no failed marriage, no strained relationship with my daughter, no questions about what happened at Volition and why I'm not at PGC anymore, no background checks and arrest records. Just me doing what I'm best at.

Before I know it, it's morning. I print out the files, put on a suit, and head into my office at PalmerSpaces. As I'm driving, I pass by the Blue Rock factory in South Maddox, and in the lot, I see a black Escalade next to a line of black Range Rovers and then a matte black BMW with the windows tinted and a license plate reading, "CPLWYR 3." Charles's car. He must be inside with his Japanese investor client.

I park, smooth my jacket, and walk up to the front door. It's locked. I call Charles. No answer.

I find a side door and creep in through an office space onto the main factory floor. I step inside, expecting to hear Japanese, but it's dead quiet. I walk a few more steps in and then hear the grumbling of distant voices.

And then, down the conveyor belt, I see Charles, Rome, their Uncle Mac, and another big Black dude, much bigger. He's tatted and his arm is in a sling. As I look closer, I recognize him from the music video Brianna showed me. It's Truck Palmer.

Along the factory walls are a dozen or so angry-looking jacked Black dudes in black pants and t-shirts, and none of them look like they work for a Japanese investment group. Each one of them, including Truck, pulls a pistol and points it at my head.

I'm silent as I assess what the fuck I just stepped into. I raise my hands, trying not to make any sudden movements.

Then Charles's voice cuts through the tension like a blade. "Stand down."

The goons hesitate, then slowly lower their weapons. Truck keeps his pistol up.

"Truck, put it down," Charles says.

The gun stays up.

"T," Rome says softly.

He finally puts the gun down.

"Fuck is he doin' here?" Truck turns to the goons. "Grab that nigga!"

Grab that nigga. Those words ring in my head. The voice sounds so familiar but I can't place where I heard it. I didn't hear his voice in the music video. He seemed more like a Suge Knight type. He didn't rap, didn't speak. He was just in the video, flexing like your typical gangsta rap mogul.

"Wait." Charles walks forward and the goons stop in their tracks. "Adrian, you picked one hell of a time to stop by."

"This a family meeting, Chuckie!" Truck hollers from afar as he lights a blunt.

That voice…

"What're you doing here?" Charles flashes what looks like a nervous grin.

"I–I was just driving by and saw your car. I got the files you wanted on this place—all the financial records and an action plan to get the new business up and running."

I hand him the binder of files.

"Wow, great work, Adrian." He thumbs through it, still flustered. "You have no idea how helpful this'll be."

Charles notices me staring at Truck. He takes a deep breath, glances at him, then at me. "Why don't you… come on over and meet the family."

"The fuck!" Truck barks.

Holy shit… I figured it out. "That's the voice."

"What voice?" Charles asks.

"The voice on the tape!" I try to speak softly but I can feel myself nearly screaming. "The voicemail Tim Rouchard sent me before he disappeared. The voicemail I gave you after you had me bring him here."

My heart jumps out of my chest and then back in before pushing down and out of my ass. Brianna was right. Of course, Charles isn't just a fucking litigator. These guys are gangsters. Their father was a gangster. Of course they're fucking gangsters. How could I have missed this?

"Shit," Charles mutters.

That's the first time I've ever heard him cuss.

I look over at Rome. His eyelids slowly drop, almost as if he's ashamed. My eyes move to Truck standing next to him. His eyes have glazed over, and his face is curled into a twisted smile as he gives a slight head nod.

Charles's eyes widen as they lock on something behind me. "No!"

I turn and, emerging from behind a steel vat, I see a tall, stringy, light-skinned Black woman, fully tatted from face to fingers—fingers that are curled around a black 9mm pistol pointed at my head.

I don't even register fear. I hear nothing. I see Riley. I see Brianna. I see Josie. I see my dad. I see my mom. And then everything goes black.

47

CHARLES PALMER

THE PROCESS TOOK a few months, but I got it done. Through a chain of shell companies, we acquired Blue Rock's real estate assets and machinery out of bankruptcy. Six facilities across the East Coast for $4.2 million. A relative steal.

These factories, this company, is going to be our ticket to regaining control. On paper, we'll bring it back to life and make it a legitimate operation with some illegitimate product lines. It'll be business as usual at Blue Rock, just the way it's been for four decades, before Adrian had PGC take it over. Ironically, we now need Adrian. He has the business acumen to establish the front and broker a connection to a wholesale firearms parts supplier.

I enter the South Maddox facility with Uncle Mac. Rome and Truck follow, each with their own entourage of RF9 members, as usual. Truck's still recovering from the gunshots he took a few weeks ago, but he's stronger than an ox. Now, he doesn't travel anywhere without at least four RF9 soldiers.

Rome, quiet and calculating as usual, just stands by the window, taking it all in, while Truck paces, lighting a blunt.

"The light-skinned nigga gon' fuck this family over," Truck mutters.

"Relax," I say. "Adrian's looking for a payday and an opportunity to put deals together. We give him that, he'll be in our pocket."

"Yeah, except he ain't one of us," Truck says. "He's soft, and as soon as he can, he'll run to the pigs."

"He won't," I shoot back. "Adrian's not some yuppie and not as soft as you think. I had Mac do some digging." I turn to Uncle Mac. "Tell 'em what you found."

Uncle Mac steps forward, his voice deep and raspy from decades of doing the work he does as he says, "He's from the Ironbridge District, probably one of the toughest hoods in all of PA, shit may be the country back in the day. My contacts on the Eastside say he used to run with Makari Griggs and the Stronghold Killaz before his father came home from the pen and snapped his ass back into the house. But before that, they said he was a major factor in these streets. A young'n but respected. Fifteen years old and had grown men—heavyweight dope pushers—workin' for him. For a minute, him and Griggs ran everything that came in and out the Ironbridge Homes. And as y'all might remember, that was a whole lotta business back then, before they tore those towers down."

Rome's face has a look of surprise, as if he's found a new respect for Adrian. "If he ran with MG da General, he not gon' snitch."

Uncle Mac nods. "Brothas from Ironbridge are trained to hate police."

I let out a small huff. "Maybe because police are trained to hate brothas."

"I don't give a shit where he from," Truck says, "or which washed up, locked up gangsta he used to run with. We need to be finished wit that sellout."

"Can we be straight here, gentlemen?" I ask. "Truck, you're just jealous because he's sleeping with Josie. Envy has no place in this business. You know that, big brother."

"You know what, Chuckie." Truck puffs his blunt. "You right. But I give no fucks. I don't want him round my son, don't want him round Josie, and definitely don't want him round my money. Josie know if she needed anything, I'd get it for her. Tell me why we need him to invest in her shit?"

"After everything you put her through?" I'm beginning to lose my patience with his intellectual challenges. "I've been trying to get her to let us invest in Geraldine's since before she went on Shark Tank. But she doesn't want our money. She knows where it comes from. As far as she knows, Adrian's fund is backed by legit investors in his network."

"Yeah but don't forget he's the reason we in this shit," Truck says. "If he didn't fuck with Blue Rock, nobody would've known what was goin' on here."

"He wasn't acting against us when he made that deal," I say. "He didn't know John Bing was working for us. But right now, he's the key to fixing that problem."

Suddenly, Adrian walks in, unannounced, uninvited, and clueless as to what he's stepping into.

"What the hell is he doing here?" Truck growls, reaching for his pistol.

The guards posted at the door have their guns pointed at Adrian before I can say anything. He freezes but handles himself well. I've trained myself to assess the fear in any man or woman, and I see none from Adrian. Just shock.

"Stand down," I order, keeping my voice steady.

Adrian gives me the files. As I thumb through them, I can feel him staring at me, confused, and then at Truck and all the armed men.

Then, he places Truck's voice as Tim Rouchard's kidnapper on that voicemail.

As soon as I turn back to Adrian, I see Getz behind him with a 9mm pistol aimed at his head.

"No!" I command, trying to stop her from killing him.

Adrian turns, and she strikes him square on the forehead with the butt of the pistol. He staggers and drops.

"Goddamnit," I snap.

He's out but still breathing, slowly blinking.

"This is our business partner." My words are hurried as I crouch down next to him.

Truck glares at Adrian on the ground. "You think he's gon' walk outta here and keep his mouth shut after this? He can connect me to Rouchard. We gotta pull the plug on him, Chuckie."

I stand up, rubbing the back of my neck. "He's an accomplice on that hit. He stole confidential files for us. He's invested over $25 million of dirty money from us and our partners. He's smart enough to know there's greater upside in working with us than against us. We don't need to kill him." I glance at Rome. "Rome, come on."

Rome takes a deep breath as he rubs his forehead. "Wake him up."

Getz slaps Adrian awake before two of her guys pick him off the ground and place him onto a metal folding chair. He groans as he sits up and blinks through the haze of what is likely a concussion. His eyes lock on Truck, then me and Rome. Still no fear. Not an ounce.

"Sorry about this incident." I lean in with a half-smile. "We obviously weren't expecting you. But now that you're here, we should have an honest conversation."

Adrian glares at me, but I know that look. He's angry, sure, but he's thinking. Calculating. "You're not capable of an honest conversation, Charles. I see that now."

I brush past the insult. "As you can probably surmise, my family is—"

"RF9." He cuts me off. "The Black Gods. There is no furniture empire, is there?"

Truck hisses through his teeth and shakes his head as he puffs.

"RF9," I repeat. "Like our furniture chain, our real estate holdings, our various small businesses… and our investment in Community Capital Partners SPV I LP… is just one of the many assets in our family portfolio."

"I should've known," he says, scoffing. "Retail furniture millionaires in Maddox, Pennsylvania, in 2025?" He starts laughing. Before long, he's hysterical. "I'm a fucking idiot."

"Listen, Adrian." I keep my voice calm. "I'm going to level with you. When Volition failed, it put pressure on our organization in a number of unexpected ways. My family is currently embroiled in a war for the East Coast arms market. We need our gun supply back and the only way we can get it without upsetting a very delicate balance is if we take over this factory and make the firearms ourselves."

"But you need the parts from Blue Rock's supplier." Adrian's eyes jump from me to the binder on the table.

"And you've already delivered that," I remind him, "so now all we need from you is assurance that you'll keep the truth you've learned today to yourself."

Adrian's quiet as he looks around the factory floor at my brothers and the armed guards stationed along the walls.

Truck steps forward, his gun drawn.

"T," Rome drawls out, cautioning him to stop.

"Nah, fuck this shit." He puts the barrel of the gun to Adrian's temple.

"Truck, don't," I plead, but he doesn't listen.

"My brothers want you alive, and you lucky I respect them," Truck growls. "But if you don't keep your mouth shut, I won't just kill you. I'll kill your baby momma, your little girl, and your daddy. I got niggas watchin' their every move. Therapy, basketball practice, grocery store, mall, and then back home to that big ass crib at 334 North Fairlawn."

Getz shoves a phone in Adrian's face, showing him photos of Riley and Brianna in their daily routines as she snarls, "We can have 'em scooped up and cut open whenever."

Finally, I see the fear in Adrian's eyes. "You've been watching my kid?"

Truck scoffs. "What I just fuckin' say, nigga?" Truck presses the gun tighter to his head. "And if you keep fuckin' wit Josie or even speak to my son, I'll rip you limb from limb. You hear me?"

"Josie?" Adrian looks up, confused. He clearly didn't know she and Truck have a kid together.

Adrian seethes. "I'll burn you motherfuckers to the ground!"

Getz lets out a chuckle of disbelief. "He think he tough. Ayo, let's dead this bitch ass nigga."

Truck's gaze turns lethal. "He a liability, Rome! Lemme do it!"

Rome sighs, rubbing his head.

My eyes jump to Rome in a slight panic. "Rome, he's holding our $6 million."

"We'll get it back from Josie," Truck interjects. "We can't afford another enemy that'll run to the feds."

"This is an important man," I plead with every shred of dignity I have left in a situation that is spiraling out of my control. "He has family and friends in very high places who will ask questions."

Truck turns back to me and then looks at Rome. "So did Tim Rouchard, and we got away with that shit. We'll make this nigga vanish the same way. No body. Won't come back on us."

"And what about our mother?" I ask frantically. "You willing to kill her when she asks why her husband's son disappeared less than a year after going into business with us? You do this, she'll know it was you and she won't stay quiet."

"Moms ain't a snitch," Truck yells. "Rome, gimme the word!"

Adrian's eyes dart around as Truck pulls the hammer back. "You kill me, you don't get your guns."

"Wait," Rome says.

"The information you need isn't in that file," Adrian continues.

Truck pulls back, huffing and puffing as he drops his gun to his side.

"Even if it was there," Adrian says, a look of newfound confidence on his face, "if you start making guns in this factory, the city will shut you down and serve you up to the FBI."

"What are you talking about?" I ask.

"Charles, if you had been straight with me, I would've just helped you. But you led me to believe this was a legit deal. So, I sold it to my good friend, Mayor Deanie Howard."

"What do you mean you sold it?" Rome asks.

"She's under pressure over unemployment. I told her I'd get the Blue Rock jobs back, and in exchange, she'd give me the parking contract. She'll need to keep a close eye since she plans to tell the media it was her idea to bring in new investors to reopen this place."

Adrian pauses, measuring our reactions, before continuing. "You won't be able to make your guns in here without me running interference. If this abandoned factory suddenly starts emitting plumes of smoke from its stacks,

Deanie's city inspectors will be crawling through this place to make sure everything is above board so she can put her name behind it."

Adrian's eyes continue to dart like he's assessing whether we believe him, but I no longer see fear in him. He knows he has leverage.

"This needs to be a real company," he says. "Not a front. And you need me to run it."

Rome steps forward. "You saying you have Deanie Howard in your pocket?"

Deanie is probably one of the few people in the city with access to my father's sealed case file. She's stood by her "anti-corruption" stance, refusing our campaign contributions and denying my requests for a meeting. Her predecessor was on our payroll, and protecting the family name has become much more difficult without that insulation.

Adrian stands with a surprising vigor. The look in his eye is one of near-absolute strength. "I control Deanie Howard. And I control this deal. Blue Rock had hundreds of raw materials suppliers. Even if I gave you the full file, it'll take you weeks and a team of forensic accountants to figure out where those gun parts were coming from. But I know exactly who the supplier is. It's a manufacturer located outside of the U.S. They aren't gonna do business with some guys they don't know and have never heard of, telling some bullshit story about Japanese investors. But someone with my resume will get a meeting in half a second."

"We can find another plug, Rome," Truck says.

"That'll take time," Adrian says. "I haven't been tapped into the streets in a long time, but I know how turf wars work. You can't afford any more delays."

"Okay," Rome concedes. "What do you need to get this done?"

"Other than assurances that the giant psycho back there won't murder my family?"

"He won't." Rome shoots Truck a look.

"You need to fire Brianna from your foundation," Adrian says. "I want her far away from RF9."

Rome nods. "That's easy."

Adrian's hurried breath returns to normal. "I also need full ownership and control over the legit business. I'll procure your gun parts. We assemble them at night here in South Maddox after hours. We limit the gun production to this facility only. The two factories in East Maddox, the bottling plant in Harrisburg, the industrial park in Trenton, and the food processing plant in Wilmington stay legit. After you get back the money you spent to buy them, they're mine. You guys keep this facility and get your gun business. I get a legitimate contract manufacturing company, and I'll make sure Deanie and her people stay in check."

Rome slowly shakes his head. "We can't give you full ownership of assets we bought. We can do fifty-fifty on the legal manufacturing money."

"How about a hundred percent of the profits to you until you double your money?" Adrian says. "And then it's mine?"

"Triple," Rome says. "And then you can have it. But Adrian, my brothers and I have every right to monitor our investments in the ways we know how. And from what Charles has told me, you're managing capital for some of our partners as well."

"Your partners?" Adrian asks, his head tilted and eyebrow raised.

I explain to him how the "small business investors" I introduced him to are fronts for the Italian mafia, the Triads, a Jamaican weed cartel, and an outlaw motorcycle club, none of whom will rely on the terms of a limited partnership agreement for their remedies if they think Adrian is hiding their returns on the parking deal.

I can see Adrian seething as he registers the reality. And then he shouts, "You have me laundering money?"

Getz steps forward and pistol whips Adrian again, this time across the mouth. He staggers but doesn't fall. The anger in his face is abundantly apparent as blood oozes from his lip.

And then she growls, "Don't ever raise your voice to the Black Gods."

I step forward with a calming tone. "Adrian, the money you invested was processed long before it touched your account. Taxes paid. Audits survived. You might want to do your own layering of entities to make it tougher for regulators, but on paper, your LPs are successful small businesses unconnected to organized crime. I've even had the government investigations lawyers at Linder Boykin stress test the structuring. It's solid."

Adrian's face settles, the anger slowly subsiding.

"Somebody patch him up please," I order.

"You set up our gun operation and 10X our money as promised, you'll have nothing to worry about from us," Rome says. "But if you don't deliver, if you play with my money, you talk to the feds, or if I find out anything you said here is a lie, I'll let Getz cut your little girl's head off."

Adrian looks Rome in the eye, his jaw tight as one of the guards brings a first aid kit forward. He thinks he's a tough man, but I can see his raw, simmering fear return at the mention of his daughter getting hurt. His weakness, like most men, is the fierce love he has for his child.

But to me, all this really means is Adrian Channing belongs to the Black Gods.

48

ADRIAN CHANNING

MY MIND RACES as I walk out of that factory. I'm lucky to even walk out at all, but I didn't fear them the way maybe I should have. The Ironbridge projects taught me not to flinch when someone pulls a piece on you. I don't care what happens to me, but Riley...

The thought of going to the police crosses my mind for about half a second. Maybe I flip this whole thing to get protection for my family, for myself. But then I remember where I come from. I grew up in a neighborhood where cops weren't a solution, they were just another gang. And given that MPD is in RF9's pocket, my family would be dead before the ink dries on my witness statement.

For the first time in decades, I feel like I need guidance. I get in the car, start driving, and somehow find myself at my father's house. I haven't seen him since that dinner nine months ago when Charles offered to invest in my fund.

I walk up the steps feeling like I'm crossing enemy lines. The house is sturdy, well-kept, with a couple of flowerpots by the door that Reeda probably tends to. Charles bought her the house, after all.

I knock on the front door. No answer, so I go around back and enter through the back door.

Reeda's helping my dad walk across the kitchen. It's as if he can't walk on his own two feet. When my eyes focus on him, he looks older and paler than I've ever seen him. His hair is a stark white now, his once thick jawline softened and wrinkled, but those hard blue eyes of his still cut through me. He doesn't look good. He looks sick.

"Son," he says, barely above a mumble.

"Dad."

The place smells clean, too clean for someone who used to come home stinking like cheap booze and stripper sweat. I guess Reeda really is keeping him in line.

"Adrian," she says, straining under the weight of his body, almost a foot taller than her own. "What a nice surprise."

I move closer and take his arm, placing it over my shoulder before helping him into his chair.

I don't say anything for a while. I just stand there observing him. His arthritic hands and sunken shoulders. I can sense his bones quivering.

"What's going on?" I ask.

"Nothing I can't handle," he says.

Reeda steps forward, fastening her purse strap, her car keys jingling. "Talk to your son, Paul." She turns to me. "Adrian, will you sit with your father for a while? I need to run some errands."

"Sure." Best she not be here. I need to know what my dad knows about her sons.

She leaves and we sit silent for a few minutes.

My dad breaks the silence as he eyes my busted lip and then the bandage on my forehead. "You look worse than me."

"I feel it too," I smirk a little, but my voice feels tight, like I'm choking on the words. "Seriously, what's going on with you?"

His mouth opens to form words but struggles to voice them. Finally, he says it, his words slurred. "Multiple sclerosis."

For a split second, I think, *you deserve it*. But then, I don't know. I feel bad for my piece of shit father.

"But I'm fine," he grumbles. "Just had a minor episode. Don't need pity, that's for damn sure. Now, what's going on with you? Haven't seen you in months."

I hate needing him. I hate that he might be the only person I can actually trust to see the strings I'm tangled in and maybe help me cut them loose.

"It's nothing. Just work shit. Thought I could use your take on something—"

"*You* need *my* take on your work shit?" His eyes narrow. "You, who's never needed me for anything? Your words. You can't bullshit me, Adrian. You could always run your games on everyone else, but not me. What the fuck's goin' on, son?"

I sit down across from him. "I think I'm in trouble." My voice is barely more than a whisper.

He scoffs with that condescending sound I can't stand. "This must be déjà vu. What kind of trouble you got yourself into this time?"

I hesitate, my jaw tight. I can feel the anger bubbling, the old wounds flaring up. And then it comes out, harsher than I intend. "Same kind of trouble you're into. What do you really know about Reeda?"

He looks up at me with a seriousness in his face I haven't seen in a while. "Nareeda's the best thing that's happened to me since your mother."

"What about her sons? Rome? Truck? Charles?"

He doesn't answer.

"Dad!"

He doesn't flinch. "What are you into with them?"

"They invested in my fund. I thought they were legit but—"

"Fuck no, those boys are not legit," he snaps. "Rome and Truck are deep in the game. They own these streets. They have for years. They're stone-cold murderers, son."

"And what? Reeda's the Queenpin?"

He shakes his head as much as he can with the MS restricting his movement. "Absolutely not. My Reeda has gone no-contact with Rome and Truck. It kills her to not have a relationship with her own grandchildren, but she won't go back to that world. The torture that their father put her through... If I could, I'd beat him to death slowly. I would've told you all this if you showed your face around here more often."

"Tell me now, Pop!"

He sighs. "Big Palm trained his children on a military form of respect. They worship him. But he was a grade-A sociopath. He brainwashed them as kids. Had 'em delivering drugs and guns, plotting kidnappings and armed robberies. He forced 'em to lie to their mother about what they were up to. Reeda had no clue who Jerome really was until Truck and Charles murdered an FBI agent. She's convinced Truck put him up to it as a gang initiation. Truck showed no remorse, but Charles was just a boy, so Reeda moved him up here to North Maddox, away from his brothers, and put him in therapy. She believes she saved him from the life his father and brothers were leading him down."

I shake my head. "She didn't."

"Charles is a lawyer, son." His slurred speech turns the word 'lawyer' into 'liar,' though maybe it's intentional. "One of the best. He says he ain't tied up with his brothers, which is the only reason Reeda entertains a relationship with him. I could always see through his act, though."

"Why didn't you say anything?"

"Because it'd break her heart," he says. "Now, what do you know?"

"Everything. The three of them control RF9. The furniture store, the real estate, all their businesses are fronts. Charles pretends he's just an advisor, but he pulls the strings. They killed Tim Rouchard. They threatened to do the same to Riley and Brianna if I don't do something for them."

"Do what?" he asks.

"I shouldn't say."

My father's face contorts in anger. "Why the hell did you fuck up your family, boy!"

"What?" I bark, standing abruptly.

"If you hadn't gotten sloppy with your dick, your wife wouldn't have left you to come here, and you wouldn't have followed them. You made it out of this shithole! And now look at you. In bed with gangsters after everything I did to move you off that path."

"Everything you did?" I'm so angry I'd knock his ass out if it weren't for the MS. I pound my fist on the coffee table, then push back and rise to my feet. "You think this is what I wanted? I had everything before they took it from me."

"*They*... it's always *they* with you. 'They made me sell dope...' 'Makari made me shoot that boy.'" He pitches his voice up, mocking a fifteen-year-old me. "When will you learn to take accountability, son?"

"When will you?" I shoot back. "EMSK was the only family I could find after you drove me and my mother into a fuckin' wall. I got my ass beat in the foster homes so I lived on the streets, Dad! I was eating out of a trash can under the Destin Street Bridge when Makari found me. The fuck was I supposed to do?"

Tears begin to well up in my eyes. I hate talking about this shit.

"You hate me for what I did," he says. "Fine. I get that. I was a drunk, and I killed your mother. You love to remind me of that, but I'm reminded every moment of my existence, son. I've spent over thirty goddamn years living with that regret. Thirty years letting the demons torment me. It's the biggest regret of my life, and I know I'll burn in hell for it. I've accepted that. Salvation is beyond me."

He coughs, spitting mucus into a handkerchief.

I pace the room, my hands running through my hair. I don't want to hear this. I don't want to hear his guilt.

"It's not just about your salvation." I hate that my voice is trembling. "Even when you got out of prison, you weren't there. You left me to raise myself in a fuckin' concrete jungle. You made me study. You made me go to school, but I was broken, Dad."

"You think I don't know that? You think I haven't blamed myself every single day?" His voice cracks. It's the first time I've ever seen him look vulnerable.

"I'm sorry, son."

That's definitely a first.

"For everything. I was a shit father, and I failed you in more ways than I can admit. I probably should've said it sooner, but I am who the fuck I am, and we are where the fuck we are. You're a grown man, son, a goddammed titan." His voice is weakened but laced with something like pride. "And that's through no doing of mine. I know it."

He struggles to lean forward as his voice falters. "But you've got a daughter who I'm quite fond of, by the way. And if you don't want to lose her, you need to get out of whatever you're into with those boys. If you lose their money or piss them off, they will hurt her to get you in line."

I stop pacing. For a second, it feels like the room isn't spinning. "I can't just stop. It's not that simple."

"No, it's not." He sighs, rubbing his face. "And the Channings have never been simple people. But son, sometimes the most logical choice is the one in front of you. Get your family the hell out of here and don't look back."

I stand there, staring at him, my heart pounding in my chest. I shake my head. "If I run, they'll think I'm stealing their money or snitching."

"So, you run fast, son."

"They have people damn near everywhere. They'll find us. I can get this under control from here. I can get *them* under control. Just a couple more years. I'll make enough money for them and walk away."

"A couple years?" He rasps a laugh, but there's no humor in it. "You think that's how it works? The price will always increase. The debt won't ever be fully paid, not if they need something from you. You think you can just walk away from these kinds of people clean and leave them standing? I know for a fact Makari taught you better than that—"

"Exactly!" I snap. "Everything you heard about me when you came home—about who I was in Ironbridge, how I ran those towers, what went down that day twenty-five years ago... whatever Makari told you when you were locked up together... it's all true. It all went down exactly as they said it did, and I came out standing. I'm not some dipshit pencil pusher who doesn't know how the game is played. I can handle this. I'll beat them."

He stares me down, his face as serious as I've ever seen it. "Knowing you, Adrian, you're probably right. But just consider what it looks like if you're not, and what you're willing to lose in the process of testing your will."

49

ADRIAN CHANNING

I'M ALREADY IN too deep.

I helped them kill Tim Rouchard. Even though I thought I was bringing him to Maddox for a good reason, I'm not sure a jury will see it that way, especially if Charles has his way in court. He'd find a way to pin the whole thing on me, painting it a revenge plot to kill the guy who leaked the scandal that ruined my career.

So, I quickly made peace with the arrangement. Blue Rock could be a golden opportunity disguised as a noose. But I'm not hanging myself, and I'm not letting Riley or Brianna get hurt. I'll run it for the Palmers, keep things looking clean on the outside, and use every trick I know to protect myself and my family.

But first, I need to make sure I'm covered on paper. Last thing I need is for the feds to come after me for money laundering.

Mitchell Lowenstein is a tax lawyer, an all-around manipulator of laws, systems, and technologies, and one of my oldest friends. I meet him at his row house in the new Arts District of West Maddox. The game is muted on the flat screen while we sit on the couch, two half-empty beers sweating on the coffee table.

I told him everything, and in true Mitchie fashion, he's working on a fix. He's got his laptop open, tax filings up on the screen, scanning through PDFs and spreadsheets like he's hacking the Pentagon.

"So," he says, tapping his fingers on the keyboard, "your investments are legit, but the cash ain't?"

"Legit fund, legit companies. But the guy who introduced me to these investors failed to disclose they were shadier than the sand under a fuckin' palm tree."

"You never could resist dancing with the devil, could you, A.C.?"

"I don't know what to tell you, buddy. I got played."

"It's all good, brother. I'll clean this up for you nice and tight."

I take a sip of my beer, watching as Mitchie's fingers fly across the keyboard. "So, what's the plan?"

"The paperwork for these LPs is decent, but you need layers to protect yourself," he says. "What we should do is set up an offshore feeder entity."

"Offshore where?"

"Cayman, maybe Mauritius, somewhere presentable but without the elitist banking standards we have here."

"Go on."

"The feeder will pool all that dirty cash along with your and Harry's clean cash before it hits your fund. And then you get some schmuck to manage the feeder as a nominee, your LPs put the money in the feeder, and the feeder invests in your fund. If regulators do an audit, they see a single investor."

"Can't they subpoena the identities of the underlying investors?"

"Only the investors who put in more than ten percent of the fund are subject to an AML look-through. Based on your LP list, only 'Paxton Investments LLC' meets that threshold. Looks like she put up thirty of your fifty Marys."

I laugh as I remember Mitchie's naming conventions. He refers to a million dollars as a "Mary" and a billion dollars as a "Brenda," combining the two things he loves the most: women and money.

"The rest of these limited partners are small peas," he says. "If anyone sees Harry Paxton at the top of your LP list, they'll assume the whole thing is above board seeing as how her money is far from funny. Perfect cover."

I push out my bottom lip, impressed. But then I raise an eyebrow. "And the IRS, SEC, FinCEN won't see through this?"

"Only way they can tell where these Marys are coming from is with our cooperation," he says. "If any of those bureaucratic fucks get so bored as to ask for records, we only need to serve 'em up with Harry's docs, showing perfectly legitimate capital. And then they'll back off or my name's not Mitchell Shaquille Lowenstein."

I blink a few times. "Your middle name is Herman."

"Don't worry about my middle name. Sometimes I wanna feel tall, alright? Fuck you." He grins.

I chuckle before the reality of this intricately designed fraud hits me. "And you're sure this'll work, Mitch?"

He looks up from his laptop, grinning at me like we're kids again. "I've hacked the federal government more times than I can count. They're idiots. Just stick to my plan and we'll be gravy. Trust me, brother, I've had your back since we were twelve."

I tap my foot against the wood floor as I contemplate that true statement. Let's just say as a youth, I may have engaged in certain activities that could've derailed my admission to Harvard. Mitch was my willing alibi on a few occasions. There's no one I trust more.

"Set it up," I tell him.

I'm still in a world of shit, but there's something satisfying about having my childhood best friend become my most trusted ally in business.

50

ADRIAN CHANNING

LAUGHTER FLOATS THROUGH the haze of smoke from fire-roasted meats. Voices in rapid-fire Portuguese buzz under the clink of glasses and the clatter of knives. Wine flows freely, hands clap on shoulders, and the steaks just keep coming, sizzling and dripping, adding to the intoxicating smell that fills the night air on the patio of Bistrô Sereno.

Mitchie's charm fills the space, his jokes hitting just the right edge of inappropriateness, pulling our potential business partner closer with every chuckle. Mitch has a knack for making friends wherever he goes, often without even trying. His eyes follow a group of beautiful women in tight dresses passing by, almost prancing to the sound of samba music in the streets. But his attention snaps back to the table after a glance. He knows we're here for business, but São Leopoldo, Brazil is doing its best to distract us.

"So, Mr. Pereira, I assume you understand the nature of my proposal?" I ask, leaning forward in my chair, the soft clink of silverware ringing in the air.

Bruno Pereira, Chief Revenue Officer of Metaliga S.A., takes in his surroundings before turning his attention back to me. He's dressed in a dark suit, his slicked-back hair and neatly trimmed mustache adding a touch of ostentation to his polished appearance. He takes a sip of his wine and sets the glass down carefully.

"Yes, I believe I do, Mr. Channing." His voice is smooth, and his accent is thick. "But I will say it seems a bit... How do you say? Peculiar."

"First of all, call me Adrian." I flash him my business smile.

"Then call me Bruno," he says, returning one of his own.

"I can appreciate the peculiarity, Bruno. Frankly, the LinkedIn message was a long shot."

"It was, but the tickets to Copa do Brasil were a nice touch. My kids were thrilled." He slices through his steak and takes a bite. "And of course, your resume speaks for itself."

"I appreciate that, Bruno." I take a small bite of picanha. "Our investment group has acquired Blue Rock's assets out of bankruptcy. That company was once a valued customer of yours. Without its orders, there must be a hole in your revenue projections."

"Yes, we took a significant hit when Volition went bankrupt," Bruno says. "Those purchase orders were vital. High-grade steel and precision aluminum components for aircraft, industrial machinery, tools, car parts—"

"Firearms." Let's just cut to the fuckin' chase.

Bruno flashes a knowing smile. "Yes, of course, we supply those components as well. Frames, barrels, firing mechanisms, everything made of metal that brings a firearm to life and ready for assembly." He pauses. "Provided you can show proof of your manufacturing license, a registration with Polícia Federal, tax verifications, and, of course, your Type 07 FFL License. I presume you'll be taking these materials to the States, yes?"

I nod and flash a confident smile. I, of course, don't have any of that shit. But I do have the world's best all-in-one hacker, forger, and tax lawyer.

Mitch flags down a cigar vendor and procures a box of fine Cohibas. With a flick of his wrist, he hands one to me and Bruno, expertly cutting the end before smirking and lighting them for us.

"Bruno, baby." Mitch smirks between puffs. "The docs are in your email."

I lean forward. "We're going to pick up Blue Rock's entire slate of purchase orders and plug those leaky projections for you. It'll be business as usual for Metaliga S.A., and you'll be able to report to your board that you made the deal happen to shore up your earnings. Perhaps it'll help you beat out Eduardo Tavares for the open CEO spot your board is looking to fill."

Bruno laughs as if he's impressed. "How do you know about my internal politics?"

I don't tell him Metaliga S.A. is a subsidiary of a company called Martex Properties, which is owned by a private equity firm out of London called Sentry Asset Management, which was quietly acquired by PGC three years ago in a deal I led. Tessa gave me the intel I needed.

I laugh with him, but keep it controlled. "I've been in business a long time, Bruno. I've done a lot of deals, and I know a lot of people. A customer like me is good to have. But a friend like me is invaluable."

"I can drink to that." Mitchie briefly raises his glass of caipirinha, his cigar set between his lips.

"It's a fair proposition, Adrian, but I am hesitant to do business with the same company that was using our products to break the law. We were fined by your government for that nonsense."

Bruno casually blows a smoke ring.

Mitch matches it, prompting light laughter from the two fast friends. "Same real estate? Same machinery? Yeah, sure. But not the same company. Blue Rock Industries is no more. John Bing was the reason for your regulatory problems, and he's obviously out of the picture. We're rebranding the company. There's new ownership and new management. You'll be dealing directly with A.C. and myself. He's the man who'll keep purchase orders in your inbox, and I'm the man who'll make sure the entire operation is fully compliant with applicable laws across this beautiful country and our own. We don't fuck around, Bruno."

"And we'll need to leave here tomorrow with the first shipment," I add. "Enough for ten thousand assorted assault rifles, high-caliber pistols, and submachine guns."

"The purchase order is in your inbox as well, Bruno baby." Mitchie smiles as he brings out his phone. "You say we have a deal, and I'll wire the deposit."

A look of realization crosses over Bruno's face as he sits back in his chair, a slight smile playing at the corners of his mouth before he extends his hand across the table. "I look forward to working with you both."

The next morning, we make the pickup at Metaliga's private airfield. I borrowed Harry's Boeing 747, a private jumbo jet perfect for transporting entire deal teams to site visits. It's also suitable to move gun parts into her private airfield.

I don't love implicating Harry in this, but maybe she shouldn't have fired me. On second thought, I could give two shits about Harry right now. The Palmers will kill my family if I didn't get this done for them. So, I got it done.

51

ADRIAN CHANNING

THE BACK LOT of the old Blue Rock factory in South Maddox is dark and quiet except for the sound of these thick tires on the gravel. Mitch kills the lights and rolls to a stop. We sit idly for about twenty seconds before I look across the loading bay lot and see two black Range Rovers, one black Hellcat and a tricked-out early 2000s Escalade. RF9.

I hop out and walk to the back. The locks clack as I turn the key, and then I swing the doors open. I shine my flashlight on the rows of wooden crates stacked tight to the roof.

Getz and Frank Madigan step forward, leading four more RF9 guys toward the truck. They each have their hoods up, ski masks on and gloves tight. But I can tell from the slits in their ski masks that they're teenagers. Without a word exchanged, they start unloading the haul.

The light above the loading bay flickers as Truck steps out from behind his Escalade, flanked by two more RF9 soldiers. I can smell the blunt smoke curling from his lips. His eyes drag over me with the same murder lust I saw the last time I met him here. He says nothing as his eyes move to the stack of crates beside me.

And then he turns and nods to one of his boys. The kid steps forward and with a crowbar, he breaks open the crate to find rows of unmarked barrels and grips wrapped in plastic and ready for assembly.

Truck pulls out a receiver designed for an AR-15, turns it in the light, checking the fit before handing it off. The kid assembles the weapon in a matter of a few minutes. Another joins him, screwing in bolts on the barrel, sliding the charging handle, and locking it down.

They continue inspecting the wares, piecing together one of each model. A 9mm pistol, AR-15, M4, MAC-10, and an M82 sniper rifle. The parts click into place without complication. Magazines are unwrapped, and ammo boxes are cracked open. Getz, Frank, and a few of their guys slot in rounds by hand. Others slap loaded mags into place, checking chambers and toggling safeties.

Mitch has already got the targets tacked up across the loading bay against some old drywall and dented sheet metal from the factory.

One nod from Truck, and the shooters raise their weapons. I plug my fingers into my ears before the bursts of gunfire break out in an uncontrolled rhythm, lighting up the far wall. The factory grounds fill with the loud cracks of suppressed fire and the dry clinks of brass hitting the floor. After the chambers empty and the ringing in my ears subsides, I hear grunts of approval ripple through the crew.

Frank watches smoke float from the barrel of the MAC-10 as his lips curl into a slight grin. "Shit's smooth, Big Truck."

"Clean enough to drop a few bitch-ass Albanians," Getz says, still gripping the AR-15 in her arms.

But Truck doesn't say anything. He watches the display with his giant arms folded and his eyes narrowed, locked on mine the whole time, as if he hates that I'm adding value to his operation.

Well, I hate it more.

Finally, he steps closer to me, face-to-face. He's not loud this time, but everything in him feels like a threat. "How's our other business? Hope you got my money makin' mo' money."

I keep my voice as steady as possible. "Projections are trending in the right direction."

"And Josie?" he asks, like it's casual. "How's she doin'?"

"Wouldn't know. Haven't spoken to her since our last quarterly call."

He doesn't respond, just smirks. He knows I'm telling the truth since his people follow me everywhere I go. By the casual way he lights his blunt and blows the smoke in my face, I can tell he's satisfied, sitting comfortably in the power he has over me. He set the terms, and he's ready to enforce them. Dying to enforce them. I know that. I need to be careful. Just keep it business, A.C.

I nod to the crates being wheeled into the factory. "This is enough for two thousand units of each model. We'll start assembly tomorrow night. Should be ready before week's end."

"We'll need another shipment bout the same size once summer comes around," Truck says. "Frankie'll be in touch."

The last crate hits the loading bay. Mitch swings the truck latch shut with a hollow clang. Truck's gaze snaps at the sound, and as he settles, his eyes find a lid that must have fallen to the ground. He walks over, picks it up, and reads it.

"Metaliga, S.A.," he says, flipping it in his hands. "São Leopoldo, Brazil. So that's your plug, huh?" He stands and moves his eyes to mine. "I bet my little brother could reach out, set up our own deal. Then, we can cut you out and put you in the woods."

"Got too many in the woods, OG," Getz says, a thin smirk on her face. "But the river real still this time of year."

Fuck. We should've stripped the crates.

I hold Truck's stare. "Is that what you're gonna do? If so, let's not waste time."

He flashes a thin smile as he slowly turns away. "Not today, bitch nigga. Not today."

Frank gets into the driver's seat of the Escalade. Getz takes the front passenger while Truck gets in the back. And then their convoy glides off like death in the night.

Mitch grumbles, "Fuck those Neanderthalic fucks," as we head for my Prius.

Once we're back on the road, he shifts in the passenger seat, squinting at the dashboard.

"Christ, how do you even fuck in this tiny shit car?"

"I'm in my forties. I don't."

"Fair point," he says. "But God damn, if I'm uncomfortable in here, I know your lanky ass—"

"Now's not the time, man." My voice is a mutter, but it's sharp. "I need to drop you off. Then I need to check on Bri and Riley. Need to make sure they're good. And you need to steer clear of me."

"Nah, I'm with you, A.C."

"Mitchie, if they broker their own deal with Bruno or find another supplier, they'll kill me. I don't want you in the blast radius when that happens."

Mitch chuckles briefly before sobering. "First of all, I just helped you smuggle maybe thirty Marys worth of military-grade firearms into the country. We're way past avoiding a 'blast radius.' Secondly, they're not getting another supplier today, which means you're still a vital component of their business. And third…" He looks out the window. "… Fuck the fuckin' Palmers."

I glance at him. He doesn't look back. He just seethes as he stares out the window.

"What's that about?" I ask.

"I wish you had told me Charles Palmer was your investor."

"What are you talking about, Mitch?"

He takes a breath. "You're not the first fund manager they've invested with. Remember my uncle Ray?"

"Ray Fitz? Of course. He had that mortgage business back in the day. He was my first intro to finance now that I think of it."

"Yeah, well, a few years ago, he launched a hedge fund. Nothing crazy. Large-cap, long hold stuff. Secure, easy. Took on the Palmer Foundation as a client. One day, he gets a call from Charles Palmer telling him to go big on NFTs. Some tip he had heard from one of his clients."

"Idiot," I murmur.

"Yeah." Mitchie sighs long and deep. "It was a bad bet. Hindsight being what it is, he was likely using that trade to wash some nasty fuckin' money for some nasty fuckin people."

"More than likely."

"Anyways, Uncle Ray pushed back as hard as he could, but that guy, Charles, has got that quiet kind of scary. And it was his money, so 'hey fuck it.' My uncle executed the trade. Things were fine for a bit... then boom—"

"The fraud was revealed."

"In a major way," Mitchie says. "NFTs were exposed as the sham that those of us with a fuckin' brain knew they were. They lost close to fifteen Marys in an afternoon."

I can't help but groan.

"Charles lied to his brothers and said Ray stole the money." Mitchie's near tears now. "He couldn't just own up to the fact that he made a bad call and lost. Next thing my uncle knows, some RF9 YNs are tearing up his office, saying they'll kill his wife and kids if he didn't pay the Palmer family the money he took."

"Jesus Christ. What did he do?"

"What could he do? Ray couldn't make that money back on their time-line, so they ended his ass. One morning, I get a call from MPD saying he was shot eight times in what they called a 'random robbery.' But no one gets shot that many times just for the fuck of it."

"Charles has the police chief in his pocket." I shake my head. "What about the family?"

"I got 'em out," Mitch says, his temper calming just a touch. "I set them up with new identities and got them to an offshore location I'll never name out loud."

I look him in the eye as I turn onto Brianna's street. "You're a good man, Mitchie."

"Yeah, well, I'm not letting the same damn thing happen to you, brother. I've got your back."

Mitch reaches down into his backpack, pulls out two freshly assembled 9mm pistols wrapped in an old rag, and sets them on the center console.

"The fuck are you doing, Mitchie? Where'd you get those?"

"Relax," he says. "I built them while those RF9 dummies were lighting up the wall. They won't notice the missing parts, and if they do, we chalk it up to breakage. Take one."

I don't touch it. I just pull the rag over to cover them. "I don't need that. I can outsmart these guys. That's how I stay alive."

"These guys don't give a fuck about 'smarts,' A.C. They don't play by the rules. They kill first and sort it out later. You gotta be prepared, brother."

I stare at the gun. Then at Mitch. He's right.

I nod once. "Put it in the glove."

He does and then shuts it. Neither of us says a word for the next few miles.

As the last haze of the sunset fades, we pull into Brianna's driveway, past the basketball hoop and neatly trimmed hedges lining the wide concrete path.

Riley brushes past us, nearly running on her way out. She's dressed in her team hoodie, basketball bag over her shoulder. Her face lights up as she sees Mitch.

"Uncle Mitchie!" She gives him a hug. "It's been forever."

Mitchie cackles as he strains his neck upward at Riley. "For the love of everything that matters, who gave you permission to grow taller than me?"

Riley snorts out a laugh. "Sorry, Unc."

She glances at me and forces on a smile. "Hey, Dad." But she doesn't stop, just continues down the steps past us.

"Where you headed?" I ask.

"Team dinner," she calls out, already halfway down the driveway.

I let her go, although I want to hug her, hold her close, and maybe ship her somewhere far away. Somewhere safe.

I watch her get to the street and pull open the back passenger side door of a waiting Uber before hopping in. The engine revs and pulls away.

As my eyes linger on the street, I look a few houses down and see two black Hellcats parked across from each other. One takes off, lurking slowly behind Riley's Uber. The other idles with the lights off, waiting.

I turn to Mitch. "You need to go home. Call an Uber and lay low for a bit."

He eyes the car down the street. "You sure you're good?"

"No. But I'll manage."

"Alright," he mutters, pulling out his phone and opening the app. "But hit me if you need me."

"I appreciate it, brother." I start up the steps, then stop and turn back. "Hey Mitch?"

"Yeah?"

"What you did for your uncle's wife and kids… Promise me you'll do it for Bri and Riles if it comes to that."

"I already made new identities for the three of you," he says. "I got you covered."

"But if the shit really hits, don't wait on me. Don't waste time worrying about me or looking for me. Just get them out. Far from here. Far from the Black Gods. Can you do that for me, man?"

He nods as his voice gets low. "Yeah, bro. Of course. I got your back." He pauses, then adds with a crooked smile, "From the first Mary…"

"To the last Brenda." I finish our old mantra with a weary grin.

Back when I was slinging weed at DuBois High School and he was running bets at the football games. We used to say we'd have each other's backs from the moment we made our first million, all the way until our last billion, whether that meant we retired fat and rich or lost it all.

I grip his hand and pull him into a hug as his Uber pulls up.

I watch him get in and pull off before I turn towards the front door. But Brianna opens it before I can even ring the doorbell. Her eyes jump toward the street as she lets me in.

"We need to talk." She pulls me by the wrist into the house.

Inside, the kitchen is spotless, the temperature is warm, and it's quiet.

"Why are they escalating?" she snaps, her words almost running over each other. "They've been parked there every night for weeks. Different cars, but each one black, tinted, and matted out. But they never bothered Riley before. Only me. I had the Jahlil situation under control. They knew I wasn't a threat. They knew I wasn't going to talk to the police."

I stare back at her. "Bri, what the hell are you talking about?"

She studies me for a brief moment, then exhales hard. "What did you do, Adrian?"

"I didn't do anything, Brianna. I invested what I thought was their clean family money. But you were right. The Palmers are criminals."

"God dammit, Adrian! I told you to give them their money back."

"It sounds like this isn't all on me, Bri! You seem very worried about Jahlil, but I haven't spoken to the kid since I got him that job at Blue Rock two years ago."

Her jaw tightens. "That job got him killed."

I take a step back. "Hold on. What?"

She looks away and presses her fingers into her temple. "Jah was RF9."

"What?" I blurt. "Why didn't you tell me that? If people find out…"

I let my voice trail off because if I continue, I'll have to tell her I just smuggled a bunch of illegal guns for them. And that if the government comes after RF9 and learns I helped one of their people get a job at Blue Rock, they'll say I was involved in the gun-running scheme all along. They'll point to my relationship with Charles and say I brokered the deal while at PGC. It would take me from forced accomplice and victim to co-conspirator. I can't implicate Brianna in that.

"He had no idea they got their guns from Bing," she says. "It was above his pay grade. So, he let it slip to one of his friends that he got a job there, and they used him as their inside man. To keep Bing in line."

"What the fuck is wrong with these people?" I mutter. "Using kids to do their bidding."

"When Blue Rock collapsed," Brianna continues, "he had nowhere to go for money, so he went back to the gang. His first job back was putting a bullet in Bing's head before he could testify. But he couldn't do it."

The silence between us stretches for what feels like minutes before she speaks again. "I went to Charles, thinking he had gotten a few RF9 members off on charges, so maybe he could make some inroads. I didn't know who he really was back then."

I stare at her. "What did he do?"

"Nothing… But Jah's mom told me he disappeared the day he was supposed to go to his office. I didn't know then that the Palmer brothers were actually in charge of the whole thing. I just thought they were, I don't know, affiliated… Respected by the gangs because of who their father was back in the day."

"When was this?"

"Last year," she says. "Around the time we had that dinner with your dad and Reeda. I think you had just launched your fund."

"That's when Tim Rouchard went missing. Charles told me he thought RF9 was cleaning up loose ends. I didn't realize he had an inside perspective."

"He's a very skilled liar," she says. "It took me longer than I'd like to admit to catch on to him."

"How did you figure it out?" I ask.

"A woman named Getz came into my office for counseling. It was obvious she was there to intimidate me. To let me know what would happen if I told anyone what Jah shared in therapy. But she made a mistake when my intake assistant wouldn't let her in, saying she worked for the Palmers and that Charles cleared her appointment. When I saw her RF9 tattoos, that tipped me off."

"Are you still seeing her?" I ask.

"Only when she books a session to threaten me," she says, suddenly blinking like she's hiding something.

"What, Bri?"

"But I am counseling Rome. He's not my patient, technically. He's never booked a session. Just comes to pick up his son. Mostly, it's just me talking at him. He hardly engaged. Then one day, he accidentally admitted his involvement with RF9—"

"Wait. What do you mean accidentally?"

"I may have tricked him into thinking I already knew everything."

"Jesus, Bri, you love to play with fire."

"I was just doing my job, Adrian. But then he threatened me. Said if I ever mentioned what I knew about his family… Well, I'm sure you know the rest."

"And if he wasn't technically your patient, you can be forced to testify against him." I move to the wall and pound it with a hammer fist. "Brianna, why didn't you tell me about any of this?"

"I did!" she fires back. "I told you not to take their money."

"Yeah, after I already took it and invested it." I start pacing as I feel the heat rising in my chest. "And you were vague as fuck, hiding behind your doctor-patient privilege bullshit."

Her laugh is short and bitter. "Maybe if we still had *spousal* privilege, I could've told you more. But you shattered that when you started screwing half the models at Ravelle Lingerie. Oh and don't forget your boss's daughter."

"Dammit, Brianna, you always skip the part where you cheated first."

She doesn't flinch. "You were gone. You might've been coming home at night, but you were… nowhere. Nowhere for me, nowhere for Riley—"

"Was it Charles?" My voice is almost a hiss.

"What?" Her face twists into a confused rage.

"Did you cheat on me with my fucking stepbrother, Bri? I know something's going on between you two. Is that what you two were talking about when I saw you through the window at my dad's house last year? How to cover up your affair now that I'm back in Maddox."

"No, Adrian! I've told you a million times, mine was an emotional affair with a guy in our old building in Manhattan. It never got physical. I wasn't even working in Maddox back then."

Suddenly, she's quiet. Her lips tremble as if she's reliving an ugly memory. "But…" Her voice trails off.

"But what, Bri?"

"Charles and I hooked up a few times. After our divorce. It started shortly after Riley and I moved here. But it ended once he showed me his true colors."

"Oh good, so you didn't step out on me with the gun kingpin. Just some dickhead neighbor." I immediately regret the sarcasm.

"How dare you?" Her voice rises again in anger. "I came clean. I owned it. I apologized for hurting you. I was ready to fix what I broke. You said you were too. You said you wanted to go to counseling, to get back to us. But you couldn't do that without hurting me back."

I stop moving. There's nothing I can say. No defense. If I had taken therapy seriously and fought for us instead of punishing her, maybe she would've stayed close enough to check me, to keep me from drowning in my own ambition. Maybe she would've stopped me before I bet my life savings on Volition. Maybe none of this spirals the way it has. But now isn't the time to unpack all that.

"Bri, we need to figure out what we're gonna do."

A heavy silence stretches between us.

"We both should've known better," she says finally. "We don't get to play fast and loose like that. Not when we have a kid to take care of."

I place my hand on her shoulder, and then slowly pull her into a hug. She doesn't resist. In fact, she dives into my chest. I can feel her tears slowly soaking my shirt.

"I've been thinking about running," she murmurs in between sniffles. "Just taking Riley and going."

"To where?"

"I don't know. Anywhere."

"They'll find you, Bri. The Palmers may seem local, but RF9 has almost a national reach. They have crews nearly everywhere."

"I know," she says. "And I won't force my child to live a life on the run. Not this close to college. She'll hate us forever."

We're still for what feels like minutes as I hold her. Two people who once had a life together, now balancing on the edge of losing everything.

I take a deep breath. "So we stay. We figure this out."

"How?" she asks.

"I'll get them their return on investment. That's what they want. If I make them enough money, they'll leave us alone."

"Are you sure?"

"Smart money can solve any problem, Bri."

"You've always said that but—"

"It's the only thing that's ever consistently worked in my life. The more of it we have, the more leverage we can put to use, the faster we can move."

"And until then? Riley's not a dumb girl, Adrian. She'll realize something's up if they keep following her."

"I just helped the Palmers out in a major way."

"Helped them how?" she asks.

"I shouldn't say. No spousal privilege, remember?"

She's quiet, making that face that says *you're right.*

"But it should buy us some goodwill," I say. "I'll talk to Charles and convince him to pull the tail off Riley. Trust me, Bri. I won't let them hurt our baby girl."

"Okay." She pulls back and wipes her tears with her shirt sleeve. "I trust you, Adrian. I have no choice but to."

I lean down and kiss her softly on the forehead. "I'll fix this. I promise."

PART THREE

52

ADRIAN CHANNING

One Year Later
Two Years Since Volition Crashed

Twelve months after launching and it's starting to work. The six factories are up and running across Pennsylvania, Delaware, and New Jersey. The workers, mostly locals, are showing up in droves, happy to have steady pay again. I secured a credit facility from Maddox Savings and Loan to buy newer, more environmentally-friendly technology and hire more employees.

I rebranded Blue Rock Industries, Inc. to Ironbridge Industries, Inc., an homage to my old hood. The name gives people in the city something to root for and hopefully cleanses the stench of John Bing's illegal operation. Ironically, now it's my illegal operation.

From the outside, everything is clean. I'm marketing Ironbridge as a revival of local US manufacturing, and it seems to be working. Legitimate revenue from legitimate customers that I personally procured. Apparel brands, car parts distributors, electronics, and more. It wasn't difficult convincing Blue Rock's old customers to jump back on board, except for the U.S. Military, of course.

Our food processing plant is boosting Josie's profit margins since we package her products at a significant discount. Hopefully, after another year or two of this kind of growth, we'll be able to sell the company at the 10X multiple the Palmers are expecting. And then I can be done with them.

Ironbridge Industries has just one highly illegitimate customer, and luckily, it controls the police. And I control the mayor.

Once I brokered the deal with Metaliga and got the South Maddox gun factory operational, RF9 hit the Albanians back hard, effectively ending the war in brutal fashion. Thanks to me, their arms business has been restored, and twelve months later, their initial investment in buying Blue Rock's factories is close to being repaid three times over, per my agreement with Rome. Turns out, the illegal firearms business is extremely lucrative, though I'm, of course, not seeing a dime of that revenue.

I incorporated a new company under CCP called MaddCom, Inc., short for Maddox Communities, to operate the parking contract. I'm in the final design phases, and then Tori Bonetti and her "family" construction company will handle the meter installations and lot renovations, putting the final touch on this recipe of organized crime and corruption.

• • •

Cameras flash from the front parking lot of the flagship Ironbridge Industries factory in East Maddox as Mayor Deanie Howard gives her campaign speech. The place is busy, workers on the floor, machines whirring. It looks like the kind of business that people can believe in.

Deanie smiles for the cameras, talking about job creation, local growth, and how this factory is a reflection of the city's resilience. She's taking credit for my work, but I don't care. I need her on my side.

She introduces me but doesn't pass the mic. She describes me as "another victim of the corruption perpetrated by organized crime in this city, an entrepreneur rectifying the neglect of his former Wall Street firm, which he left upon learning the extent of their immoral practices."

Not entirely true. Not total bullshit either.

With this deal, Deanie Howard increased her political clout. She got jobs, economic growth, and a nice headline around taking back the power from organized crime.

That is total bullshit.

To the public, I'm a savvy businessman trying to build an economic legacy for my community. But of course, I know the truth. This business was funded by dirty RF9 money. One wrong move, and it can all unravel. It's wrong for me to compromise Deanie. I know that. But I don't have a choice.

Deanie drones on about the budget savings the city will enjoy due to our public-private parking venture, and the fact that Blue Rock reopening allows us to manufacture state-of-the-art meters, toll barriers, pay stations, and automated arms at cost and in Maddox, keeping that money in the city. It was the key to winning the deal, since my competitors planned to source those materials from China, adding to the macroeconomic strain cities like ours are under.

My phone buzzes in my hand. I shift slightly on the dais behind her as I glance down.

Josie: Wow, Adrian. You said you'd be at the new Tatiana Craig product launch. I didn't think you would break up with me and just ditch Geraldine's.

Me: It's not like that, Jo. I'm just slammed right now with another investment.

No response.

Sure, I'm busy, but it's just an excuse. Truck Palmer will "pull my plug" if he thinks my relationship with Josie is anything other than professional. So, I've gone from boyfriend and business partner to ex and very silent investor.

Another text comes in.

Riley: Where were you???

Me: I'm sorry, buttercup. Work's been crazy. I'll make it up to you, I promise.

No response.

A year in, and I barely recognize myself. My days belong to this business. My every waking moment is tethered to the arms-dealing empire I'm rebuilding for the Palmers. They and my other criminal investors have made clear what'll happen if I don't multiply their capital, so every ounce of my focus is here, in meetings, phone calls, and high-stakes decisions I can't afford to mess up or delay.

Meanwhile, the life I'm missing is slipping right past me, piece by piece. Brianna agreed to cover for me, telling Riley I have a new job that makes it difficult for me to drive her to games and practices. Those moments we had, just the two of us, meant everything to me. She tells Riles I'll make it to her games when I can. But I see it in her eyes when I show up late, or don't show up at all. She's pulling back, thinking I'm choosing my business over her. Again. She doesn't know the danger, she just sees her dad breaking promises.

But now, the last straw. She was named the number one high school girls' basketball player in the nation. And I missed the ranking ceremony. That's a moment I should have celebrated, but instead, I was knee-deep in parking lot blueprints, budgets, and meetings with the zoning board. I didn't forget on purpose. But to her, that doesn't matter. Why should it? It's just another promise I broke, another big moment in her life I missed.

And the most painful part is we'd been getting close again before this mess hit. I'd shown her I could show up, really show up, but that version of me feels like a stranger now.

I have to focus completely on the fund until I have enough to give all of my criminal investors the return on investment they're expecting. Riley will understand someday. Or maybe she won't. It doesn't matter as long as she's alive. And if I get myself killed over this shit, then oh well. I had Mitchie put my ownership of CCP in an offshore trust for Riley's benefit, so whatever I ultimately make from my investments will go to her.

CCP's portfolio is growing in an organic, albeit unconventional, manner, and I can feel my reputation rebuilding. But the irony isn't lost on me. Two years ago, I moved home to reconnect with my daughter and build some semblance of a life away from private equity. Yet here I am. My business is beginning to thrive, money is coming in, and I can finally see a path back to the financial freedom I once had. But I'm alone, I haven't spent quality time with my kid in months, and on top of that, I was forced to ghost the woman I love almost immediately after we slept together for the first time.

It's all fucked.

53

HARRIET PAXTON

THE SIXTIETH FLOOR of PGC's NYC headquarters offers a panoramic view of the skyline. But inside this glass-walled boardroom, it feels like a battlefield.

I sit at the head of the table, my gaze sweeping the room: Derek Graff, Niles Tannenbaum, Terrence Weiss, Leora Mencham, Martina Hayes, and another handful of shareholders who sit on PGC's board of directors. Behind me is my granddaughter, Reanne, acting as secretary, and Tessa Summers. Adrian put in a good word for her so I stole her from Martina and put her on my personal comms team. I've taken a liking to her, so I'm allowing her to sit in on this board meeting.

"A ten billion dollar impact fund to revitalize blue-collar America?" Derek glances around the room, gauging reactions. "We should reconsider. Raising money for social impact while our chairwoman is being hammered in the media for her corporate greed? It doesn't compute."

Social media has been trying to cancel me for two years, relentlessly attacking my business tactics. The internet labels me an out-of-touch billionaire, highlighting the layoffs at PGC companies as I fly in private jets and attend opulent parties. They ignore my investments in underprivileged communities and still throw the Volition-Blue Rock disaster in my face.

I keep my tone even, my expression inscrutable. "Derek, we've never let the media, let alone social media, sway our investment decisions. The strategy is sound, and the market wants it. We can show the world that PGC has learned its lesson. Doing good and doing well aren't mutually exclusive."

He shrugs and shakes his head. "Half a billion maybe, even a full billion we could swing, but a ten billion dollar fund? Our investors will see it as a distraction from our higher-performing strategies. We should concentrate on returns, not virtue signaling."

"I tend to agree," Niles says. "We need to refocus on this firm's bread and butter. Tech, real estate, energy and infrastructure, pharmaceuticals. You think our investors—"

"They want to see impact, Niles." My voice rises a notch. "We're deep enough in those male-dominated sectors you just rattled off. We've been pivoting from impact since Adrian's departure. He laid the groundwork for this strategy, and it's solid. We need to pick it back up."

Martina leans forward. "I agree with Harry. We can transform lives and protect our bottom line. It's a trend we can lead, but we need the right talent."

"I'm not so sure, Hayes," Derek says.

"Look at the numbers," Martina says. "Since Adrian's exit, our consumer portfolio has dipped significantly in performance. Marquee brands like Stanton Sporting, Bonder Foods, and Arcadian Media are losing momentum. He was practically acting as the CEO of those companies. We need seasoned leadership like that to come in and right this ship, while committing to impact."

"I've been interviewing managing partners from BlackRock and KKR," Derek says. "Names with the track record to boost our returns and help with fundraising."

"Why not just bring Adrian back?" Martina suggests.

The room goes silent as we consider the idea I told her to offer. I can't be seen showing favoritism to Adrian. Not yet. I know he hasn't delivered Derek yet, but I've come to realize it would be better to have Adrian inside PGC, where we can take him out together. If the board backs his return, I'll have my most trusted and most capable ally by my side once more, and we'll be in a stronger position to finally push Derek out for good.

"Adrian Channing is a drug addict who brought an arms dealer into our network and crashed our biggest investment ever," Derek says, scoffing.

"He's not a drug addict," Tessa blurts out, causing the room to stop and assess where the unfamiliar voice is coming from. Her face quickly flushes with red as she realizes it's not her place to speak at this meeting.

But I back her up. "She has a point. Adrian has always been a man in control of his vices. Unlike some at this table." I briefly glance at Derek.

He looks away as he says, "Well, that's what the industry believes."

Martina taps her iPad to life. "Actually, my team did some polling at SuperReturn New York last week. After two years, folks don't really remember Volition. Not with the slew of high-profile corporate fraud cases that have happened since."

"You've done a good job managing that media exposure, Martina." I nod at her.

"Thank Adrian for acquiring Arcadian Media," Martina says. "It wasn't hard to redirect the news cycle elsewhere. If we were to bring him back, I can work my contacts to get his record expunged so it doesn't come up in any LP background checks."

"We all know he has the deal chops," Leora Mencham says. "He could lead this impact strategy, retake the reins at the investment level, and repair our image."

Niles Tannenbaum's expression darkens. "You can't be serious. We can't just hire him back after everything he did."

"He's made a full recovery in public perception," Martina pushes. "Imagine the narrative: 'The prodigal son returns to leadership.' It would not only boost our portfolio but restore our credibility and make PGC look like a culture that takes care of its own, rather than one that discards them in their worst moments. It'll help with recruiting."

I watch Leora continue the pitch the three of us rehearsed last week. "Adrian's new firm out in Maddox is small, sure, but he's proven he can build something both meaningful and profitable. Investments in vegan food brands, contract manufacturing, and municipal services. It aligns perfectly with our impact objectives. It wouldn't be a big buyout. We could just offer him the same stock package he would have received as CIO and let him manage out his Maddox investments under the PGC banner."

"No," Derek snaps. "It'll kill us with our LPs, who I can assure you still remember the $50 billion that went down the drain on Volition because of his carelessness. Garrett Declan only agreed to keep investing with us if Channing was fired."

"I'll talk to Declan," I say. "He's already complained to me about the dip in performance. I'll get him to understand we have a solution. Adrian Channing is still the best dealmaker I've ever seen. And I've seen a bloody lot. He comes back as CIO, and we pitch our original succession plan to the LPs. I retire when I turn eighty, and then Adrian takes over as chairman."

The board murmurs its agreement.

"Let's put it to a vote," I propose, feeling the tide shift.

As the votes are cast, I notice Derek's simmering frustration. He and Niles vote against it, but the others fall in line. The motion passes.

I smile. "Perfect, I'll reach out to Adrian and let him know the good news."

54

DEREK GRAFF

I LEAN AGAINST my office door, arms crossed and eyes locked on Tessa Summers as she sits there, indignant. This blonde bimbo… Adrian's former assistant turned lowly PR director. Harry's latest "shatter the glass ceiling" project. She had the nerve to speak against me in a board meeting she had no business even attending. So, I did some digging and found her credentials all over a digital landmine: confidential records from our acquisition of Blue Rock Industries being downloaded from her company account onto an external drive without permission. Harry tried to save her, but the evidence is clear.

"You can't deny it, Summers."

She lifts her chin, a misguided look of pride in her eyes. "What are you talking about?"

I step forward, lowering my voice to a near whisper. "I've seen the news out of Maddox. I know Channing somehow found the money to buy Blue Rock's assets. And I know you stole those files to help him."

She crosses her arms and stares straight ahead, refusing to acknowledge me.

"Corporate espionage is no trivial matter, Summers. A young woman like yourself doesn't belong behind bars. Admit that Channing put you up to this, and he'll do the time people like him deserve."

Silence fills the room as the determination in her gaze hardens. "A young woman like yourself? People like him?" She mocks me. "You know what? Just do what you're gonna friggin' do, you racist prick."

With one call to the lobby, police officers move in, arresting her and carrying her out of my sight. Her colleagues freeze, whispering in shock.

But then, she looks back at me with an odd smirk playing on her face.

A few hours later, I'm on a video conference, pitching Prince Hafez of Morocco on a five-hundred-million-dollar investment in our new oil and gas fund when the door swings open like the gates of hell.

Lawrence Hadington storms in like a raging bull, filling the room with rage. He's flanked by four bodyguards who could each pass for NFL defensive linemen, but somehow, he's the largest in the group.

Hadington is a force of nature. He was a Green Beret, CIA director, Senate majority leader, Secretary of Defense to two presidents and Secretary of State to a third. Many are calling for him to run for president but he's too busy conquering nations from the private sector as a foreign policy advisor to governments and multinational corporations. There's power and influence, and then there's Lawrence "the Hawk" Hadington.

I swallow hard, as I can feel the weight of his fury from the elevator bank on the sixtieth floor, reserved for the PGC C-suite and board members. This floor can't even be accessed by guests or junior employees without special clearance from my office. But I gave none.

"Derek Graff!" he bellows from the hallway as he steps in, his voice rich with a Memphis twang, each syllable laced with incredulity and rage. "Are you outta your no-good-Central-Park-West-daddy-gave-you-a-loan-of-a-billion-dollars-and-put-a-silver-spoon-up-your-bunghole motherfuckin' mind, boy! You arrested my granddaughter?"

I can see his lips getting chapped as small droplets of spit fly out of them with every word, landing on my suit jacket.

I had no idea Tessa Summers was Lawrence Hadington's granddaughter. Someone in HR will lose their job for this.

"Are you hearin' me, Graff, or should I lend you some aid?" he screams, grabbing me by the collar, his knuckles whitening as he pulls me in.

I see my minions watching me through the glass walls as I crumble to this titan.

"M–M–Mr. Hadington, this is a misunderstand—"

"Shut your fuckin' mouth!" He releases me with a shove that sends me stumbling into my desk. "I know who you are, boy. I know about your 'investor dinners,' the drugs, the escorts, the blackmail. I know about your deal with Arjun Kodra."

My stomach drops. Every nerve in my body tightens, and I suddenly can't breathe.

Arjun Kodra was a friend of my father. Until his assassination a few months ago, he was the head of the Albanian mob in New York. His organization, Kodra Krew, has kept my LP parties stocked for years: pills, powder, escorts, and just enough hidden cameras to keep the money loyal. Their girls bring the drugs and record the leverage.

That's how I keep the capital flowing in and regulators quiet. Garrett Declan only stayed with PGC after the Volition scandal because I reminded him how fast a video of him with a barely legal escort could find its way to his wife. It's a strategy the Graffs have employed for generations, controlling the wills of men through their most debased vices.

I glance at Hadington, who's still fuming and just finished cursing me out.

"H–how do you know?" I ask.

He scoffs, pacing in anger before turning back to me, his voice near a scream. "You think you're smart enough to play on either side of the law, but not smart enough to know you shouldn't talk on the phone with the nephew of Valmir Kodra, a man on the CIA's most wanted list. Boy, I got wire taps from here to South Antarctica. How do you know?" He mimics me.

Hadington turns to one of his aides, almost chuckling but still angry. "This cocksmoker wants to know how I know about his dirty dealings."

He turns back to me. "You own companies, Graff. I own the federal government! You ever heard of an alphabet suppository?"

I hesitate, unsure if it's a rhetorical question, but he's silent, waiting.

"N–no, sir," I stammer. "I haven't."

"It's when I push the full weight of the FBI, DEA, SEC, CIA, ATF, and IRS up your motherfuckin' ass!" he screams. "The only reason you're not somebody's chubby prison girlfriend right now is on the strength of Harry P.'s reputation and the money this little outfit makes for state governments across this great land of ours. But I don't give a damn when it comes to my grandbabies. You drop those charges and have that arrest wiped clean from my Tessa's record, or I swear I'll bring this little empire of yours to the ground and then I'll make ya disappear, boy."

His bodyguards step forward, their demeanor clear that they're prepared to execute on that promise.

Panic surges through me as I pick up my phone, already scrolling to my contact at the NYPD. "I'll have the charges dropped right away."

"That's what the fuck I thought." Hadington storms out of my office.

I seethe quietly, thinking through my next steps. My plan was simple: pressure Tessa to implicate Channing in their corporate espionage conspiracy, have him arrested, and keep him far from PGC. Now, I'll have to take an alternative approach.

55

ADRIAN CHANNING

IT'S EARLY ENOUGH that the streets are still empty. I strap on my helmet, then scroll through the usual flood of emails, orders, deadlines, and site inspections. I slip the phone into my pocket and get on my bike, forcing myself to focus on the road ahead.

I pedal down the neglected streets of East Maddox, my 9mm pistol holstered to my handlebars, rattling as my tires traverse the cracked pavement. I don't love being strapped. Never did. But it's a necessary function of life on the Eastside. And life in the Palmer circle of influence.

I get a text and look down at my Apple Watch.

Bruno Pereira, Metaliga S.A.: Adrian, I just met your business partner, Charles Palmer. Very nice, gentleman.

My pulse quickens. If Charles establishes a relationship with Bruno on his own, I'm a dead man.

I leave the message unanswered, giving myself a moment to think. No need to tip my hand just yet.

I continue my ride, traveling down Rawley St. along the stretch of blues bars and jazz lounges the East Side is known for. I ride by Lorenzo's Bar & Grill, my dad's old stomping ground and the last place I saw my mother alive before he drove us into the traffic barrier coming up on my left.

Traveling down the empty road, I stare up at the tall, wide concrete industrial behemoth of a building that houses my office. It's Saturday morning, but I have a ton of work to do.

I coast toward the parking lot.

Suddenly, a van accelerates right behind me, nearly touching my rear tire. I swerve just before hitting a ditch, and then I pedal hard, barely avoiding a collision.

I dismount my bike and grab my pistol. I don't see the van anymore, but I can hear it in the distance. A quiet unease settles in as rain starts to fall. I catch a glimpse of movement to my right. Two masked men, their eyes cold and focused, and their guns leveled.

I guess Rome and Truck decided it's time to kill me.

I crouch behind a concrete divider about waist high. As they approach, I raise my gun and fire twice. They scatter for cover, but immediately a third shooter flashes behind me.

I turn and pull the trigger three times. The gunshots crack through the air, piercing him in the abdomen. Blood jumps from his chest as he hits the ground.

I have no time to register anything else when more gunfire erupts. I duck behind the barrier as bits of cement chip around me. The rain is pouring down in sheets, making it difficult to see my surroundings. My mind races as I try to assess an escape route.

And then the gunfire stops. They're reloading. I poke my head up from behind the barrier, raising my pistol. The shooters crouch behind wooden slats in the lot, steps away from me. I fire five shots before they return fire in my direction.

I duck back down for cover and ready myself to see my mother when the roar of a muscle car tears through the air before screeching to a halt. Then, the deafening cracks of rapid assault rifle fire erupt, followed by the ragged screams of men as they're hit.

And then, only the sound of rain.

"Clear!" a deep, raspy voice yells. "A.C., you good?!"

I stick my head out and see a burly Black man, average height and muscular, with a bald head and full beard. He's younger, maybe in his mid-thirties, and wearing black military fatigues. His tactical pistol is still raised with the red laser from the scope bouncing about as he scans the lot.

Beside him, there are three more similarly dressed Black men armed with assault rifles. They have their guns drawn on the last assassin, who's been shot in the arm and leg but is still alive, lying on the ground with wide eyes.

Before I can say anything, the leader moves forward. He grabs the assassin, picks him up and slams him into the wall. He frisks him and then one of the other guys drag him into the warehouse.

I stand nearly frozen, my heart still racing. The adrenaline is clouding my thoughts. I'm grateful I'm alive, but who the fuck are these guys?

"What is this?" I ask, still clutching my pistol.

"We're friends," he says, holstering his gun. "MG sent us."

"MG?" I ask. "Makari?"

I lower my gun. As I look closer, I see tattoos reading "EMSK," "Stronghold," and "Ironbridge" on the arms, necks, and hands of each of the men.

"East Madd stick together." The leader winks, extending his hand. "Demarcus Teague. Homies call me Red Dot. That's Q, Ducky, and Monsta over there."

We shake hands and walk onto the factory loading dock around the back of the building, where his crew is holding the captured assassin.

"You RF9?" I ask.

"Fuck no," Demarcus says. "Stronghold Killaz still run the Eastside."

"I haven't spoken to Makari since I was a kid. How'd he know I was here?"

Demarcus shrugs. "All I know is MG da General sent word, asked us to keep an eye out."

We walk toward the loading dock, where the assassin is seated on a stack of wooden slats, his eyes darting around before they land on Q, Ducky, and Monsta wrapping the corpses in tarps.

Demarcus steps forward with an unsettling calm. He rips open the assassin's shirt and reveals a tattoo of an Albanian symbol.

Q takes a picture of the tattoo and runs it through some kind of image recognition software on his phone. "Kodra Krew."

"Any idea why the Albanians wanna kill you, A.C.?" Demarcus asks.

I shake my head. "Not a clue." I'm not going to admit that I'm running guns for RF9, Kodra's top competitors.

Demarcus nods at Ducky, and I can tell they've done this before. Ducky runs outside to their car and moments later shows up with a black pouch. He opens it and brings out a syringe.

I raise a brow. "What is that?"

"A mixture of Midazolam and Scopolamine," Ducky says in an almost military-like cadence.

Demarcus glances at me, his voice steady as he says, "Truth serum."

Ducky inserts the needle in the assassin's upper right arm. His eyes go wide, and his pupils dilate. His breathing turns ragged as the serum takes effect, and I see the fear take hold.

"Who hired you?" Demarcus asks, a forceful edge in his voice.

Blood drips from the assassin's lip as he gasps for air. "It was some Wall Street guy."

I feel a surge of anger rise up in me. The only person on Wall Street who'd want to kill me is Derek Graff. But he already ruined my life. Why the hell would he try to have me killed?

I pull out my phone and start filming the assassin, zooming in to ensure Demarcus and his team are out of frame.

"Say the name!" Demarcus orders.

The assassin glares at us in a daze. "Derek... Derek Graff hired us to kill you."

"Why?" I shout.

The assassin gasps for breath, his voice desperate. "I don't know. Just a contract."

I turn to Demarcus. "I need him alive."

Demarcus narrows his eyes. "Respectfully, A.C., nah, we don't leave witnesses. Cut the camera, please."

As soon as I stop the recording, Demarcus raises his tactical pistol, aiming the red laser scope at the assassin's head, demonstrating why he's nicknamed 'Red Dot.' He fires and the Albanian's head snaps back as blood spatters the concrete wall behind him.

Demarcus holsters his pistol and turns back to me. "Can't have this clown running his mouth. Some of us got priors."

I nod slowly, realizing he's right. "I work for some folks who can deter the police from here."

"No need." Demarcus gives me a hard look. "This the Eastside. Maddox PD don't give a damn 'bout some gunfire round these parts."

"Fair point."

Demarcus pulls the assassin's phone from his pocket, a burner with only one contact and one text conversation showing my name, my old PGC website profile picture, and my work and home address.

We stage a photo of me lying still, eyes closed, with blood streaming from my head, and send it off with a text that reads, *It's done.*

"That should buy us some time," Demarcus says.

"Thank you, Demarcus." I shake his hand again.

"All good," he says. "MG say Adrian Channing and his people still in the family. So, Stronghold got ya back."

"And you guys haven't been taken over?" I ask. "I know EMSK used to pay dues to the Black Gods. Before RF9 hit the scene."

"Nah, we kept our independence," Demarcus says. "Got out the dope game some fifteen years ago though. We define ourselves now as a community group… vigilantes, neighborhood watch, private security, whatever you wanna call it. We protect the Eastside and the folks who call it home."

As I stand in this cold, empty factory with corpses being dismantled and disposed of all around me, I'm silently enraged by the fact that my life has become a struggle to survive as if I'm still that homeless preteen slangin' weed and pills on the project steps for MG da General and the East Maddox

Stronghold Killaz. That history that I've spent my entire adult life trying to forget... without it, I'd be dead right now.

Having just stared death in the face, I know now. Life's too short to be distant from the people I love.

56

DR. BRIANNA WRIGHT

OUTSIDE MY LIVING room window, the rain pours heavily on a black Range Rover, it's windows tinted. They don't follow Riley anymore, but they show up every week now, park down the street and just watch us. RF9 wants me to know they can hurt us at any time if I don't keep their secrets, or if we try to run with their money. They don't seem to understand we don't even have access to their money. It's all tied up in Adrian's fund.

I hear a knock on the door. I peer through the window and see Adrian. I open it and notice how awful he looks. His windbreaker is torn to shreds, he's soaked and his hands are covered in dirt. Beneath that, his skin is unusually light, almost pale and drawn, a stark contrast to his normal medium brown complexion.

"Adrian, what's going on?"

"Sorry. I should've called," he says, running a shaky hand through his disheveled dark brown beard, his tall frame slumping slightly.

The stairs creak as Riley comes down. "Dad?"

"Hey, buttercup." His deep voice quivers as he glances up.

She's sixteen and is growing into a beautiful young woman but she'll always be his buttercup just like she's still my RileyBear.

Adrian starts shifting on his feet, his eyes fixed on the floor as he drips rain all over my hardwood.

"Dad, what's wrong?"

"Nothing, Riles." He hugs her tight. "Nothing's wrong. I'm good."

Adrian's head jerks back slightly as he glances up and down at our daughter. He chuckles softly before saying, "Jesus Christ, you're almost as tall as I am... How are you?"

"I'm fine, Dad." She looks confused but, surprisingly, she isn't pulling away from the hug.

Something compels me to move closer. He reaches out and pulls me into a group hug. We're still for a moment as if we're the same family we were in Manhattan before the divorce. It's as if none of us wants to let go. When we do, we're all in tears. I'm not sure what's going on with Adrian but it's clear he needs us.

"I've been so mixed up in my own shit," he says, wiping the moisture from his eyes. "It's not an excuse. I can't say enough how sorry I am, Brianna. I've been a terrible co-parent. I'm gonna do better, I promise."

"It's okay, Adrian."

He shifts his gaze. "Riles, you still wanna go college tripping in California? We can tour the entire country, I don't care. Me, you, and your mom."

"I committed to UCLA already," she says.

"Best women's basketball program in the country right now," I add. I pushed her toward the West Coast. RF9 doesn't have much of a presence there.

"Oh shit! Full ride?" Adrian asks.

Riley nods, subtly blushing.

"Goddammit, I should've known that," Adrian says. "I'm beyond proud of you. Should we celebrate? You tell me. What can I do to celebrate you? What can I get you?"

She smiles coyly. "I'm good, Dad. I don't need anything."

"Jeez, Bri. How'd you raise such a brilliant human being?" A tearful smile comes across his face as he wipes snot from his beard.

"Therapy." I start laughing. Adrian and Riley soon start laughing with me.

"How's work going?" he asks.

"Not bad. I took a teaching job at UPenn. It's a tenured position, and I have the flexibility to open my own practice if I want."

I don't tell him I'm still quietly counseling Rome and Getz. I know Adrian's already wound tight. He doesn't need another thing to worry about.

"Is that something you want? I can help you set it up on the business side."

He notices my brow rise. If this man hears anything related to business, he'll always try to muscle in and make it his.

"Or not," he backtracks. "Just let me know how I can help."

"I'm good, Adrian. But you... you don't look good."

"Yeah, Dad, like at all." Riley's eyes move to the specks of blood we've all seemingly just noticed on his windbreaker.

"I was uh... I was in an accident just now... on my bike. Some maniac came out of nowhere and—"

"Someone hit you?" Riley's voice betrays her anger and mounting concern. "Are you okay, Dad?" She steps back, inspecting the cuts and bruises on his hands and wrists.

"I'm fine," he says. "Strangely, I've never been better. I just wanted to see you."

"Sit down, Adrian." I take his arm and lead him to the living room couch.

Riley brings him water and sits next to him, resting her head on his shoulder. She doesn't say it, but I can tell she's missed him.

57

ADRIAN CHANNING

BRIANNA LEAVES TO run errands while Riley and I sit and catch up. We're quiet at times, talking, laughing, and crying at others. I feel every bit of the distance between us. Riley moves like someone who has grown up in my absence. She's calm, composed, and much more mature than the miserable teenager I remember. Sitting here, it feels like I'm trying to catch up on a life that has evolved without me.

"You need a shave," she says.

I let out a dry laugh. "Yeah, well, it's been a hellish few months. Haven't given much thought to my physical appearance."

"That's not like you, Dad." She laughs quietly. And then a semi-awkward quiet settles between us.

"Coach Trent still have you at power forward?" I ask, breaking the silence with basketball.

"Yeah." She picks at a loose thread on her sleeve. "But the offense is fluid. I run point like most of the time."

"That's awesome, Riles. And UCLA, huh? You're going to love it there, Riles. People in LA can be kind of crazy, but it's a great city."

She shrugs, looking at me sideways. "I've been on a few visits with Mom."

"I should've been there." I sigh, leaning back against the couch. "I don't want to miss anything else, Riles."

She doesn't say anything for a minute, just stares down at her hands. Then, slowly, she says, "Okay. But Dad, you've said that before." Her words are gentle, though they carry the weight of my broken promises.

"I'm gonna work on it, Riles. I'm serious this time. Therapy, church, whatever it takes. I don't wanna lose you."

She gives me a small smile, one that isn't entirely hopeful but not hopeless either. "You're not gonna lose me, Dad." Her smile slowly fades. "I've just learned not to expect anything from you anymore."

Her words hit me hard, but I can't blame her. She's still trying to reassure me, but I can hear that quiet acceptance of disappointment. "I get it. If I were you, I wouldn't expect much from me either. But I'm gonna fix it."

After a moment, she changes the subject. "How's Josie?"

"Pretty sure I've screwed that up too," I admit, rubbing my face. "I don't even know if she'll talk to me again. I was a grade-A fuckboy to her."

"I'm not surprised." She smirks.

"Smart ass." I nudge her knee with mine, and we share a laugh that settles into another semi-awkward silence.

"You know," she says slowly, breaking it, "I used to be so angry. At you, at Mom… at everything. I'd think about running away, or just screaming until someone finally got it. But then I'd remember those stories about you growing up here after Grandma Adanna died, when Grandpa Paul was in jail. And I don't know. I realized maybe no one ever showed you how to be consistent. So how could I expect you to be?"

She looks down. Her expectations of me are shot, and even though she's giving me grace now, I know I'm the one to blame.

Then she takes my hand. "But after a while, I realized that when you're around, when we're all together, it's—it's the best… I don't know… I think I was just angry that we couldn't have that anymore. I don't even know where I'm going with this… I guess my point is, you're not someone who's easy to stay mad at."

I look at her, taking her in. My daughter is becoming an adult. She's grown into someone so wise, someone I can learn from.

"I know that me and your mom splitting up—"

"It was the right thing," she cuts in. "Mom and I have talked about it. I realize now that you two weren't your best selves with each other. I get it. And I think I'm getting to a place where I just want you both to be happy. Does Josie make you happy?"

"To be honest, Riles. This right here, being with you on this couch, just talking… This is the happiest I've been in years."

Riley smiles softly and places her head lightly on my shoulder for a moment as she asks, "But what about Josie? Do you love her?"

"I do."

"Then go to her."

"I blew it, Riles. I don't think she wants anything to do with me anymore."

"Maybe stop assuming you know what's best for the women in your life. Just try. You don't have to fix everything at once. But show up, let her know you're serious, and see what happens…"

"You're right." I rise to my feet and grab my tattered jacket. "You're always right, kiddo."

"I know," she says with a perk to her voice.

I smile, lean down, and kiss her forehead before crossing the room toward the front door.

"But Dad…"

I turn back. "Yeah, Riles?"

"Take a shower and get a haircut first."

58

ADRIAN CHANNING

I PULL UP to the Downtown Maddox location of Geraldine's Homemade, where Josie typically spends her Sundays experimenting with new recipes. I walk through the double doors into the back prep area.

There she is, in baggy purple sweats covered in vegan flour and almond milk stains, flipping through old recipe books. Even in grind mode, she's just as statuesque and serene as when I last saw her in person six months ago.

I watch her in awe for a moment, wondering if this is reckless. Truck's threat still hangs in the air, but his people don't even bother hiding anymore. They show up at the factory when it's time to re-up on guns. That's when they make their presence known; they rarely make house calls anymore. I've studied their patterns. I know the rhythm. Maybe I can rekindle my relationship with Josie under their radar, at least until I figure out a way to get out from under the Palmer's thumb.

But as we make eye contact, I can feel the chill of her demeanor before she even says a word, and my stomach twists with nerves.

"Adrian, what are you doing here?" She looks me up and down like I'm someone she's seen in a dream once. Before it turned into a nightmare.

I swallow hard and give her my best smile, the one that usually works.

"Josie," I start, my voice cracking a little. "I'm sorry."

She crosses her arms and leans against the wall. "Sorry for what? I haven't seen you in months. I've barely heard from you outside of our quarterly calls. And even in those it's just 'yes,' 'no', 'I agree.' You've made it clear how you want this relationship to work."

I step closer to her, but she kisses her teeth and walks into the freezer room without another look my way.

I follow like a guilty schoolboy. "I know I've been absent. Work's been a mess. I've been putting out fires left and right."

She rifles through tubs of ice cream before her eyes briefly flick to me. "Yeah, well, that's what you do, right, Mr. Rainmaker? Mr. 'god of PE.' Jet in, jet out. No warning. No explanation."

"I know I messed up. And I'm not trying to make excuses. I just–I got caught up. Things spiraled in a way I couldn't control. I thought maybe it was better to stay away than to complicate things."

Her laugh is short and bitter. "Complicate things? Adrian, sleeping with me, leading me to believe you wanted to build a future together, and then randomly ending things and disappearing for months… That didn't simplify anything. It just made this whole thing really shitty."

I can't help but smirk for a moment. I love it when she cusses, though I hate that I'm the reason for it.

"This isn't a joke, Adrian."

My smirk turns into a wince. "I do want a future with you, Josie. That's never been the question. I think I just convinced myself that I'd drop the ball if I tried to do everything at once—be with you, show up for Riley, for Allen, fix my career. So I picked the one thing I thought I could control. But all I did was push away the only parts that made any of it matter. I see that now. And I don't want to keep getting it wrong."

I can see her digesting the sentiment.

I take a deep breath. "I disrespected you, and I'm so sorry. If I need to spend the rest of my life making it up to you, I will, because I'm not going anywhere."

I take her hand in mine. She shakes her head slightly but doesn't pull away.

Her gaze softens, though she still looks angry. "Adrian, you know I don't do drama. I don't need someone who's here one minute and disappears the next. My life is my son and the brand. I need stability. Not this. Whatever this is."

She pulls her hand away.

"I know." I lean in closer. "And I can give you that. I want to. I just want to pick up where we left off. You and I were building something amazing. And I don't mean the company. You were building that just fine before I came along. I just want to be with you. I want to be your partner in business and everything else. I'm all in, and I won't leave you again."

She looks at me like she's weighing every word. For a moment, I think she might just tell me to get out. But then, her eyes soften, just a fraction.

"You're all in, huh?" Her tone is still wary, though there's a trace of something warmer. "I've heard that before."

"Josie, I'm crazy about you. I fall asleep and wake up with you on my mind. When I'm working on a deal, I wonder what you would think about it, what insightful and fresh perspective you would bring. When I'm on my bike, I picture you pedaling next to me, leading me down a path I've never been down, reminding me to enjoy the journey. When I'm eating, I think about feeding you a bite and watching your nose wrinkle as you register the flavors."

She blushes softly.

"Josie, I am so deeply and completely in love with you. And like I said, I'm ready to spend the rest of my life proving it if I must."

I reach into my pocket and feel my mother's wedding ring. I usually wear it on a chain around my neck and under my shirt, but it snapped when my bike crashed. It's the only physical thing I still have of hers. When I proposed to Brianna, I told myself she deserved an extravagant diamond, but in reality, I couldn't bring myself to let go of this one. But here, staring at Josie, I can't help but feel like my mother would want her to have it.

I wasn't expecting to do this, but I can't help myself. I need Josie back. I pull out the ring, take a knee, and present it to her. So much for keeping things under the radar.

Her lips twitch as she sees the modest diamond ring, as if she's holding back a smile.

"It was my mother's."

"Jesus, Adrian." She wipes away a subtle tear. "Are you serious?"

I reach for her hand again, my touch light but deliberate. "As serious as a billion-dollar buyout."

She laughs. There's a long pause as she stares at our hands. The silence stretches between us. Then, slowly, her fingers curl around mine.

"But I'll give it all up. CCP, my companies, my career. It means nothing to me without you. I know it's crazy after everything but… will you marry me?"

She searches my face, her hesitation lingering just a moment longer before a small, genuine smile breaks through.

"I can't believe I believe you," she murmurs, now fully in tears. "I'm not saying yes… I'm not saying no… I'm saying I'm willing to give you another chance."

"I'll take it." I pull her in, kissing her like it's the first time all over again. It deepens and she jumps into my arms, wrapping her legs around my waist. I lose myself in her embrace, and this time, I know this is where I'm meant to be.

I won't fuck this up. And no one is going to stand in my way.

59

ADRIAN CHANNING

On Monday morning, I head into work at Ironbridge with a new awareness. The snow falls in thick, heavy flakes as I spot Demarcus and his crew in their black '72 Buick Electra, windows tinted. They're watching the factory from across the street. I've seen the car parked there for a while. I always thought it just belonged to one of the factory workers.

I pull my coat tight and start toward them, my boots crunching against the snow. As I get closer, Demarcus cracks the passenger side window.

I crouch down. "What's goin' on, fellas? Wanna come inside? Grab some coffee?"

After a second, Demarcus nods, gesturing for one of his crew to stay behind as we make our way inside.

Demarcus, Q, and Monsta follow me through the warehouse, where just thirty-six hours ago we killed and disposed of three Albanian hitmen.

We step into my office where a space heater in the corner warms the room. I pour four mugs of coffee. Demarcus takes a seat, his eyes scanning the space. I start to speak, but he raises a hand, silencing me, as Q wands a small black device over every item in my office.

The bug detector emits a high-pitched beep as he sweeps it over a vintage metal desk clock, crafted to resemble the Downtown Maddox skyline. Charles gave it to me when we closed the Josie investment. When we opened

Ironbridge, he had a team transfer my belongings from PalmerSpaces for me. I thought he was being nice, trying to smooth over the relationship. Of course not. He was keeping tabs, making sure his listening device stayed close to me.

Demarcus drops the clock and stomps it flat under his black Timberland boots. Q finishes the sweep and gives the all clear.

"We can get this place secure for you, A.C.," Demarcus says. "Advanced anti-listening technology, encrypted surveillance, real-time monitoring, and we've got soldiers who can patrol each of your factories."

I raise an eyebrow, impressed. "I think I can find room in the budget for that."

Demarcus sits across from me, and his eyes never stop scanning.

"So, you've been watching my family?" I ask. "I saw the Buick at my ex-wife's house."

Demarcus takes a slow sip of coffee. "We keep our distance. They don't know we follow. My units know how to blend in."

"What have you seen?"

"RF9 soldiers on occasion, maybe once a week. They'll follow Riley to school, sports, and back. They don't interact, but my team stays ready to intervene just in case. Dr. Wright sees RF9 on the regular, mostly youth patients, but we've also picked up Rome Palmer and RF9 Getz entering her office at UPenn on separate occasions."

"Jesus..."

Brianna didn't know about my demand that the Palmers shut down her youth facility. Knowing how much she cares about those kids, I get why she's still seeing them at her new job. But Rome was supposed to stay away. Clearly, that was another lie.

"Demarcus, I can't thank you enough for looking out."

"It's what we do," he says.

"Tell me about your team."

"We run about a hundred deep, some former military like me, but mostly ex-bangers just lookin' for a new way. We operate patrols in units of four, taking a surgical approach to security. Threats come in, we neutralize. Measured. Precise. We don't go in guns blazing unless necessary."

"How do you vet a threat?"

"Advanced surveillance. Biometrics. We can hack into phone networks, scrape social media data, and track movements with GPS down to the foot. Every person in our perimeter gets tagged. Facial scans and voice prints. We can determine who's a threat before they even make a move. And when we lock in on one, we don't hesitate. But we're still building out our capabilities. We're workin' on facial recognition software, heat mapping, drones with night vision, and real-time satellite feeds."

"And the physical aspect?"

Demarcus sets his mug down and looks at me with sharpened focus. "All my people are trained in armed and hand-to-hand combat. When we shoot, we shoot to kill. But our focus is threat elimination. No brutality, no unnecessary casualties."

"How do you fund this operation?"

"Donations mostly. We've got a few private security contracts with local businesses. But we need to grow. Hire more soldiers with clean records. More artillery, better tech. The only reason you had to take down that first shooter on your own was because our drone was broken. We caught the van tailing you too late. Plan is to build this into a real business with investors so that doesn't happen again."

I nod as my mind maps the angles. "It makes sense."

"MG said that even when y'all were kids, you were the best businessman on the block. Would you be down to partner up?"

"The wheels are already spinning, Demarcus."

Private security can be a lucrative industry with the right strategy and connections. Celebrities and high-net-worth individuals are increasingly turning to tech-driven security services for their protection. Trusted, rapid-response private security can command premium fees, especially in industries where personal safety is non-negotiable. Like mine, apparently.

Beyond that, a partnership with the Stronghold Killaz feels right. Makari was both a big brother to me and my first business partner. I technically came up with the name "Stronghold," so it feels only fitting that I reclaim it and help with their new mission. A private security company operated by reformed gang members looking to protect their community from crime would make socially progressive investors salivate. I can invest in their expansion and help them get more contracts.

"Alright, we can make a deal. But Demarcus, if you're gonna work with me, I'll warn you now. As you've seen, my enemies are dangerous and unpredictable. Things might get a bit complicated. But you ask anybody who's ever been in the trenches with me, they'll tell you. I wouldn't ask you to do anything I wouldn't do myself. And when I win, you win. That's my word."

Demarcus smirks as if he's recollecting a fond memory. "My boys and I grew up on the stories of MG da General and AC 'the man Always in Control'. How y'all practically started this gangsta shit in Maddox. Built it on a code of honor, respect, and community."

"That's an exaggeration, brother. Makari was the gangster. I was the hustler." My voice is soft, reminiscing about memories I've long locked away.

"Doesn't make much of a difference as far as my generation is concerned. You've earned the right to my loyalty. MG vouches for you, and my respect for him goes to the grave."

I place my hand on my chest where my EMSK tattoo is and tilt my head down slowly as an acknowledgment of his respect. I never thought I'd be back in this world governed by street codes and gang ties, but here I am.

Demarcus continues, his tone getting angrier. "These RF9 clowns are using your little girl and baby momma to handle the problems of men. There's no more honor in this game. Bodies need to drop, and Stronghold ready for whatever comes with that. But if we're going to war against the Black Gods, you should pay MG a visit."

The drive to Riverville Correctional is long and quiet, the snow coming down harder as we move toward upstate Pennsylvania. Demarcus sits in the passenger seat, calm as ever, while Monsta drives.

I peer out of the back window as the bridge opens up to reveal the view. Factories and rusted steel rise against the river. Past that, Downtown Maddox buzzes with blocks of color, energy, and rhythm. People moving fast and talking loudly. Bars with music spilling out even on a snowy Monday afternoon, embodying the motto of Mad Dog City: *Work hard, play hard, love hard*. Maybe it's the new awareness, but I can't believe I forgot how much I love this place.

After a while, I ask, "So, how'd you link with MG? He must've gone inside when you were a little kid."

"He's my uncle," Demarcus says. "My momma's little brother."

I'm quiet for a moment before I make a realization. "Wait. You're Deronda's baby boy?"

"Yessir."

"Holy shit, I remember when you were born. I had a huge crush on your mom. I was mad as hell at your pops."

"Guess that makes the two of us," he says. "Wherever the fuck he at…"

"How's your mom doing?"

He's quiet for a second and then says, "She been better."

I can tell he doesn't want to talk about her so I leave it alone. An awkward silence ensues before I break it. "You said you served?"

"Two tours in the Marines. You?" he asks. "I saw the way you handled that nine milli'."

I laugh. "Nah, that's just East Maddox muscle memory I guess."

Demarcus chuckles, loud and deep. "East Maddox muscle memory, I like that. Me, I came home from Iraq and couldn't find a job worth a damn, so I got down with the Killaz. Put in a lot of work behind this shit." He taps an EMSK tattoo on his inner forearm.

"How'd y'all manage to transition?" I ask.

"Got tired of going to war over shit that benefitted everybody but the warrior, everybody but our people. At some point, I looked around and saw I was one of the last OGs still active in this shit. So I took leadership but lost interest in protecting turf on blocks we don't own."

"Got tired of the violence?"

"Nah, I ain't never had a problem with violence," he says. "Nations are built on conflict. It's necessary for growth. And some folks just deserve to die. Perhaps in a way, we all do." There's a distant tone in his voice, as if he's recounting every kill, every lost soldier.

"But when RF9 started takin' over hoods left and right, killin' women and children to keep their enemies at bay, I had no choice but to strap my boots again. After a bloody winter in 2014, I negotiated a peace treaty with Mac Palmer. We got out the dope game, gave them the market share, and RF9 agreed to leave our kids alone. No more attacks. No RF9 recruiting on the Eastside. Our boys could go to school, play sports, live without being pressured into pullin' a trigger. The Killaz had no choice but to think differently. We ran these streets so we know 'em better than anyone. We reformed, became protectors."

"Security specialists," Monsta says, laughing to himself.

I'm almost speechless. These guys aren't just rebuilding the community, they're fighting for it, pulling it up piece by piece.

"And the cops?" I ask.

Demarcus scoffs. "They don't give a damn 'bout the Eastside. The few not on RF9's payroll were happy to see us take over, keep the violence down. If they don't have to get their hands dirty, they don't care."

It makes sense in a twisted way. Corruption runs deep in this city, and if Demarcus and his guys are doing the work no one else would, who's stopping them?

• • •

Makari's already waiting for us in the visitation room. I haven't seen him since the night things went sideways when we were kids. As I approach the table unsure of what I'm walking into or how he feels about my lack of contact, one thing is clear, I'm about to face a part of my past I thought I buried long ago.

He's still larger than life, in his late forties now, but looks ten years younger, thick in the shoulders and built like a brick wall. He sits across the table with a white kufi resting on his bald head, his thick salt-and-pepper beard spilling over the collar of his blue jumpsuit. His eyes scan the room with the quiet authority of a man who's survived decades of animal captivity, now cloaked in a calm, almost spiritual dominance. He wears his time well, his face hardened, the kind of face that's seen too much but never cracked.

"Been a long time, A.C." His voice is gravelly and there's a scowl on his face.

A thick silence settles between us as he looks at me, sizing me up My pulse thuds a little harder, like I'm bracing for words I don't want to hear.

But then, he breaks into a grin, his whole face softening as he stands and wraps me in a bear hug, all the tension evaporating in a wave of relief.

"My young nigga!" he bellows. "Not so young anymore. You look strong, brother. All things considered."

I hug him back, feeling the strength in his arms and in our brother-hood. "I could say the same for you, Makari."

The "No Physical Contact" sign is clear as day, but no guard says a word. They don't even flinch. He rules this facility. You can see it in the way they barely look him in the eye, in the way the other prisoners watch him. He doesn't need to speak to hold the room.

We sit down and catch up for a bit. I learn about the history I escaped. Turns out incarceration never stopped Makari. He runs everything: drugs, cigarettes, porn, alcohol, whatever people need in here. Guards are on his payroll, and other inmates are either loyal or too scared to move against him.

"I heard about your situation with those brothers from the Southside," he says.

"Yeah, I got a few situations going on right now. I appreciate the support you sent."

"Red Dot and his boys are as solid as they come. But I might be able to help you out even further."

"How so?"

"You ever heard the name Russell Gates?"

I shake my head. "Doesn't ring a bell."

"Russell was number one in here until a few months ago. He still got a grip on some parts, but that's slippin'. We've been in what you might call a power struggle. I could've got to him and finished this by now, but I've stayed my hand."

I raise an eyebrow, curious as to what this prison beef has to do with me. MG never hesitated when it came to getting rid of competition. He wasn't the type to drag things out unless there was a reason.

He leans in, his voice lowered. "Turns out, Russell ain't just any old prison gangsta. He's got ties. Big ties. Those brothers you've been dealin' with? They his sons."

"You're talking about Jerome Palmer? Big Palm?"

"Jerome Palmer. Russell Gates. One and the same."

"He's dead."

"Nah, A.C., he ain't. He's doin' life in here just like I am. When their gun pipeline got shut down on the outside, RF9 dope stopped flowin' in this bitch. So, Big Russell's money stopped. You remember all that cash you put on my books when you started pilin' up that Wall Street bread?"

"I do."

"I never touched it," Makari says. "I let it stack up, played those stock tips you gave me back then. When I saw my opening, I took it and traded it in. Bought out his guards from under him. Bought some secrets as well. He came for me and missed. I hit back, took out his lieutenants, most of his protection, then took over his cell blocks."

Makari grins, watching my reaction. "I could've had the man taken care of completely, but then your pops gave me a call, told me what was goin' on and asked if I could help."

"My dad called you?"

"Yeah," Makari says, nodding and chuckling lightly. "Shiiiet, I miss that old dude, man."

I raise an eyebrow. "He mentioned you two shared a cell block during his last bid. Think I was still at Harvard then. Didn't realize you got close."

"Yeah, he helped me broker an arrangement with some folks I couldn't exactly be seen breakin' bread with. In here, it can be very helpful to have a white man in yo crew who love Black folk more than his own." He lets out a hearty laugh. "Anyways, it ain't like I needed convincing to help out my little brotha, but your pops made a strong case for why you needed a hand."

I resent my father more than I can express in words but that call saved my life. And I'm not sure what to do with that.

Makari leans forward again, his voice lowering even more. "A.C., you gotta use Big Palm. But you gotta be quick, and you gotta be smart. When you're ready, you let me know and I'll send the message the Stronghold way. It ain't pretty but sometimes when they send fire your way, you gotta send it back."

I didn't expect to find leverage here, not like this.

"Why are you doing this for me?" I ask. "After everything that went down."

He glances around, then locks eyes with me. "I know what they say about niggas who get locked up young. Resentment, self-pity, despair. I felt it all at one point. Then I got over it. I don't blame you for where I'm at."

"Yeah, but if I had vetted that fuckin' buyer—"

"Stop," he says, sternly, glancing at the surveillance cameras overhead. "I marked my place in this world long before that deal went south those years ago. I pulled the triggers that killed those people, not you. You were a kid, and you did what you was supposed to. You got out. And even though I ain't seen your high-yella ass in nearly thirty years, you still showed love with the dollaz and cents. You ain't have to do that."

"All these years, I felt like I turned my back on you, on the Stronghold, on Ironbridge."

Makari shakes his head emphatically. "Let me tell you something, A.C. Stronghold was never about being kingpins of the city. It was about making sure our kids ate and survived long enough to try somethin' different. You did that. All I ask is that you help my nephew and his crew continue that mission. Put 'em on business the way only Adrian Channing knows how."

I leave the correctional facility with new leverage against the Palmers that I need to use carefully.

60

DEREK GRAFF

THIS MEETING NEEDS to end.

Lipstein, my personal attorney, sits to my left, flipping through his notes with smug precision. Schwartz, my divorce lawyer, sits on my right, wearing that cautious expression that all lawyers wear when they're giving you useless information that won't stop the vultures from circling. At this point, their words are almost as nauseating as they are repetitive. For a year, Michelle and I have been fighting over my assets.

"PGC's purchase of your five percent stake has been finalized," Lipstein says. "While we're happy to bill you, I have to be honest. Suing now to reverse that transaction has a low probability of success."

"Once the divorce is final, the proceeds from the sale will be released from escrow," Schwartz adds. "You're looking at a multi-billion-dollar payout, even after splitting with your—"

"Shut up." My voice is low but sharp.

My hands grip the armrests of my chair, the leather creaking under the pressure as my heart rate slowly increases. "Hand half of it over to my succubus of a soon-to-be ex-wife? I'd rather burn it all to the ground than let anyone think they can push me out of *my* firm."

Not Harry, not my wife, not Hadington, and definitely not Channing. He's a dead duck. Final and confirmed. I wish I could frame that photograph the Albanian sent me and hang it on my office wall.

"This isn't about the money," I clarify, mostly to myself. "It's about the next four decades. File the suit. I want my shares back."

Schwartz exchanges a glance with Lipstein. They don't get it. None of them do. PGC isn't just a private equity firm to me; it's my birthright. And I won't stand idly by while Harry takes it from me and gives it to some thug. She thinks that making PGC the first mega firm to be Black-owned somehow compensates for her legacy of corporate treachery. Please. She's just a power-hungry son of a bitch like the rest of us. But after this meeting, I'll hire Kodra's guys to take her out like they did Channing.

Lipstein leans forward. "If the divorce court rules in your favor, then you may be able to file an unconscionability claim against PGC to unwind the buyback, but I'd query what an internal lawsuit at the top would signal to your investors and the market at large—"

"Lipstein, stop talking." I can feel the pressure building behind my eyes as the walls of my office start to close in. The air feels heavy, as if it's pressing down on me. My heart's pounding, faster and faster, and my vision is subtly blurring.

"I need some air," I mutter, standing abruptly.

I don't even look at them as I walk out to my personal office terrace, already loosening my tie. The cold breeze hits me as soon as I step outside, but it doesn't help. I lean over the railing, staring down at the streets so far below. It feels like I'm about to fall.

I pull back from the edge, wiping sweat from my forehead. I need to get out of here. Away from the lawyers, the contracts, the divorce settlements and lawsuits, all of it. I head for the elevator, barely registering the sound of my assistant calling after me.

The city streets feel more real. Grounded. The cold air wraps around me, clearing my head as I start to walk. As I move down the sidewalk, trying to calm my breathing and force the panic down, I can't shake the feeling of eyes watching me. I'm used to paranoia. It comes with the territory. But this is different. This feels real.

And then I see them. Two tall, muscular Black guys, both wearing tight black shirts and cargo pants like military operatives. The one on the left has broad shoulders, his arms bulging under his sleeves, his expression blank behind sunglasses that look like goggles. The other has dreadlocks tied back, and his eyes are locked on me.

My instincts are telling me to run, but I know better. Running will only speed up the inevitable. These guys aren't amateurs, and I'm obviously not going to outrun them given their youth and... persuasion.

I duck into an alley. My pace quickens as I try to think, to strategize. But every glance over my shoulder shows them closer, stalking me like wolves stalking prey. My pulse throbs in my ears, and for the first time since boarding school hazing, I feel the cold grip of fear around my throat.

I veer down another alley leading to the park. If I can just get lost in the crowd, I might have a chance. But my chest is tightening, my breath growing shallower. My legs keep moving, slower now. They're still following me, closing in.

Panic continues to surge through me. Who could these guys be? I know Harry wants me out. My father told me she's had more than one of her enemies buried. But Harry beat me. I have no moves against her. I'm not a threat. Perhaps Lawrence Hadington got bored and decided to take his revenge for having his granddaughter arrested. Perhaps it's one of my investors, a target of my blackmailing, but none of them have the stones to make a move like this. I'm at a loss.

I glance around, hoping for help, but the alley is empty. My heart pounds faster, the panic crawling up the back of my neck. I glance back and don't see them. Maybe, this was all in my head.

I see the end of the alleyway and start to jog. But as I reach the street, a black sedan pulls in front of me, blocking my exit. The door opens just as the two men reappear behind me.

One of them has his hand on my shoulder before I can react, pushing me forward with crushing force. I struggle, my hands flailing for anything to grab onto, but the second guy sends an uppercut into my stomach, knocking the wind out of me. I gasp, the air rushing out of my lungs as they stuff me into the backseat of the car.

"Let go of me!" I shout, but my voice is hoarse and useless.

The dreadlocked one gets in after me. The car eases forward and then stops as the second assailant enters on the other side, pinning me in the middle. They frisk me, take my phone, and then raise it to my face, unlocking it. They then bind my hands, gag me, and place a hood over my head, plunging me into darkness. I squirm, but they're too strong.

The car doors slam shut. The adrenaline surges, every muscle in my body tenses, and my heart pounds in my chest so hard it hurts. I'm trapped, unable to see or hear anything but the rumble of the engine and my own frantic breathing.

The car speeds up, accelerating through the streets. We take a series of twists, presumably through the city, then hit a long stretch of road that feels like highway. The minutes turn into an hour, maybe two, maybe three. The car rocks and sways with each bump in the road. I try to calm myself, to think. I'm not dead yet. That's something.

Finally, the car stops. I have no idea how far we've gone, or in which direction. The sudden silence after the long drive makes my blood freeze. I hear the doors open, and rough hands yank me out of the car. My feet scrape against dirt and gravel as I'm dragged, and the cold air bites through my suit jacket.

I stumble, nearly falling, but they hold me upright and shove me forward. I still can't see a thing and have no idea where we are, other than that we're likely far away from where anyone can hear me scream.

We enter a structure of some sort, and I'm pushed down into a chair, the metal cold against my body. My hands are still tied, and the hood is still on, suffocating me with the smell of sweat and burnt metal. The seconds stretch into eternity, the silence oppressive, until finally, the hood is yanked off.

I blink, the sudden brightness blinding me. When my vision clears, I'm in the middle of a warehouse floor.

And then, like a vision from hell, Adrian Channing steps out from the dark of the back office. I can hardly see his face, but there's a menacing look in his eyes, something that makes my stomach churn. The fear hits me like a wave, so visceral I can taste it. I freeze at the sight of him, a ghost come to life. His presence twists in my stomach like a tight knot. How can he be here, alive and well?

My mind scrambles for a way out, but there is none. The two men who abducted me stand behind him. One holds a pistol, the other a shotgun, both standing silent like executioners waiting for their cue. A third man, also with dreadlocks but skinnier and younger, stands off to the side, unzipping a black pouch.

"You know why you're here." Channing's voice is unnervingly calm.

I swallow, my mouth dry, but I force myself to speak. "I don't know what you're talking about." My voice cracks, betraying me. I sound weak and helpless.

"Cut the bullshit," Adrian snaps, stepping closer. "You framed me, ruined my career, smeared my name, and then tried to kill me. Are you out of your fuckin' mind, Derek?"

"You're insane," I hiss, though even I don't believe the words. My chest tightens. "You have no proof. And soon the authorities will track me here."

"No one knows you're here," he says. "We turned off location data on your phone and emailed your assistant with instructions to clear your schedule because you're going off the grid on a wellness getaway, which the whole firm knows is just code for one of your LP sex and cocaine retreats."

He pulls out a phone and shows me a video of the Albanian hitman I hired. The idiot says my name on tape, for the love of God.

Channing steps back, and the third goon brings forward a syringe and jabs me in the arm with it. The moment the needle leaves my skin, I feel an unnatural warmth creeping through my veins. They're drugging me.

"You've taken this way too far, Derek, but I'm prepared to end it," Channing says.

He pulls my cell phone out of his pocket and shows me my "Hidden" folder. After a moment, he's swiping through dozens of photos and videos of me partying with PGC investors, politicians, and bureaucrats, taking drugs and engaging in certain lascivious acts. He's found all of the blackmail ammunition that I keep on file.

"I recognize quite a few of these folks, Derek." The smugness in his voice is making my heart beat even faster.

And then he shows me the folder on my phone titled "Niles Files", and in it are dozens of PDFs of draft articles about PGC portfolio companies alleging some very unpleasant illegalities, dating back to the eighties.

Child Labor Nightmare: PGC-Backed Company, Condura Chocolates, Exploiting Minors in Overseas Factories

PGC-Appointed Studio Executives Caught in Trafficking Scandal, Embezzling Millions from Gilded Pictures for Underage Prostitutes

Thirty Dead, No Charges: How Holliman Agrochemical Hid a Toxic Leak. And the Private Equity Firm That Backed It

And then, emails to Niles Tannenbaum asking him to have his news outlets bury them and replies from him agreeing to do so.

"I've already uploaded the contents of this phone to my encrypted drive," Channing says, "and I have emails drafted to Nora Hendricks at the New Journal and Senator Marcia Calderon. I haven't attached these files yet, but I will—"

"Don't," I rasp.

"I can bury you with what's on this phone, Derek."

"No, please don't."

"Then, we're going to make a deal," he says, pulling up a metal folding chair.

"I'll give you anything you want. Name it."

He turns the folding chair around and sits with his forearms resting on the metal backrest.

"I want your confession. I know you planted drugs on me. I know you had me pushed out of PGC, and then you hired someone to kill me. I want to hear you admit it, and I want to know why. And then you're going to pay me the thirty two million dollars I'm owed, and we'll forget any of this ever happened."

"B–But..." I can feel myself stammering. "Come on, Channing. Let's be reasonable—"

The stout, bald, bearded one cocks his shotgun and barks, "Speak!"

My breath comes in short, shallow gasps, my vision blurring. My lips twitch, but I can't stop the words, the entire truth spilling out, slowly but almost uncontrollably.

"I needed you out of the way, okay? I needed to be chairman. So, I had cocaine planted on you at the Volition IPO party. I called the cops and had you arrested."

"No," Channing snaps. "I was at PGC for a long time. I remember when our old CFO drove his car into a fucking police cruiser after Harry's Christmas party in the Hamptons. He was arrested on a DWI and wasn't fired. Like me, he didn't disclose it until your security team found it during an internal audit."

"You're right." I suddenly feel an unnatural urge to tell the truth. "The arrest by itself wouldn't have been enough. I needed to prove you had a drug problem that caused the firm a massive loss."

Channing squints as if he's in disbelief. "Volition?"

"I leaked Bing's operation to the New Journal."

"What?" Channing blurts, his eyes wide. "Why the fuck would you do that?"

I hesitate, still fighting what I've surmised is some sort of chemical truth serum the dreadlocked baboon stuck me with.

Channing unholsters a black pistol and holds it over the chair's back-rest. He doesn't point it at me. He just holds it loosely in his hand, letting me know how comfortable he is with it.

"Derek, I swear to God, I will leak these photos right now and watch PGC crumble right here with you. And then I'll fucking kill you."

"I always knew you were a thug."

His eyes settle on mine as he cocks the pistol. "I am whatever I need to be, Derek."

"I had a deal with the Albanians," I spit out. "Kodra Krew supplied my parties with girls and drugs; they'd record hidden footage and give it to me to keep LPs and regulators in line. Two weeks before Volition went public, Arjun Kodra told me he wanted to short the IPO. He threatened to expose my blackmail scheme if I didn't help him crash the stock price."

"That's why Tim Rouchard said you were in the office for some bullshit 'portfolio company audit'?" Channing asks. "You were just sniffing around for issues. That's why you told him to bury his suspicions. We take the company public, the scandal breaks, Wall Street reacts negatively… the stock crashes, and your Albanian friends make money on their short."

I nod slowly, trying my best to clear the daze in my head. "I later learned that Kodra's plan was two-fold. He didn't just short the stock, but he used me as an instrument to have Blue Rock exposed and its facility shut down by the FBI…"

"Killing RF9's supply chain," Channing finishes. "And the Albanians take control of the arms market."

A light chuckle escapes me. "I'd be angrier if I didn't appreciate the genius in that deception."

"Do you know how many lives were ruined over this?" Channing barks. "An innocent kid I put in Bing's office was killed over this shit, and Tim hasn't been heard from in over a year. All because you told him to bury what he knew, and he did. That's what made the feds think he was involved. That's why he cooperated with them. Your bullshit put him on RF9's hit list."

"An unintended consequence."

He shakes his head. "I still don't understand why you'd take that kind of risk. You cost your own firm billions in cash and reputational value. PGC might not have survived Volition."

"Bullshit," I snap. "My father built that firm to last. I knew PGC would survive the losses, but the scandal would apply enough pressure to get you ousted. And enough to force Harry into retirement."

"Clearing your path to chairman," Channing says, scoffing. "And it didn't even work. I know Harry killed your little coup."

I feel my rage returning. "She wouldn't have if my cunt wife didn't divorce me. Kudos, by the way. Didn't think you'd make good on that threat."

"That was Harry's work. She's the one who told your wife about your dirty deeds and convinced her to go after your shares. Had nothing to do with me."

The sharp heat of rage crawls up my spine as the bastard's words settle in. I can feel my chest tightening with every passing moment.

"Even if she hadn't," Channing continues, "Harry controls the board and the LPs worship her."

"That's why I had Niles hire a pack of digital influencers, social media bloggers, AI bots—whatever you call them—anyone who could make noise. The goal was to drown that old whore in a cancel campaign, keep public sentiment negative, and create a distraction that would shake the firm's faith in her."

Channing's eyes suddenly widen as his voice elevates. "None of this explains why you tried to fucking kill me, Derek! I need the truth."

"Because Harry and the board wanted to bring you back and give you my birthright after everything."

"They voted to bring me back?" he murmurs, as if he can't believe it.

"So, yes," I snap, "I paid the last standing Kodra soldiers a few bucks to hunt down your meaningless Black head and hang you!"

Channing pauses for a moment, flashes a smirk, and then turns to his goon. "Cut the camera."

The man presses a button on his phone. I hear the sound of mechanical whirring. I look up to the rafters and see a surveillance camera powering down.

"Hey… Hey you were filming?" I ask. "Thought we just made a deal. I tell you the truth, you keep this quiet—"

"Just like I had a deal with PGC." He stands and slides his gun into the back of his waistband. "The deal that was supposed to pay me thirty two mil for ten years of my hard work. The payment you stalled, so you could frame me and put me out on my ass with nothing."

"That was Harry's call," I mutter. "She had me delay your distribution so she could convince you to stay. I would've much rather had you take your money and left PGC."

Channing leans in. His face is inches from mine as he studies me. "It doesn't really make a difference at this point, Derek. PGC's board is going to see those files and this footage. Well, a heavily edited version of it, but I'm sure it'll be enough to get you terminated for cause and ousted from ownership."

A gasp escapes me before I can contain it. My voice is a breathless murmur. "I–I–I'll pay you—"

"Knowing Harry," he continues over me, "she'll keep it quiet to avoid the media storm, so you probably won't even be arrested. But if I ever again hear of you speaking my fucking name, I'll send everything I have to the cops, the media, Senator Calderon. You'll lose everything—your birthright, your reputation, and your freedom."

The finality in his voice makes the air in my lungs seize. I've lost. Completely.

Channing's goon unties me, and as he picks me up by the arm, every muscle in my body falls limp. I crumple against the concrete floor. Sharp pains shoot through my knees as I catch myself. I gasp for breath, but my lungs burn as I try to process the humiliation, the defeat.

My hands tremble, and my vision blurs as I watch their figures fade into darkness. The sound of their boots crunching against the floor is drowned out by the deafening roar of my heartbeat. I reach for my throat, trying to catch my breath, but something's wrong.

Pain explodes in my chest, sharp and relentless, like a vice squeezing tighter and tighter. I double over, clutching at my shirt, but the pain only intensifies, radiating down my left arm, paralyzing me. My breath comes in ragged gasps, each one more desperate than the last.

I can hear Channing's panicked and profane voice. "What the fuck is happening?"

But the world around me continues to darken at the edges, as if the ground itself is pulling me down.

No. Not here. Not like this.

I try to stand, but my legs buckle beneath me. My mind races, scrambling for a way out, for something, anything to hold onto, but all I can feel is the crushing weight in my chest. My pulse hammers too fast, and my heart struggles under the strain.

I sprawl on the floor, my body convulsing as pain overwhelms me. I can feel the cold concrete against my face, the taste of dust on my tongue, but everything else is fading. The air feels thin, my fingers claw at the ground, but they're growing limp.

I think of everything I've worked for, everything I've fought for. But none of it matters.

The pain surges one last time, ripping through my chest like fire, before everything goes dark.

61

ADRIAN CHANNING

"He's dead, A.C.," Demarcus says, calm as ever. "Looks like a heart attack."

"Fuck." I freeze as he inspects Derek's body lying still on the floor of this abandoned Baltimore warehouse. It's a storage location I secured for RF9's gun deliveries, rural and secluded.

This wasn't supposed to happen. The plan was to scare him and extract a confession on tape that would corroborate the video of his hired gun. It would trigger an investigation and force PGC's board to terminate him.

Demarcus takes a deep breath and kneels down, checking Derek's pulse one last time. "We need to move fast."

He's right. I try to shake the fog from my brain. If anyone finds out about this, we're all going right back to Riverville, but not as visitors.

"What do you propose?" I ask.

Demarcus stands up, his eyes focused, a calm determination settling over him. "I know a man with an incinerator nearby. We'll dust him and spread the ashes in the river." He turns to Q, Ducky, and Monsta. "Strip him, burn his clothes, and the car. And get the bleach."

I nod, the fog starting to lift as the crew cleans up the mess. Strangely, my fear lasts only a moment after I realize Derek is actually dead. I've already lured Tim Rouchard to his murder and organized an illegal arms production.

Then I shot and killed a guy, kidnapped another, and now, I'm likely guilty of felony murder. I'm escalating in a major way.

My phone rings. It's Josie.

I step outside, forcing myself to calm down. "Hello, my love."

"Hey, baby." Her voice is soft and sweet as usual. "What time do you think you'll be over? I made lobster. I was gonna open a bottle of wine, but figured if you're close, I'll wait."

Shit. It's getting late, and I'm in Baltimore, a three-hour drive from Maddox.

"That sounds delicious, but I'm sorry, babes, I should've texted. I'm chasing a deal right now in the city and have a meeting here in the morning. I'll grab a hotel and take the train back tomorrow."

"Oh." She sounds dissapointed. "Okay, yeah, that would have been nice to know."

Fuck. This perfect woman just agreed to give me another chance after a whole period of fuckery on my part. She's now cooking me lobster, for Christ's sake, and here I am, already disappointing her. But I need to secure my freedom. Our freedom.

"I know." I soften my voice. "I'm sorry, I got caught up, but I'll be back early afternoon and I'll make it up to you, I promise. I love you."

She's quiet for a moment, and then says, "I love you too, but I don't want to spend the rest of our lives hearing you say you're sorry."

"You won't, Jo."

She sighs. I can tell she's trying to give me the benefit of the doubt. "It's alright. I should've called earlier, but I wanted to surprise you. Just be safe, okay? And text me."

"I will."

I hang up and step back inside the warehouse. "We need to make this look like he skipped town."

Demarcus tosses Derek's iPhone to Q. "Handle it."

"We can use his banking app to move cash offshore," Q says, tapping away on the phone. "Just chartered a jet to Bali, where there's no extradition. Private mansion accommodations all booked."

"Good." I exhale slowly, feeling the pieces start to come together. "Give me the phone."

Q hands it to me. I draft an email to his daughter, Charlotte, explaining that he's done something terrible that could put him in prison and that he believes the Albanian mob is after him, so he's fleeing and can never return. I set it to send automatically next week.

"My boys will take care of the rest." Demarcus says. "You need to get out of here. I'll take you back to Maddox."

"No, not yet. Back to New York."

• • •

I have Mitchie meet me and Demarcus in the city. He brings me a suit and some necessary paperwork for this next step.

The wind cuts cold against my face as I stand in front of the massive stone columns, the gold letters of PGC above the door shining in the gray morning air.

As I pass through lobby security, the guards hesitate for a second, then smile.

Reggie, the head of building security, calls out, "A.C.! Long time, brotha."

"Reggie, my man. How's the family?"

"Everyone's good," Reggie says. "Junior is loving Harvard. Can't thank you enough for that recommendation you wrote."

"I'm glad to hear it." I smile as we enter the elevator.

We reach the sixtieth floor. Walking through the office, I catch glimpses of familiar faces, all doing a double take before breaking into grins, like they can't believe I'm back.

When we get to Harry's office, I take a seat across from her. The space is quiet and as pristine as I remember it. Stan Titus stands behind her, his brawny arms crossed as his eyes flick between the three of us. Reanne sits in the corner, eyes fixed on her laptop. Stan and Demarcus remain tense, sizing each other up.

"Adrian darling, why the bodyguards?" Harry eyes Demarcus's hulking form and then Mitchie's miniature form. The latter is far from my bodyguard but much-needed backup.

"Same reasons you have yours," I reply. "It's not so hard to make enemies in this business."

"No, unfortunately not," Harry says.

I take a seat across from her. "Look, I know you wanted me to manipulate Charlotte into suing her father, but that wouldn't have worked, so I found another way."

"Please do share." Harry's eyes sharpen like a hawk's.

I lean forward, keeping my voice steady. "I have evidence of Derek's crimes. Hard evidence that could eliminate him forever. Drugs, sex trafficking, blackmail, stock manipulation... attempted murder."

Harry doesn't react. It's as if she knows exactly what Derek was capable of. I play her the video of the assassin implicating Derek in a murder-for-hire scheme, and then the audio of his confession. I then show her the photos of him and PGC investors engaged in debauchery, and then the buried articles.

Her eyes widen as she finishes reviewing the evidence on the phone. "We can't afford another publicity storm. I'll take this to the board and discreetly trigger his morality clause. I wouldn't even be required to buy him out. I can strip his shares on ethical grounds."

She glances up at me. "Jesus Christ, Adrian, how did you get this?"

"An anonymous source." I fight to hold back a smirk.

Her eyes widen and then narrow again like she doesn't believe me. "Doesn't matter, really. Send the files to Reanne."

"Before I do that, there's the matter of my compensation." I snatch the phone from her hand.

Stan's posture stiffens, and then he steps forward. Demarcus does the same, meeting him. Harry and I remain calm, both waving off our respective muscle.

"The agreement was for you to help me take out Derek," she says, "and then you'd return to PGC."

"I have no interest in working for you again."

"So, what do you want?"

"First, the five percent allocation of PGC stock I would've gotten as CIO. You'll put it in an irrevocable trust for the benefit of my daughter."

Harry raises an eyebrow. "First?"

"Just a few more things." I pause, letting her mind race. "Martex Properties. It's a portfolio company I bought a few years back. I want it. You'll also use your connections to get my record expunged, as well as the records of a few friends of mine whose security company I'm investing in."

"For bloody fuck's sake, Adrian. Anything else?"

"And then you'll make warm intros to PGC's investors when I'm ready to raise CCP's first full-fledged PE fund. I won't compete with you. I'll even keep bringing you lucrative deals to co-invest in, the kind that'll help you save your reputation in the eyes of the next generation."

Harry's expression doesn't change, but I can see the tension building in her shoulders. "That is quite a tall order."

"Not for you, Harry. You'll make it happen, or these files go to Nora Hendricks at the New Journal and then Senator Marcia Calderon, both of whom hate PGC and would have a field day with these files."

Harry shifts in her chair.

"No investor will ever again commit capital to PGC and the federal investigation will drive your portfolio into the ground," I continue. "Your firm and your legacy will go the way of Lehman Brothers. But if you agree to my terms, you'll get what you want. Derek out of the picture permanently, full control of your board, no one to block your granddaughter's ascent to chairwoman. And your secrets safe."

She stares at me for a long moment, then slowly nods. "Fine. It'll take some time to get it all together—"

"Needs to happen now," I demand. "Or I release everything. I want the stock transfers made immediately. No signing period. No delays."

"Come on, Adrian, this isn't a bloody episode of *Suits*. I need lawyers to draw up the agreements and run their process. You know how these things are done. It takes time."

Mitch steps forward, pulling a thick folder of documents out of his briefcase. "Mitchell H. Lowenstein, attorney at law. You'll see here we've taken the liberty to draft the necessary agreements. It took me all night, but these are bulletproof."

I take the folder and set it on the desk. "Harry, you're going to hand me Martex Properties today because it means nothing to you. It's a relatively small company in a portfolio of hundreds. Or I'll let the media, the regulators, and then your competitors take down the legacy that means everything to you."

"I don't understand. Why the hostility, Adrian? I was prepared to bring you back."

"No hostility, Harry. This is just me *carrying my own water.*"

"You can't still be bitter." She has the nerve to act offended. "I taught you everything you know. I raised you in this business, and you've rebuilt yourself in record time. Let's let bygones be bygones."

"Harry, you may have taught me everything *you* know. But East Maddox raised me. Don't worry, though. There's a sweetener in there for you. As consideration for the Martex shares, PGC will receive a ten percent equity stake in Ironbridge Industries, Inc., my manufacturing company that we've already marked at a 2.3X multiple in only a year of operation."

She takes the folder with a look of curiosity on her face. Her eyes narrow as they skim across the pages. On paper, it's a merger between the two companies, making Harry an indirect minority owner in an illegal gun manufacturer. With her private jet on record taking delivery of gun parts in São Leopoldo, it would look like she was a knowing participant in the deal. It'll serve as additional insulation in the event the federal government comes after me. I know she'll use all of her money and influence to avoid prosecution and public scrutiny. If it comes to it, she'll bury the whole thing like she did with PGC's involvement in Bing's conspiracy.

"Reanne!" she hollers. "Martex Properties. Valuation?"

Reanne pushes her glasses back and starts typing with that nerd-like fury. "We're marking Martex at eight point two billion as of last quarter."

"Why the bloody hell have I never heard of it?" Harry asks.

"We own it through Sentry Asset Management," Reanne says.

Harry looks around, drawing a blank.

"It's an investment firm out of London I acquired when you were on that 'eat the competition' kick a few years back," I remind her. "I structured the deal to obscure PGC's ownership."

"Why do you want it? I won't sign anything until you tell me, Adrian," she says staunchly.

"I bought Martex because it was a good deal, a conglomerate with holdings in an array of unsexy but lucrative regulated industries. I used it as a platform to acquire some Maddox-based assets. Factories, warehouses, chemical plants, mills, shipping yards. My plan was to rebuild my city's economy through deals like Volition, forcing the big tech and consumer brands in our portfolio to outsource production to these facilities. Creating jobs, innovating the city, the whole spiel. The Volition-Blue Rock merger was my proof of concept. Derek wrecked that experiment for PGC, but CCP will continue it."

"Fine," Harry says. "I'll have to pay our LPs back personally."

"Eight billion is peanuts compared to what you would lose if this all comes out," Mitch says.

"I suppose I can't argue with that," Harry says.

"And to think this could've all been avoided if you paid me the thirty-two mil you owed me."

Harry hastily signs the contracts as she says, "All I know is you better keep your word on this, Adrian. I want those files destroyed."

"They won't see the light of day. But if anything suspicious should happen to me, or if I'm served with any lawsuit from PGC or any other party trying to unwind these transactions, the scenarios we just walked through will play out. I keep contingencies in every deal I do. You taught me that."

Harry keeps it cool, but I can tell by the shortness of her breath and the beads of sweat starting to form in the wrinkles on her forehead that she's caught off guard. "I guess I taught you well."

Martina Hayes calls in a favor, and within an hour, papers are filed to have my record and the records of each of the EMSK members' expunged, allowing me to pass background checks run by potential institutional investors and allowing Demarcus and his team to legally carry firearms, taking their security business to the next level.

But my focus right now is on Martex Properties and the variety of industrial assets it owns through its seventeen subsidiaries, each thriving on my favorite source of revenue—government contracts. Data storage centers, windmill fields, nuclear plants, metals producers, chemical production facilities, ports, railways, and, importantly, private prisons.

As we walk out of the PGC office, I turn to Mitchie. "No one can know we own those prisons."

"You got it, A.C.," he says. "I'll siphon 'em off into a new offshore company and put in a mountain of shell entities between you and this thing."

The plan became clear to me when I left my meeting with Makari at Riverville. I saw a placard on the wall: "A Martex Property." I forgot I actually bought Martex to help him, to improve conditions inside as much as possible. But back then, I was so caught up in market domination that I lost the thread after realizing what it meant to manage investments at the highest level. Where profit is king and reform is expensive, social change will always get left behind in the pursuit of returning capital as quickly as possible.

But I've just acquired Martex for exactly zero dollars. I'm playing with house money. Annual cash flow of approximately $163 million. I didn't raise outside funds to purchase this company, so I'm not obligated to share any of it. I can use it to reform the criminal justice system from the inside. No more forced labor. More education. More therapy. Better healthcare. I could even influence parole boards to release non-violent, non-threatening offenders, transfer the rest of them elsewhere, and convert the real estate into something that actually benefits society.

Importantly, Martex gives me cash to invest in other CCP deals, primarily Demarcus's security company. And I can treat it as my personal ATM.

With this one move, I've become a billionaire in asset value. As for how I acquired it, Derek Graff's heart exploded as a result of the guilt he carried for being a racist, deceitful, murderous waste of breath. His regular cocaine usage probably didn't help.

Larger fortunes have been taken in far worse ways.

62

SPECIAL AGENT
REGINA COURTLEIGH

I DON'T MEET my sources in diners or on dim corners. I meet them in spaces we've already wired and secured, inside operational blind spots we control. This one's a leased storage unit in an underutilized municipal transit garage. It's publicly dull, making it logistically perfect. We sweep it twice a day.

She's already inside when I get there. Her bottle girl outfit is showing under the zipper of her hoodie.

"She's clean," my guy upstairs tells me through the earpiece. "No tails."

I enter, shut the door, lock it, and check it twice. "Status?"

She exhales. "Nothing new."

"Still not talking?" I ask.

"Not about anything that matters."

"Is he still trying to fuck you?"

She nods. "He's obsessed. Keeps inviting me on his jet. Miami, Cancun, Turks. Says I've got 'energy.' Says he wants to make me his 'main thang.' He's three drinks away from proposing, but he never says shit about his brothers. Just the label. Streaming revenue. Press releases. Concerts."

I watch her closely. She's been working as a bottle girl in an RF9 night-club for eighteen months, moving pills along with tequila and sparklers. Given her coke-bottle physique and near-flawless bone structure, Truck Palmer has taken a liking to her.

"And if you let it go further?" I ask.

"Then I'm in his bed," she says. "Or my cover's blown."

I let that sit.

She paces. "I'm close, but I know he thinks he's closer. And if I don't give him what he wants, he'll freeze me out."

"No, keep your proximity. You let him chase. You let him talk. But if he puts a hand on you, we pull you."

"Copy."

An hour later, I park under a scaffolding at a municipal equipment yard and watch Lot C.

He shows up just before dusk. Hoodie. Work boots. Vest with the same city contractor logo as half the crew moving pylons across the lot. He's in far deeper than my other agent, so extra precautions need to be taken.

He stops at a locked electrical panel, pulls a screwdriver from his vest, opens the panel, slides in a sealed envelope, then re-locks it before walking away.

I get out and retrieve it ninety seconds later. Inside is a printed sanitation work order sheet from the city's central office, listing a half-dozen addresses. Garages. Warehouses. Abandoned plants. Two strip malls.

Scrawled at the bottom: *Gun factories and dope labs*.

On the back is a crude drawing of a pickup truck and another hand-written note: *Keeps talking about a "light-skinned nigga." They hate him but trust him with big $. Might run laundry. Find him.*

I fold the note into my jacket and keep walking.

Two years inside and still not a single shred of hard evidence that can tie RF9 to the Palmer family. Just a tattoo on Truck Palmer's arm and some loose affiliations. But now I have a name or a nickname or something. The "light-skinned…" word I can't say.

I don't know who he is yet. But the way he's described, like a necessary evil to them, tells me he's someone I can exploit.

63

CHARLES PALMER

THE WIND IS biting at the back of my neck as I step onto the cracked pavement. The spot he chose is an old, dilapidated dock at the Port of Maddox. It's empty and silent save for a lone seagull flying around in the night air and the sound of waves slapping against the wooden beams beneath us. Adrian insisted on meeting with me, Rome, and Truck.

We've completely eliminated the Albanian threat, and our arms customers are happy. So, it's just the three of us, our Uncle Mac, and Frank Madigan. No need for an army of bodyguards anymore. Unfortunately, the escalation of violence, our assassination of Arjun Kodra, and the increase of ghost guns on the street has put us back on the federal government's radar. It took us fourteen blocks and six decoy cars to lose the FBI tail, but we made it clean.

I look towards the parking lot and see three black SUVs roll to a stop, their engines still rumbling as the doors swing open.

Almost in unison, six guards emerge from the other SUVs, each clad in black military fatigues with M4 rifles slung across their chests. They move across the parking lot with the precision of a private mercenary unit, their eyes and barrels scanning the surroundings.

And then Adrian steps out, draped in a sleek black Burberry trench coat over a fitted black turtleneck, flanked by two more guards as he walks onto the dock. It throws me off. A man fully under the control of the Black Gods walking in like he's untouchable.

Uncle Mac leans over, pointing out the man standing closest to Adrian. "Demarcus Teague. Stronghold Killaz."

Demarcus follows closely behind Adrian as the other trails, securing a perimeter but staying close enough to remind us he's not here alone. In fact, we're outnumbered.

Truck scoffs as he puffs his blunt, watching them approach. "The fuck this nigga think he is?"

"Anybody can muscle up," Rome says.

Adrian has always been confident, but this is different. There's a calm in the way he's moving, like he knows something I don't. That bothers me.

I don't say anything at first. I just let him come closer. My brothers stand a few feet behind me. Adrian's crew is posted at strategic vantage points, spaced out, all with their rifles readied. But Adrian doesn't even seem like he needs them.

He looks me straight in the eye. "Charles, I appreciate you and your family for meeting me here. But I'm here primarily for Truck."

Rome and I exchange glances. We don't have any problems with Adrian. He's proven loyal and extremely valuable. And returns from the contract manufacturing business are excellent. But Truck still wants him dead. He still has RF9 members watching Adrian and his family under the guise of "protecting our investment," but I know he's looking for any excuse to kill him.

"Really, this isn't about business at all," Adrian continues.

"Then, what is it about?" I ask.

"Family, Charles. It's about family." He shifts his gaze to my brother. "Truck, I'm here as a man to put you on notice. Josie and I are together. I bought a house and she and Allen are moving in with me."

Truck pauses for a moment as he registers the statement. And then his eyes widen as he roars, "What, nigga? I told you what would happen if you touched her."

He steps forward, face-to-face with Adrian.

Adrian doesn't flinch. "And that's why I'm here. You've made clear what you're willing to do to me and my family if I didn't follow your rules. But Josie's a grown woman who can make her own choices. She's chosen me and wants nothing to do with you."

"Don't make no difference!" Truck screams. "I ain't gon' have my son callin' you daddy."

"I don't want him to," Adrian says. "Allen's a great kid, and I'll be there for him should he need or want my support for anything. And when it comes to you, he'll hear nothing but respect out of my mouth. That's my word. I just want to run my business and live my life in peace, with Josie."

"What about our business?" I ask.

"You guys have a fully operational gun factory in South Maddox with legitimate manufacturing contracts acting as a front for your gun assembly. I separated it from Ironbridge Industries and transferred ownership to you."

Demarcus hands me a manila folder stuffed with paperwork. I thumb through and see an asset transfer agreement granting ownership of the factory to one of RF9's shell corporations. A few pages in, I see it's been backdated to just before our gun production shifted into full assembly.

"You don't need me to run it," Adrian says. "I want out of the arms business, and I'll pay you back your $6 million right now, plus interest. But the threats on me and my family, the RF9 surveillance on them, the fake-ass Tony Soprano therapy sessions Rome and that psycho bitch Getz have been having with my ex-wife. It all stops now."

A silence hangs as I slowly exhale the cold night air.

"Or what?" Truck sneers.

Adrian steps closer, the wind catching the edges of his coat. "I'm not here to negotiate, gentlemen. I'm not here to posture. I'm here to communicate to you how this partnership is going to end."

"How's that?" Rome asks.

"Russell Gates," Adrian says slowly.

Truck and Rome look at me with a subtle shock written on their faces. I look at Uncle Mac. No one is supposed to know that name.

"You've been telling everyone your dad is dead, but we all know that's not true, and I know exactly where he is." The confident ease in Adrian's voice sends a slight chill through me.

"Bullshit," Truck says.

Demarcus steps forward and hands me an iPad. On it is a live feed from my father's prison cell at Riverville Correctional. He's in solitary confinement, curled up on the floor, shivering, noticeably skinny. It looks like he hasn't eaten. It looks like he's in pain.

Adrian turns to Demarcus. "Do it."

Demarcus pulls out a phone and pushes a button. I look down at the live feed and see the cell door swing open. Two guards enter and start beating our father with batons. Rome, Truck, and I huddle around the tablet.

"How?" I'm genuinely confused.

Rome is silent, his eyes narrowing as he stares at the feed.

"Ay, cut that shit out." Truck's voice is loud but quivering. "Make 'em stop!"

He raises his gun to Adrian's head. Demarcus raises his tactical pistol, and the red laser fixes on Truck's forehead. The other guards raise their rifles, and I see red lasers on each of our heads.

Truck's head swivels, and his eyes dart around. He slowly drops his gun, likely realizing that if he pulls the trigger, we're all dead. Demarcus confiscates his weapon. I've never seen Truck look so defeated in my life.

I look down and see the guards still beating my father. Even on the pixelated screen, I can see blood spilling from his face. Rome remains silent as he watches, quietly seething.

"Adrian, please." My voice is heavy with fatigue. "You've made your point."

Adrian stares straight ahead, silent with no emotion as the beating on the screen continues. Finally, he speaks. "That's enough."

Demarcus sends another text, and the beating stops.

Adrian's eyes flick between Rome, Truck, and me. "Let me make this very clear for you guys. I now own Riverville Correctional, both in the sense of cell block respect and in the sense of legal possession."

"What do you mean?" I ask.

His voice rises, sharp with anger. "Its guards, its inmates, its walls, and its cell doors, the fucking mush they serve for breakfast, its entire economy. They're mine. I know exactly how much money RF9 makes through the prison drug trade at Riverville, Torrance Penitentiary in Jersey, Marley Hill down in Maryland, Johnston Fields in Ohio, all private prisons owned by Martex Properties, a company now in my portfolio. I can shut down your pipeline with a phone call. More importantly, I can make sure Big Russell Jerome Palmer Gates or whatever the fuck his name is. I can make sure his time in prison becomes even more painful."

He pauses, letting the words sink in. "I can have him tortured along with the eighty-three other inmates sporting RF9 tattoos, according to my prison records. I can make sure every day until their miserable deaths is worse than the last. And then we'll see how the streets react to the fact that the Black Gods can't take care of their soldiers, the ones expected to take life sentences in that hellhole for your freedom. Loyalty can be a slippery commodity, gentlemen."

Rome steps forward with a cold scowl on his face. "Adrian, we don't respond well to threats."

"Neither do I." Adrian's eyes narrow. "But this isn't a threat. It's a fact. Back off my family, and Big Palm and all your people inside will continue as they have been. You don't, and I make their lives hell and then I have 'em all killed… I'm done being fucked with."

"Adrian, you—th—this is not you, not your lane." I'm flustered and hate it.

"Charles, I've never been the type to stay in a single lane. I'm the type who owns the fuckin' highway. I know you've been talking to Bruno Pereira at Metaliga, trying to broker your own parts deal so your brother can slice my head off. Well, Metaliga S.A., coincidentally, is also a Martex company, and Bruno, who I've just named CEO, won't do business with you unless I allow it."

I blink, trying to mask the creeping frustration behind a façade of stoicism.

"But wait, there is more." Adrian pauses as if he's hosting a game show. "I also control your precursor supply. Fentanyl, MDMA, methamphetamine, all the raw chemicals you need to produce your poison. I know you get it from Canderton Chemicals, also a Martex subsidiary. That was actually one of the last companies I bought at PGC."

"The fuck's he talkin' about, Chuckie?" Truck asks.

Truck doesn't quite understand and likely won't, regardless of how I try to explain it to him. He just sells whatever Rome tells him to sell. Adrian's acquisition of Martex Properties, a company I didn't even know existed, gives him the keys to maybe eighty percent of RF9's entire infrastructure.

"It took me a minute to figure out, but I know who's selling you off-spec precursor at Canderton," Adrian says, "and I can end your business with a series of emails firing them. But let me not stop there. This port here in Maddox, the Port of Philly, Port of New York and New Jersey, Baltimore, Miami, New Orleans, are all owned by Martex Properties. I'll stop every 'private label furniture' shipment with your name on it and make sure none of your mattresses or the drugs and guns stuffed inside them reach their destinations."

"And if we just kill you?" Truck asks. "You think your 'lil fake ass militia gon' stop RF9 soldiers from sliding through your window?"

Demarcus and his soldiers raise their weapons again with military precision.

"Say the word, A.C.," Demarcus says. "We can end this right now."

Adrian doesn't flinch, he just lightly shakes his head, and his gunmen lower their weapons. "No need, Red Dot. Don't wanna make a mess on my new real estate."

Adrian glances at my brother. "Truck, I have contingencies in place. If I'm dead due to anything other than old age, not only will your father still get fucked up the ass every hour on the hour courtesy of the boys in cell block D, but the gun parts manufacturer you rely on, the chemical producer that supplies your drug business, the prisons where you peddle them, will all get shut down and sold for parts. Your business will be done, and your enemies will come for you. Again."

"What the fuck is this shit…" Truck murmurs.

"Oh, and everything I have on you," Adrian adds calmly, "everything I know about your operation goes straight to the feds."

"I thought Stronghold Killaz don't snitch," Truck says.

Adrian lets out a slight scoff. "I don't give a fuck about street code if I'm in the ground or my family's dead. And I give two shits what you think about it. Your choice is simple, fellas. Leave me and my family alone."

He then turns his head and looks directly at me with a fierce intensity. "That means everyone I love, including my ex-wife. What I know and what she knows about how your family makes its money will be kept in confidence. You can continue running your business, keep making your guns with my parts, keep buying your pills and powder from… well, me… or I can cut you off and watch your half-assed furniture empire crumble without the dirty cash that keeps it propped up."

I study him, trying to find a crack in the armor. But there isn't one. He's dead serious. And worse? He's right.

Rome's hand brushes my arm, a subtle gesture, but I know what he's thinking. If he's telling the truth, and from the look in his eyes, I have no doubt he is, then we can't afford to push him anymore. We've tried to take the 'clean money' route. My investments in real estate, retail, and tech startups, regrettably, are all failing. Luxury real estate works well for laundering money but it's not a great business in a city that mostly can't afford such luxury. The market is in decline, and our once-reliable furniture revenue is nearly non-existent. RF9 is the only business we have generating consistent cash flow. We have far too many people depending on us to call his bluff.

"Okay, we won't bother you," Rome says. "Ain't that right, Tracy?"

Truck is silent for a while. Adrian looks over to Demarcus, who pulls out his phone, presumably to order our father's beating once more.

"Aight," Truck finally says. "You win, nigga."

Adrian pulls out a flash drive from his pocket and hands it to me. "$8 million in untraceable cryptocurrency. Your initial investment in CCP, plus $2 million in interest. We're done."

"No," Rome counters swiftly. "You promised a 10X return. That's fifty-two million dollars short, Adrian."

Adrian scoffs, a faint chuckle escaping him. "I didn't promise anything, Rome. This partnership isn't working out. Two mil is a more than fair return for two years of doing nothing."

I turn to Rome, keeping my voice low so Adrian doesn't hear. "It's a reasonable compromise."

"No, C," Rome whispers. "This was supposed to be my way out. I need enough clean money so my family never has to work again. If you, Truck, and Frankie wanna keep slingin' dope and guns, then my kids will need money the feds can't take in a RICO. I've seen the articles, the ads. Geraldine's is gonna be a big exit."

"Eight million is enough, Rome. I can grow it without Adrian."

"You've tried that before," he whispers back, but his frustration pushes his voice louder. "We got sixty-eight family members to feed. Eight won't cut it. Not forever. I don't want my kids to ever even think about picking up a pistol or a brick of dope."

"Okay." I turn to Adrian. "The terms of our agreement are binding. You don't have the right to kick us out of the fund."

"I do if your money has the potential to cause legal issues for my fund or its investments," Adrian says. "I don't care how clean you think your furniture money is, it's not."

"Well, that would need to be proven in a court of law. Are you willing to stand in trial and testify to what you think you know about my family?" I lean in close to him, lowering my voice. "That would make you a snitch, and if you enter that territory, neither I nor Rome would be able to stop Truck from handling that liability."

I hand him back the flash drive. "We'll leave you alone, but we need our full return on this investment."

Adrian studies me for a moment, then glances at Demarcus, likely considering whether he should just let him kill us like he proposed earlier.

But then Adrian looks back to me and says, "I suppose a deal is a deal. But if I see any RF9 vehicle or soldier anywhere near me, my family, or my businesses, it's all off. I'll finish you guys."

64

ADRIAN CHANNING

EIGHTEEN MONTHS LATER

THREE AND A HALF YEARS SINCE VOLITION CRASHED

THE GLASS WALLS catch the morning glare as the room settles around me. Below, the plant kicks into motion. Up here, it's slate and smoked glass, vintage rugs layered over concrete, desks cut from the same loading docks we tore out and repurposed. But down below, dock doors rumble open. Robotic arms fire up in sync. Workers stream through the facility like blood through veins, each one part of the engine we built from the bones of what used to be failure.

From my office on the top floor, I can see everything—the factory space on the lower levels, the rows of CCP analysts and associates above them, the elevators carrying lawyers, bankers, and engineers between floors.

"We've got Mitch coming up the steps, A.C." Demarcus's voice is low, military sharp.

"Yeah, we've got that status meeting."

Since everything that went down, Demarcus has become my shadow. My personal unit of Stronghold bodyguards is never more than a few steps from me, at least two always armed and trained to eliminate any threats. Necessary precautions given the cards I hold now.

"What it do, Red Dot?" says Mitchell Herman Lowenstein, the wannabe gangsta rapper.

Demarcus shakes his head, holding back laughter as they bump fists.

Mitch sits down at the conference table. "A.C., I finished the crypto conversions for our feeder investors. Sixty Marys out the door. Got the wallets for you right here." He slides across a pouch with a handful of USB drives inside. "That entire structure has been dissolved with no traces."

He's alluding to the criminal groups who invested twenty million dollars in my parking deal. I'm buying them out at a 3X multiple. Expensive, but I need them off my cap table before I raise a legit fund.

I take the pouch of USBs. "Appreciate you handling that, buddy. I have a meeting with those guys next week. I'll give it to them in person. We're good on the Martex transition, yeah?"

Mitch nods. "We've got all seventeen subsidiaries slotted to move their corporate headquarters to Maddox by Q4. And I have meetings set up with all of our 'off-the-books' execs."

He's referring to the corrupt executives at Canderton Chemicals and Metaliga S.A. selling chemical precursors and raw metal gun parts to the Black Gods.

"Let's keep close tabs on 'em. Take a couple of Demarcus's guys and make sure they understand our emphasis on discretion."

"You got it, A.C."

"Anything else I should know about?"

Mitch leans back in his chair and loosens his tie like he's just come from war and won.

"The IRS audit is officially done," he says. "They barely looked at our LP paperwork. Focus was on the management company, a couple of follow-ups on fee allocations, nothing serious."

I take a sip of my coffee. "Anything stick?"

"Nah. The structure held up clean like I said it would. IRS lady even told me she appreciated the transparency."

I raise an eyebrow. "You're saying we're good?"

"I'm saying if they were looking for a reason to pull threads, they didn't find one."

"Good thing there are no reasons and no threads."

"Oh, and I may need your help finalizing those Midwest labor contracts," Mitch says. "I'm getting some pushback from the unions."

"Push back harder. We're giving their workers a real seat at the table. No other industrial company is offering the kind of comp package we are."

With the Martex acquisition, we employ close to ten million blue-collar workers across the country, each of whom receives stock in Ironbridge Industries that pays out dividends on top of traditional wages. I don't care if they're an executive, line worker, or custodian, they get a piece of the pie, and when I and my dirty investors make money, so do they. With the profits that Martex generates, the lower class who work in my factories and plants will soon be middle class, and the middle class will soon be upper-middle.

"They're just not used to W-2s comin' with that kind of wealth," Mitch says.

"That's the point, Mitchie. If they work for Ironbridge, they own a piece of Ironbridge. That's how you build loyalty. And votes… Speaking of, make sure Deanie gets a photo op on-site at the groundbreaking. Hard hat, shovel, the whole thing. I want her name tied to these new jobs before the gubernatorial filing deadline."

"Got it, A.C."

I turn to Demarcus. "You're handling security for her voter rallies, right?"

"Yessir," he says, "I've been coordinating with the mayor's people. She'll headline. You'll open."

"Good. I want local coverage, socials pushed, everything. The image is industry revival, jobs, and political momentum. Maddox, PA, is about to be the new corporate center of American manufacturing and industrials. We make her the face of it all and ride her to the governor's office. She wins, CCP companies get priority on state contracts."

"The team down at MaddComm says the rollout's ahead of schedule," Mitch says. "Our parking projects in Maddox, Wilmington, Detroit, and

Cincinnati are fully operational, and they're expanding with waste management contracts in Newark, water filtration in Flint, and sewage treatment down in New Orleans and Memphis."

I nod slowly. "Good shit. Let's make sure we mirror the Ironbridge stock option structure at MaddComm. Parking lot attendants, water technicians, garbage truck drivers, I want them all enjoying equity."

"Spread the love." Mitch nods his head as he jots down the note. "I'm on it."

I look to Demarcus. "Where are we on the STS training program?"

"We've got seventy-six in active training," he says. "Simulation rooms are full."

I've made good on my promise to help Demarcus give the Stronghold Killaz a path to a brighter future. With the cash from Martex, I've invested over $60 million into building out Stronghold Tactical Services, Inc. (STS). That means advanced surveillance technology, weapons and soldiers, turning a motley crew of former gangbangers and retired marines into a coordinated private military with protection contracts from Fortune 500 companies, celebrities, politicians, and diplomats.

"And community feedback?" I ask.

"Homeowners love it," Demarcus says. "Liberal media, not so much."

"They'll fall in line once we show them the pipeline. We're reforming gang members. Tactical certification to full employment. We're not just training soldiers. We're creating peacekeepers. That's the message."

We converted an abandoned industrial park in East Maddox into a tactical training center. It's a state-of-the-art facility equipped with live-fire ranges, cutting-edge simulation rooms, and advanced intelligence gathering systems, designed to provide private military operatives with comprehensive strategic training and real-time operational command capabilities. More importantly, it offers young people an outlet, an alternative to gangs, and a path toward careers in security and law enforcement.

"How's the policing contract in East Maddox coming along?" Mitch asks.

"Strong first quarter results," Demarcus says. "Violent crime is down almost 19%. Response times are down 48% and drones are flying."

I glance at Mitch. "Get a media kit prepared, will ya? It should highlight our use of de-escalation and conflict resolution training, with footage of STS graduates walking into police academies."

"We just placed two cadets with the U.S. Marshals and Secret Service," Demarcus says.

I turn to him. "Amazing work… What about the city crime database?"

"Updated daily. Facial recognition is tied into city grids in eight states now. We know where every known RF9 affiliate lays their knotty dread heads."

"Any movement around my family?" I ask.

"None at all since the meeting," Demarcus says. "Seems they got the message."

"Good. Once we sell Geraldine's, they get their slice, and we're done. No strings. No threats. Just silence and distance. Then we have the wedding."

"Oh shit!" Mitch shouts as he pats me on the back. "She said yes?"

I can't help but smile. "I don't just close deals, man. You know that."

"Congrats, boss man," Demarcus says.

"So, how's the sale looking?" Mitch asks. "Need to get my dancing shoes ready."

"I've got three serious bidders. I planning to close by the end of this quarter."

Mitch raises a brow. "Is that ambitious?"

"It is, but it's necessary. We're building a machine here. I don't want Palmer residue anywhere near it."

"Fair enough," Mitch says. "What's the latest on the fundraising?"

"Harry's been making warm intros with PGC LPs as agreed. We'll close Fund I at a billion, maybe a billion two."

"Sounds like they like what they see in the current portfolio," Mitch says. "Geraldine's, STS, MaddComm, Ironbridge Industries, the Urban Rehab Network, Maddox Savings & Loan."

I smirk. "I bought that fuckin' bank out of spite. Those dickheads had the nerve to reject me for a job back when I was ass-out."

"Now it's the anchor for our small business lending vertical," Mitch says. "Gotta love that story."

I rest my hands on the glass edge of the table as I look ahead at my two-person senior leadership team. "Cybersecurity, municipal services, coding schools, mental health services, microfinance. We're not just talking impact. Our portfolio is generating returns. And none of it works if we slow down now. For institutional LPs with a mandate to have their capital make an impact for the betterment of society, CCP will become the primary investment destination."

Mitch grins as he jots in his notepad. "Love the vision, A.C. I'll work with the marketing team on the deck."

Demarcus presses his finger to his earpiece and then checks his tablet. I catch a glimpse of the surveillance feed from outside the building.

"A.C., we got a bogie in the parking lot," he murmurs.

The facial recognition software runs silently on the tablet as a tall blonde enters the lobby. Within seconds, her profile pops up.

"Tessa Summers," Demarcus reads. "Thirty-three years old. Upper East Side address, but born in Paramus, New Jersey, to Rick and Lisa Summers. Divorced."

"All good, D. She's a friendly."

Demarcus presses his earpiece and gives lobby security the go-ahead to let her in. A moment later, he taps his tablet, the ballistic doors to my office slide open, and there she is.

I haven't seen Tessa in almost four years. She walks in with the same confidence, dressed in a cream Gucci pantsuit and blouse ensemble with her Louboutin heels clicking against the floor. Same old Tessa. Scrappy and polished all at once. I play it casual, but what the hell is my I-love-NYC, aspiring Met Gala-invitee of a former assistant doing in East Maddox right now?

"Hey, boss." She smiles like she just came back from lunch. "You look good. Still tall, dark, and handsome, I see."

"Thanks, kiddo. Come here!" I pull her into a hug.

"Tessa, this is Demarcus Teague, my business partner and head of security. Demarcus, this is Tessa, but you already know everything about her."

Demarcus steps forward. "Pleasure to meet you, Ms. Summers."

She bats her eyelashes as she shakes his hand and gazes at him. Then, her eyes roam to the other STS guards patrolling the factory, mostly men who get paid to keep their bodies in peak physical condition.

"I like your new business partners, boss." Tessa shakes her head, as if snapping herself out of a daydream.

Before I can introduce him, I see Mitchie's eyes light up. "Well, well, well, who is this tall drink of my next ex-wife?"

Tessa barely blinks, giving him a once-over like she's appraising a secondhand car. "Boss, who is this little old man?"

I stifle a laugh, but Mitchie takes the hit in stride, brushing a hand through his dark and graying hair.

"Just because I don't have the aging backwards gene like A.C. doesn't mean I'm old. Forty-three and more virile than ever, baby."

"Is forty-three the new sixty-three?" Tessa asks.

Demarcus, usually stoic, lets out a muted chuckle.

I cut in before they escalate into full banter. "Mitchell Lowenstein, meet Tessa Summers, the best executive assistant on the planet. Tessa, this is Mitchie, my uhh..."

"His director of special projects. Mitchell H. Lowenstein, attorney at law, CPA, software engineer, and loyal servant of yours truly, madam." He bows, taking Tessa's hand for a kiss.

"Mitchie's a jack of all trades and master of many." I grip his shoulder and shake him lightly. "One of the smartest guys I know."

"Pleasure to meet you, Mitchell," Tessa's face betrays a slight amusement.

"It's all mine," Mitchie croons. "And don't worry about the jokes. I love a good humiliation ritual."

"Um... gross," Tessa says.

"So, what are you doing here?" I ask.

Tessa explains how before he disappeared, Derek fired her and had her arrested for getting me the Blue Rock files.

"I didn't tell you because I knew you were going through some rough times yourself. Didn't want to add to your stress."

"I'm never too busy for my friends." My tone softens. "Tessa, I would've never asked you to do that if I thought it would blow back on you. I'm sorry."

"It's alright, boss. My grandfather made Derek shit himself. He offered me my job back, but I didn't want it. I hope that sicko is choking on sand on whatever island he's on."

Demarcus and I share a knowing glance.

"Who the hell's your grandfather?" Mitchie asks.

"Lawrence Hadington," she says.

"Holy shit," Demarcus mutters.

I'm equally surprised. "Tessa, how in the hell have we known each other this long and you've never told me your grandfather is Lawrence 'the Hawk' Hadington?"

"I got the job at PGC on my own merit and didn't want anyone to think I was a nepo baby."

"Oh shit," Mitchie says. "Larry fuckin' Hadington."

"Don't call him Larry," Tessa says. "He hates that."

"Wait, then is it pronounced *Haddington* or *Hay-dington*?" Mitch asks. "The pundits never keep it straight."

"It's pronounced like *Haddington*," Tessa says. "When my ancestors reached Ellis Island from Scotland, someone must've accidentally dropped the second 'd' in the paperwork."

"Wasn't ol' Larry gonna run for president until he got busted for having two families?" Mitchie asks.

"Would've won too," Demarcus says. "The man is a legend of the Beltway. Respected across the aisle."

"Yeah, that's right," Mitchie says, perusing an article on his phone as he cackles. "He had the classic blonde wife and kids but was doing the dirty deed with the Dominican nanny for years. So, are you a legitimate grand-daughter or illegitimate?"

Tessa's expression drops, as if she feels a pang of shame at the insinuation.

Mitchie notices and softens his tone. "Oh, I'm sorry, Tessa. My astigmatism sometimes makes it hard for me to see the line. Feel free to *bonk* me in the head anytime I cross it."

Tessa giggles. "I would, but something tells me you would enjoy that."

Mitchie smirks and tilts his head as if to say, *You're right*. Then, he turns to me and says, "She's sharp, A.C."

I smile hard. "The sharpest."

"My grandpa is an extremely accomplished man with flaws like everyone else," Tessa says. "He couldn't be in my life growing up because his wife wouldn't let him, but after she died a few years ago, we connected and hit it off. I know everyone says he's scary, but he's really very sweet."

"Wait, so you're part Dominican?" Mitchie asks. "I love a good mofongo."

"Only a quarter. I'm obviously white-passing."

"Hey, so am I," Mitchie says, prompting laughter from all of us.

Tessa surveys my short and pale fixer, only slightly amused before turning back to me. "Anyways, boss, I told my grandpa about you. Showed him all the press clippings on this place, the parking project, the policing, all the public works. He wants to meet you."

I'm floored. "Are you kidding me? Tessa, you're full of surprises."

"But listen," she says. "I need a friggin' job. But I don't want to be your assistant anymore. I was on Harry's PR team, and I've been handling media relations for my grandpa's company, Hawk Strategies. But foreign relations are boring, and I want to get back into private equity."

"Name your role."

"Head of PR and Chief of Staff," Tessa says. "The world needs to know what you're doing here. I can show them and help you turn this operation into a well-oiled machine."

"Welcome to the team."

Tessa shrieks in excitement. "Great! First order of business. Back to New York. My grandpa is in town on business but he's going to the Congo tomorrow. So, we gotta go now."

"Let's do it."

"Great, I'll book train tickets," Tessa says. "Traffic's gonna be a nightmare."

I look around the office and realize something. Martex Properties. "Let's take the company chopper."

•••

I step into the lobby of The Somerset Club, my tailored three-piece light gray suit drawing more eyes than the typical silver-haired patron.

The manager leads me into a private lounge where Lawrence Hadington sits, puffing a cigar and sipping a cognac. Dressed in a blue argyle sweater, khakis, and brown wingtips, he looks casual for a man of his stature.

"Adrian Channing," he announces, his Memphis twang making me feel more welcome than I anticipated. "Glad you could make it." He offers me a handshake, a glass, and a Cuban. I accept all three.

"Mr. Secretary—"

"Call me Lawrence. Or call me Hawk. Just never Larry."

"It's an honor, Lawrence."

"It's mutual, son. I've been watching your career for a while. Harry Paxton's an acquaintance of mine."

Interesting choice of words. "Just an acquaintance?"

"Well, she's made me a good bit of money over the years. She also told me the truth about that Volition foolishness." He shakes his head and pushes his lips out as if recounting a horrible memory. "How Derek Graff, that inconsequential runt of a man, was the reason for its failure and then fed you to the wolves when they needed a scapegoat. Nasty stuff."

I stay silent and sip the cognac. It's a Frapin. The bottle probably costs more than some people's rent, and it tastes like it.

He takes a slow sip of his own, his eyes locked on mine. "You and I, Adrian, we're cut from the same cloth."

"Is that right?"

Hadington nods slowly, and the silver strands of his hair catch the light like a well-worn history. "Boys from the inner city who fought their way to the pinnacle of success, only to get knocked down hard, humiliated, and left for dead. We may have laid down for a bit, might have bled for a while, but then we got up and clawed our way back. Not just because we had to or wanted to, but because we don't know how to stay down and don't give two shits whose got their foot on our back. Just not in our DNA."

"I couldn't agree more." I sip my cognac. "I've never been the type to let others dictate my station in life, or in anything for that matter."

"Mmhmm," he grumbles, taking a sip of his drink.

"I will say I've been inspired by your story, sir. How you took the media's scrutiny of a personal family matter in stride, took your time, and played your cards. Given the media coverage around this next election, it seems like your presidential prospects have been revived."

Hadington smirks as he sips his cognac. "You're not wrong, son. You're not wrong. Nations, companies, men, and women all fall at some point. But only those willing to test the limits of life itself are guaranteed to rise again. And from the research I've done on you and the stories my Tessa has shared, I can tell you're the kind of man who understands that concept keenly."

"I am, sir."

He gives me a half-smile as he eyes me up and down. "Y'know, you're taller than I expected. I don't usually like dealing with men as tall as me. Tend to think they got too much bark, not enough bite. But you?" He lifts his glass for a sip. "You don't strike me as the type that likes to bark. You're the type that just bites, aren't you?"

I give a subtle grin. "Only when needed."

"I like that kind of attitude, son, I do."

"And I appreciate you making the time. Tessa tells me that, at this stage in your life, you don't take meetings with folks you don't already know."

"Son, I ran the CIA for nine years. If I don't know everything about a man by the time I sit across from him, I'm not doin' my job." He leans back. "But you? You're interesting. Unusual combination of grit and pedigree. And I hear you know how to turn a buck into two."

"That is my specialty."

"I'd love to get in on your next fund." Lawrence swirls the last of his cognac. "I've got a few friends in government who prefer to invest through me. Quietly, of course. Hard to rail against corporate overreach on the Hill when your name's tied to a fund flipping oil fields and weapons parts suppliers."

"Weapons parts suppliers?" I ask curiously. "CCP doesn't invest in anything like that."

"Sure, it doesn't." The former CIA Director says those words slowly. "But Adrian Channing might. And I want all of that deal flow, son."

I flash my best attempt at a smile that says I'm unbothered. "Well, then, I'd be honored to have you and your discreetly principled friends on my LP list."

"That's what I thought you'd say."

After a couple of hours talking business, politics, power, and influence, we start bullshittin' like old friends in the project hallway.

He throws his head back as a booming laugh echoes through the room. "Son, I'll tell ya, that low-down shit stain was damn near cryin' for his pappy."

I'm laughing just as hard, gripping my glass as he tells me the story of how he made Derek Graff wet his pants on the sixtieth floor at PGC.

The conversation eventually shifts into something I didn't expect. He tells me he grew up in a trailer park in North Memphis and ran with what he calls "some nefarious types." He shares how, at seventeen, he got roped into an armed robbery that would've ruined his life if not for a high-powered attorney who took his case pro bono. The attorney got his record wiped clean, and encouraged him to join the Army, then law school. Then to Linder Boykin where he handled government investigations before going to work for a small defense contractor. He became CEO, grew it, and sold it to PGC in the 90s.

"How much did you make on that deal?" I ask casually, taking a measured sip of cognac.

"Son, I don't even remember the number. All I know is I got load-samoney." He says it like a punchline and downs the last of his cognac. A waiter refills it almost immediately.

I laugh. I'm enjoying this more than I thought I would.

He goes on, not with the arrogance of a man listing titles, but with the ease of someone who's lived a hundred lives and doesn't need to prove any of them. After selling his company, he won a Senate seat and then took charge of the Armed Services and Foreign Relations Committees, navigating the world of foreign affairs like a hawk, hence the nickname. After that, he became a cabinet staple for multiple presidents, from Secretary of Defense to State where he took his influence into the global stratosphere.

"You've had a hell of a run, sir."

"It was supposed to end in the White House." His voice doesn't crack, but there's weight in it. "But there was a complication... Let's just say the Hawk might be better off behind the man behind the desk. For now."

Now, he runs Hawk Strategies, a foreign relations consulting firm, technically. In reality, he negotiates with terrorists on behalf of governments around the world who publicly claim they don't negotiate with terrorists. His firm covertly topples regimes, takes out hostile elements, seizes valuable assets, and manages conflict situations before they evolve into war.

"I move quietly, but I don't move alone," Hadington says. "I've got eyes and ears in every corridor worth walkin'."

"And when something goes sideways?"

He leans forward and lowers his voice. "Then I seize the corridor or I blow it to hell."

I nod slowly as I take a sip.

"But," he continues, "we're having an issue. Too many of the groups I rely on for tactical support have grown too big, too noticeable. I don't need adrenaline junkies leaving their footprint everywhere I do business. I need surgical professionals. Soldiers who understand discretion and know how to do what needs doin' without me having to clean up their shit."

He leans forward slightly, and his eyes are locked on mine. "And I need them yesterday."

I take a slow sip of my cognac. "Now I understand why we're talking."

"I like what you're building with STS. Veterans, street-hardened operators, tacticians with something to prove and everything to lose."

"And now we have the infrastructure, the technology, the numbers, the discipline, and loyalty. We're scalable. We're quiet. And we're hungry."

Hadington lets out a low whistle.

"I'd of course be honored to have the Hawk Hadington in my fund, but I'd really love to get you on STS's board of directors. We can be your go-to provider for tactical support around the globe."

He raises his glass. "Now, that is a proposition I can get behind."

We toast to a new partnership. And as I leave the club, I know I've just secured more than an investor or client. I've gained the most valuable kind of friend, one who's not just untouchable but makes the determination as to who else is.

65

SPECIAL AGENT
REGINA COURTLEIGH

THE SURVEILLANCE VAN sits tucked between two delivery trucks across from the back entrance of the PalmLux Residences, a luxury condo high-rise three blocks off the river owned by Palmer Real Estate.

My techs are flipping between drone feeds, dash cams, and an encrypted facial recognition program that's already getting ping after ping. The building's east-facing camera catches the first arrival.

Charles Palmer steps out of his matte black BMW like he's walking into court. He gives the doorman a nod and heads in without looking back.

After a few idle moments, a white Range Rover pulls up. The windows are down just enough for me to see her before the software pings her face, striking in that predatory way that doesn't soften with money. Her brother steps out behind her, his eyes scanning their surroundings like a man who's always a second from drawing a pistol.

"Tori and Jason Bonetti," I say. "Their father is Don Daniel Bonetti. Philadelphia mafia."

They're barely in the door before a black S-Class creeps up behind them. Out steps a thin, older Asian man in a dark navy suit with no tie, flanked by two younger, beefier Asian men.

"Chen Lao," my tech says. "Eighty-nine percent match."

"Zi Wan Triad?" I ask.

"Second in command to the dragon head." He shakes his head in astonishment as he records timestamps and logs the photos.

Another ping. A late 70s Chevy Chevelle rolls in slow, then idles. The driver's door opens, and the man who steps out is all presence, donning dreadlocks, a gold chain tucked inside a black pullover, and black Timberland boots. Two younger men get out in front of him, also dreadlocked and both armed, unless my instincts are failing me.

"That's Winston Lloyd, top man of the Lloyd Posse," I murmur. "Came up in Kingston. His crew runs RF9 dope out of Florida."

Then, the rumble. Three matte-black sport bikes roll in, LED glow underneath. The leader wears a fitted black leather cut with gray stitching and a chrome skull patch. Full-face helmet. His crew flanks tight, fast, and silent.

"Rashad 'Rawbone' Hill, President of Black Metal M.C. Serious west coast drug pushers." I watch them park their bikes and then enter the building.

One of my techs mutters under his breath, "Jesus Christ."

"They're not even trying to hide," the other says.

"Why would they?" I reply, sarcasm in my tone. "On paper, they're legitimate entrepreneurs."

Then a Bentley SUV in a deep, dark, emerald green parks. Two men in black suits and mirrored shades exit first, one with a thick beard scanning the perimeter.

"Demarcus Teague," my tech says, running facial software. "Ex-Marine. Before that, did juvie time for gun possession. Expunged though. Gang database has him as a member of the East Maddox Stronghold Killaz."

Then comes a man I recognize. My tech runs facial recognition and pulls up his old file from Pennsylvania's child welfare database, showing his foster placements, caseworker notes, everything.

"Akuchukwu Paul Adrian Channing," he says. "According to his LinkedIn profile, he just goes by Adrian."

"I know him." I stare at his expunged arrest record on the laptop screen, next to his professional headshot. "Had him flagged during my investigation of the Volition-Blue Rock gun leak. He was just a potential witness then."

That was before Lawrence Hadington stepped in on behalf of Harry Paxton and made clear that PGC personnel were off-limits to our investigation, even just for questioning. Hadington told us they were "too busy making money for the many good ol' states of America to be bothered by a low-level theft of property."

Now, Adrian steps out of the SUV, holding a small leather pouch, looking like some sort of corporate mobster in a tailored slate suit, no tie, gold Cuban link chain flashing under his collar with a security detail moving like SEALs.

And when I see his face, that smooth caramel profile, I know now he's the light-skinned N-word my undercover flagged. He must be their money launderer.

Demarcus whispers something in Adrian's ear before they both pause and glance in our direction. For a long moment, they stare with an almost eerie precision straight toward our position.

My lead tech shifts in his seat as he starts typing harder. "I've got a drone overhead." Static flickers across his laptop screen. "And now a signal spike. I think someone knows we're here."

I turn back to the main screen to see Adrian turn and walk into the building without checking his six. Because he knows someone's already checked it for him.

But if he's the linchpin to the biggest organized crime conspiracy I've ever seen, then no amount of private security or anti-surveillance technology will save him from what's coming.

66

DR. BRIANNA WRIGHT

I STAND AT the kitchen counter sipping my coffee, watching Riley through the window as she stuffs her duffel bag into the backseat of her new car. The sun's barely up, just enough light to catch the shine off the electric BMW her dad bought for her birthday. Typical of him. His career is thriving again, and he's back to using money to make up for lost time. But I guess it's not just about the money this time; he's actually showing up. And that's all I care about.

Henry, the Cavalier King Charles Spaniel that Adrian got her, scampers around Riley's feet, his tail wagging furiously. His black, white, and tan fur gleams in the morning light. Riley bends down to scoop him up, laughing as he licks her face enthusiastically. It's also typical for Adrian to saddle me with that responsibility since Riley will soon go to college and can't bring a dog, but this puppy is beyond adorable.

"You ready for school?" I ask, leaning against the doorframe, my hands warming from the coffee mug.

"Yep," she says, loading her book bag into the trunk.

"Are you still going to your dad's office before your game?"

"Yeah, he has meetings set up with a sports lawyer and an agent to go over the NIL stuff." She rolls her eyes but can't stop smiling. "He's being extra, but it's cool I guess."

I watch her toss her sports bag into the backseat. "He's making up for lost time. Can't fault him for that."

"Are you coming?"

"To your last ever high school basketball game? Are you kidding me? I wouldn't miss it. You better score thirty for me."

"That's easy." She gives me that confident Channing smile as she hugs Henry one last time before setting him down. "I'll text you when I get to school. Don't work too hard, okay?"

I laugh softly. "Impossible. Have a good day, my love."

She gives me a peck on the cheek, hops into her car, and waves as she pulls out of the driveway. I watch until the car disappears down the street. There's a tug in my chest, but I push it down. She has the best parts of me and her dad and has her whole life ahead of her. She's ready.

●●●

The day was short, spent mostly in my home office with middle school students still reeling from the trauma of last summer's school shooting. Now I stand at the window in my kitchen, watching the tea kettle tremble gently on the stove. It hasn't whistled yet, but my heart is already racing.

Behind me, Special Agent Courtleigh leans on the kitchen island. Her presence carries weight, the kind that settles in your lungs.

"This isn't a game, Dr. Wright. You're too smart not to know that. You might be the only person who can connect the Palmer Foundation to RF9."

She just wants a shortcut to her RICO. And I'm the thread. The foundation's money is clearly derived from ill-gotten gains. I know that now. It's likely washed through scholarships and charitable real estate developments like parks and basketball gyms, then rerouted to local PACs and community programs, many with ties to local law enforcement. If I connect the dots, it's not just the Palmers they'll bury. It's half the city council, former mayors and every sheriff who's ever taken a dirty campaign contribution from them.

I turn around slowly and meet her eyes. "These boys trust me. If they think I'm talking to the police, I lose their trust. I lose all the credibility I've built over the last twenty years."

"I've read your research," Courtleigh says. "I know how passionate you are about your work. I'm not asking you to sell out your patients. I'm asking you to help dismantle the system that keeps them locked in a cycle of violence. You want to save them? Help me take down RF9."

"You think that saves them? RICO indictments don't save anyone. They swallow the network whole. Even the ones trying to change."

"We don't have time for idealism, Dr. Wright. People are dying. Kids are dying."

I can't help the bitter laugh that escapes. "And your solution is to lock them away instead? You think your justice system saves kids from the inner city? You'll just issue another press release about a major gang bust, get your photo op, create another generation of fatherless kids, and then move on."

"That's not my intent here—"

"My ex-husband was raised by this system, Special Agent. I've spent my adult life studying it, trying to heal the damage it causes. Don't insult me as if I don't know how the law really treats kids in gangs." My voice cracks just enough for her to hear the rage and grief fueling my words.

"They're not totally innocent," she says. "Some of these kids are murderers. Others sell assault rifles to school shooters and fentanyl to pregnant women."

"By force. More often than not, these kids are scared. When you're scared, have no other options, and are not fully developed from a cognitive perspective, you make mistakes—"

"And sometimes, rehabilitation is a necessary part of rectifying those mistakes. Especially for gang members willing to spray an entire nightclub with automatic rounds just to get one guy."

"And what about *your* rehabilitation, Special Agent? What are you willing to do to take down your target?"

She doesn't answer, so I keep going. "Like slipping a name during a raid or leaking a fake transcript, just enough to make it look like some scared kid is flipping on his gang. You let the rumor spread and wait for him to panic when his crew starts suspecting him. Then you swoop in, offer protection and a plea deal, but only after he has a target on his back, his family's back. You don't turn informants. You trap them."

Courtleigh barely reacts. "And how many of those kids would've gotten out otherwise?"

"And how many of them didn't make that 'right' choice?" I retort. "How many got gunned down before they ever got the chance to talk to you again? Before they even understood what was happening?"

"Then they should've made better choices from the start."

"You know what, Special Agent?" I lean forward, lowering my tone just a notch. "I spend my days with gang members. And right now, I'm not sure I feel like sharing tea with one."

Her eyes narrow. She didn't like that comment. Good. All cops are bastards.

"You want to play it that way, fine," she says. "I know you work closely with Charles Palmer."

I don't respond.

She pulls out her phone and slides it across the counter. It shows surveillance photos of me leaving Charles's building on the riverfront back when we were dating.

My chest tightens, but I keep my face blank.

"Are you fucking him, too?" she asks, her voice taking a more playful tone. "Can't blame you. He's hot. A criminal, yes, but I'm sure he's packin' more than just a pistol."

I glare at her, doing my best not to let her get to me.

"I'm sure he lays pipe just as good as he cleans dirty gun money. And he does that with your ex-husband, Adrian, right?"

She swipes on her phone and shows me photos of Adrian and Charles at PCA together. "You've got great taste, I must admit. You guys ever do a threesome?"

I don't answer.

"Come on, Doc. Who's bigger?"

"You're a disgusting woman," I snap.

"My money's on Charles, but something tells me Adrian's no slouch in the dick department—"

"What is your point with all of this?"

"My point is I know your ex-husband is laundering money through his fund." Her tone is suddenly devoid of its previous sarcasm. "And I know you also work with the elusive Rome Palmer."

"I work with his son."

"Not sure the U.S. Attorney will care much for that distinction. Not when you also counsel a handful of known RF9 members, including Truck Palmer's right hand, Theresa Legette, aka RF9 Getz. You don't really believe you're guiding them out of the life, do you? Maybe the pre-teens have a chance, but Rome and Getz are seasoned gangsters. Set in their ways."

She drops her voice an octave. It's crueler now. "You're just sharpening the tools they use to sell drugs and kill people. You're RF9's in-house shrink. Their insurance policy. Your job isn't to heal your patients, it's to keep them from cracking. From snitching. From running. A performance coach for organized criminals. That's how the prosecutors will paint you. And what's worse? You know exactly what you're doing. That makes you dangerous."

"I help my patients learn how to breathe before they act, how to recognize a trigger before they succumb to it. That doesn't make me dangerous. That makes me useful."

"Useful to who? Them? Or the people who use them? You're not just calming their rage. You're enhancing their control, giving them discipline. You're making these boys better soldiers."

I stare at her. She believes that. And maybe, somewhere in the mess, it's true. I don't know anymore. I thought I did.

"I've seen it work," I murmur. "I've seen people walk away from that life. It may have taken time, but it worked. Once they found another way forward."

She scoffs. "And how long does that last? How long before those good intentions buckle under the weight of gang loyalty, retaliation, or just the need to eat in this expensive fucking world we live in? They always go back.

That's why the only way to save anyone caught up in this kind of mess is to topple the infrastructure. I'm sure you know that by now. Maybe you can't admit it, but how many more kids need to die before you do?"

I almost let his name slip. But I don't. Revealing my suspicions about Jahlil would only prove her point. And potentially make me an accomplice to his murder. I told Charles about Jah. Trusted that maybe the powerful, polished lawyer who funded my program would help him. I know now how naïve I was being. I fed that boy to the RF9 killing machine without even realizing it. And now this woman wants me to help her clean up the mess. If it were just me, I'd consider it. But it's not. I can't play hero anymore, not with my daughter firmly in the crosshairs.

Yet, Adrian tells me he has it handled and there's nothing to worry about anymore. That their investment is performing well and he's nearly free of their reach. I believe him. Because if I stop believing him, I start spiraling and that's when mistakes get made. I won't put my daughter at risk so the FBI can secure their headline. Unfortunately, that means I have to live with knowing that more kids like Jahlil will meet the same fate.

The quiet clink of this FBI scrooge setting her mug down brings me out of my thoughts. "I'll keep with my approach, Special Agent."

"You think you're helping your community," she says, her perpetually raised eyebrow arched even higher now. "But you're not. You're just prolonging the poisoning. RF9 and every Black God behind them are going down. And when we file charges, we won't discriminate. Lawyers, accountants, therapists, and fund managers."

She lets those last words hang before adding, "But I'm offering you and your ex-husband full immunity in exchange for your testimony against the Palmers. Witness protection for the both of you and your daughter."

I let her think I'm considering it.

"This is your only chance, Dr. Wright. I won't extend this offer again."

I meet her eyes with all the fortitude I can summon. "I'm not breaking any laws. Neither is Adrian. Now, please get the hell out of my house."

She sets the mug down slowly, like she's making a point, then turns toward the door. But before she reaches it, she pauses and looks back. "You think you're protecting them. But sooner or later, the kids you're trying to save… they'll just end up dead or behind bars. And the ones who put them there will still be attending galas and putting their names behind shiny new buildings downtown."

"Special Agent Courtleigh, my daughter is playing in her last high school game ever tonight. I can't be late."

"Fine." She starts down the steps of my porch, then glances back. "I really hope you don't think I'm bluffing. RF9's time is up. We have what we need. Arms trafficking, narcotics, tax evasion, murder. RICO will stick, and these kinds of charges aren't easy to fight."

I don't say anything. I can sense her getting impatient.

"Look," she says, letting out a slow breath. "Full disclosure. Without you or Adrian, we've got smoke when it comes to the Palmers. Strong patterns, odd tax structuring, whispers on the street."

I cross my arms. "So, not enough."

"Not yet. Sure, we can indict RF9 today. Truck and Getz would likely go down. But if you can connect Palmer family money to the Blue Rock gun running scheme—"

"I can't violate privilege."

"I'm not asking you to. But maybe you noticed something in the foundation's books. Or maybe Rome said something, even in passing, about his family's business."

I look away, trying my best not to let anything on. But inside, I know I have exactly what she needs.

"That kind of detail," she continues, "takes this from a simple gang takedown to a full-blown RICO. We don't just get RF9. We get the Black Gods, the cops on their payroll, the judges and politicians they fund through that foundation, the ones who all knew exactly what Jerome Palmer was and where that money is coming from."

She pauses. I don't say anything.

"But if you stay silent?" she adds, softer now. "Then they stay clean, and this whole thing looks like another low-level gang bust. And you'd go down with them as an accessory. As the woman who kept killers sane enough to keep killing. You can be a key witness, Dr. Wright. Or a co-defendant."

I won't lie, she's compelling. But I've already made up my mind.

"If you need anything further, feel free to contact my attorney, Mitchell Lowenstein." My voice is calm, almost polite, but sharp enough to let her know I'm done with this conversation.

"Please reconsider. Urge Adrian to do the same. I'd hate to see your kid all alone while her parents sit in federal prison until she's sending her own kids off to college."

This bitch is really starting to piss me off. "The front gate swings inward, Special Agent."

I don't watch her leave. I lock the door, press my palm to the wood, and let the silence settle. Then I push it all down: every threat, every lie, every fatal mistake. I've got a Riley Channing fan jersey to iron and a front row bleacher seat to claim.

67

SPECIAL AGENT REGINA COURTLEIGH

THE BOSSES COULDN'T wait any longer.

Nearly five years of undercover work, sealed warrants, buried subpoenas, and quiet surveillance. All so we could creep close to the Palmer brothers without tipping our hand, but we still don't have enough to tie them all to RF9. Rome and Charles are insulated. Clean on paper. They're willing to let their soldiers, including their own brother, fall so they can stay standing.

But now that Senator Calderon, who called for this task force, is running for president, suddenly everyone's got a hard-on for results. They want indictments and headlines. Photos of RF9 soldiers face-down on asphalt with our boots on their necks, next to crates of illegal guns and kilos of fentanyl, so she can say she's done something to solve this epidemic, even if it means blowing the whole operation before we get our hands on the real power behind that gang.

So here I am after leaving Dr. Wright's house, now bouncing down a cracked industrial road in the back of an armored van, suiting up for a raid I'm not ready for.

I pull my vest over my head and tighten the straps. My sidearm's already holstered, safety off. Beside me, my tactical team is reviewing schematics of the factory. They identify six exits, three choke points. No real intel on how many men are inside, but we're expecting a small army.

When I step out, Rondell is waiting at the rendezvous point. His FBI windbreaker is flapping in the evening wind, and his radio is at his shoulder. He doesn't smile. And neither do I.

"I take it the shrink isn't talking," he says.

I shake my head. "Not a peep."

"We still have a hell of a case, Court. We'll see if she changes her tune when she's looking at ten years for aiding and abetting. Let's get this done."

I fall in behind the tactical team. But this isn't about building a case anymore. It's about sending a message.

We storm the RF9 gun factory in South Maddox, breaking through the doors like a tidal wave. The air reeks of metal and gunpowder. I'm at the front, leading the charge. My team fans out, weapons raised, with flashbangs exploding down the hallways.

We seize pallets of assault rifles, boxes of semi-automatic pistols and submachine guns, crates of hollow-point rounds, and piles of duffel bags stuffed with cash sitting next to bricks of fentanyl, ecstasy, heroin, and cocaine. This is the heart of their East Coast operation, where they're housing close to $80 million worth of contraband and blood money.

Shots ring out from one of the back rooms as RF9 soldiers open fire. My men move like clockwork, returning fire without hesitation. The crack of gunshots bounces off the concrete, and within minutes, it's over. The shooters go down, and we push forward, room by room, securing every corner. This place was a fortress, but now it's the property of the federal government.

I catch my breath as I step outside and then into the mobile command unit. My eyes lock on the wall of live feeds from across the country. We're not just hitting RF9 in Maddox. Hell no. Philly, New York, New Jersey, Baltimore, D.C., Detroit, Chicago, St. Louis, Cleveland, Atlanta, Miami, Houston, and Oakland.

I watch as various tactical units bust down doors, pulling out mass stashes of guns and kilos of pills and fentanyl. The streets are flooded with blue flashing lights as gang members are dragged out of trap houses in cuffs.

An RF9 heroin lab in Detroit is taken down with fifteen dead bodies found in vats of hydrofluoric acid. The RF9 street empire is burning.

Despite my failed attempts to secure the testimony of family members and insiders such as Shanita Palmer, Reeda Channing, and, of course, Dr. Wright, in the end, it was old-fashioned police work that made this possible. Undercovers, surveillance, wire taps, and forensic accounting. In total, we've arrested 182 members and seized approximately $300 million in drugs, guns, cash, real estate, and illegal crypto accounts. RF9 is finished.

This should feel like victory. But the Palmers, the Black Gods—the real masterminds—are still out there, untouched. My undercovers are deep on the inside. Those two agents are the reason we're standing here right now. They infiltrated Getz's core crew, following her around the country as she managed RF9's drug and gun shipments. They uncovered these locations, and their evidence secured the arrest warrants. We have enough to bring her and Truck Palmer down, but we've left them out for now, hoping they'll make a mistake that'll get us to Rome and Charles.

Still, the clock is ticking. Rondell wants them out. It's too dangerous to keep them in since once the news of these raids hits, the Palmers will likely be paranoid and start hunting for a snitch. But I can't pull them. Not when we're this close. The Black Gods will slip up. They have to. And my people will be there when they do.

• • •

The task force war room is alive. Phones are ringing. Boots are thudding across the floor. Agents are talking over each other as the adrenaline still hangs in the air. Laughter cuts through the noise in quick bursts, but beneath it all, the tension hasn't quite let go.

I barely get the chance to sit at my desk when he walks in like he owns the building. Which, in a way, he does. I can hear Lawrence "the Hawk" Hadington congratulating agents on his way through. His voice takes on that low, clipped, Southern drawl that's been polished by an Ivy League rearing and half a dozen intelligence briefings a day for four decades straight. He smiles like he likes you, even if he's here to end you.

Rondell stands to greet him, which tells me everything. Rondell doesn't even stand for judges.

"Davis," Hadington says. "What do you say we get right to it?"

"Of course, Mr. Hadington." Rondell waves a hand at me. "Court, get over here."

I step inside the conference room and close the door behind me.

Hadington pulls out a chair at the head of the table like his name is engraved on it, opens a slim leather folder, and glances at a page that looks like a signed arrest warrant. "I understand you've just taken down much of the RF9 network. Is that correct?"

"As of this evening, sir," Rondell answers. "We've got all but the Palmer brothers in custody."

"And a few affiliates to pick up," I add.

"Like who?" Hadington asks.

"Some Palmer cousins we have on record running gun deliveries," I say, "a few folks who manage their fronts… as well as their in-house doctor and one of their money launderers. Plan is to get one of them to flip on the Palmer brothers."

Hadington nods, but not like he's satisfied, like he's digesting the update. "I need you to strike Adrian Channing from any and all aspects of this investigation. Effective immediately."

I keep my voice steady. "With respect, sir, Channing was present at a summit of five separate criminal factions the Bureau is actively investigating. He's in our surveillance logs—"

"I've seen the logs," Hadington says. "Very thorough. But irrelevant."

I glance at Rondell. He looks just as confused as I am.

"We are literally about to go pick him up," I say.

"On what grounds exactly?" Hadington asks. "I don't see enough for an arrest in this file."

"Just questioning for now," I say. "I'm sure a subpoena on his financials would give us what we need for an arrest. He might be willing to testify against the Palmers if we put some pressure on him."

Hadington's tone stays calm, almost amused. "Adrian's proximity to these Palmer hoodlums is purely coincidental. Rooted in distant family affiliations. Any attempt to include him in your RICO indictment will be viewed as an overreach."

"Overreach?" I snap.

"Do you have any evidence of his involvement in any crimes?" Hadington asks.

"He walked into a Palmer-owned building flanked by mercenaries," I say. "I believe he was meeting not only with Charles Palmer but with representatives of the Zi Wan Triad, Bonetti Mafia, and two other drug syndicates we suspect acquire their product from RF9."

"He was seen in a building open to the public," he drawls out as if trying to prove how absurd it sounds. "Did he arrive with them?"

"No. But am I supposed to believe he was there for a family brunch? He's laundering their money."

"Did you witness him engaging with them at all?"

"No." I sigh. "But I have it on good authority that at least one of RF9's money launderers is a light-skinned Black man."

Hadington raises an eyebrow and then chuckles. "Do you hear yourself, Special Agent?"

I don't speak. He's right. I need more evidence.

"Let me put it plainly," Hadington says. "Unless you have evidence of legitimate violent crimes he has committed, Mr. Channing is an asset to certain national interests. He is not your concern. He is not to be surveilled, researched, subpoenaed, or so much as named in your paperwork."

"This is obstruction." I can't help but fidget with the badge hanging from my neck.

"No," he says, calm as ever. "This is the business of the United States of America. Go after the Palmers. Take out every Black God, every gang and crew under RF9, every drug pusher, gun runner, and killer you can put a case on. Burn it all to the fuckin' ground. But Adrian Channing, his wife, his ex-wife, all of his people… They are out of bounds. And that is not a request."

I'm getting fed up with this shit, so I stand and say, "With respect, Mr. Hadington, you're a private citizen. We don't need to comply with your orders."

He smiles. "Then I'll have the FBI Director, who I put through college, pull your badge so fast your coffee won't have time to cool. And if, for some stupid reason, he won't, I'll have the Attorney General, who's life I quite literally once saved, pull his. And if you speak Channing's name in a press room or to a member of the media, I'll personally make sure you both spend the rest of your lives in a federal maximum security prison for treason."

I sit back down and the room goes still.

Rondell exhales through his nose. "Understood, Mr. Hadington."

I grit my teeth. "You're protecting a criminal."

Hadington rises and adjusts his cufflinks. "He's a fund manager, Special Agent. They're all criminals. Take him off your list until I tell you otherwise."

68

CHARLES PALMER

I MADE THE call. Black Gods and senior shot callers only. That's me, Rome, Truck, Uncle Mac, Frank Madigan, and Getz at a patio table in the backyard of a vacant suburban home in Chester, PA. It's registered in the name of our half-sister Raylene Jenkins. She's my father's daughter from before he met our mom. Big Palm wasn't in Raylene's life. There's no birth certificate or any evidence that she's a Palmer. So, no one will look for us here.

"Everything we built," Truck says, his voice trembling in anger. "Just wiped out." He pulls out a bag of cocaine and sprinkles it into the blunt he's rolling.

I lean forward in my chair. "Chief Collins doesn't think the federal task force has any solid evidence on the Black Gods."

"Why ain't he tell us we had snitches in our camp, C?" Rome asks. He looks more tired than I've seen him in a while.

"The feds boxed MPD out of the task force when John Bing and his men were killed in their safehouse. He only knew about the raid because it was happening in his backyard."

"Who else did they get?" Truck asks.

"Two shot callers out of RF9 Maddox," I confirm. "Slim Choppa and Lil Nutty, both of whom can testify to the identities of the Black Gods and our involvement with RF9. If I recall, Slim Choppa was involved in Rouchard."

"Nah," Getz says, shaking her head. "Them niggas solid. They'll do the years. Just gotta keep they families straight."

"But we got no cash on the street," Truck snaps, his frustration bubbling over. "No product. Nothing to keep niggas loyal. How long until the streets start questioning the Black Gods?"

"Not long," Rome says quietly. "C, how much cash do we have in the trust?"

"A little under two million dollars."

"What about the returns from the Ironbridge Industries deal?" Rome asks. "That should be more than twelve million."

"We put the bulk of it back into the street to fund the West Coast expansion," I explain.

"So the feds just took that shit?" Frank spits out.

I nod. "I've got another one point five I can take out of my firm, but that's not nearly enough to take care of the families and legal fees of over 180 RF9 members."

"Get in touch with Adrian," Rome says. "Tell him we need that eight he offered."

"He was my first call." I sigh heavily. "He said it would be 'unlawful' to cash us out while we're under federal investigation. He's playing it by the book. Holding our piece in escrow, hiring a forensic team to trace the source of funds."

"But he's knee deep in this shit!" Truck shouts. "He's part of the fuckin' RICO."

I exhale deep, scratching the top of my forehead. "I reminded him of that. He's cooked the books well. There's no record of his involvement in the South Maddox factory the feds just raided. On paper, he never held owner-ship. I don't know how he pulled that off. He's acting like he knows he won't be prosecuted no matter what happens."

Truck blows a plume of smoke, his eyes red and dark. "I told you this shit would happen, Chuckie! We got played by another thief you gave our money to! This is your fuckin' fault!"

Truck and I proceed to bicker. He calls me a "wannabe gangsta in a suit." I call him a "big dummy with a gun." We go back and forth until—

"Enough!" Rome slams his fist on the table, rattling the bottle of Hennessy and glass tumblers. "We need a solution."

"We gotta move on that light-skinned nigga and take our fuckin' money back," Truck says, before turning to Getz. "G, tell the Black Gods what you got."

"Yeah, OG," Getz says. "Press release say he got a billion-dollar fund now. He guaped up forreal. My young bouls got the crypto account set up. He can get us the bread without the feds flaggin' shit."

"We go in with every RF9 soldier still standin'," Truck says, smoking and pacing. "We force Adrian to give us the money, then we kill his ass. Tonight."

I shake my head. "Truck, you're still angry that Josie moved on with Adrian. You need to let that lust for revenge go."

"This ain't about that," Truck says. "This ain't even about business, Chuckie. This is survival. This the legacy our daddy built. What we built. We take what the fuck is ours. That light-skinned nigga think he the king of Mad Dog City. He ain't."

"If you go after Adrian Channing, you'll die." I glare at him. "Have you been to East Madd lately? You won't even get close to him."

"He's right, Big Truck," Frank adds. "The Eastside's a fortress. STS Police roam the streets like commandoes. RF9 is not allowed. It's like they tagged us. The furniture trucks, utility vans... Anytime one of our shipments goes past Rawley Street, they get stopped by STS. They don't search but they make it clear if we come back through, they will fire on us. And those boys are surgical."

"The white Black God ain't lyin'," Getz says. "STS cleared all our corners on the Eastside. We get no money over there."

Truck sighs, his voice a low growl. "He'll make his boys stand down if we got guns to his kid."

"This is why Daddy told us to never smoke this stuff." I slap the bags of cocaine, fairy dust, and weed off the table. "The drugs are corrupting your brain, Truck."

"Fuck you, nigga," he grumbles.

"The feds won't stop until they have a Palmer in cuffs," I say, "preferably all of us. They'll be watching our every move, waiting for a mistake. If you get caught in a ransom scheme, the prosecutors will argue it was on behalf of our organization and tie us all into a RICO. Not just us in here. That's Shanita, the cousins, uncles, and aunties who all own a piece of Palmer Holdings LLC and all work for our various fronts, laundering our money—"

"Shut the fuck up, Chuckie!" Truck shouts. "If I get caught, I'll eat the charges. Ain't nobody but me gon' see years behind this RF9 shit, you hear me? This gang shit is my shit! I built it and I'll die wit it if need be."

"No!" I shout back. "We don't have to lose anyone! We just need time... Rome, tell me you agree with me on this."

Rome sits at the head of the table, staring at the floor, silent, like the weight of the conversation is crushing him.

"Let me worry about how to rebuild our business," I continue. "This is not the first time the federal government shut us down. They did it in '04 when Big Palm went away, and we rebuilt. They did it four years ago when Volition crashed, and we rebuilt. We can do it again."

"How?" Frank asks.

"When the heat dies down, I'll reason with Adrian. He's a man of his word. He'll pay us our rightful proceeds on the Geraldine's investment once it's safe for him to legally do so. But if you kidnap his kid, there's no walking that back."

"Nah, I don't trust that nigga to do anything to help us," Truck says, still fuming. "Not without leverage."

"And what if he doesn't give in?" I ask. "What happens if he calls your bluff? Are you willing to kill a teenage girl?"

Truck's eyes narrow. "I'll do what I gotta do. We was just watching him and his family, making sure he didn't skate wit our bread. He escalated when he had hands put on Big Palm."

"Are you ready to spend the rest of your life in Riverville with him until they give your big Black ass the needle?" I holler, flustered.

"I made peace with that possibility a long time ago, Chuckie. They say everything happen for a reason, right?"

I sigh, shaking my head. "Yeah, and sometimes the reason is you made a stupid decision."

"Who the fuck you think you talkin' to like that—"

"Enough," Rome cuts in. "C, what does it look like without the dope and guns? Our legit businesses. Can we live on that?"

"You know as well as I do the Emporium is bleeding. Without RF9's cash flow, I'd give it a year before we start shutting down locations. Everything else in the portfolio is either illiquid or purely for laundering. We'd have to downsize in a significant way. Sell all the real estate. All of the family members would need to find real jobs. Forget private schools, forget luxury. But it would be temporary. Once the heat settles, we could rebuild."

I study Rome's face, watching the tension pull his features tight as he rubs his beard, now more salt than pepper.

He looks at me and sighs. "Look, we need cash. But we don't hurt civilians anymore. That's not about risk. It's about who we are, and who we're trying to be."

I nod with vigor. "I couldn't agree more."

"C, sell everything as quickly as possible. Truck, let our soldiers know we'll take care of them in due time, but if we can't and they spill on us, then we can't protect 'em on the inside. And they got plenty of Albanians doin' time in Riverville who hate RF9."

"It's the right move, Rome," I say. "I'll get as much as I can for the real estate. Everyone just lay low until the heat dies down. We'll survive this."

After the meeting adjourns, a round of brotherly embraces ensues, signifying the tense times we're in. Our business has been eviscerated, but by the grace of God, we still have our freedom and each other.

69

TRUCK PALMER

As SOON AS the front door of Raylene's house shuts behind Chuckie, Rome's demeanor shifts. He's angry in a way I haven't seen in a while.

He stands and paces as he rubs his head. Then he stops, looks at me, and then at Getz, and back at me. He waits until he hears Charles's car pull off before speaking.

When he finally speaks, he has that tone he uses when it's time to regulate. "This shit took forty years to build, T. Three hundred million vanished in a day. All that money, all that power gone because we let one bitch ass light-skinned nigga into our house. He fuckin' put hands on our father and stole our bread. This shit can't go unanswered."

The old Rome is back.

"Do it," he orders, his voice low, "but don't hurt the girl. You hear me? Take her but nothing happens to her, T. You make Adrian give us that crypto, everything he fuckin' has. Not just our six million. I want it all. Then, put a bullet in that nigga."

He pauses for a moment, looking at the ground like he's fightin' whatever he 'bout to say. Then, real slow and real quiet, he says, "And kill the therapist. She can put me and Chuck in the RF9 RICO. She needs to go."

"Why you ain't say this shit five minutes ago?" I ask.

"Chuck needs plausible deniability, so he can represent us in court if it comes to that. But I'm serious, Tracy. You don't hurt the daughter. Mask up so she can't ID you. If Adrian hesitates or tries to negotiate, just draw him out and kill him and his baby momma. You let Riley go. Once you get the bread, I'll take my third, and I'm out for good. I'm takin' my family and leavin' the country. The business, the family, it's yours, T."

I look back at Rome with fire in my eyes. "Say less, big bro."

• • •

Getz put the call out to about a dozen RF9 soldiers, pretty much everyone who ain't get caught in the RICO. Not much time to plan, but we got 'em waiting at the Trenton warehouse. The feds didn't even touch this spot, only the Black Gods and a few shot callers knew it existed.

Soldiers fill the space, the air clouded wit smoke and chatter, plotting our next moves over brown liquor, weed, and dust.

I step to the front of the room. "Me and Getz take the girl and her momma after the basketball game at PCA. We'll tail 'em from the parking lot and grab 'em out they whip."

Getz steps forward. "Frankie, your crew will pull up on Rawley Street, just outside the light skinned nigga's office. Once Truck and I have the girls, we'll send him footage of his family tied up and make him call off his shooters. You go in, make sure he sends the crypto and don't pull any funny shit. Then, you bring him here."

"Gotchu," Frank says, jamming an extended clip into a submachine gun.

"Keep him alive," I say. "I'ma be the one to pull his fuckin' plug. No one else."

We roll out, piling into a caravan of SUVs and Hellcats. Kareem hops in my Escalade with Getz and me. He held it down when the Albanians tried to smoke me. He pretty much saved my life, so Getz moved him up. He's been one of her right hands for the better part of the last year. From what she's told me, he's proven himself.

I park in the lot across the street from the basketball gym at PCA and shut off the engine. As we wait, the tension builds. My fingers tap against the steering wheel. Getz double-checks her 9mm before snorting a bump of white. She passes me the bag, I take a bump, and then sprinkle some in a blunt and light it up.

"We just grab em, G." I puff, the high hittin' me slowly. "Don't rough 'em up or anything like that. I know how you love to pistol whip a muhfucka."

"Like I did that white boy? His ass was cryin' like a bitch." She laughs as she takes another bump.

Kareem leans forward from the backseat, laughing as he takes a bump himself. "G Getta livin' a nigga dreams. I ain't never shot no white boy. Would love to, though. Bet that shit felt good than a mothafucka."

"Fake ass Elon Musk nigga ain't know what was coming." Getz laughs along.

Kareem's quiet for a minute, taking a bump before he starts again, excited. "Oh shit, you talkin' 'bout that electric airplane dude that went missin'? Richard or Rouchard or some shit? That was us? Oh shit!"

He's hyped up. Too hyped up. Too much powder.

"He ain't missin', K," Getz brags. "Cracka ass cracka knew too much. We put dude in the river on da gang."

"Ay, can y'all shut the fuck up and focus? Once the daughter and baby mom get in the car and turn onto Destin Street, it'll be quiet. I'll pull in front of 'em, you and Kareem hop out and grab 'em. Once they see guns, they should do as you say. We'll pull the plug on the light-skin nigga and the baby momma after we get the crypto. But the Black Gods want the girl taken peacefully. No extra shit."

"Got it, OG," Getz says.

"The Black Gods? Oh shit, Rome in on this?" Kareem asks, more excitement in his voice.

"You think we take orders from Charles L. Palmer, attorney at law?" Getz mocks Chuckie's white boy voice as she snorts another bump and wipes her nose.

"I don't know what the fuck y'all talkin' about." I puff hard, eyes half-lidded. "My brother Rome sells furniture and coaches football. Charles is a lawyer. I'm the only Black God in dis bitch."

The gym door opens up, and Brianna and Riley walk out. I move to turn on the ignition. That's when I hear a soft click and my heart skips.

Kareem has two pistols drawn from the backseat, one aimed at the back of my head, the other at Getz's. "I can't let y'all do this."

I turn my head just slightly. "What the fuck is you doin', nigga?"

"I'm FBI," he says. "I can't let you two psychopaths kidnap innocents. Toss the guns out the window!"

I look to the center console where my piece is sitting.

"Don't try it, Truckie!" Kareem presses the barrel tighter to my head. "I've got units closing in. It's over! Guns out the window! Now!"

I look around and see nothing. The parking lot is filled with parked cars, but no squad cars are closing in, no movement at all.

"Bullshit," I snap back. "We put this mission together real quick. You ain't even know where we was goin'."

I look at Getz out the corner of my eye, the anger and shame spilling from her face.

"Ah, fuck you, nigga," she spits. "You ain't no fuckin' fed, Reem."

"Don't do it," Kareem barks.

Getz's hand moves fast, but his is faster. I flinch as a shot rings out. I glance over and see Getz's head slumped forward on the dashboard, her brains leaking onto the leather.

Kareem puts both guns on me. "Don't make me do it, Truck! We want Rome and Charles! Give us your brothers, and we can make a deal!"

"Okay!" I slow my breath and toss my piece out the window. "I won't resist. I'll give you what you want."

In the rearview mirror, I see him holster the gun in his right hand and reach into his jacket for cuffs. His eyes leave me for a second, and that's all I need. I ain't giving up my brothers for shit.

I lunge back, pushing his trigger hand away. The SUV rocks as we grapple for his gun. He's stronger than I thought. He slams my head against the dashboard, then moves the barrel of his gun to my dome, and fires. But I jerk forward just in time and he misses my head. The bullet crashes through the window. I grab the barrel, twisting it away just as he squeezes off another round past my ear, out the window.

I punch him in the jaw and then the gut. He gasps, faltering. I wrestle away his gun and put two in his chest. He slumps, still holding on. His eyes lock on mine like he's trying to tell me something. I don't give a damn. I fire again, this time at his face, pullin' his plug.

His body slides. I pant, feeling my veins pulsing as I try to catch my breath. I check him and see the wire in his jacket lining flashing red, transmitting everything.

"Shit!" I gotta move. I push the bodies out of the car and peel off.

Think, Truck. If the feds just heard everything, I need to blow the country. But I need some real cash to do that, and they took all the stash spots.

As I speed alongside the gym, I take a quick bump from the vial of cocaine in the cup holder.

I look up to my left and see Adrian's daughter crying for help, crouched over her mom on the ground, bleeding. Looks like she got hit by a ricochet from that fed snitch's gun. Everyone outside the gym scattered at the sound of the gunshots. She's there alone.

I need that bread. I can still pull this off. I make a U-turn and slam on the gas. The tires screech as I race through the parking lot. My hands are shakin' and my head's spinning from the dope and the noise of the shootout, making everything feel like it's moving too fast, too loud.

I see the girl in the middle of the empty parking lot, still sitting there alone, still screaming for help. She looks up at me through the windshield, and I can see the fear in her eyes as I accelerate toward her. I grip my pistol and then move to open the door so I can snatch her in as I get close.

I reach out for her, but then gunshots crack through the air, bullets shattering my windows.

Shit! STS shooters move in from the streets, dressed in black fatigues. They surround the girl and her mom as they bust shots at me.

I duck low, my adrenaline pumping as I hit the gas again. I can feel the bullets grazing by. I hear sirens closing in. I floor it and peel off as fast as I can.

I slam my fist against the dash over and over and over. I can't believe I let a cop infiltrate my crew. This mission would've been perfect if not for that fed snitch bitch. He shot the therapist. Not me.

70
ADRIAN CHANNING

I'M IN MY office, on the phone with the owner of a hospital system I plan to buy. The call stretches on as I grind him down on price. Outside the windows, the city fades toward evening. Inside, the clock keeps moving, and I'm getting more and more annoyed because I'm going to miss Riley's game.

The news on the TV is muted but the footage of the RF9 raids unfolding is crystal clear. I watch passively, although Hadington tipped me off that it was coming. Not only am I making him and his friends a lot of fucking money, but STS has already become one of Hawk Strategies' primary providers of mercenary services. If I'm taken down over a misunderstanding like taking capital from a well-polished, highly effective, sociopathic liar, it benefits no one.

Suddenly, Demarcus storms into my office. One look at his face, and I know something has gone terribly wrong. I hang up the call, and he gives me the news.

The room spins, and for a moment, I can't think straight. I thought I was clear with these Palmer fucks. I tell them to leave my family alone, and they do the exact opposite.

When I make it to the emergency room, Brianna is in a bed, fresh from surgery. She's pale and unconscious with wires and tubes running everywhere. Riley sits beside her, still in her basketball jersey, staring ahead with a numb look, the mix of sweat and dried tears leaving a faint crust on her cheek.

"Dad." Her voice shakes as she falls into my arms.

I hug her tight, then pull back, inspecting her for injuries. "Are you okay?"

She nods slowly as if she's not confident she is. "He tried to take me," she cries, her face pressed into my chest, tears soaking my shirt. I hold her tighter.

"It's okay, buttercup, I'm here."

After a few hours, Brianna slowly wakes up. She's disoriented, her voice more like a gasp. "Wh–what happened? What's going on?"

Her eyes dart around the room. First to me standing by her bedside, then to Riley curled up on the chair, sleeping. Then to the open door where my guards are posted, lining the halls. I'm not taking any chances.

"We're not sure yet." I try to keep my voice steady as I move closer to her. "It could've been an attempted robbery."

She tries to sit up, but then winces before laying back down. "I don't believe you, Adrian. This had something to do with the Palmers, didn't it?"

Brianna's the one person I can never successfully lie to. After a moment of hesitation, I nod my head.

"Why?" she asks, her voice weak and slurred. "I thought you were paying them back."

"It was never going to be enough, Bri. I had to do something to back them off of us."

Riley slowly starts to wake up. Brianna's head tilts back, as though the weight of holding it up has become too much.

"What did you do?" she whispers. "Why didn't you tell me there was still danger?"

"Because I beat them, Brianna."

Her eyelids twitch, a quick, fragile tremor, and after a moment, they sink closed. The monitor's steady beep fractures into a faster, louder rhythm before stretching into a single unbroken scream.

"Bri!"

"Mom!" Riley cries, clutching my arm. "Dad, what's happening?"

I scream for the doctors. The sterile hospital room feels suffocating as they swarm around Brianna, their voices urgent but detached as they determine she's bleeding internally. My heart pounds as they wheel her away for another surgery.

Hours later, the surgeons finally emerge, their faces grim. The words they deliver are like a thousand high-caliber rounds to the chest. "I'm sorry, Mr. Channing. We did everything we could…"

Riley collapses into my chest and wails as if her heart is being torn apart. Her legs give, along with mine, and we crumple to the ground. Her cries cut through me like shards of glass, but I force myself to stay steady, to hold her close, even as my own throat tightens and my vision blurs. I swallow hard, blinking back tears, trying my best to be strong for my daughter.

I hold her tighter, feeling the weight of a loss that cuts through our core as I wrestle with the guilt and regret that I couldn't protect her mother.

Brianna was the light in the darkest of worlds, a beacon of goodness that didn't deserve this cruel fate. The pain in her last moments, her fear, and knowing it was my actions that put us in this horror, makes me feel like the worst kind of monster—a man who sacrificed his loved ones on the altar of his own recklessness.

I've become the very thing I vowed not to be. I've become my father.

71

TRUCK PALMER

My HEART'S POUNDING so hard it feel like it might burst out my chest. The coke is still buzzing through my veins, and I can't stop shaking. The crib smells like blunt smoke and gunpowder. Now, I'm tearing through drawers, tossing clothes, cash, dope, and a pistol into a duffel bag while Zaida stands in the corner, watching me with wide eyes. I forgot we was finally supposed to get it on tonight. I set that up before the raids.

"What the hell is goin' on, Truckie?" she asks.

"I fucked up," I mumble, wiping sweat from my face with trembling hands. "I had it all planned out, everything was good. Grab the girl, get the crypto. Almost had her, then Kareem raised up on me. Nigga was a fed. I had no choice. Had to dead 'em on the spot. But *he* shot the therapist, not me!" My voice cracks as I try to keep it together, but the fear and the dope racing through my veins are making it hard. "I gotta skip town."

"Where are you gonna go?" Zaida asks.

"I got a boat. I'ma slide up the Delaware, cross into Canada. Got a connect up there who can get me to Africa on the low."

She doesn't say anything, just nods. The sirens in the distance are getting louder. I freeze when I hear heavy boots on the steps outside, the metallic clink of guns being readied. They're coming up the front porch steps. Back door is covered, too. Every exit is sealed.

How the hell they find me? I switched cars, took back roads. I was careful. They shouldn't have been able to track me here this fast.

I drop the duffel on a chair by the door. As I rummage through it for the gun, I realize. If the feds got one undercover, they might have another. This bitch, Zaida, must be a cop too. No wonder she wouldn't let me fuck until tonight. Only way they have my location right now since my name ain't on this deed.

My fingers graze the grip of the 9mm at the bottom of the bag as I feel a sharp jolt in my back. My muscles seize as electricity sears through them. I drop to my knees, gasping for breath. The duffel bag falls open and the gun and cash slide across the wood floor. Zaida stands over me, a pistol in her hand, her face cold. She kicks the gun out of reach and slams the butt of her gun over the top of my head. A sharp crack reverberates through my skull, and I collapse. I'm too high for the shock to knock me out, but I can't move either.

"FBI!" she screams. "Don't fucking move, Palmer!"

The door bursts open. Cops swarm in, weapons drawn. I'm pinned to the ground in seconds. A half-dozen pigs jump on me, jamming their knees into my back and legs while they cuff me.

A white bitch fed busts in, gun drawn as she hollers, "Ortiz!"

"Courtleigh, I'm good!" Zaida yells. "He's alive. I got him on the wire saying he killed Kareem. Is Galloway really dead?"

Courtleigh nods, and they both start crying. I guess Kareem was they homeboy. Fuck that sellout.

72

ADRIAN CHANNING

Two Weeks Later

THE WRIGHT HOUSE in North Maddox is filled with the quiet murmurs of people offering condolences, their faces blurred together in a haze of grief. Brianna's funeral drew a crowd of friends, family, clients, and members of the community who admired her work.

Now at the reception, I barely hear the soft voices and don't even register the soft pats on my back or the sympathetic nods. I'm stuck somewhere between rage and regret, between sorrow and fury, and each new face that comes through the door only makes it worse.

Riley's a mess. She won't leave my side but won't talk to me either. I'm beyond worried about her. Josie's been my rock, taking care of the arrangements with Mitch and Tessa, and making sure Riley and I are good. This whole thing is weighing on her as well. Truck's her child's father. I know it's not easy on her and Allen.

I had Demarcus explain to Josie that Truck was likely looking for a ransom. He heard about my success and needed cash to skip town after the RF9 raids, his vitriol being fueled by our relationship. It's not totally a lie, but not the full truth. Josie's smart, and I can tell she's not buying it, but she's not asking the questions that I can almost see brewing in her mind.

I look to my right and see Mitchie standing at the bar with Tessa before he beelines my way.

"Looks like feds, A.C." He nods toward the front door discreetly. "I'll get rid of 'em."

But I had already noticed the two people standing awkwardly by the doorway, out of place. The older one, a Black man with a receding hairline, graying beard, and hard expression, wears a dark suit too stiff for the room. Next to him is a younger white woman, late-thirties maybe, her blonde hair pulled back in a tight bun, eyes sharp, scanning everything. It's Special Agent Courtleigh of the FBI. Hadington got me her file, and apparently, she has a hard-on for me.

"It's all good, Mitch." I pat him on the back. "They probably just want to pay their respects."

The agents approach me, Riley, and Josie.

"Mr. Channing, Ms. Channing, ma'am," the older Black agent greets us.

"It's Wright-Channing," Riley corrects him softly, holding back tears.

"Of course. Ms. Wright-Channing, my apologies." He flips open his badge with a practiced motion. "Special Agents Davis Rondell and Regina Courtleigh, FBI."

Courtleigh gives a tight nod, her face serious. "We know it may not help, but we wanted to let you know that we've charged Truck Palmer for the attempted kidnapping and murders of your ex-wife, our undercover agent, Jabar Galloway, and Tim Rouchard. He's confessed to everything and is expected to plead guilty."

"Thank you for letting us know, but my daughter's been through a lot." I glance at Riley and then at Josie. "My family's been through a lot."

"Of course, Mr. Channing," Rondell says. "We just thought it might bring a bit of closure to know the scum who did this will never again see the light of day as a free man."

He taps Courtleigh on the arm as a signal to leave. But she's not having it.

Her determination is clear in her eyes as she asks, "Do you have any idea why Truck Palmer would want to harm your family? We understand his mother is married to your father and you're now engaged to the mother of his son." She glances at Josie. "Was this a family feud of some sort?"

I turn to my daughter. "Riles, go sit with your grandparents, okay? Try to eat something. Josie, can you..."

"Yeah, babe," Josie says. "I got her."

They head for the dining room. I lead the agents through the kitchen and out into the empty backyard. The winter sun is low but sharp as it bounces off the frost-bitten grass. We stop under a bare sycamore tree, its shadow thin and useless. I slide on my sunglasses—not for the sun, but because something tells me I'm about to have to lie like my freedom depends on it. Best if they can't see my eyes.

"First of all," I begin, "the Channings and the Palmers are by no means family. From what I understand, Truck is estranged from his mother. I have no idea why he'd want to kill Brianna or kidnap my daughter. Only thing I can think of is he thought he saw an easy target for a ransom."

"That would make sense, but there's just something I can't put my finger on about that motive," Courtleigh says. "Like I said, Truck confessed to murdering your former business partner at Volition Aeronautics to silence him."

"I'm glad Tim's children now have that closure. But I'm struggling to see what you need from me right now. On this day."

"Well," Courtleigh says slowly, "we know you led the acquisition of the company that was selling dirty guns to RF9, known to be controlled by a group referred to in the streets as the 'Black Gods.' But Truck is claiming he's the sole 'Black God' and that his brothers and cousins had nothing to do with any of it. He says he forced them to ship his guns and dope through the family furniture store and provide legal services, threatened to kill them and their families if they didn't go along with his scheme."

Just a family of liars... "I'm not sure I heard a question, Agent Courtleigh."

"Does that strike you as curious?" she asks. "Given your involvement in the company and with the family that we believe to be the buyer of your dirty guns. Excuse me, Blue Rock's dirty guns." She's being cute.

I should let Mitchie run their asses out of here with legalese. But it's better to keep it cordial and avoid a scene.

"I spearheaded that acquisition in my role as a Managing Partner at PGC years ago. I've long been cleared of any wrongdoing in connection with that theft of property, and until the news of your raids hit the airwaves two weeks ago, I had no knowledge of any group called the Black Gods. But maybe you two should be out there doing your jobs, instead of here asking me to do it for you."

Courtleigh smirks but then her face hardens. "Look, that piece of shit and his gang of degenerates killed my father, killed my agent, killed your business partner. Then, they killed your kid's mom." Her tone is growing in fervor with every word. "These guys do nothing but leave trails of dead bodies across the entire country. I don't care what you knew back then or what your involvement was. As far as I'm concerned, you're a victim in all of this. But I need to know what you know about Rome and Charles Palmer."

I nod, but keep my jaw clenched tight.

Rondell steps in. "We have most of Truck's RF9 crew on RICO, but nothing on those two, who we believe to be the real power behind the Black Gods criminal empire. None of their people are talking. Anything you can share would go a long way."

"I'm not close with my father, so I wouldn't be close with his new wife's adult sons. But..." I pause briefly as I think about how much to give them. "As you know, Charles is an attorney. He helped me with a couple of discreet legal matters a while back. But we're not friendly, and I no longer employ his services. As for Rome... I bought some furniture from him a few years ago. Other than that, I don't know anything about their family or their business."

They're silent, eyeing me.

"Of course, Mr. Channing," Rondell says, gruffly. "If you can think of anything, please do reach out." He hands me his card.

"Just one other thing," Courtleigh says. "In his confession, Truck said he carjacked Tim Rouchard when he was here in Maddox. But Tim didn't live here. He had no business here after Volition folded. He was scheduled to give us his testimony the morning after he went missing. He said he had digital evidence of John Bing's dealings with RF9 that he could only share in person. We specifically told him not to leave New York. Any idea what he was doing in town that night?"

"Not a clue."

"Was he here to see you?" She's not trying to hide her suspicion.

"Tim Rouchard was the CEO of one of the fifty-three portfolio companies I managed for PGC at the time. We weren't friends, but I admired his vision, his mission to leave the world in better shape than how he found it. Unfortunately, his desire to do the right thing made him another victim of this dangerous criminal conspiracy that for too many years flew under the government's radar. Tim was failed by the law enforcement agencies charged with protecting us. He was an American hero, as was my daughter's mother. That's all I have to say about that... I need to get back to my daughter now."

I give Mitch a look, and he ushers them out.

Josie stands on the back porch, watching the interaction, eyeing me closely. I can sense her concern. It doesn't help that Charles Palmer, the liar, just arrived. It's not a coincidence. I'm sure he was waiting around the corner for the FBI to leave. The sneaky shit.

He strolls through the side gate into the backyard, his old, fat shit body-guard, Uncle Mac, accompanying him as usual. Demarcus and two STS guards stop them before reaching me, frisking them for weapons. I can't believe he has the nerve to show up here.

"They're clean, A.C.," Demarcus confirms.

Wanting to avoid a scene, I allow them into the backyard, still empty except for Mitch and my security. Charles and Mac approach as Demarcus trails, his hand resting on his holstered pistol.

"Adrian," Charles says his voice soft, carrying a feigned earnestness that I can now hear clearly. "I came to pay my respects. Brianna was a brilliant woman, an amazing practitioner. She didn't deserve this. I'm truly sorry for your loss."

My eyes are fixed on the liar, but I say nothing.

"I know my brother's actions are inexcusable." His eyes stay low. "He was out of control and this shouldn't have happened."

"Bri—" I stop myself. Just saying her name brings tears. "My daughter's mother is dead because your idiot brothers couldn't control their ego. Because you couldn't control them."

"Rome had nothing to do with this. He shut Truck down, but Truck was on drugs and not thinking straight. He thought he could use Riley and Bri—"

"You don't say her name. I know everything, Charles. I know how you lied to her, how you manipulated her when she asked for your help. Just like you did me."

"I'm not here to argue." Charles takes a tentative step closer, desperation edging his tone. "We just needed our money out of your fund. Truck thought the only leverage we had was your family. Rome and I stood against it."

He pauses and for a moment we stand in silence, staring at each other.

"Now I know what you're thinking right now," Charles continues. "That once Truck gets to Riverville or one of your other prisons, that you'll have him killed, but I'm ask–no… I'm begging you not to do that. I'm begging you not to retaliate against my family."

He glances around the yard at the eight armed STS guards, each capable of neutralizing this talking headache and his Steve Harvey-suited uncle upon my word. He likely chose this moment, amidst civilians, to approach me because if it were anywhere else, I'd kill him.

I stay silent, staring at him through the black of my sunglasses, hoping he'll make himself disappear.

Finally, I speak. "If Rome didn't sign off on the kidnapping, then he has nothing to worry about. But Truck is gonna die in prison. And that's his doing."

"I'm asking for a chance to resolve this without more bloodshed. There must be something we can work out."

"The time for dealmaking is done." I keep my voice calm but stern. "You should leave."

He drops his head, likely in a solemn acceptance that he has no influence over me anymore. As he turns to leave, he looks through the French doors into the house where Riley sits with Josie, both peering over at our conversation.

"If it's alright, I'll just briefly give Riley and Brianna's parents my condolences," he says. "It's a request from my mother and Shanita."

I raise my eyebrow in disbelief. "Charles, if you go anywhere near my daughter, Demarcus will shoot you in the fuckin' head. I don't care who's watching."

Demarcus steps forward, almost shoulder checking Charles, letting him know he's ready to carry out that promise.

Josie, again, watches the entire interaction, her face showing concern and curiosity as two STS guards escort them out.

After another few hours, the guests go home. The living room is quiet, with just the soft ticking of a clock and the weight of grief hanging in the air. Riley sits on the couch, staring blankly at the floor, her eyes swollen from crying. Brianna's parents hover nearby, looking unsure of what to do with themselves.

I clear my throat, my voice barely above a whisper. "Come stay at our place tonight, buttercup."

She doesn't even look up. Her hands are clenched in her lap, her whole body tense. "No." Her voice is like ice. "I don't want to be near you right now, Dad."

The words hit me like a hammer. I try to respond, but she cuts me off, her voice rising with emotion.

"This is all your fault. I heard what Mom said to you in the hospital before she… She would still be here if it wasn't for you. You—" Her breath hitches. "You did this. Whatever you're involved in did this! And now I'm supposed to come with you? No, Dad. I can't. I won't."

I stand here helpless, feeling the full weight of the truth in what she's saying. The pain in her voice, the way she can't even look at me. It's like a punch in the gut.

"I loved her too." My voice breaks. "Riles, I promise I will make this—"

"Just stop it!" she screams, finally looking up at me, her eyes filled with a fury I've never seen before. "What? You'll make this right? You can't! All you do is lie! You say you'll do better. You promise this and you promise that. You buy gifts, but you only care about yourself and your precious business. Just... just leave me alone." She wipes away her tears with the sleeve of her dress as she turns her body away from me.

I want to reach out, to hold her, to tell her I'll fix everything, but she's right. That would just be another lie.

• • •

At home, Josie and I sit at the kitchen island as I cycle through old family photos of me, Brianna, and Riley.

"What did Riley mean when she said whatever you're involved in killed her mom?" she asks.

Angry tears well up in my eyes as I contemplate how to deflect. "I'm not sure, babes. I think she just meant the way we split up. After we divorced, Bri felt like she couldn't be near me. She moved back here with Riles to start fresh. If I had been a better husband, she wouldn't have been in danger." I slam my hand on the kitchen island. "Dammit!"

Josie caresses my back, but her eyes linger on me like she's waiting for the rest of a story she knows isn't coming.

After a long quiet moment, she asks, "Are you somehow involved with the Palmers?"

I shake my head in feigned disbelief. "Other than through my dad and Reeda, no."

Josie met my dad after I proposed. Strangely, he and I are in a good place and he agreed to keep my secrets. Still, it was awkward with Josie and

Reeda, given the Truck history. They knew of each other but had never met. So, Reeda had never met Allen, her grandson. We had a long conversation about the Palmers, her knowledge of their crimes, and my connection to them through my dad. I told her how Charles helped me with my legal issues but left out everything that happened afterward.

"If you're involved with them, you can tell me," she says. "You can tell me anything."

"Like what?" I retort. "What do you think I'm involved in?"

"I don't know. Laundering money—"

"I'm a legitimate businessman, Josie. I can't believe I even have to say that to you of all people."

"I'm not accusing you of anything, baby," she says quietly. "It's just... nothing seems to make sense."

"I can't talk about this anymore, Jo. I won't waste my energy trying to understand the reasoning of a sick man like Truck Palmer."

She drops her questioning, but she won't let it go. I know her too well.

73

TRUCK PALMER

I STAND IN court, shackled at my wrists and ankles. The judge is talking, but I'm not really listening anymore. It don't matter. The sentence is in. The judge apparently has a moral issue with execution, so she gave me five hundred consecutive life sentences instead.

I wasn't expecting anything different after they got me on the murders of a tech CEO, a "hero" undercover agent, and a doctor. Can't forget the racketeering, narcotics, arms trafficking, money laundering, and attempted kidnapping charges.

It's a spectacle. The leader of RF9 apprehended. A Black God taken down. The feds ain't even really do shit. After a week of detox, I see that it was my own carelessness that brought me down. As corny as it'll sound, I broke the first rule of dope dealin': Never get high on your own supply.

Chuckie's still doing his best. God bless him. Even though we squabble, I love my baby brother to death. He's not a soldier, but he's done more to protect our family than any gun.

He addresses the judge one more time, his voice soft, almost pleading. "Your Honor, my client's family, his son, lives here. We ask, respectfully, that you allow him to serve his sentence at Lower Maddox Correctional, where they can visit him. It would offer them some small mercy in this difficult time."

The judge looks up from her papers and then over to the pews. My eyes follow hers to a little guy in a sharp suit with a slight grin on his face. Charles tells me it's Mitch Lowenstein, Adrian's fixer.

The judge refocuses on Chuckie with a face that tells me she's been reminded of the fat stack of cash waiting in her chambers. And then she announces, "Brianna Wright's daughter won't get to visit her mother, will she? Neither will Agent Galloway's family. What about Tim Rouchard's kids? You must be joking, Mr. Palmer. Request denied. Your brother will serve his sentence at Riverville Correctional. Court is adjourned."

The gavel comes down, and just like that, it's over.

• • •

Processing at Riverville is worse than the trial. Stripped, searched, and prodded like cattle. They give me a blue jumpsuit with a number. I'm no longer a person, just a piece of meat to be chewed on by the system.

The guards are gruff, giving me those sideways looks like they know exactly who I am and how many cops I've killed. Like they can't wait to make me pay for it.

They put me in a cell with no windows, no light. Just cold concrete walls. The first few weeks, I keep my head low, and I don't say much. They got me on twenty-three-hour lockdown. I assume on orders from the light-skinned nigga.

It's a Tuesday night, and everything's quiet. My cell door clicks open like it's on a timer. Six dudes, all my size or bigger with "EMSK" and "Iron-bridge" tats on their arms and necks, steppin' in like they have permission.

But Big Truck ain't no ho. I don't care how many they got, I ain't goin' down without a fight. "Well, let's get to it then, niggas."

I swing hard, feeling my knuckles crack against one of their jaws. I swing again and again, landing each time. But there are too many. They hold me down, and their fists rain down on me from every angle. My vision blurs as my legs give out. When I finally hit the ground, breathless and tired, they stop, just standing over me, waiting for me to realize I'm done.

Then I see him, MG da General, leader of the original East Maddox Stronghold Killaz, a legendary gangsta. I see the glint of a shiv in his hand. Real talk, I'm glad it's him instead of some fuckin' bitch ass C.O.

He takes off his kufi, sticks it in his pocket, and leans down, whispering in my ear. "A.C. say whaddup, fuck nigga." He sticks the shiv in my gut. "This for Brianna." He plunges the shiv in again, over and over and over and over and over.

He stands, and then one after another, they all join in, stabbing and slashing. The guards don't come. I don't expect 'em to.

I don't fight back. I can't. The pain is setting in. My body's numb.

The last thing I see before everything goes dark is Makari's face, leaning in close. "And this is for Riley."

He slides the shiv across my neck. Blood squirts from my jugular, but I don't feel pain. I don't feel anything.

Dying in prison is a reality I accepted when I pulled my first plug as a shorty. What's throwing me now is the fact that I got got by some high yella pretty boy corporate sellout. It is what it is, I guess.

I'll give him his credit, though. It's some cruel shit from Adrian. Letting me live for a few weeks, fooling me into thinking he was taking the higher road. Maybe I'd eventually get yard time, have some sort of a life, maybe see my pops, build some type of brotherhood with the RF9 soldiers in here who still worship the Black Gods. Hope is a painful thing to rip away with the blade of a rusty shiv.

Fuck it, though. Out of the 84 human beings whose plugs I pulled, I never thought about a single one of 'em again. Their souls never haunted me.

Call me a monster, I'll agree. I don't know why God made me this way. But he made me in his image just as much as he did you.

74

ADRIAN CHANNING

One Year Later

Five Years Since Volition Crashed

I sit back, letting the weight of the signed term sheet settle in my hands. $212 million cash in exchange for ninety-five percent of GH Sweets, Inc. Josie's vegan dessert brand is officially in the stratosphere and about to be acquired by Jennison Brands, one of the largest food conglomerates in the business. I should feel something bigger, something more monumental, but instead it feels like the next logical step. Like business as usual.

Josie and I had the wedding this past summer under the open Paris sky where we first met years ago. When she walked toward me, her gown caught the breeze like something out of a dream. Riley was there, even though she made it clear she attended for Josie only. She was her maid of honor. It was almost the perfect experience, but we missed Brianna's presence. That's clear every time I look at our daughter and the grief that marks her features.

Now, here she is, my wife, standing by the expansive bay window in the kitchen of our eight-bedroom estate in the North Maddox Hills, the nicest neighborhood in the city. Her hand rests on her stomach as she stares out at the sun dipping below the horizon. I watch her, the way she gracefully cradles our future in her belly. She's six months pregnant with our son, and I haven't seen a more wonderful vision yet.

Allen is growing into a perfect gentleman despite the trauma left by his father's legacy. Josie accepted the explanation from Riverville Correctional when they told her that Truck was killed by a rival gang looking to get revenge for a murder he committed. Now that I think of it, that's not a total fabrication. She still doesn't know I own that asset.

And now, Josie and I have plans for the next phase of our lives.

"I can't believe it's actually happening," Josie says.

I set the offer sheet down on the kitchen counter between us. "Believe it. You pulled it off. This deal's gonna change everything."

She glances at me and smiles faintly. "For the five of us." Her hand drifts over our unborn child.

I move toward her, wrapping my arms around her. "Yeah, babes. For the five of us... if Riley ever returns my calls or texts me back, that is."

"Just gotta give her time, baby."

I offer a soft smile and kiss her on the forehead. "I know."

Her eyes move to the papers. "I have to start working with the lawyers, coordinating due diligence and everything else. There's a lot to handle."

"You got this, Jo. I already locked in the price and material terms. The rest should mostly be formalities."

"What do you have today?" she asks.

"Office and then meetings in the city. The PR from the sale is getting LPs excited, and Harry wants to do a PGC-CCP impact fund joint venture at ten billion."

"How's that gonna work?"

"CCP finds the deals and does the work, PGC funds them."

Josie furrows her brow. "Profit split? If CCP's not putting up capital, won't PGC want the lion's share of returns?"

"God, I love it when you talk deal to me." I put a playful seduction in my tone. "Is it too early to make baby number two?"

I pull her tighter and slap her lightly on the ass. She giggles before our lips meet briefly. "Don't start, boy." She turns to the fridge and starts packing Allen's lunch.

"Well, Harry and I still need to iron out those details. But if it's not fifty-fifty, it's not happening. But it could skyrocket our AUM without sacrificing our own cash. That plus Fund II… A lot of work ahead."

"To the stratosphere." She mocks me playfully. "Seriously, that's amazing, baby. I wouldn't expect anything less from you."

She's quiet for a moment, just turns and looks at me, as if she's searching for something deeper. Her hand moves over her belly again. "But I need you here too, you know. With the baby coming, with the deal. I can't do it all on my own."

"I'll be back tonight, Jo. Mitchie and Tessa will get a team to help with the sale process. You'll just have to sign the papers."

"That's not what I mean," she says.

"Then, what do you mean?"

"You keep saying it's all for us, but we both know that's not true."

"This *is* for us," I insist, stepping closer. "For you, for the baby, for Riley and Allen. With the Geraldine's profit and CCP growing the way it is, we'll be set for life."

"I get that, Adrian. I just want to make sure you remember to be present and grateful for what we have today."

I feel a twinge of guilt but bury it quickly. "I'll be present, Jo. I just need a few weeks to close some important deals, and I'll be back fully focused on you and the baby."

"It's just that the more CCP grows, the more I wonder if we'll ever find balance. It feels like I'm constantly losing you to the next big thing."

"You're not losing me. I'm just building my dream."

She studies me for a moment longer. "You once told me you'd give it all up for me. Is that still true?"

"Is that what you want?"

"That's not the question."

"But it kind of is, no?"

"I want you to be happy, Adrian, but I also just want... you... us. I don't need to be the wife of some billionaire business mogul. We make more than enough money with Geraldine's. We don't even have to sell it. We can just run it together as husband and wife, keep it family-owned and live off the profits."

I can't believe what I'm hearing. "That wasn't our deal, Josie."

"Our deal? Adrian, we're married and having a baby." Her tone betrays a growing annoyance with me. "You're not just my investor anymore."

"You don't want to sell this company now? 'Monetize your father's legacy,' that's all you've talked about since I've known you."

"I know, but I'm just thinking—"

"No, Josie. We're selling this company. We've signed the term sheet and have an agreement in principle. We back out now, we'll have to pay Jennison a termination fee. Not selling is no longer an option."

I've invested close to $1 billion across twenty companies out of CCP Fund I, but I'm still growing them. We need this exit to prove my concept.

"I'm worried that Geraldine's is the only thing keeping you here with me," she admits. "And not out there doing whatever it is you do to build your portfolio."

"What's that supposed to mean? 'Whatever it is you do.' I haven't done anything that others in my position haven't."

"Like what?" she asks.

Josie doesn't know about the illegal transactions, shootouts, and dead bodies. At least I don't think she does. Perhaps Truck told her about my criminal involvement during the course of their co-parenting before I had his throat slit a year ago. But if that were the case, Josie and I wouldn't be having this conversation. She'd have been long gone by now.

"Josie, the only thing I'm doing is trying my hardest to build something that my mother and my children can be proud of. Something you can be proud of. I'm not going anywhere."

I move closer and caress her belly. "We don't need to run a company together to stay close. You can just be my wife. We can start that foundation, invest in Black girls like we've talked about. You'll be the queen of this castle."

She shakes her head lightly. "Sounds like you want me to be another asset in your portfolio."

"What? How can you say that, Jo—"

"We need to go before we hit traffic." She calls for Allen, gives me a kiss and leaves. I watch through the window as their STS security detail trails her Mercedes.

I can't shake the feeling that Josie knows more than she's letting on. That maybe she's starting to see through the cracks. I'll have to keep that suspicion from her, like I've kept everything else.

75

ADRIAN CHANNING

SIX MONTHS LATER

THE LIVING ROOM of our home is flooded with soft evening light, a beautiful, sprawling space where everything feels right. I'm sitting on the plush sofa, AJ cradled in my arms, his tiny fingers grabbing at my shirt. Josie is somewhere in the house, probably working on the Channing Foundation, her next big project. We're committing big dollars to drug and gang intervention.

After taxes and expenses, Josie and I are flush with around $115 million in cash from the sale of Geraldine's. Shortly after the sale closed, Josie gave birth to our son. Adrian Channing Jr. was born ten pounds, twenty-two inches. Tall and strong like his dad, yet graceful like his mom.

"Jo!" I holler. "Riley's game is about to start!"

I hear a faint reply. "I'll be down in a sec."

This place is actually too big for just the four of us.

Allen shoots around on a toy hoop in the living room, just enjoying himself. Despite the fact that he's starting to look more and more like his piece of shit father, I love him like my own son. A child shouldn't be judged by their father's sins. It's the parents' responsibility to make sure he doesn't repeat them. Josie's doing an amazing job with that.

As Allen plays and AJ naps, I watch Riley tear up the court for UCLA in an exhibition game. She still doesn't return my calls or let me come to her games, but I know she's safe and thriving as much as a kid can, especially given what she's been through. It kills me that I have to root for her from afar, but I'll root, nonetheless. And I have the jet gassed up to see her whenever she's ready to see me.

Despite the tragedy of Brianna's murder, I feel like I've made it out the other side. God's favor, maybe. My firm is growing rapidly, and money's pouring in. My son's laughter fills me with a joy I haven't known in years.

Josie's done everything she set out to do since we teamed up. She monetized her father's legacy, and Geraldine's continues to be a rocket of a food company. We retained a five percent stake, and Josie now sits on the board of Jennison Brands. She seems happy, and she loves our son. I'm convinced she still loves me, too.

The game ends with Riley hitting a game-winning buzzer-beater from three. Allen and I run through the house screaming in excitement. Henry, Riley's puppy, chases us around, his tail wagging almost violently.

It's about nine p.m. when Allen goes to bed. I realize Josie never came down to join us for the game.

"Wanna go find Mama?" I ask AJ in a baby voice, bouncing him lightly.

I turn off the TV, and we wander through the house. Her home office is empty, the kitchen is still, and the bedroom is dark. I call out for her, but the house stays quiet. This is odd. Even though it's a big house, we can usually hear each other with a light holler.

I find her in my study, at my desk, staring at the screen. My blood turns cold. She has my encrypted drive open. She must've guessed my password. She doesn't look at me, just keeps scrolling through, her face like stone. She tells me she was looking for my tax returns for the foundation's tax filings and didn't want to bother me with the boys.

I freeze as the video of the assassin Derek Graff hired to kill me plays. And then the video of Derek confessing. All of Derek's dirty photos. The headlines.

"What is all this, Adrian? And please don't lie to me again."

I tell her the truth of the matter, that Derek tried to kill me out of jealousy. She seems to accept that explanation, but then she pulls up the original bank statement from when The Palmer Family Trust wired me the exact amount I initially invested in Geraldine's.

And then she shows me the Martex stock transfer agreement that documents my ownership of that company, including a schedule showing Riverville Correctional as one of its assets.

"Jo, this is all out of context."

"Give me the context, Adrian."

I have no choice, I tell her everything. The dirty Palmer money, their threats, the gun deals, the criminal LPs, Derek's death, the way I got out from under the Palmer's thumb, the hit I ordered on Truck—the reasons why both of our first-born children had to suffer the devastation of losing a parent so tragically.

I'm foolish to think she's grateful for my honesty. But maybe she'll vow to keep my secrets, to be the Bonnie to my Clyde, and help me uphold this illicit empire of mine.

I watch her face register the devastation. She grabs AJ from my arms, her breath quickening, her eyes wild. She screams for Allen and packs their bags frantically.

"I gave you every chance to tell me the truth." Tears are streaming down her face. "But you're just a liar. And a murderer. You killed my son's father."

"Because he killed my daughter's mother," I shout, unable to control my emotions.

She looks me up and down, the disappointment evident. "You're no better than he was. Actually, you're worse."

"How can I be worse than that guy?" I ask. "He did nothing but poison and murder innocent people!"

"Truck never lied about who he really was. He was nothing but flaws, but he owned them."

She finishes packing and barrels down the stairs toward the foyer.

"You can't take AJ from me." I move to stop her. "Please, Josie. Don't go."

"You're a monster. And you'll never see AJ or Allen again."

"They need their father, Josie. I need them. Don't do this."

I gently reach for her arm in hopes the physical touch will remind her we're a family, connected by much more now than some dirty money. She pauses for a moment but then abruptly draws her arm away.

"I'll fight you for custody, Josie."

She pauses, staring at me with a venom I haven't seen before. "You do that, and I'll tell the police everything."

My eyes widen in rage. "I own the police, Josie."

"Then I'll tell the press."

I stand speechless as she leaves through the front door and piles her bags and the baby stroller into the trunk of her SUV. I follow her out, pleading, but she's not having it.

She looks me dead in the eye through a crack in the driver's seat window and says, "Stay away from us, Adrian."

I hear AJ and Allen both crying in the back as she drives away, and just like that, they're gone.

76

CHARLES PALMER

ONE YEAR LATER

EVERY ASSET IN our portfolio has been seized. Palmer Furniture Emporium and all of its locations around the country, the real estate, and small businesses that employed dozens of Palmers, even my law office and the money in the family trust, have been deemed assets illegally funded by Tracy "Truck" Palmer and the RF9 gang.

For the first time in five decades, my family is living life completely aboveboard, yet dangerously below the poverty line.

Rome stands on the sidelines of the football field at South Maddox High School. His arms are crossed and his eyes are locked on the players sprinting across the field. His face is hard, but his demeanor is calm and peaceful, the same way it's been for over a year now, since the FBI shut us down and Adrian had our brother killed.

I watch him focus on the scrimmage like he's forced his mind to live only in this simple world of high school football and family barbecues. It feels too small for me. Too inconsequential. I can't shake the feeling that we're failing the Palmer legacy, that we're meant to rise again, that Truck's death shouldn't be the end of everything we built.

"I've been talking to Tori Bonetti," I start, keeping my voice low as we step further from the playing field, toward the quiet of the oak trees at the edge of the facility. "She wants to meet. Says she can get us a line on product."

Rome doesn't look at me. He just subtly shakes his head. "I'm out, C."

"I know you're out, but things have changed. I've worked every legal strategy I can think of to get the Emporium back, but Community Capital Partners acquired everything the feds seized. Palmer Community Athletics is now Channing Community Athletics. He's taking over our family's legacy, Rome. He even bought your mansion on the North Side and demolished it out of spite. We have no assets, no money in the bank and none coming in."

He keeps his eyes on the field, but I can hear him say, "Jesus Christ," under his breath.

We walk a few steps along the endzone as he monitors a group of quarterbacks warming up. "What about the clean six million we invested with him? I saw they sold Geraldine's. The fed heat is gone. We should get our return now."

"He won't answer my calls. I've thought about suing him, but I'm confident he hacked into my bank records because there's no evidence of my wire to CCP, and I'm sure he's cooked his fund's books. The investment is gone."

Rome shakes his head in confusion. "How can he hack into a bank? Don't they have the best cybersecurity?"

"He bought Maddox Savings & Loan. He's likely covering his tracks with bank regulators, hiding our investment and obscuring the participation of the other investors I brought him."

Rome sighs, not looking at me. His tone is steady but resigned as he says, "Let him have it, C."

"What? How can you say that?"

"We knew it would be expensive to get out. I didn't think I'd have to give up my baby brother for it, but…" His voice trails off, and even through his sunglasses, I see the moisture in his eyes. "But we did it. We can find success in other ways, brother."

"You don't really believe this is success, do you? We lost everything. Our money, our businesses, our influence, our respect. And he's out there sitting on top of a city we made, all because Truck couldn't just leave it be. He had to go after that man's family."

Rome finally turns to me, and I can see the fire simmering beneath the surface of his stoicism. "Truck did what he thought he had to do. But me, I'm done living two lives, C. The only influence I care about now is the one I have with my family. Shanita's happy. Momma's finally talking to me. My kids know their grandmother now, bro. I'm not giving that up."

"But we could get it all back." I step closer, my voice sharpening. "Truck made the sacrifice, and I'm grateful too, but now the feds have gone on to the next big case. They're not focused on Maddox anymore. Tori says her family has a new supplier out of Nigeria—"

"Nigeria?" Rome's eyebrow raises.

"Yeah, I asked around. It's legit. New outfit out of Lagos with a serious catalogue. Streets refer to them as 'The Control.' They're already supplying the Bonetti's, Black Metal M.C., the Triads, the Jamaicans, a few other groups around the country."

"And I imagine the Italians need an East Coast distributor with a pipeline into Black neighborhoods." Rome picks up the thread like the seasoned contraband executive he is.

"That's exactly right... We can work with them, start small and slowly rebuild our market share, our infrastructure... And then take 'em out."

For a moment, I think he's convinced, but then he shakes his head again. "I tried my best to keep you out of this life, but you're your own man, Chuck. You don't need me. You've got a good relationship with Tori. You're more than capable of doin' this on your own."

"But Don Bonetti respects you, Rome. He asked for you specifically. I think he'll give us better pricing if you're at the meet. I just need you to set up the deal. I'll have Frank run the street business. Mac and I will manage the supplier relationship."

Rome takes off his sunglasses, turns, and finally looks me in the eye. "Why you so eager to take this risk? You can make good money as a straight-up lawyer. Get back into the civil rights stuff you used to love. Those police brutality cases pay well, don't they?"

"The decision came back last week." I avoid eye contact, hoping to hide my shame.

"What decision?"

"I've been disbarred," I admit. "Adrian told the state bar about the voicemail from the Rouchard grab. I was his lawyer then and violated ethical rules when I buried that evidence. I placed RF9's interests over his. If it wasn't for Truck saying he forced us to work for him... I still had to call in every old favor to escape prosecution. I don't know how else to make a living."

He's silent for a long moment, turning back to the field where his players are huddled. "I can get you a job coaching basketball here, maybe even teaching. You got the resume and the mind for it."

I think about it for only a moment. "I appreciate the offer, but that's not for me. I can get us back to where we were. I need to at least try."

He blows his whistle for the next drill, and as he does, Shanita and the kids arrive at the school to pick him up since they only have one car now. They wait in the lot, but my niece, Amaya, just five years old, runs toward us.

"Daddy! Daddy! Uncle Chuckie!"

"There's my baby girl!" Rome lets out a hearty chuckle as she jumps into his arms. He flings her in the air before setting her down. "Go stay with Mommy, okay? We'll go home soon."

He lets out a deep sigh, his shoulders slumping as he watches her run back. "Aight, C. I'll sit down with the Italians. But after that, I'm done. I'm not dragging my family into that life again."

77

CHARLES PALMER

IN THE BONETTI warehouse in South Philadelphia, boxes are stacked haphazardly, some marked, others not. The ceiling rises almost out of sight. Steel racks climb toward it, row after row, stacked with crates and pallets likely holding stolen artifacts, paintings, and bundles of precious jewels.

I step into the back office with Rome. Uncle Mac and Frank Madigan are backing us up. Just the four of us since RF9 is defunct and we can't afford bodyguards.

Across a heavy mahogany table sits Don Daniel Bonetti and his two kids, Tori and Jason, each dressed in black with diamonds hanging from their wrists, ears, and necks. Behind them, three of their leather-jacketed guards stand watch.

Jason Bonetti leans back in his chair, his eyes glinting with cold amusement. "Isn't this an intriguing twist of fate? You used to be the ones supplying us with dope and guns. Now, it's the Black Gods seeking the pleasure of moving our wares. Feels like pigs are flying." He lets out a sharp, biting cackle that cuts through the air with unapologetic arrogance. His lips curl into a smug grin as if daring anyone to take offense.

A thin smirk sneaks onto Tori's lips. "Power shifts in the most unexpected ways, Jase."

Unbothered, Rome locks onto the decision-maker. "Don Bonetti, we appreciate the audience and hope we can continue our business relationship, even if certain roles are reversed."

Don Bonetti nods but remains silent behind his diamond-encrusted shades.

"We'd like to discuss how your new product line will fit into our distribution network," I say, trying to mask my nerves with an air of confidence.

"Our new supplier has opened his full catalog to us," Tori says. "Methamphetamine, fentanyl, uppers, downers, fairy dust, dopamine, pretty much every synthetic narcotic that exists. We can also sell you guns. But we have an eight-million-dollar minimum buy-in for all customers."

"We're going to ask that you sell us this first shipment on consignment," Rome says. "As you can understand, our business is rebounding."

Jason presses a cigarette to his mouth and lights it with practiced ease. "Can't do consignment, fellas."

"We've let you purchase product on consignment on several occasions over the last two decades," Rome says. "The Black Gods have made a number of concessions for your organization. Surely, you can offer the same courtesy."

"The Black Gods are finished, aren't they?" Jason says, his South Philly accent piercing the room as he cackles again in our faces.

"I can assure you," I say, "the Black Gods are far from finished."

"Well, RF9 certainly is," Jason replies. "At least according to the feds."

"Don Bonetti." Rome ignores Jason, raising his voice slightly to address the aging kingpin. "You're a man of tradition, but I believe, first, you're a friend. I'm asking, as a friend, that you make an investment in an organization that has dominated these markets for decades. We might be down now, but my brothers here, Charles and Frank, will re-establish that dominance. I have no doubt about that."

"Absolutely." I keep my face calm and resolute.

Don Bonetti doesn't respond. He looks lost, as if his dementia has progressed since we last saw him.

Frank, standing guard behind us, steps forward and adds, "My uncles in Boston have already agreed to work with us again. They're letting us service our old territories in the northeast once we lock down a new supply. We'll build our network back up quickly."

"Can I just say it's good to see Charlie here stepping into his true light." A sly smirk creeps on Tori's face. "The world has too many dirty lawyers. Just be dirty. But to be honest, I'm not sure we can afford the lack of liquidity. Even with the promise of the Irish sharing their territory. Too risky."

"Don't forget I was your plug for a long time," Rome says. "I know market pricing better than anyone and can guess what you're paying this new Nigerian supplier and what you're charging downstream. You're making great margins."

"And we know how much you made on the Maddox parking deal I brought you in on," I remind them. "You can do without the upfront cash."

"And to be clear," Frank says, "we're just looking to service our old corners. We'll respect your new position atop the food chain."

For now.

"That's right," I say. "Our business will remain in the territories that members of your organization don't blend so well in. The Black and Brown neighborhoods."

Don Bonetti raises an eyebrow and finally speaks. "The Blacks are good people. Some think we Italians hate them, but I don't hate them. I love Black pussy. Brown pussy too." He chuckles softly before a look of confusion overcomes him. He turns to his daughter and says, "I'm sorry, sweetheart. What are we doing here?"

"That's okay, Daddy." Tori rubs his back in slow, soft circles before she snaps her eyes back to us. "Look, we see where you're coming from, but here's where we're coming from. Our new supplier gave us extremely attractive pricing on the guns and dope. I mean, we pay him almost nothing. As a condition of the deal, we needed to give certain assurances."

"What assurances?" I ask.

"Well, just three really," Tori says. "The first is no consignment deals, of course."

"The second, no more trafficked women in our strip clubs and massage parlors," Jason says.

Tori sighs and shrugs her shoulders. "Tough for profit margins but eh it's a new day. Whaddaya gonna do?" The Philly girl from the block slips through in her tone. "We'll make up for it with the extraordinary margins on our dope and gun business."

"And the third assurance?" I ask.

She pauses, looking around the room as if she's searching the warehouse shelves for the third assurance. They're stalling, but I'm not sure why.

I glance at Rome, who has an uneasy look on his face. Out of the corner of my eye, I can see Uncle Mac subtly unbuttoning his trench coat, preparing to draw his pistol.

"Are we good here, Tori?" I ask.

"Rome…" Don Bonetti says, seemingly snapping back to lucidity, "you've always been a good boy. A strong man like your father. I'm truly sorry about this."

Rome is silent as he studies Don Bonetti's face.

Tori leans forward, her voice cutting through the stillness. "The third assurance is no more Black Gods."

For a moment, confusion flashes across Rome's face, but then a look of eerie realization appears as he shouts, "C! Run!"

Before I can move, the muted pops of silenced sniper rounds pierce the air, followed by two dull, nearly synchronized thumps—the sound of bullets penetrating the skulls of Uncle Mac and Frank. A split-second later, I hear the heavy thuds of their lifeless bodies hitting the ground in unison. Rome and I turn our heads to see their bodies on the floor.

I turn my head back to the table, and Tori has a pistol aimed at Rome's head. Without hesitation, she pulls the trigger. The sound of the gunshot echoes through the warehouse. Rome's head snaps back and then juts forward. His upper body slumps onto the table as blood and brain matter spill from his forehead.

"No!" I scream but it feels more like a gasp.

It's all happening so fast. I barely have time to process anything before snipers glide silently from the warehouse rafters. Then, the room's heavy doors burst open and a dozen mercenaries storm in, each with their assault rifles trained on me. Despite the laser scopes blurring my vision, I recognize the bulky figure of Demarcus Teague.

He quickly disarms me while he presses the cold steel of his pistol against my head.

"Hostiles down," Demarcus mutters into his earpiece. "All clear for the Controller."

The commotion is deafening, and amidst the chaos of STS mercenaries securing the space, I see Adrian Channing stepping into the room, calm as ever, flanked by two more guards.

He seems bigger than when I last saw him, as if he's been spending time in the weight room, a contrast to his slender biker's frame. He's dressed in a black three-piece Zegna suit, custom-fitted with a black shirt and a black tie. A pair of dark Cartier sunglasses mask his eyes but not the coldness that radiates from them. The diamond cufflinks on his wrist dance in the light, next to the rare Rolex Daytona 6263, a watch worth more than some homes.

He scans the warehouse, quietly surveying the carnage, letting me sit with my panic as Demarcus presses the barrel of his gun to my forehead.

He doesn't need to say anything. Everything about him—the way he stands, the cut of his suit—says more than words could. As his eyes lock onto mine, the admiration for me that I recognized when we used to politic in my old law office is nowhere to be found. There's no hint of anything but calculation. He wants me to know exactly where I stand in his world and exactly what he can do to mine.

Not long ago, this man was a bundle of raw nerves and a desperate pawn in my network. I exploited his weaknesses, used his vulnerability to my advantage, but clearly pushed him too far.

I think until this very moment, I still underestimated him. I'm not sure why. But now, it's obvious that Adrian Channing is the embodiment of danger wrapped in wealth, someone who can buy lives as easily as he can take them.

Tori stands and greets Adrian with a kiss on the cheek. He barely reacts, just keeps his eyes fixed on me through his designer frames.

Tori turns back to me and says, "Charlie, I believe you've met our new Nigerian supplier." She glances back at Adrian. "Wait, are you really Nigerian?"

"Half," he says quietly, still showing no emotion, still staring me down. "We'll take it from here, Tori."

The Bonetti crew exits the warehouse.

"Why?" I shout. "You already got Truck! It was him who hurt your family. Rome told him to leave you alone." I slam my fist on the table in front of me.

Demarcus presses the gun tighter against my head. "Let me know, boss."

"It's fine, D. He can't do anything to me, and he knows it." Adrian pats Demarcus on the shoulder, who then withdraws the pistol from my head and holsters it in an almost robot-like fashion.

"I thought we had an understanding!" I cry.

"Maybe *you* did, Charles." Adrian's tone remains cold as he looks down at me. "Do you really think Rome was innocent in Brianna's death?"

"He was."

He begins pacing the room, his hands clasped behind his back. "As you probably figured out by now, I gave the Bonetti family your supply line—chemical precursors for dope and parts for guns. They'll take your market share and pay Martex Properties for the pleasure. But the real beauty of that quiet little conglomerate is the millions of dollars in campaign contributions it makes that bought me a number of new friends in some very high places."

"What are you saying, Adrian?"

"I heard the wire recordings that Agent Galloway, aka Kareem Temston, took before Truck killed him. They all but confirm that Rome ordered the kidnapping and the hit on Brianna."

"I don't believe that."

Adrian nods in his direction, and Demarcus plays the tape of Truck, Getz, and Agent Galloway in the Escalade the night Brianna was killed.

Truck refuses to implicate us by name, but it's clear him and Rome acted together when I hear him saying, "*We'll pull the plug on the light-skin nigga and the baby momma after we get the crypto. But the Black Gods want the girl taken peacefully.*"

"Why?" I mutter, mostly to myself. "We had a plan."

"I suspect it's because Rome wanted out of the life," Adrian says. "If Truck went after my kid, Rome knew he would get caught and fall on the sword for the two of you just like he did. The feds already shut down RF9, but they wanted the Black Gods and wouldn't stop until they got at least one of them. So, Rome sacrificed his own brother."

"He wouldn't do that."

"He knew I would shut down your supply, leaving your family with nothing to sell. And then he would be free to act like he's the Black Bill Belichick of Maddox, PA."

He stops pacing, his gaze fixed on me again. "You know, Charles, I've thought a lot about that night three years ago. When I showed you my cards, had Big Palm beat up, and let you know what I was willing to do to protect my family."

"I remember."

"You should've just taken the $8 million I offered. Or maybe I should've listened to Demarcus and killed you all right then and there. My daughter would still have a mother if I did. That was my mistake. And that..." He nods to Rome's dead body, then abruptly roars, "... THAT IS AS CLOSE AS I CAN GET TO FIXING IT!"

He takes a step back as he catches his breath. "Rome should've just come to me like a man. I could've brokered a sale of your business to the Bonetti's and got him out peacefully, along with the sixty-plus million dollar return you would've received from the Geraldine's exit."

He unbuttons his suit jacket, exposing the grip of a pistol tucked into a shoulder holster, and resumes pacing with measured steps. "No one would've gotten hurt, and you guys would've gotten rich with clean money. I could've even pulled some strings and gotten you clear of the fed heat. But instead, your family went after mine."

"That wasn't my doing—"

"Shut the fuck up, Charles!" Adrian screams. He draws what looks like a nickel-plated Colt .45 from the shoulder holster and lets it hang at his side. I can see it in the quiver of his lip and the twitching of the trigger finger. He's psyching himself up to kill me. Or maybe fighting to hold himself back.

"Because of your family, Brianna's dead, Riley doesn't talk to me, and Josie left me. Took our son after she found out about everything I was forced to do because of your lies and his threats. Rome doesn't get to enjoy his family after he ruined mine."

"I didn't know, Adrian." My heart rate increases as I stare death in the face. "I fought against Truck's plan."

Adrian nods slowly. "You know, I actually believe you, Charles." He slowly holsters his pistol. "You're smarter than them. And that's why I'm willing to let you live. But it happens on my terms."

"What terms?"

"You'll work for me. You'll use your skills, your strategies, and connections to represent my interests in the black market."

I shake my head, trying to make sense of the offer. "Why not just kill me?"

"Because you're worth more to me alive. I have no interest in organized crime, no interest in playing neighborhood drug games. I left that shit in the Ironbridge towers when I was fifteen. Not to mention, a number of city governments are paying me and Demarcus handsomely to police their streets. I can't be seen movin' weight."

He pauses, letting those words linger before starting again. "But Martex Properties quietly controls the country's largest producers of chemical precursors and gun parts. I've diverted all of the off-the-books business into an entity called The Control. With my strategy, it'll be the ultimate supplier of raw materials to American narcotics and firearms traffickers. The plug of all plugs."

"Why? You have a legitimate private equity firm, billions in assets. You don't need this kind of income."

"That's right, Charles. I'm in private equity, which means I'm in the business of business. And given the relationships I have now, there's no such thing as dirty money. Not for me. One hundred percent of The Control's profits get reinvested into community improvement programs and initiatives designed to solve problems in underserved neighborhoods. And then I'm going to use this asset to make sure psychopaths like your brothers never hurt innocent people again."

"How?"

"The Control will offer its supply for dirt-cheap prices, and in exchange, its customers will adhere to its rules," Adrian says. "Any mass shootings with a Control firearm, any children or pregnant women being sold dope made from Control chemicals? We shut off the tap. Any Control customers trafficking humans for any purpose or recruiting children to do their dirty work? We shut off the tap. Any gang wars spill into the streets and harm innocents? We shut off the tap, watch their market share dwindle, and let their competitors take them out."

"Use pricing to control behavior." Now I understand the name, and I'm starting to see his vision. "They'll get used to the enhanced profit margins, the cash flow, and do whatever you say in order to stay rich. The gangs will police themselves."

"Exactly," he says.

"But there'll be groups that don't take kindly to your rules. The cartels for one. And other groups that rely heavily on human trafficking."

Adrian shrugs as if he's considered that risk and isn't concerned by it. "If they don't fall in line. Demarcus will send in a kill squad to eliminate the entire fucking trap house or hacienda. STS has private policing contracts in almost every major drug market across the country and a mercenary arm with operations around the globe. If I also control the flow of drugs and guns, I say which gang, mob, or crew gets to move *my* contraband on *my* streets without police scrutiny. And if they do, they better do that shit with some decorum."

"And you want me to run this operation?" I ask, the intrigue setting in. "Help you juke the stats for your private policing business?"

"I obviously can't run it," Adrian says. "Outside of managing CCP and its twelve billion in legitimate corporate assets, I'm far too busy trying to get my family back…" His voice trails off, though the simmering anger is still clear in his tone. I can sense him recalibrating, trying to calm his temper.

And then he continues, "Charles, you'd be the CEO of the largest contraband operation in the country, shit, maybe the world. At least top ten. You'll have all the power you've ever wanted, but you can never forget who the fuck controls you. And who the fuck can end you at any moment?"

I sit silently for a moment, studying his posture, trying to judge the sincerity of the offer. Then, a realization sets in. "And my father? If I don't toe the line, you'll have him raped and killed, right?"

He chuckles under his breath. It's almost a sinister sound. "Charles, I want you to hear me when I say this because this is what you made." He finally takes off his sunglasses and makes me look into his eyes. They're empty.

"That $60 million return you would've gotten on my first fund?" he says. "I'll put it into a grant for those nieces and nephews of yours and for all of the victims of the violence that your brothers were responsible for. I'll reopen the Furniture Emporium, and the innocent members of your family can all have their jobs again. But if you cross me… if you try to run one of your classic Charles Palmer plays, your lies… if you even think about fixing your sophisticated, nuanced, tactical brain to accomplish anything other than what I order, I'll kill every motherfucker named Palmer that springs from your bloodline. Or I can blow your brains out right now. Your choice."

For a moment, I contemplate standing and telling him I'd rather meet my brothers than be the puppet of a high-yella sellout. But the weight of the offer presses down on me. The power and respect I fought so hard to grow and protect, only to lose, are now being handed back to me by the man who killed my brothers. Death would be the easier escape, but I can't do that to my mother. With a heavy, resigned nod, I accept that my only choice now is to serve the man I once believed I could control.

"Alright, I'll be your puppet."

"Not a puppet, Charles. A proxy."

As Adrian and his men start to walk away, I realize he's once again stealing the strategy Rome and I employed for years.

"You're just using me to keep your hands clean," I murmur. "That's all this is. Making me what RF9 was to Rome and me. But trust me when I say that sooner or later, it'll all crash down around you. It always does."

He stops and pivots slowly. "It may be a similar strategy, but you and I are not the same, Charles. I was born the only son of a trafficked Nigerian immigrant and a trailer trash white American. While you were getting therapy from the city's best doctors and flaunting your daddy's dirty wealth like a badge of superiority, I was clawing my way out of public housing, out of foster care and juvenile detention, all the way to the top of the global economy."

I raise an eyebrow, but he's not waiting for my response.

"And even when the evils of institutionalized corporate greed and organized crime blocked my ascent, I found a way through and put myself at the helm of it all. And that's because the path of a titan can never be deterred by the wills of mere men."

He steps in closer now, taking off his sunglasses again so I can see the full weight of determined anger in his eyes. "I'm building my empire my way. And no matter the cost—no matter the lies I may need to tell, the illicit assets I may need to manage, the politicians I may need to put in my pocket or the enemies I may need to put in the ground—I am never losing control again."

78

SPECIAL AGENT
REGINA COURTLEIGH

THREE YEARS LATER

I DID SOMETHING most agents only dream of, bringing down a national crime syndicate in a sweeping RICO case. I've had many drinks for my partner, Agent Galloway aka Kareem Temston. An unwilling sacrifice.

Truck Palmer's arrest was the pinnacle of years of relentless work. But when I heard about his murder in prison, I couldn't help but feel it put a blemish on my so-called victory. A year later, Rome Palmer's body washed up on the southern banks of the Delaware River, and Charles Palmer has seemingly vanished from existence. His loved ones are unaware of his whereabouts. There are no traces but for a few sightings here and there, usually of him cavorting with a member of the DEA's most wanted list.

I'd love to keep searching for him, but the Justice Department closed the file on Maddox and moved me to New York with Rondell and my new partner, Agent Winnie Ortiz, who helped bring down Truck Palmer. In the end, it was lust that nailed his coffin, letting "Zaida" into his safe house based on the promise of sex. Her bravery sealed off his escape and secured his apprehension without a firefight.

• • •

Ortiz and I stand in front of Rondell's desk. My heart's racing, knowing we have nothing solid, just a series of coincidences, whispers on the streets, and a gut feeling.

"Look, I know it sounds crazy," I start, catching the skeptical look on his face, "but I'm telling you, we missed something big in Maddox."

Rondell's voice is deep and hoarse as he says, "Court, I'm sick of hearing about that city. We won. It's over. I need you focused on the Rivas Cartel."

"Davis, I'm telling you it's all connected. The pieces don't line up perfectly yet, but if I'm right—and I am right—Adrian Channing is this 'Controller' that we've been hearing so much chatter about. Help me get a task force, just a small one, to dig deeper. I know we can crack this wide open."

"It's a myth, Court," grumbles Rondell. "The Control or Controller or whatever? It's bullshit. I find it hard to believe that a single organization controls the entire narcotics and arms market across the country. It's a work of fiction. Bad guy folklore."

"I don't think so, Davis." I move closer. "I'm certain this organization killed Rome and Truck Palmer and took their position in the market."

Rondell sighs as he leans back in his chair, swiveling lazily. "Run me through it. And this better be good."

Ortiz pulls up photos of Adrian as a youth in the 90s, backward baseball cap, Eagles Starter jacket, and sagging Karl Kani jeans. He's standing with Makari Griggs in front of the Ironbridge Homes, concrete high-rises with broken windows and rusted balconies. Around them stand more grown men with dead eyes and hard faces, the kind who look like they'd kill for less than what it cost to rent a unit in that shithole. Adrian's just a kid here, but he looks like he's running them.

"Before he became a private equity icon," Ortiz begins, "he was a dope boy. My sources tell me he was a founding member of the East Maddox Stronghold Killaz, one of the first organized street gangs out of Maddox."

"This is all well-documented, ladies," Rondell says, already losing his patience. "Everyone knows of Adrian Channing's 'streets to the boardroom' story."

"But what they don't report in those puff pieces is that in '94, allegedly, Adrian set up a drug deal that turned out to be a police sting," Ortiz says. "Makari Griggs, backing him up, killed two confidential informants while Adrian got away. Makari, at nineteen, got life. Adrian, at fifteen, turned his around. But the detective who ran surveillance swore that young Adrian pulled the first trigger."

"All rumors?" Rondell asks. "Nothing corroborated by actual evidence, I assume?"

"No," I say. "Forensics were a wash, and Makari said he was alone. But we pulled his prison file, and Adrian's been putting money on his books for close to four decades now. We figure those are guilt payments."

I step toward the screen and pull up surveillance photos from Adrian's meeting with Makari in the visitation room at Riverville Correctional six years ago.

"It's not illegal to help a friend in prison," Rondell says. "I'm not hearing anything worthy of further investigation, ladies."

"Riverville's a private prison owned by Martex Properties," I say, "which in turn was owned by Sentry Asset Management which was owned by PGC up until just a couple years before the Palmers were taken out. When we were looking at this, state business records showed that Martex was merged with Ironbridge Industries, Inc., one of Adrian's companies. We think he acquired these prisons as a power play against the Palmers, who controlled its drug trade through their father, Big Palm."

"However," Ortiz says, "today, if you search for those same merger filings that were once publicly available, they're nowhere to be found. No mention anywhere on the internet of Adrian Channing or CCP investing in private prisons."

"It's an ugly thing to own for someone committed to uplifting the Black community," Rondell says. "But not a federal crime, ladies."

"Hey boss, can you stop calling us 'ladies'?" Ortiz snaps.

"Apologies, ladie—" Rondell catches himself. "Apologies."

I pull up surveillance footage of Adrian arriving at the same building as representatives of the Black Gods, the Bonetti Mafia, the Lloyd Posse, Black Metal, M.C., and the Zi Wan Triad, all within ten minutes of each other. "This is from when we were investigating the Palmers."

"Now that was peculiar," Rondell murmurs.

"It's a who's who of organized criminals, all of whom used to buy their guns and dope from RF9," Ortiz says.

"Anything tying him to these groups on paper?" he asks.

"I had a friend at the IRS audit his firm," Ortiz says, "but it came back clean. No red flags, no mismatched wire trails. But the structure… Offshore feeders upon offshore feeders, nominees fronting a bunch of sub-ten percent LPs, just small enough to stay anonymous."

"That kind of layering doesn't show up unless someone's hiding something," I add.

"Yeah," Rondell says, "could be drug money. Or it could be money from one of these ultra-private Saudi royal families. Or maybe money from a Fortune 100 CEO who doesn't want his name tied to a competitor CCP is investing in."

"Or it could be drug money," I say flatly. "But he's graduated. He's not just laundering money anymore. Our theory is that Adrian Channing has filled the vacuum created by RF9's extinction."

"But why?" Rondell asks, shaking his head. "And how? No one just starts selling drugs in their forties and becomes Pablo Escobar overnight. Doesn't make sense."

"Martex Properties." I can feel the anger in my voice growing. "Firearms manufacturers, chemical plants, pharmaceutical companies, cannabis companies, private prisons, ports, shipping, private military. All mechanisms that would give one the ability to mass-produce firearms and narcotics, and the means to distribute and protect them."

"Hmm," Rondell grumbles.

"Can't forget the political relationships to evade regulations that prevent companies like these from selling shit to criminals," Ortiz adds.

"Look at it, Davis." I point to the screen. "The Italians, Jamaicans, Chinese, bikers. His father has ties to the Irish mob as well. He could be laundering their money through his fund, sure, or he could be selling them the materials to peddle their contraband around the country. I believe we're looking at a new kind of kingpin, one hiding in plain sight as a private equity billionaire, using his portfolio companies in a shell game to control the black markets."

Rondell is silent for almost a minute, his face expressing the mental gymnastics he's doing. And then he asks, "To be clear, all of this is purely speculation, correct? All based on perfectly legal corporate transactions and a checkered childhood?"

"That's technically correct," I reply.

"We couldn't bring charges even if we were absolutely positive of this theory," Ortiz says. I can tell she's still on the fence about the theory.

"So, let me get this straight." Rondell's tone of skepticism returns. "He's a wealthy businessman who uses his money to influence government so he can make himself more money? Other than the fact that he's a Black man doing this, what makes you think this qualifies him to be a drug and gun kingpin, instead of just your normal-course American tycoon?"

I take it Rondell is tired of seeing prominent men who look like him being taken down. Many call Adrian Channing an icon and the "savior of inner city America" for what he's done to revitalize blue collar cities across the country. As a white woman agent of the historically racist federal government, I realize how my accusation looks, but I've never had a hunch that didn't lead to a conviction. And if I'm right, he's just another criminal.

"Do you have anything of substance to support this theory?" Rondell asks.

I go to my desk, pull out the printout of Adrian's senior thesis at Harvard, and hand it to Rondell. "How about motive?"

"The Power of Private Capital by Adrian Channing," he says, reading the title. "What is this, Court?"

"Ninety-eight percent of it, he's arguing that private companies and the billionaires that control them can solve the world's problems if they stopped caring so much about lining their own pockets. But if you look at fourteen, he digresses into a theory about how a single actor could control the entire illegal drug trade in America with a series of strategic corporate acquisitions."

"And a collection of massive cojones," Ortiz adds.

"He wrote the blueprint years ago, and now he's executing it," I say.

Rondell reads the chapter. "This isn't motive, Court. It's theory and hypothesis." He hands the paper back to me. "Do you have any leads on actual evidence?"

"No, but let us put a small team together and I'll get it," I insist. "Just a junior agent or two and a couple of forensic accountants."

"Absolutely not," Rondell says. "Can't open an official workstream on this. Hadington will end us if we take a shot at his buddy."

"But he basically told us if Adrian crosses the line into violent crime, he's no longer off limits," I say. "Money laundering is one thing, but I can't imagine his other activities are being sanctioned."

"You might be right," Rondell says. "If Channing has a deal with the government, it's likely contingent on non-violence." He goes quiet again as he strokes his beard. When he speaks, it's in a low voice. "Fine. You and Ortiz can work it on the side. But keep it quiet."

What I don't tell him yet is that I already have an undercover team infiltrating Adrian's fund and a snitch working her way into his inner circle.

Friend of the new president or not, I will take Adrian Channing down.

www.ingramcontent.com/pod-product-compliance
Lightning Source LLC
Chambersburg PA
CBHW020648110726
47901CB00001B/90